W9-AYL-407

Bubbles Betrothed

Also by Sarah Strohmeyer

Bubbles Unbound
Bubbles in Trouble
Bubbles Ablaze
Bubbles A Broad

SARAH STROHMEYER

Bubbles Betrothed

DUTTON

DUTTON
Published by Penguin Group (USA) Inc.,
375 Hudson Street, New York, New York 10014, USA
Penguin Group (Canada), 10 Alcorn Avenue, Toronto,
Ontario M4V 3B2 (a division of Pearson Penguin Canada Inc.)
Penguin Books Ltd., 80 Strand, London WC2R 0RL, England
Penguin Ireland, 25 St Stephen's Green, Dublin 2,
Ireland (a division of Penguin Books Ltd.)
Penguin Group (Australia), 250 Camberwell Road, Camberwell, Victoria 3124,
Australia (a division of Pearson Australia Group Pty. Ltd.)
Penguin Books India Pvt. Ltd., 11 Community Centre, Panchsheel Park,
New Delhi - 110 017, India
Penguin Group (NZ), Cnr Airborne and Rosedale Roads, Albany,
Auckland, New Zealand (a division of Pearson New Zealand Ltd.)
Penguin Books (South Africa) (Pty.) Ltd., 24 Sturdee Avenue,
Rosebank, Johannesburg 2196, South Africa

Penguin Books Ltd., Registered Offices: 80 Strand, London WC2R 0RL, England

First Printing, April 2005
10 9 8 7 6 5 4 3 2 1

The treatments contained in this book are to be followed exactly as written. The publisher and author are not responsible for your specific health or allergy needs that may require medical supervision. The publisher and author are not responsible for any adverse reactions to the treatments contained in this book.

 REGISTERED TRADEMARK—MARCA REGISTRADA

LIBRARY OF CONGRESS CATALOGING-IN-PUBLICATION DATA

Strohmeyer, Sarah.
  Bubbles betrothed / by Sarah Strohmeyer.
    p. cm.
  ISBN 0-525-94864-3 (acid-free paper)
1. Yablonsky, Bubbles (Fictitious character)—Fiction. 2. Women journalists—Fiction. 3. Beauty operators—Fiction. 4. Pennsylvania—Fiction. I. Title.
  PS3569.T6972B825 2005
  813'.54—dc22   2004019698

Printed in the United States of America
Set in Janson Text

PUBLISHER'S NOTE
This book is a work of fiction. Names, characters, places, and incidents either are the product of the author's imagination or are used fictitiously, and any resemblance to actual persons, living or dead, business establishments, events, or locales is entirely coincidental.

This book is printed on acid-free paper. ∞

For the sexy sirens of ADWOFF, who have been nice enough
never to consider a day without Bubbles

ACKNOWLEDGMENTS

This book could not have been written without the extraordinary homemade beauty tips generously offered by the following readers: Robyn Beckerman, Sara Cambreleng, Kathi Jones-Hudson, Roberta Ann Pane, Joni Langevoort, Leslie Rossiter, Lisa Spencer, Carol Spigner, and Tracey Wellman. In addition, I would like to thank Phyllis Banks, Deb Mundy, BJ Smith, and, of course, the great, welcoming Sue Noyes. Special hello to those hot mamas, the Two Jeans.

And last, but hardly least, many, many thanks to the ever patient, hardly ever controversial, always upbeat Bubblesheads. Can't wait to see you all when Bubbles hits the road once again.

Chapter One

Of all my favorite getups—tube tops, short shorts, leopard-print blouses, and mini skirts—I never expected that the one to get me thrown in jail would be my first business suit ever. Specifically a thirty-dollar skirt and jacket by You Go Girl! in hot pink acetate.

I'd bought it on layaway from Almart, months before I finally landed a full-time reporting job at the *News-Times*, the daily paper of record in my steel town of Lehigh, Pennsylvania. I hadn't required a suit as a hairdresser at the House of Beauty. Too risky what with all the chemicals we used.

But seeing as my days of perming and coloring were on the decline, I figured that being a professional woman now, I should get myself upgraded. So I ransomed the suit out of layaway, stuck it in my closet, and waited for the right debut.

Turned out the right debut was a few days later at the arraignment of Julia Simon, aka Crazy Popeye, for murder.

Crazy Popeye got her nickname because she was, well, crazy, and she bore an uncanny resemblance to Popeye. I don't know if she squeezed open spinach cans with her bare hands, but I do know she dressed in a sailor's suit and shaved her head bald. And, being homeless, she slept in a garbage can. Honest.

Six months ago, while snoozing in her garbage can at the corner of Polk and Mechanic, Popeye was rudely awakened by a sanitation worker doing his job. Reacting like any home owner would to an intruder, Popeye attacked the poor man who, upon witnessing a bald sailor of indeterminate gender lunging for his throat, immediately suffered a fatal heart attack.

A merciful judge agreed with her court-appointed public defender, Stu Kuntz, that Popeye had not been in her right mind, and Popeye was shipped off to the local loony bin until she was sufficiently rehabilitated.

Unfortunately, the loony bin had no room for yet another occasionally homicidal homeless person, and Popeye was back on the South Side within weeks, belting out the theme song of her namesake and begging for spare change.

No one wanted to cross Popeye, not after what she'd done to the garbage man. So we'd give her coffee and let her use the bathroom whenever she stopped by the House of Beauty. We'd wave good-bye to her and she'd wave good-bye to us, and, as we all predicted (and the more cynical of us wagered), Popeye was soon arrested for murdering another innocent man.

In this case the victim was sixty-four-year-old Rudolph Schmidt, Liberty High School's longest-running and most highly esteemed principal. Popeye had been caught red-handed—literally—stuffing Rudy's throat with his trademark navy and maroon, official Liberty High Alumni tie. It was a sad finale, yes, but also a fitting one, since even to the end, Rudy upheld his reputation as a booster.

Normally, Lawless, the ultimately lazy *News-Times* court reporter and recovering Ho Hos addict, would have covered Popeye's arraignment because he was investigating the Schmidt murder. But Lawless had a conflict. Specifically, he had a conflict with leaving his chair.

"I don't trust Popeye," he told me. "She could stuff a sock or something down *my* throat."

"I've known Crazy Popeye off and on for ten years," I said. "Last I checked she doesn't even wear socks."

"I don't care. I'm not taking chances." Lawless handed me Popeye's file. "You can cover her arraignment, though you better not screw it up. You're still on probation."

Probation is a kind of corporate purgatory between "You're hired" and "You've got health insurance" where I could get fired for no reason. Though I had broken more front-page stories in the past three months than most of his staff members, Managing Editor Dix Notch refused to cut me a break.

That meant the pressure was on and, therefore, the You Go Girl! suit was too.

The You Go Girl! suit turned out to be a big disappointment. The pockets and the back flap were sewn shut, making it hard to walk. More expensive suits, I decided, would have real pockets, not imitation, and working back flaps. I'd have to be well out of probation before I could afford one of those.

It fit okay, though, especially with a tasteful pair of pink pearly plastic earrings and matching hair clip. Luckily, I had just the right cotton candy eye shadow to complete the ensemble and a nifty new lipstick called Electric Raspberry.

Lorena Ludwig said nothing about the suit when we met on the sidewalk in front of the county courthouse the afternoon of Popeye's arraignment. This was no surprise. Lorena's not a girly girl. At best she's a talented news photographer wrestling with what she terms a "character flaw," but what the rest of us behind her back call "a freaking psycho temper."

"You're parking there?" Lorena pointed to my Camaro in front of Delarusa's Bail Bonds. "Delarusa will tow. He'll get his brother to do it and you won't have a front end left."

I shrugged. "Delarusa knows me. Dan sends most of his clients to him." Dan was Dan Ritter, my ex-husband, a slimebucket lawyer who changed his name to "Chip" and traded me in for Wendy the cheese-ball heiress. "And anyway I'm only going to be here for an hour."

"Don't say I didn't warn you." Lorena tossed the thick brown ponytail that stuck out from the back of her head, and made for the courthouse. The photo equipment in her bag clinked and clanked around her neck as she bounced ahead of me. I minced behind, unable to step more than a few inches on account of the sewn shut You Go Girl! skirt.

It was late November gray going on dark and miserable. That happens to be the average forecast for the Lehigh Valley, by the way. Dark and miserable with pockets of acid rain. If that sounds depressing, think again. "Dark and miserable" means "pollution," and "pollution" means the steel plant is still chugging and that means there'll be dinner on the table. We usually feel flush when the sun's gone.

Lorena and I walked past the courthouse lawn filled with TV reporters and other vermin from the national press who were intrigued by a "hometown story" of a cartoon character gone bad and a principal with a limited wardrobe. I knew they would pounce on Popeye as soon as she stepped out of her lawyer's car and that, if there was a God, she'd lunge at *their* throats.

"How come your Steve Stiletto's not here?" Lorena asked, taking two desperate puffs of a cigarette before going inside. "This story not big enough for him?"

"Stiletto's in New York tying up loose ends before going to England next week."

So soon, I thought, feeling instantly depressed. This week Steve Stiletto, the studliest Associated Press photographer ever to fill a Banana Republic photo vest, would be leaving me for an overseas assignment. "I'll be back to being single."

"Woo-hoo." Lorena opened the courthouse door. "That means me and you can make Ladies Night happy hour at the Tally Ho. Buy-one-get-one-free strawberry daiquiris on Thursdays."

For Lorena, one woman's tragedy is another woman's free cocktail.

I passed through the metal detector after surrendering all my valuables—nail file, car keys, spare change, and ankle bracelet—to the paunchy deputy sheriff doing security.

Lorena followed, grumbling steadily about the inconvenience of having to empty her photo bag and take off her belt.

"What's wrong with your skirt?" she asked, threading her belt back through her black pants. "You walk like you got a wedgie."

"It's a suit. It doesn't have a full flap. It's cheap."

"It's not cheap. You're ignorant." Lorena shoved her camera back into the bag. "You're supposed to cut those threads before you wear that. I bet your pockets are sewn too." She tugged at my pockets. "Oh, yeah. This your first suit?"

"No," I lied. "I've owned lots of suits."

"Good thing I got my Swiss Army. It has scissors. I keep it between my boobs. All that silicone keeps them hidden from the scanner."

But no sooner had Lorena reached in her bra to pull out her Swiss Army than she was surrounded by deputy sheriffs. I'd never seen two men each pushing three hundred pounds move so fast. Bloodlust filled the air. They'd apprehended a live one.

"You wanna step over here, miss?" A brown-suited sheriff appeared on either side of Lorena, like magic. The sheriff who had wanded us in was on his walkie-talkie, calling for backup of a female officer to do a body cavity.

"Body cavity!" Lorena howled. "No one's sticking no hands in no cavities."

If they weren't careful, Lorena was going to forget her anger management classes and start karate chopping law enforcement. "Deep breathe," I advised. "Repeat your calming words."

"Buzz off, Yablonsky. No one tells me what the fuck to do."

Trust me. In our part of Pennsylvania those were classic calming words.

A deputy sheriff approached me. JOHNSON was engraved on his

brass name tag. "You with her?" He pointed to Lorena, who was snarling and snapping her teeth.

"She's our photographer." It was like Lorena was our pet. "And she's got to get a photo. You have to let her go."

"I don't *have* to do anything. What's your name?"

"Bubbles Yablonsky. I'm a—"

Johnson didn't let me finish. "You got some ID?"

I opened my purse. The deputy peered in as I fished through makeup cases and tampons and a notebook to find my wallet with my license. I handed it to him. He studied it.

"This is all my doing," I blathered, one half of my brain concentrating on Lorena, who was beginning to kick wildly. "She was helping to cut my—"

"Cut? Did you say cut?"

"Don?" asked the other deputy, who was at the end of his rope trying to subdue his catch. "Mind giving me a hand here before this turns into a free show?" He inclined his head toward the crowd of spectators gathered by the metal detectors.

Johnson chucked his chin toward me. "What about this one?"

"Lock her up. This is a two-man job." He gave Lorena's wrist a twist.

"I'd kick you in the nuts if you had any," Lorena shouted. She turned to the crowd. "Do you see this? They're subverting my rights. My rights are being subverted. Is there a lawyer in the house?"

Every hand shot up.

"C'mon," said Johnson, taking me by the elbow. "You're gonna have to wait in lockup."

"Lockup? What did I do?"

"You violated Pennsylvania Consolidated Statute Title 18, subsection 6111S, carrying on your person a lethal weapon into a courthouse, punishable by up to one year in jail and a three-thousand-dollar fine." Johnson was now practically dragging me down the hallway.

"I've got a story to cover." I was failing miserably at keeping my voice calm and professional. "I've got to get a seat before they close the hearing."

"You should have thought of that before you concealed a pocketknife." He punched some numbers in the black lock, opened a thick wooden door, and shoved me in. "You wait here, Miss Yablonsky. By the way, you got a lawyer?"

"No." Then I remembered my ex. "Wait. There's Dan. Dan Ritter. Of Ritter and Ryjeski." This was like the *Twilight Zone*. All I'd wanted was to clip my skirt and now I was in jail.

He shut the door, locked it, and left me. Now what? Now what was I going to do? The biggest day of my career, covering the arraignment of Rudolph Schmidt's murderer, an article everyone in town was going to read, and I was stuck in the tank. The paper would have no story at all. No photos, even. They'd be forced to use some lifeless brief from the AP wire.

This was going to get me shit-canned. Then I remembered the Camaro in front of Delarusa's. This was going to get my car towed, too.

"You stay away from me," a high-pitched voice hissed from the corner. "You stay way over there. I got my eye on you."

I swung around to find myself with Lehigh's most famous celebrity of the moment.

Crazy Popeye. With socks.

Hey, Crazy, I almost said, before catching myself. "Julia. What are you doing here?"

Crazy Popeye winced. "What the hell do you mean, what am I doing here? I'm the main attraction." She slowly approached me. "I'm the murderer."

I took a step back. Crazy Popeye had never been renowned for sparkling dental hygiene or liberal use of deodorant. She was still in her sailor suit and her bald head was nubby from recent shaving mishaps. I'd have expected her lawyer, Stu Kuntz, to have bought her a floral dress and perhaps a wig, persuaded her to take a sponge bath at least, but maybe Crazy Popeye was a stickler for routine.

"Are *you* against me?" she asked, her red-rimmed eyes darting. "Everyone else is."

"No way." I took out my Reporter's Notebook. "I'm Bubbles Yablonsky, remember? Bubbles from the House of Beauty. I'm not against anyone."

Popeye tried to place me. "Oh, yeah. The dumb one."

"Pardon?"

"Nothing." Popeye flashed her five teeth proudly. "I always did like you. You had good gum."

"Cinnamon Trident. The best."

She held out her hand. I found a stick in my purse and, after blowing off a couple of crumbs and tobacco leaves, gave it to her. She chewed awhile and studied me unabashedly from head to toe. "What's wrong with your suit?"

"It's fine."

"You need to cut those threads."

"So I've been told." I clicked my pen and opened the tablet. "What do you mean everyone's against you?"

Popeye scratched her throat. "I mean everyone's against me. The cops, the judge, the prosecutor. Even my own lawyer. He's the worst."

I wrote this down.

"They're making up stuff." She peered at my notes. "Like that part about me killing Rudy Schmidt. It's all a bunch of lies."

"But Doctor May, Rudy Schmidt's podiatrist, walked into her waiting room and caught you with your hands down his throat."

"I was trying to save him. See, Doctor May lets me use her bathroom whenever I want. Lets me sleep in her waiting room, even. That's where I was, in the bathroom, when I heard this awful gurgling noise and chairs turning over and voices, voices, voices." Popeye slapped her hands to her ears.

"Men's voices?" I was writing like a demon. "Or women's?"

"Both. I tried to get out of the bathroom, but the door was locked. Then someone unlocked it. When I come out I see him there. On the floor choking on the tie. I did what I could. I was trying to save him, not kill him."

Popeye dropped her hands. Her face was clammy gray and she was sweating profusely.

"You hot?" I asked.

She nodded and ran her finger around her sailor collar.

"You want me to open a window?"

Popeye thumbed to the window. It was barred. "Can't. I don't know what's wrong with me. It must be the gum. Too spicy." She spit it onto her hand, a juicy red blob. "Want it?"

"No thanks," I said.

"Your loss." Popeye stuck it under the table. "How come you're writing down what I'm saying?"

"Because I'm a reporter now. A full-time journalist at the *News-Times*."

"You're kidding. You?"

"Don't look so shocked."

"It's like me being a psychiatrist. Where'd you learn how to be a reporter?"

"Two Guys Community College."

Popeye nodded in approval. "Good school. Wasn't a bad department store, either. Delicious pretzels."

I tried to get back on track. "You tell the police what you just told me?"

"They're the most evil of all." She clutched my arm. "They're against me too. I don't trust any of them."

"If you don't trust your lawyer, the cops, the judge, and the prosecutor, then how come you trust me?"

"Because you're a hairdresser. Every woman knows she can trust her hairdresser. It says so in the commercials. Only a woman's hairdresser knows for sure." Popeye staggered a bit.

"You're not feeling well." I led her to the one chair in the room, an uncomfortable wooden number with no arms. "I'm going to call someone."

"No!" Her eyes were wild. "They'll kill me. They'll kill you, too, if you put what I said in the paper. Mark my words. They'll be after you as soon as they find out you talked to me. I'd run for my life if I was you."

I smiled maturely. Popeye was a paranoid schizophrenic. Her emotions were irrational and her fears a product of her brain-wasting disease.

"No one's going to kill anybody," I said serenely.

"Oh, yeah?" challenged Popeye. "Then how come . . ."

Suddenly her body went rigid, her eyes became unfocused, and before I could do anything to help, Popeye keeled over and died.

Chapter Two

They must have heard my screams down the hall because, almost on cue, the door burst open and Sheriff Johnson rushed in along with Stu Kuntz. Stu Kuntz took one look at Popeye and said to me, "What did you do to her?"

"I didn't do anything to her."

Kuntz popped a radio off his belt while Johnson, the county's finest, remained immobile, mouth agape.

"I'm on the EMT squad," Kuntz explained, requesting an ambulance. "I'd give her mouth-to-mouth but . . ."

But it was Popeye, I thought, and who knew where her mouth had been?

Johnson knelt beside Popeye and put a finger to her neck. "No pulse, anyway. She's dead," he said astutely.

"Oh, crap." Kuntz slammed the walkie-talkie on the table. "Are you sure?"

"I'm sure," said Johnson.

"This is highly irregular," said Kuntz. "This won't do at all."

Kuntz was in his mid-forties with a slightly receding hairline of curly black hair and a neatly trimmed beard peppered with gray. He was lean from running—marathons and races of other sorts. Kuntz had designs on becoming the next federal defender in Eastern Pennsylvania and finding the most famous client of his career dead on his watch would not further that goal.

"Go get someone. Stat!" Kuntz barked to Johnson, who scrambled up and hustled out the door as he'd been told. "Okay. Tell me everything that happened."

I felt like I was on the witness stand. "It wasn't much. They put me in here because of a mix-up at the scanner. Popeye and I got to talking and I gave her some gum and suddenly she got hot and didn't look well."

"Let me see the gum, please."

I searched in my purse. There was no gum. "That was the last stick. It was all cruddy." Then I remembered Popeye disposing of it. "She stuck it under the table when she was done."

Kuntz stepped over Popeye's body and looked under the table. "There's tons of gum."

"Yeah. But this stuff was wet."

"I'll alert forensics." Kuntz straightened himself. "Then what?"

I tried to remember, even though I was beginning to feel sick myself. "We chatted about Schmidt's murder and—"

"You *chatted* about Schmidt's murder!" Kuntz's eyes bugged. "Without me? I'm her lawyer."

She didn't trust you, I was tempted to say. "I didn't force her. Popeye talked of her own free will. She said she didn't do it and she told me why."

Kuntz's hands balled. "If she had lived you could have queered the entire case. She had no business talking to a reporter, and you, as a reporter, should have known better than to interview her. I could sue you."

Take a number. Besides, I didn't know too many reporters who would demur from interviewing a high-profile murder suspect.

"There's only one recourse left." He held out his hand. "Surrender your notes."

I clutched my bag. "No way."

He snapped his fingers. "Come on. Don't make me pursue legal action."

The door opened and Johnson was back with District Attorney Reggie Reinhold, also known as the Putz. Behind them was a cacophony of reporters, shouting questions and flashing bulbs. Johnson slammed the door in their faces.

"Holy mother," blurted Reinhold, staring at Popeye's corpse. "How did this happen?"

"Ask her." Kuntz pointed to me. "Bubbles Yablonsky, the *News-Times'* newest rookie."

"We've met." Reinhold glowered. I'd burned him bad in my most recent exposé. "What was she doing in here with Julia Simon?"

Johnson whispered in Reinhold's ear. "Imbeciles," Reinhold said. "Putting a newspaper reporter in with a murder suspect. Think of the risk."

"Yeah," I said, "she could have killed me."

"That, too," he said.

"Yablonsky won't surrender her notes as mandated by law," Kuntz said.

"What law? There's no law that says I have to turn over my notes." I never saw *that* on *Law & Order.*

"Oh, yes there is." Reinhold, who was as undersized as his ego was oversized, stepped closer to me so that he was eye level with my bust. "This is an ongoing murder investigation and your notes are evidence."

I turned to Johnson, who was looking off, probably thinking about what would be on TV when he got home. "Where's my lawyer?"

"Who?"

"My lawyer. Dan Ritter. You said you'd get him."

"Oh, yeah. Right." Johnson blinked. "Can't make it over. Too busy, he said."

I bit the inside of my cheek. Had I been *too busy* to give birth to our daughter, Jane? Had I been *too busy* to put him through law school? Or to work two jobs when he was starting his career?

"What did he mean, 'too busy'?"

"Car accident." Johnson scratched his head. "Or explosion. I forget which."

I gasped. Take back every bad thought I just had. "Dan's been in an accident? His car exploded?"

"Either his or his kid's. I wasn't paying attention."

Oh my God. Jane's car exploded. But wait! Jane didn't have a car. Then I remembered. Dan had loaned her his old BMW so she wouldn't ride with G, her slack-jawed boyfriend who went by one letter, G—for God or genius, depending.

"Get me out of here!" I banged on the door. "That's my daughter who's in trouble. Get me out of here!"

"Do what she wants," agreed Reinhold. "We'll take care of her later."

"Absolutely," said Kuntz. "This isn't over yet."

West Goepp is a typical steel-town street of row homes either in dark red brick or white aluminum siding. My home, not to be outdone, has both, along with the de rigueur pot of geraniums (now inside because of the cold), a fraying aluminum lawn chair, and a faded green Astroturf welcome mat on the front porch.

While our front yards on West Goepp won't win any *House Beautiful* awards, our postage-stamp gardens in the back are freaking cornucopias in the summer. Tomatoes, beans, and zucchini—enough to make all sorts of pickles, breads, and relishes. We tend not to eat our fresh vegetables fresh in Lehigh. We'd rather boil them in jars until they're mush, and throw them in later with overcooked meat.

Now that winter was here, the gardens were mulched and there wasn't a speck of green on the street. There was, however, lots of red, mostly in the form of plastic: big red Santas, red noses on Rudolphs, and red illuminated candy canes the size of large dogs. All were weathered and slightly sun bleached, having been first put out as soon as the Halloween candy had been consumed.

Yes, Thanksgiving was three days away and already the neighborhood looked like a North Pole junkyard.

I had used Lorena's cell phone to call home from the courthouse and found that Dan and Jane had survived and were at the house recovering from what Jane described as "a minor but suspicious car fire."

"What does that mean?" I said.

"I don't know. That's what Dad said. And he won't let me call the police because neither of us was hurt."

Oh, brother. I handed Lorena back her phone. "My ex has gotten himself in some sort of trouble," I said, "and he doesn't want our daughter to call the police."

"Go home," said Lorena, who'd been released from custody with numerous apologies by the deputy sheriffs. "You'll feel better seeing everyone alive. Also," she made a fist, "this might be a good excuse to knock your ex's lights out."

I parked the Camaro with its *Ask Me About Donkey Sucking* graffiti (long story) and hustled up the front steps of my house.

The front door swung open and out stepped Dan. He was wearing an expensive camel cashmere coat—purchased by Wendy—and matching Burberry scarf—again, Wendy. His Grecian Formulated black hair was slicked back to a hard shell and he reeked of CK cologne.

"Hey, Bubbles. What's up?"

"What's up?" My head felt light from stress and a spike of maternal alarm. "What do you mean, 'What's up?' Your car blew up is what's up."

"Relax. Jane and I weren't even in it. It caught fire when I turned it on with the remote starter."

"Something wrong with the remote?"

"Either that or"—he cleared his throat importantly—"I'm a targeted man."

I frowned. "Oh, please."

"What can I say? I live a life of danger." Dan squinted into the setting sun. "All part of the job."

"You must have a new job, because last I checked you were a boring slip-and-fall lawyer. There's not a patch of ice in town without your business card next to it."

"That's just my cover, toots. You haven't a clue about the real Chip Ritter."

There wasn't a *real* Chip Ritter; Dan had changed his name to Chip to make it sound WASPy. But it takes more than a name change to make a WASP. Dan had the dumpy body and predilections of a true Lehigh Valley bohunk. He couldn't pass up a plate of halupkies or miss a World Wrestling Entertainment match on cable.

"Skip it," I said. "What happened with the car?"

"I'm not free to discuss it. Attorney/client privilege." He flung his scarf over his shoulder. "Let's just say that I'm involved in an extremely high-risk case. I've been, ahem, getting death threats."

"I thought Wendy quit with that already."

He ignored this comment. "The radiator explosion was a warning shot fired by the enemy. Next time, I might not be so lucky. Next time, they might succeed."

"Promises, promises." I pushed past him into the house. Jane was at the kitchen table writing furiously. Her hair was a blinding pink, her nostrils were accented with rings and studs, and her clothes were black leather, ripped. There were fewer pimples on her face today, thanks to the various homemade acne recipes she'd been trying (see pages 290–291). Clear skin or no, she was still stressed.

She looked up. "Not today."

"Damn." I put down my purse and shrugged off my fake-rabbit fur jacket. Jane, our brilliant though punked-out daughter was waiting to hear if she'd been accepted early admission to Princeton University—home, as she reminded me every day, to Albert Einstein.

"And," I would chime, "don't forget alma mater to Brooke Shields." For some reason, this never impressed her as much as it did me.

Secretly, I wished Jane would attend my alma mater, Two Guys Community College. It was cheaper and much closer to home. Plus it had a superb physics program. It's where I learned that light and heavy things don't fall at different speeds in a vacuum, though Jane says every third grader already knows that.

"What are you doing?" I went to the refrigerator for a Diet Pepsi.

"Working on a speech for the Rudy Schmidt memorial service. I've been asked to eulogize, along with two other students and a couple of community members. I'm dreading it."

I popped open the Pepsi. "Why?"

"Because I'll actually have to go to a football game. Worse, the big Liberty/Freedom game on Friday. The memorial service is at halftime."

"I'm sorry." I rubbed her back.

"It ruins my record. Three years at Liberty and I never attended a football game once."

"Football's good for you," said Dan, coming in through the front door. "You meet real men at football games. Not wimps like that pathetic hair-cutting monkey you're dating."

Jane stuck out her tongue at him. "Where have you been?" she asked me.

I told her about getting thrown in jail with Popeye and my interview, the horror of witnessing Popeye collapse, and getting harassed by Reinhold and Kuntz for my notes.

"Does Kuntz have a kid named Jason?" asked Jane. "He applied to Princeton too. And Harvard. And Yale. And anywhere else with a sprig of ivy on the walls."

"Actually, on Thanksgiving I'm doing a feature on tricks for getting into the Ivy League—"

Dan interrupted. "They have no right to ask you for your notes, Bubbles. This is a First Amendment issue. Your rights need to be preserved for the sake of the integrity of the Constitution. Did you call the *News-Times* lawyer?"

"No, I called you."

"Dad was handling his own problems, Mom. He's getting death threats." She winked. "Maybe there's an angry filing clerk on the loose, upset because Dad stapled his papers on the wrong corner."

Dan turned red. "I'll have you know, Miss Smartypants, that it's not so safe being a lawyer. My career is just as dangerous as your mother's. Maybe more. Even *you* could be in danger."

"That's it." I put down the Pepsi. "If these death threats are real, then I'm calling the cops."

Dan beat me to the phone, clamping his hand over the buttons. "You'll do no such thing."

"Take your hand off the phone. It's mine."

"Listen to me." Dan put his face up so close I nearly passed out from cologne intoxication. "If you tell the police that I'm getting death threats at work and that someone intentionally blew up my car, they'll swoop into my office like shopgirls at a Victoria's Secret sale."

"So?" I said, though I was thinking, Ooh, Victoria's Secret sale.

Dan lowered his voice. "So . . . maybe I don't want them uncovering my, um, self-compensation program."

I shifted feet. "What does that mean?"

Dan took me aside, out of Jane's satellite ears. "It means that Wendy's been leaning on me to make more money. And, well, I've been making more money by taking a bigger share of what's rightfully mine."

"In other words you've been embezzling."

"Please." Dan turned up his nose. "Such a loaded term."

"How much?"

"Twenty grand."

I was speechless. That was more than I made in a year.

Dan hurriedly explained. "You don't understand. Wendy's very high maintenance. We can't live on just the money she's inherited. It's emasculating."

"You're confused," I corrected. "Ripping out your testicles with Mama's weed claw, that's emasculating."

Dan crossed his knees. "Ouch."

"It's also what awaits you if you don't return that money."

"Oh, c'mon."

"Embezzling's illegal, Dan, and it's wrong. Plus, if Jane's about to go to a big, expensive school like Princeton, we can't risk you being out of a job, or worse, in jail. I'll give you twenty-four hours to put that money back. I don't care if you have to grovel to Wendy for it. Get it or else."

"Or else what?"

"Or else I'll go to the cops myself."

There was a rap at the kitchen door, a demanding open-up rap made by tiny Polish-Lithuanian knuckles. My muscles snapped to attention as though they'd been caught slacking off.

"Grandma," said Jane, running to where two figures waited silhouetted in the frosted glass, one short, one tall. The Mutt and Jeff of the Lehigh senior social circuit. Mama and Genevieve.

"Is it Monday already?" I checked my watch. Four-thirty on the dot. Dinner would be on the table at five. From the smell of it, smothered chicken. All of my mother's food was smothered. For all we knew she could have been serving us road-killed squirrels with a can of Campbell's poured over it all these years and we'd never known.

"Not those two. I gotta get outta here." Dan made for the front door. "Wendy's gonna be here any minute to pick me up."

The phone rang.

"I'll get that," said Dan. "It might be the cops."

This time I was faster. "Nice try." I answered it.

"Bubbles? You okay?" It was Mr. Salvo, my night editor at the *News-Times*.

"Okay about what? Okay about witnessing Crazy Popeye's death or okay about learning that the car my daughter was in nearly blew up?"

"Whoa, whoa, whoa. Back up. Your daughter's car nearly blew up? Is, uhh . . ." He searched for the name of my daughter which, considering we'd known each other for a year, I'd have expected him to remember.

"Jane," I coached.

"Is *Jane* okay?"

I eyed Dan, who was sniffing the aroma of what smelled like Mama's Golfer's Chicken. (One bottle of Russian dressing, one packet of Lipton's onion soup mix, and one jar of apricot preserves. Mix. Pour over chicken pieces and bake at 350° for an hour. So yummy and plebian, Wendy wouldn't have made it if you put a gun to her head.) "She's fine."

"Good." That mushy family stuff out of the way, Mr. Salvo got down to the nitty-gritty. "You get a chance to talk to Crazy Popeye before she croaked?"

Editors are rarely known for their sensitivity.

"I did. Popeye told me she was locked in the bathroom of Doctor May's office and overheard the murder. She claimed she's innocent."

"Stop the presses. An accused murderer proclaiming innocence. Say it ain't so."

"I, for one, believe her, and there must be something to it, since Reinhold and Kuntz would sell their mothers to get my notes."

"Notch's been fielding phone calls from the DA's office and the public defender's all afternoon. Brace yourself. Stu Kuntz is playing the irate attorney. He's making a big stink about you being cocky and arrogant back at the courthouse."

I let the words sink in. Cocky and arrogant. I'm never cocky and arrogant. The accusation was so unfair it was almost incomprehensible.

"That's a total lie, Mr. Salvo. I was frightened and slightly sick over seeing a woman die before my very eyes."

"I know. I know. Notch and I think the complaint is just a straw man to get at your Popeye notes. Kuntz and the DA are demanding you turn over all information and/or material Popeye gave you today and they're willing to go to court to get it." Mr. Salvo paused. "That could mean incarceration, Bubbles, if a judge finds you in contempt."

I didn't know what to say. I tried to recall my Journalism 101 course from the Two Guys Community College and what we learned about reporters' privilege, but all I could remember was the episode where Mary Richards was sent to jail on the *Mary Tyler Moore Show*. And how ugly—yet still perky—she was in prison garb.

It gave me hope.

Out of the corner of my eye I could see Dan gesticulating with his hands, grimacing and dancing about like a chimpanzee, impatiently wanting to know who was on the phone.

"It's my editor," I said, covering the mouthpiece. "You can go."

When he was gone, I said to Mr. Salvo, "I don't want to go to jail."

"It's unlikely, but it's something you'll have to prepare yourself for. We can talk about it when you get into the office. Uh, you are getting into the office, aren't you? I'm planning on running your Crazy Popeye interview tomorrow, Kuntz be damned. I'm not going to let the *Morning Call* beat us on this one."

Dan returned holding a plate of Mama's cooking, a napkin tucked under his chin. He was inhaling the slop like pure oxygen, completely violating Wendy's rule against consuming food that wasn't organic, free range, fat free, and cooked by someone in a puffy white hat.

"Of course I'll be in to write the story, but I'd like to get out early, in case Stiletto comes back from New York."

"Congratulations on that, by the way," Mr. Salvo said heartily. "I just got off the phone with Stiletto's editor at the AP. I had no idea."

My heart stopped. Knowing Stiletto, that could mean anything from "I had no idea he'd been nominated for a Pulitzer" to "I had no idea he'd been crushed in a Bombay bordello brawl."

"No idea what?"

"That you were the lucky girl."

"Excuse me?"

"Come on, Bubbles. Don't play coy. I'm an editor, a journalist, a muckraker for twenty years. I can ferret out any scheme. Now fess up. Stiletto and you got engaged secretly over the weekend, am I right?"

It was such a stunning statement, so out of the blue that I choked. Dan even patted me on the back.

"Well, he got engaged to someone," Salvo said. "The AP practically put it on the wire."

"Honestly," I managed to say. "Stiletto's been in New York since Thursday night. I haven't heard a thing."

There was an awkward pause, and then Mr. Salvo said, "Okay, be that way." And hung up.

What way? I wondered, hoping the answer was not *jilted*.

Chapter Three

"I think Stiletto got engaged," I said out loud.

I was still holding the phone, dazed, Mr. Salvo's sentence swirling around and around inside my head.

Well, he got engaged to someone. The AP practically put it on the wire.

My chest felt crushed. Steve Stiletto—who had managed to wear me down with his innate sexuality, who had sworn that I'd be different from all the other women all over the world who'd thrown themselves at him, that I was special—had found someone else. Someone he wanted to spend his life with.

How could this be? Hadn't he said he loved me just before he left for New York? Hadn't we been indulging in the most intense, the most joyous and thoroughly satisfying lovemaking over these past few weeks? And though he may not have put it into actual words, hadn't he implied a lifetime commitment?

Or had that merely been my wishful thinking? Blinded as usual by what I wanted instead of what really was. Like the pore minimizer cream I bought last week that suckered me out of twenty bucks.

A harsh beeping echoed in my ear. The phone. I slammed it down.

Now I understood. Stiletto hadn't gone to New York to visit his editor and tie up loose ends at the Associated Press. He went to propose.

"What's wrong with you?" Dan's voice cut through my fog. "Did you just say Stiletto got hitched?"

"What?" I said. "Uh, yeah. Sort of. He got engaged."

"When did this happen?"

"Over the weekend. Mr. Salvo said it's all over the AP. Stiletto's getting married."

A howl went up in the kitchen. Mama jogged in. "What's that? Steve Stiletto's getting married?"

"I knew it." Genevieve followed on her size-thirteen clodhoppers, incorporating all the grace of Ma Kettle rushing a Pittsburgh linebacker. "I knew that slick Italian stud was nothing but a horny European gigolo."

"That's what you get for giving the milk away for free." Mama wiped her hands on her apron, like my relationship with Stiletto was chicken grease on her fingers. "I tried to tell you, but would you listen? And here you are, almost middle-aged. What kind of role model is that for Jane?"

I hung my ahead. Ashamed of my gullibility and my sluttiness. Though not my slut wear. I liked my slut wear.

"I'll shoot that bastard right in his roasted garlic nuts." Genevieve plunked her mitt on my daughter's shoulder. "Jane, get me my musket. It's in the backseat of the Rambler. I gotta oil the sucker."

"I'm not getting your musket, Genevieve." Jane regarded me with sympathy. "I'm sorry, Mom. What can I say? Boys are jerks." She returned to the kitchen.

"You two weren't together long enough for a palimony suit," Dan said, disappointed not to be scamming someone out of money. "Too bad."

"We don't need no palimony." Mama hugged me quickly. "We got Genevieve. Genevieve will even the field. Without testicles, Stiletto won't get very far with his new bride. That should cheer you up."

I put my face in my hands. I wanted everyone to go away. I wanted to talk to Stiletto and find out what exactly went wrong, why he kept such a secret from me, and what *she* had that I didn't.

A horn beeped outside. Not a Chevy or Ford beep. A Hummer beep. Made you think for a moment you were bouncing along the Serengeti. Wendy had arrived, and, knowing her, she had the doors locked and the bullet-proof windows up, in fear that my low-class neighbors would attempt a carjack.

What she didn't realize was that no one on my block was itching for a bright yellow minitank with pricey upkeep and zero parking potential.

"That's her come-here-now beep. I better run." Like an obedient puppy answering his master's call, Dan bounded out the door, his tongue practically hanging from his mouth.

Leaving me to ask, what is it with me and men?

Contrary to what I had expected, Lehigh Police Detective Bob McIntyre was extremely cooperative when I called for a reaction to my Popeye exclusive interview. Maybe he sensed I was a wounded bird, a fragile being in need of kindness instead of the usual cop brush-off.

"You got an interview with Popeye before she passed on?" Detective McIntyre said. "This is what you guys call a scoop, say?"

I smiled to myself. "Kind of."

"May I put you on hold briefly while I gather my thoughts?"

"Go right ahead." What a nice man.

While he put me on hold I read over my story and then tidied up my desk, throwing away an empty coffee cup and straightening my framed first article, written as a legit full-time staff writer. I tried not to think what Stiletto was doing right now.

"Hey, Yablonsky." Lawless popped his head over the divider that separated our cubicles. "Was that McIntyre on the phone?"

"Was?" I put my hand over the receiver.

"Yeah. You've been on hold fifteen minutes."

I checked the little clock at the corner of my computer screen. Fifteen minutes. So I had.

"McIntyre hung up long ago."

"How do you know?"

"Because I just got off the phone with him. He called to ask who the nitwit dame was who had the nerve to call him about Popeye. I told him to cut you some slack. You're still a rookie."

I slammed down the phone. "Rookie shmookie."

"Rookie shmookie?" Lawless raised a salt-and-pepper eyebrow. "You're in a newsroom now, Yablonsky, not the Girl Scouts. You gotta straighten up your language. I don't want to hear rookie shmookie again. Fuck that."

Fuck was Lawless's favorite word. It was "fuck off," "fuck you," "fuck this," "fuck her," "fuck him," and his favorite, "fuck this shit." Lawless was a true wordsmith.

I scanned my story and typed in a "No comment" after Detective McIntyre's name. I decided to include in the article only those statements from Popeye's interview that came close to fact, especially since I couldn't get any authorities, like McIntyre, to corroborate her more outrageous claims. I wrote that she maintained her innocence and that she had been trying to help Principal Schmidt when she was discovered with her hand down his throat.

In other words, I left out Popeye's wild opinions, her insistence that everyone was against her, including her lawyer. While I wrote that she said she was in the bathroom while Schmidt was murdered, I did not report that she thought she "heard voices," both male and female, on the other side of the bathroom door. I don't know why I didn't add that to the story. I think because I wanted to preserve what little was left of Popeye's dignity.

I read over the piece one more time, then hit the button and sent it straight to Managing Editor Dix Notch. Notch said he wanted a version of it by his 7:30 news meeting. It was 7:25. In reporter land, that was plenty early.

When I was done with that I said, "McIntyre might call me a rookie, but wait until he reads that interview with Popeye. Then he'll wish he'd talked to me. Read for yourself."

Lawless leaned over and read my story on the computer screen. As he did so I gave myself a mental pat on the back for being such a professional in such extenuating circumstances.

When he was finished reading, Lawless said, "Good going," with as much sincerity as he could muster. "It's got a few holes, but not bad for a rookie. By the way, impressive you had the guts to interview Popeye after being thrown in a cell with her."

It was the first time Lawless had ever paid me a compliment. "Thank you, Lawless. I appreciate that." I told him about Popeye hearing voices.

He picked up a tin of mints I keep by my pencil sharpener. "How many calories in these?"

"Two each. But they're so strong they burn themselves."

He proceeded to empty the tin into his mouth.

"Help yourself." I tried to hide my disgust as Lawless closed his eyes and savored the pepperminty sugar.

"So, you find out anything about Cerise May?" I asked.

Lawless's assignment had been to investigate Dr. Cerise May, the Little Warsaw podiatrist in whose waiting room Rudy Schmidt had been cooling his heels last Thursday evening when he was suffocated. Word around town was that Dr. May had ties to the Mafia. Jokes about "cement shoes" had been bandied around the newsroom ever since.

"Mafia, definitely, though not the kind you're thinking." Lawless handed me the tin. Two sticky mints were glued to the container. "Want one?"

"No, thanks." I tried not to retch. "Finish 'em off."

"What's four more calories?" He picked them out with two fingers. "According to a source of mine, Cerise May used to date Karol Smolak."

"You mean Cerise May is gay?"

"Get your head out of the gutter, Yablonsky. Karol with a K. He runs what passes for a Polish Mafia in town. Big in Little Warsaw. I don't know what the Polish Mafia does—makes you an offer you can't understand, I guess."

"I don't get it."

"No kidding."

I took the tin he'd left open on my desk and dropped it in the trash. "If Karol Smolak is head of the Polish Mafia, that's bad."

"I've heard they're pretty ruthless. Twenty years ago they used to dump bodies under the Hill to Hill, though they gave that up when the Polish Mafia tried to go upscale. Happen to know anyone in it?" he asked cagily.

"Because my last name's Yablonsky?" I narrowed my eyes. "Watch it, buster. Next thing I know you'll be asking how many of my people it takes to screw in a lightbulb."

"Two to spin the chair, is what I heard."

"Or ten thousand to spin the house."

"Anyway, they don't need lightbulbs because they invented the first solar-powered flashlight," Lawless said.

The Polish invented the solar-powered flashlight? Now that was a great idea. It'd never run out of batteries. Jane had a solar-powered calculator and swore by it.

Lawless studied my expression. "You don't get that one either, say?"

"Let's skip the jokes. What happened between Karol and Doctor May?"

"Word was that Karol's mother never took to May. She wasn't Polish enough or something. Not the spitting image of the fucking Black Madonna of Czestochowa. Karol said no wedding and May immediately dumped him. Then again, from what I heard, Smolak isn't the marrying kind. A Polish playboy, you could call him."

My fingers involuntarily gripped the handles of my chair. This subject was hitting a bit too close to home. "How long ago did she dump him?"

"Don't know. I got this from a police source, Bubbles, not one of your ladies' gossip groups."

Mr. Salvo was making his way toward us, a dreaded press release in his hand. Lawless spotted him and slinked back into his cubicle to hide, lest Mr. Salvo hand him an assignment requiring actual work.

"There's a miracle in Hellertown." Mr. Salvo waved the paper. "Seems the Virgin Mary has been making regular appearances on a North Side Chevy Impala, right in time for the holiday shopping season."

As usual Mr. Salvo's countenance was pasty white and his armpits were stained with sweat.

"Catch is, she only appears at dawn. Seeing as I'm all out of three wise men awake at that hour, I'm looking for a volunteer."

I clamped my lips tight and busied myself organizing paper clips. I'd planned on sleeping in tomorrow. I'd planned on never getting out of bed again.

Lawless laid it on thick. "Wow, that sounds like a killer story. Page-one material. I'd love to do it. Unfortunately I'm swamped." He cast a regretful glance at the press release. "I'll be busy for days digging up dirt on May's connections with Karol Smolak. How about Yablonsky? This piece could be a rookie's dream."

I stuck my tongue out at Lawless.

Mr. Salvo didn't notice. "Okay, Yablonsky, you're on at five A.M. tomorrow, got it?"

Five A.M.? "Got it." I tried not to say that with a whine.

"You know who once had a run-in with Smolak?" Mr. Salvo said. "Your buddy Stiletto."

"Really?" I said. "That so?"

"I don't know the details. You'll have to ask him. Some bad scene in Philly with Smolak's brother, Cosmo. Nearly got Stiletto whacked himself."

"And then where would you be, Yablonsky?" Lawless asked. " 'Cause without Stiletto's help, you wouldn't have a job here, would you?"

I glared at him, hoping that a dirty look would say more than dirty words, and the tongue hadn't proven very effective.

"Of course, once you rope the famous Steve Stiletto into wedlock, my bet is you'll give up reporting altogether." Lawless took our silence for rapt attention. "Yes, I can see it now: Mrs. Steve Stiletto, barefoot and pregnant, waiting with her feet up for hubby to bring home the bacon."

"Ahem." Mr. Salvo cleared his throat pointedly.

"YABLONSKY!" Notch was at the door to his office, sleeves rolled up, grease pencil behind his ear. "Now."

"Fuck," said Lawless.

"No," I said, grabbing my notebook and ecstatic to be called away from Lawless. "I think he just wants to go over the story."

Notch was back at his big mahogany desk. His sunburned bald head, the color of the fireballs he kept in a fishbowl nearby, was bent over my story.

"Close the door." He didn't look up.

This was not promising. Notch and I had never liked each other. But he'd come far since I'd first entered the newsroom in hot pants and a tube top to discuss a lawsuit in which I'd landed the paper. Both of us had come far, inching toward a common ground where we could almost tolerate the other.

"This is okay." He tossed me the printout. It was marked in red and black. It didn't look okay to me.

I stared at his scrawls—delete and question marks. Despite computers, editors still printed stories and marked them viciously. I felt low. So much work. And with me trying to get out of the office so I could finally be by myself to think over this Stiletto development.

"Make those corrections. Also, I faxed it down to the lawyers. They want to know if you called Doctor May."

"Doctor May? Why?"

Notch reached in the fishbowl and pulled out a fireball. "Because until this story, word on the street has been that Schmidt was stalked by Popeye, that Popeye broke into May's office and murdered him.

"According to your interview, however, it appears that Doctor May and Popeye had an understanding where it was okay for her to use the restroom." He crunched the fireball. Cinnamon sparks shot from his mouth. "I don't think that's gonna sit well with May's patients."

"I'm not sure Doctor May has any patients," I said. "My mother hangs out with people who organize fan clubs for local doctors. She and her friends have never heard of Doctor May."

Notch took on a patronizing tone. "Yes. We all like to think of our mommies as the ultimate authorities. And to that I say, grow up! Call Doctor May. Visit her office if you have to. Just get her on the record about Popeye. And another thing." He regarded me sternly. "I understand Tony Salvo told you about Kuntz and Reinhold filing complaints with Garnet about your blue language. I don't like my reporters being rude."

"Like I told Mr. Salvo, I wasn't even close to rude, even though the sheriffs threw me in a jail cell with Popeye for no reason. Despite that, the worst thing I said was 'hell.' "

"All I care is that my reporters keep it clean, and that means no swearing of any kind." He ticked more no-nos off his fingers. "No threats. No trespassing or breaking of any local ordinances. No obvious indications of bias. No violence. And no gossip."

No gossip? How was I supposed to do my job? Scratch that. How was I supposed to live?

"Now, as for that notebook you're holding, that contain the Popeye interview?"

I stared at the notebook, still too worried about that "no gossip" rule to focus on exactly what Dix Notch was saying.

"I'm not supposed to tell you to get rid of that, the lawyers would kill me," Notch said, "but I encourage you to keep your desk neat.

We don't have much storage in this newsroom and so we've instituted a strict policy of incinerating spent materials, including notebooks. Got me?"

I thought of the newsroom desks piled high with papers, notebooks, coffee cups, municipal documents, etc. "Out of curiosity, how long have we had this strict policy of neatness?"

"Officially, as of five minutes ago."

Outside his office I ran into Lorena. Lorena was on cloud nine due to my interview with Crazy Popeye and her photos of Reinhold running to the lockup with Johnson upon hearing of Popeye's demise. No other photographer had been in the courthouse. They'd all been on the front lawn.

"We slam-dunked everyone." Lorena lifted her hand for a high five. "I got you an exclusive interview. You owe me, Yablonsky. You owe me big for getting you in that cell with her."

I did not high-five Lorena, but kept walking to my desk. "This is not a matter to celebrate, Lorena. Popeye died. She was probably murdered."

"Autopsy results tomorrow," added Lawless as I passed by.

"You're just trying to weasel out of owing me." Lorena ripped open a bag of peanuts with her teeth.

I looked up Dr. May's telephone number in the phone book. I dialed and waited for her to pick up. "What makes it even more of a tragedy is that I'm convinced Popeye was innocent."

"Either way," Lorena said, "you still owe me."

"Cerise May here."

I was startled to get a live person at such a late hour—and Dr. May herself, no less. So startled that I didn't know what to say.

"Hello?" Dr. May asked again.

I quickly rattled off my name and introduction and that I'd like to discuss the Crazy Popeye case with her.

"I'm sorry," Dr. May said, her tone still warm. "I'm not granting any interviews. But you can call my lawyer."

Lawless zipped to my side and hastily scrawled a note. ASK HER THE BIG QUESTION. DON'T FUCK AROUND.

He was right.

"Did you give Popeye permission to use your bathroom?" I said.

Dr. May said nothing.

"Because that's what Popeye told me today." I looked over at Lawless. He nodded as he wrote another note. "It's going to be in the story we're publishing tomorrow."

ASK HER ABOUT THE VOICES, Lawless's note said.

"Also, Popeye told me she heard several voices outside the bathroom that evening. Male *and* female."

"Oh," Dr. May said. "Oh. But the police are still confident that she's the one, aren't they? I thought they were sure she was his killer."

I scribbled this on the back of the notebook I was supposed to destroy. Otherwise I remained mum—a very effective tool for getting the other person to say more.

Lawless scratched off another order: GET HER TO MEET WITH YOU.

Lorena mimed herself taking a picture.

LUDWIG TOO, Lawless added.

"Perhaps we should meet," I suggested again, "to discuss what Popeye said."

"I can't do that. This situation has already been very stressful on me, as I'm sure you can fathom. It's—"

"I'd like to discuss," I braced myself, "what your relationship with Mr. Smolak might have to do with Mr. Schmidt's murder."

Lawless raised his eyebrows, impressed.

Lorena gave me the thumbs-up.

Cerise said nothing for a while. When she spoke again, the smooth doctor veneer was gone, replaced by a hissing wet cat. "What would my relationship with Karol have to do with this? What are you saying?"

I stood my ground. "Mr. Smolak is a known ringleader of the Polish Mafia and, as such, has a history of being involved in violent crime."

Dr. May abruptly got off. It sounded as though she was talking to someone in the background, a man. Their voices were muffled.

"Absolutely not," she said. "You're not coming here. And if you get within one block of my office"—her voice reached a hysterical pitch—"I'll call the police and have you arrested. You have no business writing about me or my personal life. No business at all."

She slammed down the phone.

"Where'd you get that Smolak is a *known* ringleader of the Polish Mafia?" Lawless asked as soon as I hung up. "And this business about a history of violent crime?"

"That's what you told me."

His expression remained blank. "Really? My source was just talking off-the-cuff over drinks last night. And he didn't say diddly about violence. I checked the court records. Smolak's never even been arrested."

"Oh, no!" I bit a knuckle. "What if Doctor May calls Dix Notch? Five minutes ago, he gave me a lecture about no bias, no gossip."

"Screw Notch," Lawless said. "What if May rats you out to her ex, Karol Smolak?"

"*Karol* Smolak!" Lorena exclaimed, now part of the conversation. "Oh my God. I didn't know it was him you were talking about."

"You two know each other?" I asked.

Lorena dumped a handful of peanuts in her mouth. "Karol's in my anger management class. And if you think I've got a problem, then you haven't seen nothing until you've seen Karol, hopped up on testosterone, swinging a folding chair."

Chapter Four

May I be frank? Well, too bad, I'm Bubbles. Rim shot.

Anyway, the point is that, frankly, I was not motivated to "head off Doctor May at the pass," as Lorena put it. It was already closing in on eight and I was suffering from a hardcore case of ennui.

I needed a hot bath and a defrosted Sara Lee Devil's Food Cake (though it didn't have to be defrosted). I needed A-Treat diet root beer and lots of it.

On the other hand, Lorena needed a job and that was why we were hurtling through the South Side in my Camaro. Lorena was smoking a mile a minute and I was freezing, since we had to keep the window down and the smoke out.

"What I'm thinking is that while you're apologizing . . . ," Lorena began.

"Clarifying," I corrected, clutching the wheel.

"Groveling. I get a shot of this May doctor all flustered, jamming her fist in the camera, kinda like on *Cops* . . ."

(I very much doubted Dr. May was the type to jam her fist in the camera kinda like on *Cops*, but try telling that to Lorena.)

". . . and we run that next to my pix of Reinhold running, then I'm in like Flynn. Deal?"

"Deal." I turned onto Fourth Street. "So, on a scale of one to ten, how bad is Karol Smolak's anger problem?"

"Twenty-five." Lorena considerately blew a plume out the window. "You remember that vandalism at St. Hedwig's last year? All those broken stained-glass windows?"

"Don't tell me he did that."

"Had fifteen stitches on his hand to prove it. It's how he ended up in anger management."

"How come? I mean, *why* would he do that?"

"I dunno. We're not supposed to talk about reasons in A.M." Lorena flicked out her butt. I watched it in the rearview sending up crackling sparks, hoping it wouldn't ignite the gas leak from my tank. "Reasons are justifications for unjustifiable behavior. Make the change to justifiable behavior and the reasons will be justified."

I rolled my eyes. Lorena and her repetitive twelve-step mantras.

"My beef with Anger Management is, I'm not so sure I want to get rid of all my anger, you know? Sometimes what the other guy needs is a left hook to the kisser." She thumbed through her cigarette case. "And it feels so good, too, you know, to really smack someone."

I searched for a way to get off this track. "So has A.M. changed Smolak's behavior?"

"Oh, sure. He's much better, though he threw a Tupperware container of dinner he'd brought from home at our teacher last week. Cost him fifty bucks and a month of extra sessions."

"How old is he?" He sounded no older than six.

"Forty. He still lives with her, you know."

"Who?"

"Mother Smolak. And let me tell you, she makes one heck of a borscht. I finished off what was left in his Tupperware."

I pulled up to the House of Beauty, my old stomping ground, as

Lorena lit her second cigarette in ten minutes. It was defiance of nature that she could still breathe.

"What gives?" she griped. "Why are we stopping? We'll miss May."

"I have to drop something off. You wait here." I shut the door and ran up the steps.

The House of Beauty is a pink-walled, two-sink salon lined with faded Dippity Do! posters on Fourth Street and it is where I've spent most of my adult, professional life—until recently. After Managing Editor Dix Notch offered me a full-time newspaper job, I gave notice to my boss and best friend, Sandy, who owns the place.

"Oh, get out of here," Sandy had said when I tearfully promised to try to work for two weeks. "I'm not going to let a stupid thing like employee policy stand in the way of your success."

Now, a few weeks later, there I was feeling like an outsider in front of what once was my home away from home. It was weird, me not working here. Already the place felt different. There was a brand-new Christmas decoration I'd never seen before—a twirling Mrs. Claus— and when did Sandy get that shiny green plastic rubber plant with the twinkling colored lights?

Sandy's miniature poodle Oscar leaped off his doggie mat and started yapping madly, as though he'd never seen me before, causing Sandy to rush out of the back office and scream, "Oh my God. You look so grown-up. Turn around."

I turned around.

"That the suit you bought on layaway?"

I nodded. Sandy bent down, removed a pair of scissors from the pocket of her peach polyester uniform, and snipped the threads on my pink skirt. "There. They should have done that at the store."

This is why Sandy is my best friend. I missed her.

"That new Mrs. Santa is nice," I said. I was glad to see that my vanity was still vacant, except for a half-burnt patchouli candle. "Tiffany joining you full-time?"

"Are you kidding? I don't carry that much insurance." Sandy picked up the coffee carafe and shook it, weighing whether to brew a new pot or microwave the old.

"Don't bother. I can't stay." I opened my purse and took out my Reporter's Notebook. "I just stopped by to give you this."

Sandy took the notebook and stared at it dumbly. "What for?"

"For safekeeping. Look." I flipped to a page with shimmering streaks of red, coral, pink, rose, wine, and blush. "It's got lipstick samples. From the new Clinique line."

"Hess's?"

"Mama was buying inserts. I had time to kill."

"I like this one." She pointed to the blush.

"That's called Nude Flourish. It's a semi. Fourteen bucks. I'm saving up."

"And you want me to keep this notebook for that?"

"I'm still making up my mind. I might go with Wine Whimsy. I need it for reference."

Sandy looked dubious.

"Or, alternatively, I need to hide it because the notes on the other pages could turn out to be key evidence in the investigation of Rudy Schmidt's murder and I could be imprisoned for obstruction of justice if a judge finds out I have it."

"I'm going with the Whimsy." She kicked open a bottom drawer of the makeup display and dropped in the notebook. "Not so complicated."

"Excellent choice."

Sandy shut the drawer. "Now, what's this about Stiletto getting engaged?"

Mama. Western Union could pick up pointers. "I don't know exactly."

I could feel those damn tears welling up again. Here, with Sandy, in the safety and warmth of the House of Beauty, I might actually lose it. I recounted my conversation with Mr. Salvo.

"And how does Stiletto explain this?"

"Huh?"

"Stiletto? Didn't you call him?"

"I don't know where he is." I was beginning to feel like an idiot.

Sandy frowned. Sandy is a very practical person. She opens her bills as soon as they come in the mail and if there's a late charge on the Visa, she calls the company, explains there's been a mistake, and gets it dropped.

Me, on the other hand, I wait until the end of the month, then I peek at the Visa with one eye open. Every time I try to call the Visa company and ask for the charge to be dropped, they laugh.

"Surely you have his cell phone number," she said.

In fact I had it memorized.

"And isn't he coming back today?"

"Either today or tomorrow."

"What are you waiting for, then? Call the sonofabitch and ask him what's this about him getting married."

The doorbell jingled and Lorena waltzed in.

"Who's getting married?" she asked. "Who's him?"

Sandy was fast on her clogged feet. "Nothing. I was describing a scene from *GH*."

GH stood for *General Hospital*, the soap opera that has saved me more than once. Fortunately, Lorena was strictly *One Life to Live*. If it didn't involve Viki Buchanan or Dorian Lord, she wasn't interested.

"*GH!* Blech." Lorena stuck her finger down her throat. "They haven't been able to get it together since Luke and Laura."

"I don't care," I said. "I miss *GH*. I wish they'd let us watch it in the newsroom like I used to watch it here."

"Memo Notch," Lorena said, grinning. "Bet he'd take it under advisement."

"I might just do that," I said. "They let sports watch ESPN twenty-four/seven. Why can't I watch my soaps?"

Lorena nodded. "You tell 'em, Bubbles."

"You don't need to watch soap operas." Sandy said. "New job. Elusive boyfriend. Guns shooting off left and right. Meanwhile, I languish away at the dull House of Beauty where nothing ever happens."

Lorena's eyes darted to the Styrofoam wig form she'd once put a bullet hole in and stuffed with gum and a Parliament filter. That was shortly after we'd had a House of Beauty catfight where we'd ripped off each other's nail tips. The way we saw it, what Sandy didn't know couldn't hurt her.

Cerise May's office was in Little Warsaw, in a white aluminum-sided building off Thirty-Third Street (pronounced "tirty-turd"), above Bartold's Bakery, next to Purvalowski's Deli and Meats (read: sausage), one block down from St. Hedwig's and across the street from The Polish-American Club.

Which, by the way, was really hopping for a Monday night in November. The one-story building was packed and booming with polka music. Even in the car we could smell the grilled kielbasa and heavy cigarette smoke.

"How much more Polish can you get?" Lorena asked as we searched for an inconspicuous place to dump the Camaro.

Thirty-Third was not the kind of street where you worried about parking violations. Cars were all over—on sidewalks, in front of fire hydrants. Sideways. Perpendicular. Aside from a fairly respectable shiny white Cadillac, the rest were beat-up Fords and Chevys, the kinds of cars where you didn't care if they were nicked or scraped.

We walked down the block and opened the door off the bakery that led to a narrow flight of yellowish-green carpeted stairs and Dr. May's office. Even though the bakery was closed, the oily aroma of lard-based super white frosting hung in the air.

Yum. Lard.

"Doesn't it seem strange to you that her front door is open at eight-thirty at night?" Lorena asked, huffing and puffing up the stairs behind me.

"Maybe she sees a lot of after-hours patients."

"Who? The drunks from the Polish club?" Lorena and I reached the landing that led to Dr. May's office. "Nuh-uh. Something's up."

She was right.

The lock on Dr. May's office door had been broken. Beyond the door, the waiting room was a showplace for federal disaster relief.

Cheerful, flowered couches had been overturned, the cushions carelessly thrown to the floor. One light was knocked over and the bulb was burnt out. Magazines and papers were strewn everywhere, carpeting the floor white. I was barely able to make out the yin-and-yang, black-and-white pattern on her thick Oriental rug.

Either May had been burglarized or . . . worse.

"Doctor May?" I called out. "Are you okay?"

No answer.

"And the plot thickens." Lorena got out her camera. "Now aren't you glad I made you come?"

"I'll let you know when I'm back safe at home and not riddled with bullet holes."

"Oh, don't be such a wuss." She adjusted the flash. "Think of this as the first step in a career advancement for you and a permanent paycheck for me. Good-bye, unemployment. Hello, job stability."

It floored me that Lorena had the presence of mind to think of getting a photo. I was extremely nervous being here. Nervous and more than slightly apprehensive. The hairs on my arms had risen in response to a sixth sense that whoever had done this to Dr. May's office might still be on the premises. He might be down the hall. He might be watching us right now.

"What are you waiting for?" Lorena took a wide-angle shot of the couches. "Snoop before the cops get here."

"What if the cops don't know? Shouldn't we call them?"

Lorena reached through an opening in the receptionist's window and held up a cut phone cord. "Fat chance of that. Now, c'mon. With her connections, Doctor May might be stuffed inside a closet around here. In which case, I'm asking for a starting salary of twenty-six."

I shivered. Lorena could be downright heartless, but she was right. This was a golden snooping opportunity.

I started with the semiwalled receptionist's area. Seemingly every patient file had been removed from a sliding set of shelves and emptied on the floor. It was impossible to walk without tiptoeing on someone's X-rays or insurance information. Cerise May would want to kill herself after seeing this . . . if she wasn't dead already.

"Didn't you say she was talking to someone in the background when you called?" Lorena asked, now taking shots of the paper-littered floor.

"A man." A brass letter opener glinted on the receptionist's desk, beckoning me to pick it up. "Though I wouldn't recognize the voice. It was garbled."

"This is more than kid vandalism." Lorena kicked aside a folder. "Whoever did this was searching high and low for a document, I bet. They were looking for files."

"Files of feet?" I examined the letter opener. It lay next to a framed photo of two smiling women. One woman was in a white lab coat and I recognized her as Dr. May from her photographs in the newspaper: trim, thirtyish, with shagged dirty-blond hair.

The other woman was plumper with a long, wavy brown mane pinned back in a clip. She was wearing a corduroy jumper and very little makeup, except for her naturally angelic nature. I remembered her right off.

Ruth Faithful. One year behind me at Liberty. I looked around the desk. There was another picture of Ruth with her father, the rather portly Reverend Tom Faithful, pastor of All God's Children Church. Ruth, I deduced, was now working as Dr. May's receptionist.

Though the Reverend Faithful had a reputation as a real Bible thumper, I remembered his daughter as anything but. In high school, Ruth had been busted for smoking pot on Pine Street behind Liberty and then suspended—by Schmidt. She'd been a bit of a wild woman. She'd dated Carlos Vallerico, for heaven's sake.

I still got a charge remembering Carlos Vallerico, the way his lithe, tanned body moved across the gym floor at Northeast Junior High dances. His slim hips and sultry Puerto Rican accent that put pay to the pasty-faced boys I'd grown up with. His whisper of a mustache and—

"What the hell are you doing?" Lorena hollered. "Your fingerprints are going to be all over that now."

I quickly wiped the photo on my skirt and quit dreaming of Carlos. Where had Ruth been last Thursday evening when Schmidt was murdered?

There was a sudden barking outside. *Woof. Woof. Woof.* A dog who wouldn't quit. I was surprised the babushkas in this neighborhood tolerated that kind of behavior. I know where I live a yipping dog is tolerated for five minutes before Mr. Hamel flies out the door in his T-shirt and boxers, screaming for quiet.

"That dog needs to shut up," said Lorena, looking out the window. "Oh, shit. Blue lights. It's the cops."

Chapter Five

"**N**o way can the cops find me." Lorena was already ahead of me down the hall, which was illuminated by one sickly green light from a smoke alarm. "I do not do cops."

That was a loaded statement when it came from Lorena.

"You don't have to *do* the cops." I grabbed the letter opener for protection and followed Lorena, checking quickly into what appeared to be Cerise May's office. I flicked on and off the light. Nope, no body. At least not one in full view. "You just have to avoid them. What's the big deal anyway? We'll say we came here to interview Doctor May and found the place like this."

"You don't have to worry, 'cause you're law-abiding," Lorena said.

"And you're not?"

We stopped by a door that said FIRE EXIT—ALARM WILL SOUND in red letters. Lorena was panting and it wasn't even a very long hall. We were stuck. Open the door and risk the alarm or stay and get caught.

"I had a run-in with the law." She gripped the door handle. "Once, I shoplifted a teensy-weensy bit of retail."

"Candy?"

"Bigger. More like a stereo."

I had one ear tuned to the stairwell, listening for footsteps coming up the back way. "Don't worry, Lorena. We all do stupid stuff when we're kids. Even the cops."

"I did it on Friday." Her eyes glowed amber in the yellow light.

"You *what*?"

"I don't know what came over me. I was at Circuit City and this salesman was giving me a hard time about my credit and me not having a full-time job for two months, so I stormed outside and I saw this stereo that was there, waiting to be picked up, and I took it."

"Lorena! I'm ashamed of you. Someone bought that and you stole it. Why?"

"It's part of my character flaw. I do stupid stuff when I'm angry." She sighed. "I'll have to bring it up at A.M. It'll set me back."

"Forget setting you back, how about the stereo? Have you taken *it* back?"

She shifted her hips. "Now, how am I supposed to do that? Simply walk into the store with this Sony and say, 'Um, I think I may have mistakenly picked this up'?"

Slam. From below a door shut. Hard.

"That's gotta be the cops coming up the steps," I said, fighting an urge to run back and forth crazily, like a trapped mouse in a Havahart.

"Think positive. Maybe the cops went to the Polish-American Club," Lorena said. "The party there did look like it was getting out of hand."

No such luck. Voices were entering the waiting room. We had no choice. We had to go out the emergency door.

"One, two, three." We pushed it open and I squeezed my eyes shut, waiting for the blare of the alarm.

Nothing.

Lorena and I hesitated a minisecond. "It's been deactivated," she said. "Whoever broke in here . . ."

But we didn't stop to discuss details. Before the cops tramped up the back hall we were out the back door and in the alley.

Free.

The trick, of course, was exiting Little Warsaw without arousing the babushka radar. Lucky for us, it was almost nine and the ladies were tucked in bed.

Having grown up with Mama, the Babushka Queen, I was savvy enough to keep my lights off and to drive down Thirty-Third in the dark until we were two blocks out, in the regular part of the South Side.

"I got a question," Lorena said as we passed two women in shorts leaning into a low-slung Audi. Never mind it being November in Pennsylvania and too cold for shorts, what was an Audi doing on the South Side? That was cause alone to call the cops.

"You want to know what happened to Doctor May," I said.

Lorena fumbled with the camera in her lap. "Actually, I was going to ask if my butt looked big in these pants, but now that you mention it, that is kind of strange. I mean, whoever ransacked the place did a thorough job. They would have needed time."

Time. How much time had we spent, exactly? We'd stopped off at the House of Beauty for no more than ten minutes and the total trip from the *News-Times* to Little Warsaw would have taken all of twenty. That would have given the burglars a maximum of thirty minutes to toss Dr. May's office.

That is, if she left as soon as we ended our phone conversation. Unless . . .

"They took her." Lorena pronounced this like it was fact. "Definitely." She tapped her teeth and stared out her window.

"How do you know?"

"Because there was only one nice car on Thirty-Third."

"The Cadillac."

"Did you read the license plate?"

"Nuh-uh."

"FT1ST. I remember because when I first read it, I thought, hey, that should be mine. Fight First. Then I realized it said—"

"Feet first." I parked the car in front of the *News-Times* and yanked the key out of the ignition. "And it was still there when we left."

"Hot dog," we said in unison.

Upstairs in the newsroom we found Mr. Salvo as jumpy as if he'd never put out a paper before in his twenty years of experience. The police scanner droned a mindless list of codes, of suspicious persons and ambulance calls. The presses hummed even louder, spinning off the inserts and lifestyle sections until the final run—front-page news and local sports—could be printed and packaged.

"What happened at May's?" Mr. Salvo didn't bother to look up from his white layout sheet. "You were gone for over an hour."

"We got there and found it was trashed," I said. "No sign of May."

Mr. Salvo's black grease pencil stopped halfway down the page. "What do you mean, trashed?"

"Tossed. Destroyed. Ransacked." Lorena and I exchanged glances. We'd cooked up a story in the car that we hoped Mr. Salvo would buy. "Lorena took a few photos from the doorway and then we split. We would've called the cops but the phone cord was cut. . . ."

"And they were just arriving anyway," Lorena offered. "So we felt it prudent to clear out. Give them some elbow room." She'd been A-OK, doing just fine, until she felt compelled to add, "Tell him about Ruth Faithful, Bubbles."

I cleared my throat, a signal to Lorena that she should *shut . . . up.*
It was too late. "Who's Ruth Faithful?" Mr. Salvo asked.

Lorena didn't wait for me to answer. "She's this woman Bubbles went to high school with. She's a receptionist for Doctor May and the daughter of a really strict minister in town and once Schmidt blew the whistle on her for smoking dope on Pine Street. We found her picture on her desk, she's May's receptionist, and Bubbles recognized her right off."

I started humming "If I Only Had a Brain."

"Isn't that awesome?" Lorena asked.

Mr. Salvo rubbed his eyelids with ink-stained fingers. "What's awesome is that you two violated a crime scene. That is, unless"—he looked hopeful—"the receptionist's desk is right by the door."

"Nah," said Lorena, head so thick there was no room for more stupidity. "We had to cross the office to see that."

My stomach turned. *No swearing, no misrepresentation, no bias, and no trespassing.* Notch's warning.

"I am not pleased," Mr. Salvo said curtly. "Let's just hope it doesn't get back to Notch what you've done. Let's hope the shit doesn't hit the fan."

Personally, I can't stand that expression. Who throws shit at fans, is what I wanted to know. It was so gross.

While Lorena holed up in the darkroom developing the prints that I was certain would soon, like my Popeye notes, join the Lehigh PD's Most Wanted Evidence list, I tried calling Dr. May at her home.

Cerise May was listed in the phone book as living in the Spring Street Apartments, a shingled complex built for swinging singles in the 1970s. Though I'd only been there twice, to do the hair of a client who'd been too ill to drive to the salon, I recalled it as a rather run-down development. Not the kind of place where you'd expect to find a single professional doctor with an established foot practice.

I let the phone ring eight times. Dr. May didn't pick up and neither did her answering machine, which I thought was kind of strange. Seemed to me that if anyone was required to have either an answering machine or service it would be a doctor.

That left me with no other option than to make a house call of my own.

Dr. May's apartment was fairly easy to find. The number was written on one of the small metal mailboxes by the entrance. May. 100-D. First floor. Big mistake for a woman. Easy access to Peeping

Toms. Personally, I'd never sleep on the first floor of anything. Unless Mel Gibson was sleeping next to me.

I drove around to Building D and found 100, a corner unit that looked onto a mowed-down cornfield. Probably why she rented it. Privacy. A street light that would have kept me awake nights if I lived there illuminated the otherwise empty parking lot.

I left the Camaro idling and went to the door that did not meet the Lehigh Christmas code of decorating standards. Nothing but a plastic wreath with fake snow. No lights. Not even a wilting poinsettia by the welcome mat. Pathetic. I mean, would it have hurt to hang a couple of jingle bells?

I knocked three times and rang the bell four, gambling that an annoyed neighbor would pop out and demand to know what the Sam hell was going on. But apparently the Spring Street wasn't that kind of an apartment complex. People here kept to themselves. In fact, they seemed oblivious . . .

. . . except for the man watching me from the Ford.

I don't know how I'd missed him. It wasn't until I had given up and was walking back to my Camaro that I spied the guy from the corner of my eye. He was a big black shadow in the driver's seat of a nondescript dark sedan and he was wearing a bowler. Like in *The Exorcist*. Creepy.

The sedan was parked in the space next to the one in front of Dr. May's apartment and the engine was dead.

Half of me wondered if he was too.

Still, I'm not one to go poking my head into strange men's sedans in deserted apartment complexes. (Unlike, I might add, the ladies of the night near Little Warsaw.) And just because the two of us were up late in the Spring Street, I saw no reason to introduce myself and strike up a conversation.

Careful not to make eye contact, I stepped inside the Camaro (thank goodness I let that engine run) and pulled—make that *peeled* with a screech—out as fast as I could. Not a light went on.

It was after eleven when I got home, safe and sound and not followed by an exorcist. Jane was working at the kitchen table doing calculus.

"Have a nice night?" I asked cheerfully.

She punched a number on her calculator. "Um," she said. Very unlike her. So unlike her that I began to fear the worst.

"Princeton didn't . . ."

"E-mail me. No." Jane pushed the calculator away and sat back. Her eyes were red rimmed, which meant she'd been crying, though, as the mother of a teenager, I knew better than to say anything about *that*. "But Jon Chou, that kid from New York who went to Lehigh University's summer physics program with me last year, he found out. He's in."

One space taken.

"Buck up." I opened the refrigerator and pulled out two A-Treats plus Mama's leftover Golfer's chicken. "There are lots of places you can go besides Princeton. There's—"

"Don't say it." Jane clapped her hands over her ears.

Geesh. Why was everyone so down on Two Guys?

"By the way, Stiletto didn't call either," Jane said bitterly, returning to her work. "Only Dad. He wants to talk to you about his mystery case. He says there's been a development. Also, he left his coat here. He wants you to bring it to his office tomorrow."

I'd get right on that. Perhaps I could pick up his dry cleaning, too?

The phone rang. Jane and I froze, me with my nose in chicken and her with a finger hovering over the cosine button.

"I don't think Princeton makes telephone calls at eleven-fifteen," she said. "Want me to get it?"

"Could be Stiletto." Like a teenager I dropped the plate and dashed for the phone.

Relax, I told myself. You don't want to sound anxious.

"Hell-o?"

"You might want to return that stereo," a throaty voice said. It took me a second to realize that it belonged to a woman, or perhaps a teenage boy, who was trying his or her hardest to sound like Lauren Hutton with emphysema. "Circuit City prosecutes *all* shoplifters."

Who was this? "Is this G?"

"G?" Jane said from the kitchen. "But, Mom, he's . . ."

"Is that your daughter I hear?" It was definitely a woman's voice. "Is that Jane?" Whoever she was, she knew I had a kid.

A damp chill, one that I can only describe as sinister, came over me. Even the room felt colder. What could have been a gag suddenly was anything but. I spun around and looked at Jane, who stopped writing, saw the panic on my face, and got up.

Who is it? my daughter mouthed.

"If I were you, I'd stay away from the Popeye story. 'Cause if you don't, Jane might not make it to graduation. And that would be a darn shame."

The line went dead.

Jane ran to my side and took the receiver out of my hand while I teetered against the staircase, feeling as though I'd been punched. Jane. She'd mentioned my daughter.

"What did he say?" Jane said, depressing the receiver.

"Not a he. A she."

"Who was it?"

"I don't know who it was. She made a reference to the story I'm working on." Better to keep it vague until I got the particulars.

"Let's find out." Jane started dialing *69.

"That costs a buck fifty."

Jane ignored this, listening as the computer-generated operator gave her the number. Writing it on her palm, she redialed.

"She threatened you, didn't she?"

How to tell her that, actually, she'd threatened *her?*

Then I remembered. Lorena. She'd confessed to stealing the stereo from Circuit City while we were in Dr. May's. Which meant that whoever called tonight had been in the office. She'd heard us.

She'd been there!

"Just a crank call from a drunk, Mom. Don't worry about it." Jane hung up and waved at it with disgust. "What losers. I mean, grown women drinking and dialing from the Polish-American Club. Talk about needing to get a life."

Chapter Six

Of course the Polish-American Club was right across the street from Dr. May's.

This was the first uplifting thought that entered my groggy brain as the alarm buzzed at 5:15 A.M. For about two minutes, which felt like two hours, I lay in bed trying to fathom why I would have set the clock at such an ungodly hour. It was still pitch black outside and I'd stayed up almost all night worrying about Jane, falling asleep long after three.

And then it came back to me. Madonna on the Impala.

Sliding out of bed, I slogged down to the shower and let hot water run over my body, cursing myself for my stupidity. Last night, hopped up on sugar from eating half a pack of Oreos, and about ready to check myself into the Happy Farm Retreat and Asylum thanks to a Lifetime late-night special about the mother of a child with a rare blood disorder caught in Bora Bora, who'd traded in all her worldly goods to take her kid for one last whirl around Disneyland, I'd committed the most grievous of sins.

I'd called Stiletto.

Not what you'd call my better judgment. Be kind, though. It was the act of a desperate woman in desperate straits. That phone call from the Polish-American Club had shaken me to my bones and I wasn't feeling steady to begin with. Not after learning that Stiletto had gone off and gotten engaged.

So what happened? The worst.

He wasn't in. He wasn't in his apartment in New York. His cell phone didn't ring and all I got at his mansion in Saucon Valley was the usual answering machine.

By the time I got around to the Saucon Valley answering machine, I had really worked myself into a lather envisioning him in a big four-poster European bed making love over and over again to the one woman in the world he believed worth marrying.

So—and, yes, this was another stellar moment for me, Bubbles Yablonsky—I left a message that would surely qualify for lead exhibit in the Hall of Fame of Tasteless Acts of the Lovelorn, if indeed there were such a place. (Though I suspect there is, located somewhere in New Jersey.)

Ugh.

Don't even ask me what I said because I can't bear to think of it. Suffice it to say, it was so awful, no amount of makeup could hide my embarrassment. The most I could hope was that a lightning bolt would hit his house, electrify the telephone wires, and blow out his machine.

I quickly stepped into a demure black turtleneck sweater and a tight pair of black leather pants, an appropriate outfit, I felt, for viewing the Holy Virgin on auto parts. I added the crucifix I used to wear religiously in junior high school and two tiny crystalline cross earrings. Slipped into my stiletto boots, tied back my hair with a black bow, and checked my reflection in the mirror.

Very Madonna of the Valvoline.

Rousing Jane before dawn was no easy trick, but I did it with the aid of my big lungs and a lot of warm, maternal threatening. I could not leave her alone for a minute. Not after last night's phone call.

While she struggled to consciousness, I rushed down to the basement and threw a load of wet laundry in the dryer, making sure to clean the lint filter. A week before, I'd covered a house fire and interviewed the owner, a distraught mother of three who'd done two white loads before gathering up her kids and rushing off to work. Her parting words to me were, "Don't forget. Clean your lint filter!"

I didn't forget.

Then I called Dan.

"Geesh, Bubbles," he groaned, "it's not even six. What's your problem?"

"How did you know it was me?" I shoved a Pop-Tart into the toaster.

"Caller ID."

"Call her Aidee? Who's Aidee?"

"It's too early to play games. What do you want?"

I poured myself another cup of coffee and threw in a packet of Sweet'n Low. "I want you to know I won't be dropping off your coat. I have to go over to Highland Heights to cover a Virgin Mary sighting, so you'll have to meet me there if you want it."

"Who is it?" Wendy screeched in the background.

"No one," grumbled Dan. "Is that it? Is that why you woke me up before six?"

"Jane said you called last night about a new development in your so-called mystery case. The one that's giving you car trouble."

"More than car trouble. My radiator blew up."

"James Bond's got nothing on you." I bit into the searing hot blueberry Pop-Tart, instantly burning my tongue. "What do you want me to do?"

"I want you to use your apparently intrepid reporting skills and help me investigate what's going on."

"Okay, let's start with an obvious question. What *is* going on?"

"Can't talk about it here," he murmured. "At the office where it'll be safe."

With his mini-Homeland Security system, I'd have assumed Dan could hold off an invading Martian from setting one little green toe on his lawn, let alone what appeared to be one seriously pissed-off auto mechanic.

"Listen, you should know that you're not the only one getting death threats," I said. "I got a call when I got home last night. It was made from the Polish-American Club. I can't go into details, but the caller said that if I didn't stay away from the Popeye story, Jane might not see graduation."

Dan thought about this. "That would save us a few bucks, say?"

"I might actually be able to retire." I laughed, hung up, and found Jane, still half awake, frowning at me, finding the joke about her getting bumped off not so funny. Teenagers. Very self-centered.

"If you considered Two Guys," I said, "I wouldn't have to resort to such gallows humor."

When Jane was safely in Mama's arms at the senior citizen high-rise, I gunned it over to the cushy Highland Heights neighborhood where the Madonna was appearing on the 1972 Chevy Impala.

Upscale Tudor-style homes set back from the street. Big oak trees. Lots of Lehigh professors. The Madonna house was on the corner. A Christmas tree was already lit up in the lead glass window, as was a big BEWARE OF DOG sign.

I parked my Camaro in front of Mr. and Mrs. Henry Taylor's, home to the Blessed Impala, and waited for Lorena, since no way was I going into any BEWARE OF DOG place without a bitch of my own.

A cold strip of pink was spreading across the horizon. I fogged up the windows killing time, listening to AM radio and finishing the much cooler blueberry Pop-Tart. If Lorena didn't hustle, we'd miss all the action.

Five minutes later she arrived in her raised-end jalopy with its 8ME plates. I stepped out into the frigid air to join her.

"Sorry I'm late." Lorena tossed me a *News-Times* from the top of a pile of clothes in her arms. She was still in her bathrobe. "Hooked up with an old pal of mine at the Tally Ho, and, well, you know how it is with one-night stands. I practically had to push the guy out the door."

I wasn't a one-night-stand kind of girl, except for an afternoon in the back of my Camaro with a Radio Shack repairman and I wasn't about to repeat that fiasco. It's what set me off on my vow of chastity, which only the spell of Stiletto had broken.

Stiletto. Sigh.

Lorena pulled on a pair of jeans under her robe. "Kick-ass story in today's rag. I like the way you smoothed over us breaking into May's office."

"About that." I tried to ignore the fact that our photographer was actually getting dressed in the middle of the street. "I received a nasty phone call when I got home last night. Seems we weren't the only ones in May's office."

"No shit." Lorena let the robe drop, ducked behind my car, and slipped a sweatshirt over her head. "What happened?"

I told her about the call. When I finished, Lorena zipped up her jeans and said, "Polish-American Club. That's the ticket. From now on, that's where I'm doing all my drinking. You'll see. It'll pay off in news tips."

In Polish one-night stands, I thought, certain there was a joke for that, too.

The sun was rising rapidly and, as I was not eager to wake up at five A.M. again to catch Our Lady of the Hubcap, I tossed the paper back to Lorena. "We have to hurry."

"Damn," she said, looking dejected. "Forgot the underwear. See what happens when I don't have time for coffee?"

When it came to underwear and Lorena, I had no comment.

As we walked up the Taylors's driveway, two teenage girls ambushed us in the dark. They fell into that painfully awkward age bracket between eleven and fourteen, too old for dolls, too young to drive. Lots of braces, pimples, and giggles, giggles, giggles, topped off by the familiar green-plaid-skirt-and-white-blouse uniforms of Saint Anne's Catholic School.

"I'm Samantha Taylor," said the taller one, her hair slicked to her head, indicating that it had been brushed over and over. "T-A-Y-L-O-R." She leaned over to check that I was writing it down correctly. "I saw her first."

"Who?" I asked, assuming we must be talking about the Madonna.

"I saw her too. I was sleeping over," piped up another, darker copy of Samantha. "I'm Brittany Walsh. Brittany's spelled—"

PWWWEEP! A screeching whistle sounded.

The girls leaped back, wide-eyed at Lorena, who, coffee-less and panty-less, seethed at them like a possessed demon. Lorena slowly removed her fingers from her mouth. "It's almost dawn. Where the he . . . where's the Impala?"

Samantha, still in a mild state of shock, pointed to the end of the driveway. "There. In the garage."

"*In* the garage?" I walked toward it, the BEWARE OF DOG dog leaping madly from window to window inside the house as I passed. "How does the image come *in* the garage?"

"That's why it's a miracle, silly." Samantha giggled, causing an echoing ripple from Brittany. "We're like the girls from Our Lady of the Lourdes."

"Or Sarajevo," offered Brittany, the smarter of the two.

The back door of the house opened and an energetic mother bounded out, wearing a neat white turtleneck, preppy boat sweater, and jeans. She was the type who would remember underwear, coffee or no coffee. Her hair was blond and she wore one of those hard, black, uncomfortable hair bands.

"Are you the ladies from the newspaper?" she asked, extending her hand. "Super. I'm Mrs. Taylor."

I supposed that's how she expected me to identify her in the paper. Mrs. Taylor. Or perhaps, Mrs. Henry Taylor of the Scranton Taylors, steel and scrap metal.

"If she can't take photos," Mrs. Taylor said, nodding toward Lorena, "I have more pictures that a professional took the other day. I can leave them to you."

At the insinuation that she was not a professional, Lorena let out a low growl. Maybe the rumors were true. Maybe Lorena really had been raised by wolves.

"It's almost time," squealed Samantha, lifting up the garage door to reveal the large, light-green, well-waxed car.

"Groovy." Lorena nodded with genuine approval.

"My husband's a collector." Mrs. Taylor leaned against a minivan, as if to say that she had no truck with vintage muscle cars. "He's had it since college."

Lorena pulled out a light from her bag. "Where does this, um, vision usually show up? On the hood or on the side?"

"Right there." Samantha gestured to the rear window. "It's very clear. There's no mistaking her."

"One more minute," reported Mrs. Taylor. "The almanac says dawn's at 7:12. Why don't you tell the reporters what happened, honey."

"On Saturday morning I was looking for my cat, Bozo, and Brittany was helping me," said Samantha. "I could hear him crying, like he was in pain."

Brittany stepped forward. "We thought he was trapped in the garage."

"So I opened the door and then . . ."

We all gasped. As the gray dawn lit up the dangerously unsafe small window of the Impala, sure enough the outline of a woman began to emerge.

Lorena dropped the light and started clicking photos madly.

At first there was just her head. Large and round. Then waves of soft hair. And then her arms, bare with bracelets, and cleavage, low. A bustier of some sort. Fishnet stockings and . . .

"Hold on," I said as the teeth came into view, big and gapped. "This is the Madonna?"

"Not *the* Madonna," corrected Samantha. "Madonna."

"You know," Brittany said. " 'Like a virgin'?"

"Oh, I hate that song." Mrs. Taylor rubbed her arms at the chill of it. "She's such a slut, that Madonna."

"She's a material girl, Mom."

Lorena started laughing until I gave her a slight kick. "So what kind of vision is this, exactly? Madonna the rock star. What does this mean?"

The BEWARE OF DOG dog let out a series of yips and Mrs. Taylor excused herself, mumbling about Channel 10 and the *Today* show.

"You know what I think this means?" Samantha stood by the vision so Lorena would be sure to get her in the picture. "I think it's a lesson to us girls that we should be free to be ourselves. To dress as we want."

"That it's okay to wear miniskirts," offered Brittany, seizing the opportunity to protest her religious-school uniform. "And the nuns should let us come to school with fishnets, too. At least on Fridays."

"Yeah," Samantha agreed. "At least on Fridays."

"It's what the Holy Mother would want," added Brittany.

"That's not the Holy Mother," I said. "That's Madonna."

Brittany and Samantha stood together in solidarity.

"I know what this vision means," said Lorena, standing. "It means that a soap drawing inside the window of your dad's car catches the reflection of a rising sun. That's what it means."

In a flash, the girls' demeanors changed from confidence to visible guilt. Each tried hard not to look at the other, now that their game had been exposed. Brittany, I sensed, was about to cry.

"Miss Yablonsky?" Mrs. Taylor called from the back door. "There's a man here to see you. He says he's your husband."

Dan, here to get his coat. Always I had to stop for him.

I excused myself and jogged around to the front of the house. How would he like it if I stormed into his office one day while he was with a client? Or what if I burst out in the courtroom, yelling for more child support?

"I'm sorry, he got back into his car to take a phone call." Mrs. Taylor met me on the lawn and, putting her hand firmly between my shoulder blades, steered me to a putzy Ford that wasn't his style at all.

Must be a loaner, I thought, since his BMW had caught fire.

The rear door popped open and Mrs. Taylor practically heaved me in. Before I could protest I found myself wedged between two men in white shirts and black pants with forearms like Mama's. They had shiny moon faces, blond hair, and chins that were gonna be double within a year. They could pass as twins and likely were.

There was no Dan.

"Is this what you want?" Mrs. Taylor asked nervously.

"You did good, Sophie. Your brat will be pleased," said one of the men, nodding.

What brat?

"Wait!" I protested, but Mrs. Taylor slammed the door and the car sped off. God, what was the world coming to when soccer moms start cavorting with thugs?

I noted that the rear seats were separated from the front by a pane of smoked glass, kind of like a cab. Not a good sign, I thought, seeing as this wasn't a taxi and I didn't want to go anywhere.

"I'm Jozef," said the beefy man on my left, "and this is my brother Zbigniew." He pointed to the beefy guy on my right.

"Zbigniew," I said. "That's original."

"Not where we live." Zbigniew rudely snatched my purse.

"If you're looking for a gun," I said, "forget it. I'm not that kind of girl."

But he wasn't looking for a gun. Instead, he lifted out my notebook and thumbed through the pages, smiling at his twin.

"That's mine," I said stupidly. "That has my notes from this morning. You can't take it."

"He just did," said Jozef. "Karol looks forward to reading it. Now just sit back and enjoy the ride." He removed a gun from his pocket and pointed it at me.

Nothing like a little Polish hospitality.

Chapter Seven

I'd heard some scary stories about Karol Smolak, about him smashing the stained-glass windows at St. Hedwig's and hurling his own
mother's borscht at his anger management counselor. So the last activity I expected to find him engaged in was the damp and peaceful
pursuit of horticulture.

Yet there he was in the back of Smolak's Flowers, a sweet grand-
motherly shop tucked in between a shoe repair and Kaminski and
Sons Funeral Home. I'd driven by it many times and ordered from
Smolak's at least twice for funerals.

Clearly Smolak's had a privileged, not to mention convenient, relationship with the Kaminski family. Now that I knew Karol Smolak
produced corpses as well as lilies, I was developing a new apprecia-
tion for the dynamics of business interdependence.

The Ford was parked in the Kaminski lot, in full view of bustling
Little Warsaw. One of my escorts stood guard while the other as-
sisted me out the door. Since I was in black, I supposed I looked like
any other grieving woman in the protective custody of two Polish
cousins arriving to work out arrangements with the Kaminskis, except that I was swearing up a blue streak.

"Let go of me, you overstuffed sausage," I screamed, trying to shake my arm free. Then remembering Lorena's classic line, "I'd kick you in the balls if you had any."

This did not pack the same punch as Lorena's tirade. I didn't raise an eyebrow from any passersby, not even as I was led, my feet dragging, to the flower shop.

"Mind her footwear," a meter maid advised before moving to the next car, pausing to frown with pity . . . pity only for my now seriously scraped boots.

Zbigniew and Jozef threw open the back door and shoved me into a small, cluttered greenhouse filled with plastic flower stands, red clay pots, and large rolls of ribbons and netting, along with stacks of unfolded boxes.

"Is this her?" A giant of a blond man wearing a dark green apron approached, holding the most wilted and sad cactus I'd ever seen. His hair was buzz-cut short. Very unflattering. Usually is. He had grown a pale Fu Manchu mustache and goatee in an attempt to cover his double chin which, along with the anger management issue, was an evident personal weakness.

"Bubbles Yablonsky, Karol," announced Jozef, tossing Smolak my notebook. "By the by, Sophie says hi."

"Hi to Sophie." Karol gave them a quick nod that I assumed was Polish Mafiese for "Now scram, punks."

The two dropped my arms and left the way we entered. They didn't go far, though. I could hear them right outside the door.

Smolak and I faced each other. I pegged him right off. He was a playground bully. A kid who had gotten his way in school simply because he'd been the biggest first. As a grown-up (and I use that term loosely) he may have graduated from lunch money to hush money, but he was still beating up those littler than him.

"Just where do you get off," I began, smoothing my turtleneck, "interrupting my workday for your personal whim? I was in the middle of reporting on a story."

Smolak was temporarily speechless. I guess he was used to kidnappees cowering. "I . . . I needed to talk to you," he sputtered.

"There were other ways of talking to me. There's the phone. That's a nifty invention. And, of course, e-mail." I sounded tough, but inside I was quivering, especially when I saw the size of his massive hand, which could have turned the flower pot it was holding into red dust. I couldn't get out of my mind that image of him busting church windows.

"Yeah, well, this is more important." He plunked down the cactus. "Where's Cerise?"

It was my turn to be dumbstruck. "I don't know what you're talking about."

"Bull!" He smacked his fist into a wooden table. Clay pots clattered and the Christmas cactus almost fell over. "I read your article this morning. You had to have been in her office last night. My sister Sophie saw the same story and agreed."

Which explained the "brat." Brat is the Polish word for brother. Sophie was Karol's sister, along with being the mother to Samantha T-A-Y-L-O-R.

"You were the one who called Cerise," Smolak went on. "She didn't want you to come by her office, but being a pushy reporter, you did anyway. Couldn't give the poor woman a rest, could you?"

"You were with Cerise?" I asked. "I thought you two were splitsville."

"Whether or not we're splitsville is none of your damn business. And if you don't start answering my questions, I'm gonna have to take measures." He made a fist and brought it under my nose. It smelled like dirt. I didn't have to ask what kind of measures. "Question one. Where's her gun? It was stolen from her office drawer last night."

"I don't know where Cerise or her gun is. I didn't go in her office and she wasn't there when I arrived and the place was trashed. Whoever got to her reached her before we did."

Karol dropped his fist and looked off, comprehending these words. Absently, he took to picking brown leaves from a wilting plant with drooping pink flowers.

"Is that a Bleeding Heart?" I couldn't care less what it was. I was simply trying to find common ground. If I could soften up Smolak, he might be able to tell me more about his ex-girlfriend.

"Yup." He pushed it aside. "Poisonous. You eat enough, you can go into convulsions."

I didn't know many people who went around munching on house-plants.

"It's candy compared to this." He gestured to a large pot in the corner in which sprouted a shrub with dusty maroon leaves and striking crimson burrs. "Carmencita. Attractive annual. Perennial down south. Otherwise known as the castor bean plant. Two seeds will do you in. Ricin and all."

"Appetizing." I was beginning to detect a pattern. A rather disturbing pattern at that. "And this?"

Smolak followed my gaze to another potted shrub with leathery green leaves and delightful light pink flowers. "Petit Salmon. Grows only four feet high and needs tons of sunlight. Can't grow it outside here. Can't grow any oleanders north of Virginia, really."

"Let me guess. Poisonous?"

"All parts." He slipped on a pair of rubber gloves and deadheaded a flower. "The larger varieties grow into shrubs. Texas has them all over. There's enough on the highways to wipe out the whole state."

Karol Smolak: personal gardener to the Manson Family.

"So, what is it with you and poisonous plants?" I asked.

He dumped the dead flowers in a can. "I like them. They're more interesting. And"—he stepped back and surveyed the oleander—"there's a sense of control."

Which he should be applying to his anger management instead of lethal fauna, but who was I to judge?

"Back to business." He yanked off the gloves and set to opening my notebook, flipping through the pages with his deadly green thumb. "Where are those notes you wrote when you were talking to Cerise on the phone?"

I secretly delighted in the fact that all the notebook contained were a few scribbles about Brittany and Samantha. "I don't think they're in there."

He reached page three and found it blank. "Where's the rest of it?"

"We got a tidy-up policy at the *News-Times*. All notes are disposable. Immediately."

Bang! I jumped as Smolak hurled my notebook across the small greenhouse and it landed on a plastic bag of composted cow manure. Before I could react, he kicked over a stool and shoved his fist into another large bag of potting soil.

Get a grip, I thought, retrieving the notebook and wiping off any residue of poisoned oleander.

He swung around and towered over me. His face was hypertension red. A vein across his fair-skinned forehead pulsated. "I've had just about enough of your crap, Yablonsky. You're gonna tell me right now what you know. You're gonna tell me every fucking—"

My heart was beating hard. I didn't know what this guy was capable of, if he'd actually smack a woman, in addition to church windows.

"Kar-ol?" A voice called from the front of the shop. "What's going on back there?"

Karol looked up, as though trying to remember where he was. His color lightened somewhat and he said, "Nothing, Mother."

I slipped my notebook back into my purse.

"Who've ya got? I hear a woman. Is that Cerise?"

There was a shuffle, shuffle, shuffle down the hall. Karol and I separated. He wiped dirt off his hand and we both pasted on polite smiles as a rotund woman inched toward us in a black headscarf, flowered dress, and suntan knee-highs encasing exploding ankles.

Mother Smolak.

"Who's she?" Mother Smolak took me in, as though *my* outfit was outrageous. "Ain't seen her before. She a customer?"

Karol Smolak awkwardly toed the ground. "This is Bubbles. Mother, Bubbles Yablonsky."

"Pleased to meet you." I extended my hand but Mother Smolak stared at it like it was a dead fish.

"I don't shake no one's hands I don't know. Ain't sanitary," she said. "What happened to that other one? Cerise. I liked her."

"She's gone," Karol said tersely. "I told you that already."

Mother Smolak squinted at me. "You ain't Albanian, are you?"

"No," I said. "Lithuanian. Plus a bit of Polish."

"What's your name again?"

"Yablonsky."

"With a *y* or *ie*?"

"Y."

"Field hands, bah." She waved me away. "Swine herders." Turning to Karol she said, "Stop socializing. We gotta send a thirty-five dollar Thanksgiving basket to the Grimes on Marvin Street. Also, we need to order more roses and baby's breath. We don't got no more. And we're outta strawberry plants. I forgot."

"We had four!" Karol exclaimed.

Mother Smolak stuck out her elbow. "I been using fresh strawberries on my dry spots. Notice the difference?"

We leaned forward to inspect her elbow. It was bony with ugly brown age marks, but it was smooth as a baby's butt, I'd give her that (see page 291). "Very well moisturized," I said.

"It's soothing. I make a rub with salt and—"

"Enough!" Karol tried to compose himself by deep breathing. "I'll order more strawberries, too. So if you don't mind, Mother, I'd like to finish up here."

"Suit yourself."

After Mother Smolak shuffled off, Karol yanked me to him.

"Good going. Now it's going to be all over town that I'm dating a new woman. A half-Lithuanian Yablonsky with a 'y' no less. Cerise will never come back to me. You goddamn offspring of a swine herder."

"Swine herder, my ass. I'm from a proud line of coal crackers." I wrenched free. "It's not my fault your mother overheard. You should watch your temper."

"I do. You should have met me before I took A.M."

"Ask for a refund on those classes, then. I hate to be the bearer of bad news, but you're getting ripped off."

"Shut your lip or I'll shut it for you."

"Case in point."

"You got a lot of nerve for a dumb hairdresser. Where'd you get off being so cocky?"

Mother Smolak, I wanted to answer. No way her son was going to lay a grubby finger on me as long as that old babushka was eavesdropping.

"I get cocky when men try to push me around." To prove my point I pushed him back. "So step off. I still own four-hundred-dollar scissors that—" I was stopped by a confusing realization. How had Smolak known I'd been a hairdresser?

"How'd you know I was a hairdresser?"

He grinned. "That bothers you, does it?"

I didn't want to admit that as a matter of fact it did.

"I know lots of stuff about you. I know you live on West Goepp, that you drive a Camaro, and that you got a teenage daughter Jane who is by herself *a lot*."

At the mention of Jane being by herself *a lot* I felt hot, like blood was rushing to my face. "Watch it."

"I'll watch what I want." He grinned again, victorious now that the tide had turned in his favor. He had managed to scare the wits out of me. "That's the way I operate. I own this neighborhood. No one comes in or out without reporting to me. Anything I want to find

· · · · · 69 · · · · ·

out, I do. Including when you're home, when you're not home, and the color of your white-and-purple bedspread."

I clenched my hands into fists. I was nearly blind with rage, with the audacity of this playground bully of a florist poking into my personal business, going so far as to acquaint himself with my bedroom's color combination.

"I know cops. . . . ," I began.

"Save it. I wouldn't mention my name to the cops if I was you."

"Give me one good reason why not."

"Because your daughter takes Center Street to West Goepp every day between the hours of three and four now that her Daddy's car blew its radiator, and I'm sure you wouldn't want her to go missing. By the time the Lehigh PD got around to deciding she wasn't a teenage runaway, they'd need to bring in the dentist."

I burned with indignation. I would have strangled Karol Smolak then and there if I thought I could have gotten away with it.

"Not that I'm suggesting that would happen," he said. "Just musing out loud."

We made dreadful eye contact. His eyes were gray and heartless. I pictured him being eaten alive by a Venus flytrap and felt slightly better. "You win," I whispered. "For now."

"I'm gonna cut you a break because you didn't know about me. You were ignorant." He moved closer. He smelled like his fist, dirty and sweaty. "But next time when I fetch you, I want you to be more respectful. When I ask a question, I want an honest answer. Humility is what I like to see in a woman."

I suppressed a low growl for the sake of Jane's future. "If the world were perfect," I said, "there won't be a next time."

"Maybe you're right. That's a good idea."

"KARROLLLL!" Mother Smolak's voice boomed.

Smolak winced.

"HAVE YOU FINISHED THAT THANKSGIVING BASKET YET?"

He cursed under his breath and then grabbed a basket and some red and gold ribbon. "Working on it."

"Tell your friend it's time for her to go home. You've got chores."

"Yes, Mother."

I accidentally let a snigger slip and Karol caught me with a dark glance. "Let's go," he said, dropping the ribbon. "I've had it with you."

When he opened the door the two guards were gone. Karol didn't seem to notice. He led me across the parking lot to the waiting Ford, which promptly started at the sight of us.

Karol opened the rear tinted door and shoved me inside. "Goodbye, Yablonsky. " He slammed the door shut and I heard him rap on the driver's-side tinted window. "You know what to do."

What did *that* mean?

Apparently it meant something to the driver, because he murmured a reply and peeled out of the lot. We bumped and bounced onto Helsinki Street and zipped up Fourth, crossing the double yellow line and weaving in and out of cars.

"Hold on there, pal," I said, swinging from side to side. "What's the rush?" I pulled on the door handles, but they were locked. And someone had ingeniously sawed off the locks. How clever.

The driver floored it, passing through one red light and a cacophony of blaring horns.

"That's my stop," I cried, pointing ahead to the *News-Times*. "You're going to miss it."

He didn't respond. Instead, he shot past Perkins Cake & Steak in the opposite direction. We followed a dark road.

He wasn't taking me back to work. He was taking me under the Hill to Hill. Now I knew what he was going to do. He was going to bump me off and bury me in the Polish Mafia's dumping grounds.

Oh, where was the holy Madonna when I needed her!

Chapter Eight

Forget me ever suggesting to a Polish Mafioso that we never meet again. What would that ever get me but dead? And me here with my funeral insurance not yet kicked in. Dang. Did I have bad timing or what?

I searched my purse for a weapon. And, by gum, I found one. The brass letter opener from Cerise May's office. I held it tightly in my sweaty hands, readying myself as the driver swung into oncoming traffic, took us off the bridge and onto the Union Street exit.

He hooked a quick right and then another. It was exactly as I had feared. We were headed under the Hill to Hill, to the mossy, dank, and dirty banks of the crummy Lehigh River.

Oh my God. Oh my God. I can't believe this. I ordered myself to pray and pray hard. The Our Fathers were no problem, but when I got to "Hail Mary, full of Grace," all I could picture was a soap drawing of Madonna skipping across the Chevy Impala singing "Erotica."

Then there was the crunch of gravel and the musty smell of the Lehigh. We had stopped.

"Okay, buster," I said to myself, "prepare to sing soprano."

I heard the driver get out, walk around the front, and then put his hand on the door handle. My heart was beating so loudly it was difficult for me to think, which was just as well because as soon as the door flung open, I lunged with the letter opener, driving it as hard as I could into his thigh.

Not just any thigh. A well-muscled thigh in tight blue jeans. A thigh (one of two) that I'd stroked many a late night while indulging in glorious naked ecstasy.

"Holy fucking hell!" he yelled, grabbing the letter opener and pulling it out of his thigh, then flinging it as far as he could.

Blood, I observed.

"Damn . . ." He clamped his hand over the wound and bent over in pain, leaning against the door for support. "You stabbed me! I can't believe it. You stabbed me! And here I was trying to save your ass."

I pushed past him and slid out of the car, throwing my arm around his familiar neck. "Stiletto. I . . . I didn't know it was you."

"Like hell you didn't." He closed his eyes. Of all the violence I'd perpetrated on him unwittingly, from socking him in a dark hotel room to nearly getting him blown up in a mine, this, by far, was the worst.

I felt awful until I remembered that my so-called "savior" was also the same jerk who had gotten himself engaged over the weekend. Maybe a minor flesh wound was just what the therapist ordered. Maybe a minor flesh wound was too good, in fact.

I stepped back and folded my arms, regarding him coolly.

"What?" Stiletto grimaced, which, I am sad to report, only made him look sexier. He was wearing a gray wool sweater over a white T-shirt under his old brown bomber jacket. His wavy hair, a mix of black and brown, was longer than it had been last week, and he hadn't shaved.

He was gorgeous.

"Why are you just standing there?" He lifted his bloodied hand and examined the cut. "What's wrong with you?

"Serves you right." I leaned into the Ford to get my purse. "It's what you deserve. You got off lucky."

"Got off lucky?" His dark blue eyes flashed. Really striking with the whole long-hair, unshaven, leather-jacket, Mel-Gibson-in-his-better-days package.

Control yourself, Bubbles. Stay the course.

Stiletto spoke through clenched teeth. "I saved you from those lunkheads and that two-bit Mafioso Smolak. And, I might add," he wiped the blood off his hand, "I did not barge into his shop on the off chance that you were doing an interview, that you were actually working instead of flirting."

"Flirting?" Oh, that was rich, coming from him. "Listen, Stiletto, I'm not the one who ran off—"

"Agghhhh." A deep moan erupted from the rear of the Ford.

I was alarmed. "What was that?"

"Oh, yeah. I forgot." Stiletto hobbled up to the trunk and opened it. He threw off a brown woolen blanket to reveal Zbigniew curled up in a fetal position. Zbigniew blinked with his one good eye. The other was swollen shut. He possessed the disoriented gaze of someone either very drunk or very stupid. Or, in Zbigniew's case, likely both.

"Dis is an outrage!" he complained. "Karol's gonna be very displeased when I—"

Pow! Stiletto socked him in the other eye. Zbigniew fell back into unconsciousness.

"How'd he get there?" I asked as Stiletto threw the blanket over him.

"I put him there. He wouldn't hand over the wheel when I asked nicely, so I had to take matters into my own hands. So to speak."

"So to speak. But where's his twin?"

"At the bar. I slipped him a twenty and sent him off to the Polish-American Club. Cheap date."

I peered at the lump that was Zbigniew. "I can't get over that you can throw a grown man in a trunk in broad daylight and no one calls the cops."

"It's Little Warsaw, Bubbles. When it comes to the Smolaks, no one asks questions. No one reports." Stiletto flipped open his cell phone and punched in a few numbers.

"How do you know so much about the Smolaks?"

"Had a run-in five or six years ago with Karol's brother, Cosmo. That was before the feds busted him for dealing Ecstasy in Philly. But not before he put a contract out on an *Inquirer* reporter and me."

"You? How . . . ?"

Stiletto didn't answer because he was busy informing whoever was at the receiving end of his cell phone call that they could come get their oversized gas guzzler and its occupant under the Hill to Hill. Then he flipped the phone shut.

"Come on. Give me a hand," he said. "I'll tell you about Smolak some other day. Right now I just want to get out of here."

With his arm settled across the back of my shoulders, we slowly walked toward the Lehigh. A stiff November wind whipped off the surface, making me, for some odd reason, hungry. Then I remembered. It was almost ten and all I'd had was a Pop-Tart.

Stiletto paused at the riverbanks and tossed the Ford's keys into the Lehigh.

"Let Smolak deal with that idiot now," he said as we headed south on the railroad track, taking the black-tarred wood rails two at a time. By following the track we'd arrive at the *News-Times* within minutes. The track crossed under the Hill to Hill and then Fourth Street. Trains tied up South Side traffic twice a day.

The steel mill loomed ahead of us, across the river. Rusted now, not nearly as red or booming as in my childhood, and down to only one shift a day. That's the way it was going to be from now on, I thought, one shift. It was like watching an adult I'd been frightened of as a kid wither and shrink with age and illness into a drooling invalid.

Maybe it was the ketones kicking in, or maybe I was still reeling from Smolak's angry outbursts, but I was shaking. If Stiletto hadn't taken care of Zbigniew, I'd be sinking in the river silt right now. It was hard to stay mad at a man who saves your life periodically. I'd have to really concentrate.

A frosty silence settled between us. Only the sound of my heels and Stiletto's clomping gait down the tracks broke the stillness.

"Okay. What gives?" Stiletto finally said when we got to the *News-Times*. "You've been treating me as though I've run off with the town whore."

"Your words," I said, clipped. "Not mine."

"Did something happen in the past seventy-two hours that I don't know about?"

"You tell me. This is your chance, since you weren't considerate enough to give me a heads-up before I . . ." I shook his arm off my shoulder. "I had to hear about it through the grapevine."

"Oh, shit." Stiletto shook his head. "Tony Salvo told you about the engagement and you're pissed."

"Damn right." I looked off, unwilling to grace him with my expertly accentuated eye contact.

"Let me explain."

I put out my hand. "Don't bother. There's nothing you can say. To tell you the truth, I'm floored that you didn't even consider my feelings. Don't I mean anything to you, Stiletto?"

"Of course you do." He limped to hold me, but I backed off. "I did it for you. For us."

"Please."

"Lookit. This whole thing was an accident. I never would have agreed to the engagement if I hadn't been forced into it."

"Don't tell me you're pregnant?"

Stiletto, to my shock, laughed. "Very funny."

When he saw I didn't get the joke, he got serious again. "If there's anyone to blame, blame Marla."

Marla! Who was Marla? The other woman. The nerve of bringing her into this!

"How long, may I ask, if that's not too intrusive, have you known *Marla*?"

He shrugged casually. "Years. We met in a bar in Myanmar, back when it was still Burma. Who cares?"

Drunk, I thought, picturing ceiling fans, hot sweaty nights, and white beds with mosquito nets. I bit my lip. It was so *Year of Living Dangerously*. My most favorite Mel.

Jealousy, green and vicious, now rose in me as Stiletto continued.

"Marla came up with the idea. She thought it might be a way for me to get out of going to England for six months and yet still keep my job and the London assignment. She'd read the rules."

Oh, she was a crafty one, this Marla. And hadn't Mama warned me that the world was filled with dames like Marla, always conniving, planning, calculating how to get another woman's man?

"The next thing I knew, it was all over the AP press room." Stiletto looked exasperated. "Marla told me that if I backed out everyone would think I was a skunk, so I guess I'm stuck. *We're* stuck."

I huffed. "Well, good luck then," I said, still unable to make eye contract. "Hope you and Marla are very happy. Hope you and Marla have tons of kids and a big house in the burbs and an inground pool for parties. See ya." I charged toward the front door.

Part of me, like three-quarters or maybe more, expected to hear a desperate smash as Stiletto threw himself at my feet, renouncing Marla and every other woman who had ever attempted to seduce him. I was looking for a pledge, here. A vow of fidelity.

Instead, what I heard behind me was a chuckle. A deep, chesty chuckle. I turned and found Stiletto bent over in hysterics. "You're such a Bubbles," he said, when he caught his breath. "Man, I hope you never write an exposé on me."

I could feel color rush to my cheeks. "What's so funny? You think it's a laugh riot that you dumped me for another woman?"

"No." Stiletto stood and tried to compose himself. I was glad—

yes, glad—to see the dash of dark red on his jeans. "No, I think it's a laugh riot that you think I got engaged to my editor."

"Your editor? Marla is your editor?" That was even more outrageous. No wonder he could keep his London assignment. He was marrying the boss!

"Age sixty-two with grandkids and a husband who could qualify for the Silver Ironman. Marla Cressman's one of the most famous photojournalists in the business. Haven't you heard of her?"

"No." He'd lost me on Ironman. I used to read Superman, but who was Ironman?

"I thought you knew who I was talking about."

"Nuh-uh."

Stiletto hobbled over to me, still grinning. "I have to ask you something. You do check out your news tips better than you did this one, right?"

"Oh, sure." Total lie.

He kissed me and I let him. It felt good. So very, very good to feel the stubble of his chin on mine, to feel his warm, sexy lips. He may have looked scruffy, but he smelled like fresh air and leather. To have his hard abs pressing against mine made me delirious.

"Are you okay now?" He looked down at me. "Not mad anymore?"

"Mad?" I said, momentarily confused. "Uh, no."

"We have to play at being engaged for six months. After that, I still have to go to England, but you can join me because Jane will be out of school by then. Deal?"

"Deal," I answered, not exactly sure to what I was agreeing. Had Stiletto pretended to propose marriage? "So, um, we're fake engaged?"

"Weird, isn't it? We've only known each other four months. Who gets engaged after knowing someone four months?"

I might have reminded him that Dan and I got married after knowing each other four weeks. And that was after only one date, a ten-minute encounter on the sticky floor of a Lehigh University fraternity. A date that produced our daughter Jane and cut short all my plans to graduate from Liberty High School with a waist.

"I've got to go," Stiletto said, after kissing me one more time. "I haven't even been home yet."

That's when I remembered the answering machine and the enchanting message I'd left.

"What do you mean, you haven't been home yet?"

"Came to you straight from New York. Called the newsroom and found you were over in Highland Heights on a story. Ran into Lorena, who said Smolak had taken you. Why?" An evil twinkle sparkled in his eyes. "You wanna join me at home?"

"Maybe later."

I massaged my temples to ward off a burgeoning headache. Think, Bubbles, think. Stall him so he doesn't get to his house before you do. Drug him. Lasso him. Stab him again. Yes, that was it. Stab him again. Darn. What had I done with that letter opener?

Stiletto interrupted my machinations. "Two issues we gotta deal with. One, as Marla said, we have to play engaged all the way. If word gets out that I'm pulling a scam, I'd get canned immediately."

"No Mama, though," I said. "If Mama finds out we're supposedly getting married, she'll put her life savings on a deposit for an all-you-can-eat wedding buffet at Dutch World and a boombas band from Kutztown complete with a dollar dance."

Stiletto looked ill. "You're right. No Mama. Secondly, there's this asshole I work with, Chad Kent. He's been gunning for the London assignment since it was posted. I know he suspects I'm pulling one over on management, and, considering he spends his life ferreting out cover-ups, I'm betting he'll be around asking nosy questions. Watch out."

"Okay, boss." I reached in my purse for the letter opener. It was gone. That's when I remembered Stiletto flinging it far, after I'd stabbed him.

I had to revise my strategy.

"The Camaro," I announced. "It's still in Highland Heights and"—bogus watch check here—"I've got to be at a staff meeting."

He fell for it. Stiletto never could resist a Camaro in distress. "I'll pick it up for you. Don't worry. I'll ask one of the guys in photo to drop me off this afternoon, after I get my leg sewn up."

This afternoon? I could not wait until this afternoon. I could not risk him going home and listening to my crazy message.

"Oh, no, Stiletto," I cooed. "You won't be able to drive with stitches. You'll be too sore. I'll just find someone myself."

"What? You need it now?" He flung his arm over my shoulder and led me to the door. "That's okay. I'll pick up your car before I get stitches. No problem."

"But your leg." I stared down at Stiletto's thigh. It was now soaked with blood. "It's a mess."

"What are you talking about?" He smeared a bright red patch across his jeans. "Nothing more than a paper cut. Jeez, Bubbles, when I was in Sarajevo, I lived with a cut like this for four days while accompanying a bunch of refugees to the border. This . . . this is a *luxury* in comparison."

"Well, if you feel up to it," I said with as much hesitation as I could muster. "What about a tetanus shot?"

"Tetanus shots are for wimps. Besides"—he kissed me right in front of the big glass windows where all the girls in classified ads could see—"I've had enough tetanus shots to last me until I'm eighty."

"Thanks, Stiletto, you're a savior."

"It's the least a future husband can do."

Oh my God. I felt faint, especially since Pauline, Dix Notch's evil secretary, had just opened the door—supposedly for a cigarette break, but really to catch a glimpse of Stiletto.

The look of shock and horror on her face as she overheard his words was priceless.

"How's it going, Pauline?" he said casually, shoving his hands in his coat. "You look great. Been working out?"

"Uh-huh." I caught her checking out his butt as he limped off. "You look good too, Steve. Don't be such a stranger."

Pauline zeroed in on me, her voice shifting from sweet to accusatory. "I don't believe it. Not Steve Stiletto. Future husband?"

Blushing bride-to-be that I was, I smiled demurely.

"Well, don't get too pleased with yourself," she said, sneering. "Notch has been waiting for you. Along with two plainclothes. Looks like if you're planning a wedding, you're going to be doing it from jail."

Chapter Nine

I got the impression we weren't gathered in Notch's office to discuss my safety. Notch and the two cops, along with Stu Kuntz, regarded me with sour looks as I stepped into the meeting room. I'd received warmer receptions returning a gently used thong to the snooty saleswomen in Hess's lingerie department.

One cop I knew: Detective Burge. He'd been key in investigating a fatal hit-and-run Stiletto and I witnessed in the park back in August. Among other distinguishing aspects, such as halitosis that could kill mildew and a weakness for stained tweed jackets, Burge hated Stiletto. Despised his devil-may-care attitude and that Stiletto viewed cops as fascist pigs due no more respect than anyone else.

The other cop was unfamiliar, by face but not name. Lehigh Detective Bob McIntyre. The prince who'd put me on permanent hold. McIntyre was about ten years younger than Burge and much better looking. Reddish-blond hair and Irish features. Good build likely borne of disciplined eating and exercising.

Both were seated in front of Notch's desk. Kuntz, dressed in a rumpled brown suit and bow tie, was on the couch looking particularly frail and politically correct. I was surprised he was still involved, considering that Popeye was dead. Knowing Kuntz, he'd boast he was just that committed to his indigent, disenfranchised (and even deceased) clients.

"You're late." Notch pointed to the wall clock, which read ten-fifteen.

I sat next to Kuntz on the couch. "I began work before dawn covering the Madonna sighting at Highland Heights."

The cops exchanged a muttered remark, sniggered, and broke apart.

"We'll talk about *that* later." Notch gestured toward Burge. "Burge is heading up the Schmidt murder investigation and he'd like to ask you about your Popeye interview. They know the boundaries. So I'll cut in if I hear anything that requires me to call our lawyers." He stressed the "our lawyers" as though to indicate that we had ammunition on *our* side, too.

"I don't mind discussing Popeye." I moved my butt to the couch edge so I could press my knees together and stop them from shaking. "I called the department yesterday to talk about that interview. Unfortunately, I was put on hold. Permanently." I batted my eyes at McIntyre, hoping he'd get the point.

McIntyre returned the stare with not so much as a blink. He regarded me like I was artwork on the wall. I held his stare and decided he was the living re-creation of Howdy Doody with facial hair.

"Miss Yablonsky." Burge cleared his throat importantly. "It's not the job of the police to answer *your* questions. Rather it's our job to *ask* the questions. We can't be expected to drop everything in the midst of an ongoing investigation when a suspect is at large."

"Hold on." I turned to Stu Kuntz. "Suspect at large? Has a miracle occurred? Has Popeye resurrected herself from the dead?" If so, forget the *News-Times*. I was calling the *National Enquirer.*

Stu Kuntz was about to answer when Burge interrupted. "That question's not even worth honoring with a response. If that's your idea of grim humor, Yablonsky, don't leave your day job for stand-up."

I had no plans to leave my day job for stand-up. I'd stood up long enough as a hairdresser.

"However," continued Burge, "partly because of your story this morning, we've been getting tips on other suspects who may have been either acting in concert with Miss Simon or separately to commit homicide on Mr. Schmidt." He said this begrudgingly, loath to give the press any credit.

"The suspects acted separately from my client," Kuntz said, asserting himself. "You and I and the DA's office know that full well, detective. It has sickened me to see you using a mentally ill woman as bait to lure Mr. Schmidt's real killer."

"She wasn't mentally ill," Burge replied. "She was sane and you know it."

"She took her life! Don't you people in law enforcement have any sympathy?"

"I can see your bleeding heart pumping from here," Burge cracked.

Notch raised his eyebrow at me and I took his cue. "How do you know it was suicide?"

Kuntz opened a folder on his lap and read from an official-looking white paper. "Preliminary toxicology reports and an examination by the coroner have confirmed that Julia Simon overdosed on her own antipsychotic medicine." Kuntz closed the folder. "I foolishly let Julia control her meds. I should have been paying attention."

The toxicology report left me with a dull feeling. On the one hand I was relieved that my cinnamon Trident hadn't played a role in her death. On the other hand I was saddened. Popeye was ill, like people with heart disease or cancer. And, like them, she suffered pain. I, too, should have been more sensitive.

"I'm sorry about your client, but we're getting off track," Mr. Notch said. "Let's stick to the issue that brought us here: why you want Bubbles's notes. Stu, you want to field that one?"

Kuntz brightened at the invitation. "The request stems from nothing more than my desire for justice."

Burge made a sissy face that Kuntz either missed or ignored.

"You should be aware that Julia suffered from schizoaffective disorders, including a tendency to believe that the problems of the world fell on her shoulders." Kuntz spoke slowly, insuring that Notch copied down every one of his oratory jewels. "For example, if she heard about an event, either read it in the newspaper or saw it on TV, she could convince herself that she was responsible. The closer the crime to her, the more likely she was to believe that she had committed it."

"We call that guilt," Burge said, rolling his eyes.

"This is why, Bubbles." Kuntz put his hand in the sexual-harassment-free zone—kind of midair, like he could have touched my thigh but wouldn't dare to. "This is why your notes from your interview with Julia could be key to locating the real murderer. There are subtleties that you might not notice, but that my psychiatric experts could find meaningful."

"Or our experts," Burge added.

"All I'm asking is to review them," Kuntz added, "and, if necessary, have you testify, should the Schmidt family decide to pursue action against her estate."

"What estate?" I asked, thinking, Garbage can?

"Though Julia was orphaned when she died, her parents set up a trust for her before they passed on. I'd rather not say how much is in the trust, but it is sizeable enough to be a lucrative target."

Who knew that all along Julia had been rolling in dough, as well as old newspapers?

Notch pounced. "We've been over this. I need to bring the lawyers in if we're gonna talk testimony. . . ."

"Try a judge slapping her with contempt of court," Burge said. "The Popeye interview wasn't with a confidential source, Dix. It's public knowledge Yablonsky spoke with Popeye and vice versa. No one's disputing that. Yablonsky's notes are evidence, and any judge around would agree with me."

"Please," protested Kuntz, "her name was Julia. Can't you call her that or Miss Simon at least? Anything but Popeye. It's so demeaning."

"Okay." Burge nodded. "Miss Popeye, then."

Kuntz could have socked him. "As *Miss Simon's* lawyer, I insist on viewing these notes first. For privacy concerns."

"What your client said is in the story," Notch said firmly. "I've seen Bubbles's notes and they're identical."

I nearly coughed. Notch hadn't seen my notes. Lying didn't seem to bother him, though. He summarized my story with perfect professionalism.

"The highlights of Yablonsky's interview were that Simon claimed she'd been in the bathroom when Schmidt was murdered and that she'd been trying to save him when Doctor May came in." Notch tossed his pen on the desk. "Frankly, that's all Yablonsky took down. You can put Yablonsky on the stand to verify the veracity of that. Nothing more."

A pain wrapped around my ribs and I realized I'd been holding my breath. That wasn't all I'd written down. I'd also transcribed Popeye's fears that everyone was against her and her claim that she'd heard lots of voices while she was in the bathroom. I didn't include those parts because they sounded too wacko. I was too superstitious to libel the dead.

"That's very nifty. But how can we verify the veracity," Kuntz asked, "without the notes? We need the source material."

Heavens. You would have thought I was Moses with the tablets. I mean, I write pretty fast, but I'm not a ninety-word-a-minute stenographer. There's a lot I miss.

"Then do what you have to. You're not getting those notes. No newspaper in the state would risk establishing that kind of precedent." Notch sat back, calling their bluff. "Get a judge and haul Yablonsky into court. Jail her for all I care. You're not getting the notes."

Jail her for all I care? Hold on just a cotton-picking second. "Wait a minute," I said to deaf ears.

"You're making it too hard." Burge leaned forward into Notch's personal space. "We could be done and out of your hair in an hour, since I bet the rookie over there"—he pointed at me, the rookie—"can barely take dictation, let alone define the word 'veracity.' "

I held up a hand. "I can so. . . ." Though, on second thought . . .

McIntyre said nothing. His hands folded loosely in his lap, he kept his gaze squarely on me. McIntyre had the air of someone biding his time, waiting for Burge and his generation of unprofessional, racist, out-of-shape cops to retire.

"May I ask something?" I said during the first lull in the bickering.

The men turned my way.

"I know why I'm here and why Mr. Notch is here. I know why Stu Kuntz is here and Detective Burge. But what's Detective McIntyre's role?"

Like a tennis match, they turned back to McIntyre.

"Detective McIntyre came at my request, Bubbles," Notch said. "According to Ludwig, you were taken by force this morning—kidnapped, as she overstated it—by two men working for Karol Smolak. Detective McIntyre is here to write a report."

Panic shot through me. My first concern was Jane and what Smolak could do to her if he found I'd blabbed to the police.

"Lorena got it wrong," I said quickly. "She completely misunderstood. I put in a request to interview Karol Smolak and he was nice enough to bring around a limo."

"Bring around a limo?" Notch asked, incredulous. "Ludwig said it was a Ford."

"In Little Warsaw, that's close enough."

"Who is this Smolak?" Notch asked McIntyre.

"Supposedly he's a florist, though most of his income is derived from other means." McIntyre spoke in the clipped manner of a no-

nonsense cop. "He's also known to us as Cerise May's ex-boyfriend. We've been advised that he may be responsible for her disappearance."

Notch wrote this down. I was too scared to take out my notebook, lest it be confiscated by Kuntz and Burge.

"Why do you say she disappeared?" Notch asked.

"We have our reasons," McIntyre said.

"Maybe she just went to visit her grandmother," I said, "or got carried away on a shopping spree. There's a get-a-jump-on-Christmas sale at Almart, you know."

"I don't think so," McIntyre said. "Her office was ransacked last night and there were signs of forced entry. Her car was found on Thirty-Third Street."

He had a point. Hard to go on a shopping spree without your car.

"Based on Smolak's connection to May, are you investigating his role in the murder of Rudy Schmidt?" asked Notch.

"Bob's been investigating the Smolak operation for five years," Burge said. "And, yes, we have reason to believe that Smolak might have had a hand in Schmidt's murder."

"Finally," Kuntz exclaimed, "the truth comes out."

"Is that on the record?" Notch persisted.

McIntyre and Burge thought about this. "Better not," Burge said.

"How about May's disappearance?" Notch pressed. "Can you say on the record that her disappearance is tied to Schmidt's murder?"

"For now you can say that we are investigating Doctor May's disappearance as more than a walk-away," Burge said. "That's the only statement I'm willing to issue now."

Go out on a limb, why don't you.

"Publicly clearing Julia Simon's name and alerting the community to other potential suspects like Smolak would aid your investigation," Kuntz said cheerfully.

"Thank you for telling me how to do my job." Burge shifted in his ill-fitting coat. "Anyway, I'm not going to discuss the case here, in a newspaper office with a public defender and two journalists. Come on, Bob." He and McIntyre got up to go. "I guess you leave us no choice but to seek a search warrant for those notes, Dix. That's a damn shame."

"Do what you have to do," Notch said. "Everyone's just doing their duty."

With all this talk of duty, I remembered Dr. May's own employee, Ruth Faithful, the wayward daughter of the superstrict Pastor Faithful. "Any other suspects besides Smolak and Popeye?" I said. "For example"—I thought carefully about how to phrase this—"have you investigated Doctor May's employees?"

McIntyre defrosted slightly. He stepped forward, so much taller than when he was sitting down that I scrunched myself into the couch. "Anyone in particular? Not too many people work for Doctor May."

"Yes, Bubbles. Anyone you got in mind?" Notch gripped his pencil. It might have been a signal for me to shut up, but as I hadn't been given the updated *News-Times* codebook of nasty managing editor faces, I didn't know.

"Just fishing." I examined my nails, like the last person on my mind was Ruth Faithful.

"Reporters," Burge cursed. "Always fishing."

"Pure sensationalism is what it is," added Kuntz prissily.

The only person who kept his two cents to himself—and his two eyes on me—was Detective McIntyre. He knew I knew something.

The question was whether it was Ruth Faithful.

And whether I could get to her first.

Mr. Notch asked me to stay after the cops and Kuntz cleared out. I stood in front of his desk like a schoolgirl before the principal. I just wanted this ordeal to be o-ver.

Notch closed his door and locked it.

"Okay," he said, jingling the change in his pockets. "What was that last question about?"

The thing with Notch is you can't con him. It's his tone of voice or willingness to fire you on the spot. He's not like Mr. Salvo, who's squishy around the edges. Him you can bamboozle.

"Last night when Lorena and I went to interview Doctor May, we found her gone and her office in shambles."

"This I know. Tell me something I don't."

"We, um, looked around to see if Doctor May was hurt or anything. We felt it was our civic duty."

"You snooped." Notch's face remained impassive. "Trespassed onto a crime scene like I specifically told you not to do."

I waited for the rebuke for violating Rule #1. None came, so I continued. "There was a picture there of the receptionist with Doctor May. I recognized her. She's Ruth Faithful, the daughter of Tom Faithful, who's the pastor at All God's Children Church."

"Pyramid style, Yablonsky. Most interesting news first. You're losing me."

I spoke faster. "When I was in high school, Schmidt caught Ruth with pot and called her dad. From what we heard it wasn't a pleasant scene back at the Faithful homestead. Pastor Faithful was known for being from the dark ages. Some kids said he beat her. I was just wondering if Ruth was the type to hold grudges."

Notch returned to his swivel chair. He linked his fingers behind his head and stared up at the ceiling.

After a thoughtful few minutes, he said, "I can't assign you to the Schmidt murder because that is Lawless's baby, though he's been plugging away at it for five days now and not coming up with much. He says it's because the town's been coerced into listening to endless glowing eulogies about how Schmidt walked on water. No one dares say anything negative."

Or, I thought, Lawless won't leave the newsroom and interview actual people, dig for sources and anecdotes.

"However"—Notch sat up and doodled on a tablet—"if I intuited Burge and McIntyre correctly, Doctor May's disappearance may be more than a last-minute vacation getaway. The way they put it, it sounded like the cops were investigating her disappearance as suspicious and linked to Schmidt's death."

"Sounded like that to me, too."

"You have any meetings this week?"

Municipal meetings. As a rookie reporter I got more than my fair share of them. "There's a township council in Mahoken tonight: second public hearing on the Quick Mart development and an executive session to discuss stuff that's too important to discuss publicly."

"You have time to follow up on May's disappearance and drop by Ruth Faithful's to catch up on old times?"

"Sure." I feigned a casual tone to cover my burst of excitement.

"Interview her today." Notch got up. "Chances are, if you remember Ruth Faithful, someone else will too. That McIntyre's a hound dog. He'll hunt a lead."

He walked me to the door and unlocked it. "Also, I want you and Lawless to work better together. Both of you gravitate toward the same types of stories, and it's annoying and a waste of *News-Times* money to always pit you two against each other."

That philosophy was opposite from the *New York Times* where, Stiletto told me, reporters were routinely pitted against one another, but that was okay. If I could work with Lorena the Queen of Anger, I could work with Lawless the King of Ho Hos.

"I'll be professional," I said.

"That's a start," Notch replied, and he shut the door.

I was exhausted and suffering from a serious sugar low when I fell into my chair. What a morning. Madonna in soap, a surprise fake engagement, and a threat to be thrown in jail. I called over to Lawless's cubicle.

"Hey, Lawless. Got candy?"

Lawless, always up for a diversion, swung around. "No, and what was that in Notch's office?"

I opened my drawer and retrieved a dollar fifty in change. "Walk with me to vending and I'll tell you."

We climbed the metal stairs to composing, which was dead quiet this early in the day. Waxed clips of this morning's headlines were stuck sideways on the blue cutting boards, reject misprints or misspellings tossed aside. We stepped our way through discarded newspaper hats, the quaint tradition left over from the days of hot print, and reached the dusty vending machines in the far corner.

Some newsrooms, I'd heard tell, had cafeterias where you could buy genuine food instead of stale bags of peanuts and Snickers bars that were so old they cracked when you bit into them. Not the *News-Times*.

I stood with my quarter poised in the slot trying to choose between a somewhat healthy bag of Jax (contains vitamin A but stains your fingers orange) or two Twix. This was doubly hard, as it was all I could do to stop myself from fantasizing that Stiletto had asked me to marry him for real.

"I wouldn't buy from there." Lawless hoisted up his pants to show that he'd been losing weight. "Last year Linda from Lifestyle bit into a candy bar and got a roach head."

Extra protein, as Mama used to say. I shoved in the quarters and chose the Twix. Then I got a Diet Pepsi.

Lawless eyed the Twix with lust. "Okay. Spill about what went down in Notch's office."

"Burge and your buddy McIntyre want my notes and Notch is willing to send me to jail on precedent." I bit into the Twix. No bugs so far. "What's up with him, anyway?"

"Who? Notch?" Lawless peered into the vending machine, his willpower weakening.

"McIntyre."

"McIntyre's gonna have Burge's job someday and Burge knows it. McIntyre's got a good rep with his superiors. Fills out all his paperwork and can handle the press, though he's been a prick lately. He needs to get fucked."

I flinched, still not used to the easy way Lawless threw his favorite swear into casual conversation.

"How many calories in a Milky Way?" he asked.

"A zillion. It's not worth it." I popped open the Pepsi. Already I was feeling much more rejuvenated. "Come on." I threw half of my Twix wrapper in the trash and yanked Lawless away from his candy-stuffed temptress. "McIntyre is a stud. I wouldn't think he'd have any problem getting laid."

"All married men have problems getting laid. It's the law of the domestic jungle. That's why he's divorced. Figured there was more action on the single scene. Oh, no." He stopped on the third step. "Don't tell me. You think McIntyre's a stud?"

"He is, kind of." It was a fact, an innocent observation, nothing more.

"McIntyre put the moves on you, didn't he?"

"How could he? There were three other people there, including Notch."

"Did he do the undercover cop glare? The I-know-what-you-look-like-with-your-clothes-off stare?"

"No."

"Too bad. If you flipped McIntyre's switch, then I'd advise you to turn on the juice. Ask him out on a date. Sleep with him. Just get him to talk."

I didn't know whether to feel insulted that Lawless regarded me as a slut or flattered that he thought I could have that much power over law enforcement. In the end I decided to be both, and irate as well.

"That is so sexist, to suggest I sleep with a source." Showing him how liberated I was, I let him go ahead of me through the door. "Besides, I'm engaged."

"Engaged?" said Lawless. "To who?"

"Who else? Stiletto. Steve Stiletto. *The* Steve Stiletto."

Lawless looked at me dumbly. "Am I supposed to be impressed?"

"Of course. Do you know how many women would kill to be in my shoes?"

Lawless looked at my feet, stuffed into a pair of pointy, high-heeled, black leather boots. "Not too many."

"Many! Stiletto's smart, handsome, brave, and cool." I guzzled my Pepsi. "And he's great in bed."

Lawless thought about this. "Fuck that. I'm great in bed. Unless you're comatose, everyone's great in bed. My wife's great in bed and half the time she's got her nose in a book."

I groaned and marched on while Lawless continued to argue the advantages of me sleeping with McIntyre.

"McIntyre's an opportunity you shouldn't miss. Like a stock option."

Or if you're Lawless, free cake.

"Let me try it. I'll set it all up for you. One phone call." He passed me in the hall. "McIntyre will eat it up. If you're lucky, he might even eat you up."

"I would never have sex for a story!" I shouted to him as he turned the corner and opened the door to the newsroom. "Never."

"Sure you would." Lawless climbed onto a chair in the middle of the newsroom. "I need a reality check, people." He made his hands into a megaphone. "How many of you think Yablonsky would sleep with a cop for a story?"

All hands immediately shot up.

"See, Yablonsky?" said Lawless. "It's what you do."

Humiliation poured over me like hot, thick, red lava.

"No," I countered, now seriously pissed. "It's what *you* do, Lawless. Sleep. Sit. Eat and play solitaire on your computer. Anything but leave the newsroom and work. As for me, I hustle my ass off."

The newsroom fell silent. It was quite a bit of impertinence coming from a rookie, and I knew I was treading into dicey territory, especially since Lawless wasn't the only veteran reporter who had long ago lost the hunger for news.

And then a beautiful sound. Applause. Slow at first and then building until Lawless was the only reporter not clapping.

Better yet, the person applauding the loudest was Steve Stiletto, back from retrieving my Camaro and just in time to hear the whole exchange.

Chapter Ten

Of course I should have known that Steve Stiletto did not do emergency rooms. Emergency rooms were sterile and efficient. They provided anesthesia and antiseptic and social workers who asked questions. For this reason, along with plain orneriness, Stiletto instead did Shorty.

Shorty came with no "Dr." preceding it. It was just Shorty. Or rather, Shorty in Hunklestown.

"He's a great guy. A Vietnam vet who's stitched up more legs than those Grenada Medical School dropouts at the hospital ever will." Stiletto held up an orange envelope. "You want to open this or should I?"

"Where'd you get that?" I shifted into fifth and headed west on Route 22.

"It was in your car when I picked it up. They're photos, I can tell."

"Maybe Lorena left them. Probably art from the Madonna at dawn shoot. Sure. Open it."

I didn't care. I was too focused on planning my next move: further distracting Stiletto so he wouldn't go home. There was no other choice, I decided, but sabotage. Nothing too drastic like blowing him to smithereens. Something time-consuming instead. Like tarring and feathering his Jeep.

"Nice day," said Stiletto, flipping through the photos.

"Yes," I agreed. "Isn't it."

Maybe G, I thought. G had tools, or access to them (read: steal). If I could bribe him into taking a break from Hess's salon, he could tinker with Stiletto's brakes. Wait. Not brakes. That was too drastic. That fell under the smithereens category.

"Fill me in on this Schmidt murder," Stiletto said. "I read your story this morning. It was kind of incomplete."

"Incomplete?" I glared at him. I found it very hard to take criticism from Stiletto. "What do you mean by that?"

"Keep your eyes on the road, Bubbles. Shit, you nearly sideswiped that trailer."

"I wasn't anywhere near the trailer." I touched the brakes and got my bearings.

"By incomplete, I mean you wrote a lot about Popeye but nothing about Schmidt. Who was this guy?"

"He was the principal of Liberty for years and years until he retired last spring—Pennsylvania's longest-running administrator ever. Very influential. Headed the state principals' association and even slept over at the White House. Twice."

"I don't care about credentials. What was he like personally?"

I thought back to Schmidt, to his legendary rigid frame marching down the green-tiled halls of Liberty, a whistle around his neck and a clipboard in his hand. He sported a crew cut, steel-frame glasses, and a navy suit with that blasted navy-and-maroon Liberty High tie. For as long as I knew him, he never wore anything else.

"He ran marathons before that was common, and swam in the Lehigh in January," I said. "He was a member of the Polar Bear Club."

"Sounds insane himself." Stiletto turned a photo sideways and squinted. "Why would anyone want him dead?"

I took the airport exit and immediately got us in a traffic jam, backed up by construction. It didn't matter that it was November and that road crews were forced to work in sleet and snow like mailmen. Construction on the airport never stopped. Too many people were too eager to fly out of the Lehigh Valley.

I shifted into first and wore down the clutch as we crept up the exit ramp. "If you believe the cops, Popeye wanted him dead because she was nuts."

"But Popeye didn't do it."

"Clarification. According to her lawyer, Stu Kuntz, she didn't *know* if she did it or not. She had a psycho disaffective disorder or something. Kuntz said she'd feel guilty for crimes she didn't commit."

"Uh-huh." Stiletto pulled out another photo. "And this Doctor May. What have you found out about her?"

I inched up. "Nothing much. Mama says she's never heard of her as a podiatrist."

"Your mother not knowing a local doctor? That's a red flag."

"And when I spoke with Cerise May last night she got defensive when I mentioned her boyfriend, Karol Smolak."

Stiletto put down the photo. "You mean she's involved with Smolak?"

"Not anymore. They broke up."

Stiletto shook his head. "Just watch out, Bubbles. The Smolak brothers are bad news. They're into drug dealing and money laundering. I told you Cosmo put a contract out on me, and his brother can't be much of an improvement."

"You don't have to warn me," I said without thinking first. "If you hadn't taken care of Zbigniew and what's-his-face, I'd be rotting at the bottom of the Lehigh right now."

Stiletto grinned. He loved the idea of being a white knight.

"Though I still had my letter opener, so I could have handled matters myself," I quickly added. I didn't want this white-knight stuff going to his head.

"I have no doubt." He held up one of the photos. "Are you telling me this is a picture of the Blessed Virgin at dawn?"

The photo left by Lorena in my Camaro was black and white. Typical news photo. Only it was out of focus (even for Lorena) and it wasn't of a soap drawing in the back of the Taylors' Impala. It was of a scene so obscene I nearly rear-ended the car in front of us.

If that was Madonna, then I was a virgin for the very first time.

"Who *is* that?" I asked, turning my head to connect the parts.

"I think you mean, who are *they?*" Stiletto put down the photo and lifted another. Same woman. Dirty blond shag. Long back with a slim waist. A slight scar, or maybe it was a tattoo, ran down the length of one of her calves. Stiletto flipped through the remaining two. All showed her from the back bending over a naked man.

Whoever this woman was, she took care of herself. There wasn't an ounce of fat on her.

"These photos definitely have nothing to do with Madonna on the Impala," I said. "Who left them?"

"They're stills from a video camera, possibly a security camera." Stiletto displayed the clearest one. "Recognize anyone?"

"Doctor May," I said, pointing to the yin-and-yang rug. "That's in her office. And that's her hair, at least from what I've seen in other pictures."

"Thought so." He handed me the photo. "No wonder your mother doesn't know her. Seems as though Doctor May's podiatry practice uses revolutionary techniques to raise those arches."

"Gives new meaning to sole support." I studied the grainy picture. Something was off. "Wait a minute. This might not be Doctor May."

A car behind us beeped. I flipped him the bird, moved all of four feet up the ramp until I was bumper-to-bumper with an SUV in front of me. Then I gave the photo another pass.

"It's a wig. That woman's wearing a wig."

Stiletto leaned over. "She is? How can you tell?"

"A decade in the beauty biz and you know," I said with authority.

"To be fair, it's a very popular style. We used to sell it at the House of Beauty. It's called Breathless by Raquel Welch, a favorite of housewives who need a quick fix."

"You can tell all that from a photo?"

"I can't tell that much."

Beep. Beep.

I frowned in my rearview at the rude driver behind me, who was shaking his fist and probably cursing in some language I'd never heard. You take your life in your hands when you flip the bird in traffic. Never can tell when someone's got a .22 hidden under the passenger seat. I longed for the good old days when imaginative hand gestures were considered part of the auto vernacular.

"I can't tell who she is, or who the man on the other end is, since all we can see is from his hip down," I said.

"We men are boring that way, aren't we? Seen one, seen 'em all." Stiletto handed me the next photo. "Though I'm not sure you want to see too much of this geezer."

Stiletto was right. Our lucky winner was no Brad Pitt. (Why are they never Brad Pitt?) What I could make out in the photo was mostly pale flesh, loose skin, and veins popping out all over the place."

"Yuck." I bent closer to look at the popping veins.

"Yuck, yourself. You'll be there someday. You won't be young, smooth, and supple forever, Bubbles."

I wanted to ask if that was a problem for him, but I didn't dare out of fear that he'd answer yes. Besides, we were nearly at the end of the ramp and something in the geezer photo had caught my eye.

Stripes, various shades of gray and black in the photo, lay in a heap by the geezer's right knee. In real life I was betting they were navy and maroon.

I pointed to the tie. "Guess whose that is?"

"You're kidding," said Stiletto. "Is that *the* tie? The one that got shoved down his throat?"

"I don't know. I only saw him wear the same tie every day for three years. I'm sure he had others."

"But you're fairly confident . . ."

"Yes, I'm confident. . . ."

"That the geezer," said Stiletto, "is . . ."

"Schmidt."

Gross. I was once kissed by my old physics teacher and that was bad enough. But seeing your high school principal naked . . . that required sedation.

Chapter Eleven

Shorty was a doctor, of sorts. A doctor of cars. Oh, who am I kidding, he was a grease monkey changing the oil on a beat-up pickup truck when we pulled into the driveway of his circa-1850 farmhouse.

He was neither tall nor short. Just average. Begging the question of how he got his nickname. Shorty slid out from under the truck, ran a feeder cap across his forehead, and exchanged high fives with Stiletto before examining his thigh.

"It'll take five minutes to sew up," Shorty said. "Come back in a half hour."

I was unsure about this. Stiletto imagined himself as a macho man who required only a bullet between his teeth and a fairly sterile needle to endure surgery. But Shorty was the kind of guy who cleaned apples with spit—and possibly stab wounds, too.

"You will use a painkiller, won't you?" I asked.

"Absolutely." Shorty gave me the thumbs-up. "And alcohol."

Whew.

"Whiskey?" suggested Stiletto. "Or moonshine?"

"Whichever kills the pain faster."

Not exactly what I had in mind.

Torn between supervising Stiletto's surgery or fixing the answering machine issue, I hovered about Stiletto until he made Shorty promise to run the needle through a flame. When the men disappeared inside, I got back in the Camaro, shoved all the photos into the orange envelope, and went in search of a pay phone.

In most civilized areas of the world, pay phones are hard to come by, the logic being that if you're important enough to make a phone call on the road, you're important enough to own a cell.

But this was Hunklestown—flat, mowed-down, gray farmland. Not a cell tower for miles, and if there were one it would be crawling with truant high school students looking for a cheap thrill in the boonies.

I found the nearest pay phone three miles away at a Sunoco station with rusted pumps. While there I went to the bathroom, washed my hands in the grubby sink, checked my reflection in the condom machine, grabbed a cellophane-wrapped sandwich and a Diet Pepsi, and dialed Hess's salon. *The* Hess's, in Allentown.

The receptionist—I still couldn't get over the fact that this salon had a receptionist—called for G, who took a good five minutes to get to the phone while I plunked in quarters. Did it irk me that my daughter's boyfriend, who had dropped out of VoTech and had never studied hairdressing seriously, was the golden boy at a salon that wouldn't even glance at my application? Not at all.

Hess's was too snobbish for my standards. I supposed working there was *okay*, as long as you could tolerate clients who carried froufrou dogs in their laps when they drove their Lincoln Continentals. And who didn't think it gauche to tip with crisp twenties.

"Hey," G grunted. "Whassup? I got a color and the timer's ticking."

"What would it take," I said enticingly, "for you to fiddle with Stiletto's Jeep?"

"Fiddle like explode?"

"No!" I held the phone away from my face. Who was this kid and how come he was dating my daughter? "No. Of course not. I just need to buy some time. I need Stiletto to get out of my hair so that I can do stuff."

"What kind of stuff?"

"I can't say." Darnit. "It's private."

"So you want to know what it would it take for me to screw up your old man's vehicle?"

"Yup."

"It would take you telling me what's so private."

I thought about this, about how G's brain worked, about carrots and sticks. G hated both carrots and sticks, so they weren't any good. MTV and cigarettes, yes. But as a responsible adult I couldn't be a party to those.

"How about I promise to tell you what stuff is so private if you are successful and Stiletto's delayed?"

"Plus fifty bucks."

I balked. Fifty bucks! That was an outrage. Whatever happened to the juvenile delinquents of yesteryear who cut brake lines for pure sport? "Okay," I said, giving up. "Here's where his car is."

I described Smolak's Flower Shop and warned G to be discreet. If Smolak found out that the Jeep in his lot belonged to Stiletto, who had earlier in the day bonked one of his employees on the head, stolen his favorite Ford, and tossed his keys into the river, things could get dicey.

"Whatever, Mrs. Y," G said, already bored. "There goes my timer. I'll get over there in an hour."

I checked my watch. It was one. Maybe I could take Stiletto out for lunch to stall him. Then again, Stiletto wasn't a big lunch eater. I could drive him out to the woods for a quickie. He'd like that, though it would be a little weird, especially since my lunch hour had expired and I was, technically, on company time. As a general policy the *News–Times* frowned on paying for quickies.

I got back into the Camaro, unwrapped the sandwich, and contemplated my chances of succumbing to botulism from questionable Hunklestown Sunoco gas station turkey sandwiches.

While I ate, I flipped through the photos and immediately put down my sandwich. Mama used to paste the refrigerator with photos of herself in pink stretch pants when she was on a diet. But seeing an old naked man like this was really stomach churning. I'd be a size two if I had to eat across these at every meal.

I tried to mentally re-create Dr. May's office. Judging from the angle of these photos, the security camera would have been positioned right above the door, which meant that, if it was still working, it would have caught whoever ransacked her waiting room.

Ransacked her waiting room. It triggered a memory. Lorena had said *Whoever did this sure was searching high and low for a document, I bet.* Sure enough, all the medical files had been scattered across the floor, as though each one had been opened and then tossed aside.

Could that "document" actually have been these very photos in my hands? They were the perfect size to fit in a medical folder.

Then how did they end up in my car? It now seemed unlikely that Lorena had put them there. Maybe Sophie Taylor had. She'd spoken about giving me some extra pictures, done by a professional, though I'd understood her to mean the ones she'd taken of her daughter with the soap Madonna.

Then again, Sophie was Karol Smolak's sister. Did she get these from Smolak?

Hold on. Hold on. What was I thinking? I was missing the target again, shooting up, down, and sideways and completely ignoring the bull's-eye. If the security camera was working, it would have taped Rudy Schmidt's murder.

Hell. It would have taped Lorena and me.

"Hey, babe." Stiletto poured himself into the Camaro. "How's it going?"

I flattened myself against the driver's door and pinched my nose. "You smell like Uncle Manny's on a Saturday night."

"Moonshine." He closed his eyes and leaned against the headrest. "Dandelion moonshine. Shorty's home brew. The stuff's a killer." He slapped his thigh and didn't even flinch.

I scrutinized Stiletto's thigh. The denim had been cut away from the wound, exposing a Frankenstein ladder of black stitches. No Band-Aid. Shorty, mindful of sterilization, had managed to taint the cut with only a smudge of grease. I pointed this out to Stiletto.

"Good for it," he mumbled. "Keeps it waterproof. Can we go? I'm beat. I just want to get my car and head home."

"Not in your condition," I chirped. "Besides, I'm late for an interview."

Stiletto moaned.

"Don't worry. You can stay here." I turned on the radio. Van Halen. We have *the* best radio stations in the Lehigh Valley. Van Halen, Lynyrd Skynyrd, REO Speedwagon, and Kansas, 24/7.

Stiletto flicked the radio off. "I thought of something when Shorty was cutting off my pants."

"I wouldn't go around saying that in public."

"You've got to verify the Geezer. It might not be Schmidt."

"You mean it could be some other geezer. What are the chances of that?"

"You're talking about a podiatrist's office on the South Side. All May sees is geezers."

"Valid point." I slinked through the Airport Road construction. "How are we going to find out who it is?"

Stiletto answered with a soft snore. Poor baby. The thing is, I'm hard on people, like I am on shoes. All the rubber on the bottom of my heels is worn out, and so are my men.

I was super quiet as I took the Whitehall exit and tried to figure out the shortest way to Pastor Faithful's house.

"You'll have to show the photo to Rudy Schmidt's wife."

I nearly ran a stop sign. "I thought you were asleep."

"Never in the middle of the day." Stiletto sat up looking amazingly refreshed from his two-minute catnap. "Mrs. Schmidt, if she's still around, will be able to ID her husband. Show her the photos."

"No way, Stiletto. You don't know Mrs. Schmidt. She's wrinkled and ancient and looks like the Queen Mother. Even has the hats with the netting. We ran an editorial yesterday that called her our Local Treasure. They were married fifty years, she and Rudy."

"Then she ought to be able to identify her husband naked, shouldn't she?"

I swung the car into Graceful Corners, a suburban development of 1970ish split-levels. Basketball nets on every garage bordering smooth, black-topped driveways. I found the Faithful's house immediately.

Who else would have on their lawn a blinking red-and-green electric sign that said PUT THE "CHRIST" IN CHRISTMAS? It made the neighboring reindeer and Santa Claus seem so corrupt.

"Oh, brother," Stiletto said when he saw the sign. "This looks grim."

I grabbed the envelope and filled him in about Ruth Faithful. "I'm going to find out where Ruth lives. If she's here, I'm going to show her the photos and ask if she knows who these people are and if they're connected to Doctor May's disappearance and Schmidt's murder. Maybe she'll start talking."

"That's not such a good idea." Stiletto rolled down the window and waved to a lady salting the sidewalk next door. "What if the woman in the photo is Ruth Faithful?"

"Not likely. Ruth was never small in high school and if the photo on her desk is any indication, she hasn't been pushing away many plates of brownies since twelfth grade."

"Meow!"

"Just a fact." I grasped the door handle.

"Want me to go with you for moral support?"

"That's nice of you, but . . ." I surveyed my partner. Stiletto's five o'clock shadow had sprung up to a full stubble. His longish hair was unkempt. His jeans were ripped and bloodied. On top of that he reeked of dandelion moonshine. Neighbors in this tidy suburban cul-de-sac would be madly punching their Home Alert alarm buttons if he so much as stood on their sidewalks. "That's not necessary, honey."

Before he could protest, I was out the door and up the walk. The Faithfuls' doorbell was predictable: it played "Amazing Grace." But the doormat was disturbing: DIRTY SOLES GO TO HELL. White on green plastic grass.

"Yes?"

I lifted my gaze from the mat to find Pastor Faithful's craggy face scrutinizing me over a pair of half-glasses. Scrutinizing with open disapproval. Maybe it was my crucifix earrings and matching necklace. Couldn't have been the tight leather jeans. They were black. And expensive. Thirty bucks.

"I'm Bubbles Yablonsky from the *News-Times*." I held out my hand. Pastor Faithful shook it with vigor, his face suddenly becoming animated.

"I been calling you people. Come in. Come in." He opened the door and led me to a living room with cream walls, cream carpet, a matching royal blue velour sofa set, and the largest wide-screen TV I'd ever seen.

"Now hold on." He held up a finger. "Let me get my makeup." He stopped and checked around me. "Where's your camera?"

"Camera? I don't have a camera."

"Oh, of course." He threw up his arms and pointed to my orange envelope. "Those are probably the still shots I sent you folks."

Okay. Now I was totally flipped. Pastor Faithful had sent me photos of a naked man in Dr. May's office? Perhaps I'd been too hasty in writing him off as a stick-in-the-mud. Perhaps All God's Children Church was a kinky cult of low morals and high times.

"Uh . . ."

"Never mind. Vanity of vanities. All is vanity." He shook his head, embarrassed. "I'm so human I keep forgetting this publicity is about the church, not me. The thing is, I get so excited about our twenty-fifth anniversary that I lose my head." He smacked himself on the head, as though to keep it from flying off.

"Oh." I smiled, slightly disappointed that I wouldn't be dealing with a kinky cult after all. "Actually, I'm here to talk to Ruth, not about your church's anniversary."

"Does that mean you're not doing a story on our bell-tower fund-raiser?"

"Afraid not."

He eyed the photos again. "So those aren't mine?"

"They're photos I found of our class at Liberty," I lied, realizing full well that lying to a man of God, like Pastor Faithful, would guarantee me a day pass to hell.

He looked out his bay window to my three-toned Camaro, which still had pig-sucking graffiti emblazoned on its side. Stiletto was gone. Uh-oh.

"Ruth's never mentioned your name," Pastor Faithful said, his eyes narrowing in suspicion. "You coming here wouldn't have anything to do with that story I read this morning in the *News-Times*, that Doctor May's office had been burglarized?" He was back by the door, ready to open it and give me the heave-ho.

"Why would you ask that?" I opened my eyes wide.

"Don't lie to me, missy." Too late. "You know Ruth works for Doctor May."

"Ruth works for Doctor May? Who knew? I thought she worked at . . ." I snapped my fingers, pretending to recollect.

"The county clerk's office," Pastor Faithful said, still skeptical of my intent. "Before that she filed for a couple of lawyers in town."

"I'm surprised she's not married and settled down with a passel of kids."

I caught a glimpse of Stiletto. He was engaged in deep conversation with the salt lady. She looked aghast as he lurched toward her, emanating fumes that surely violated Pennsylvania's EPA emission standards.

"Ruth works too hard. Always at the office." He put his hand on the doorknob. "I keep reminding her she'll never get a husband that way. She's even working today, helping Doctor May get her office in order."

"Of course." It seemed Pastor Faithful didn't have a problem stretching the truth, either, seeing as Dr. May was out of town. "I guess I should go then." I tucked the photos under my arm and joined him at the door.

"Now may I ask you a question?" Pastor Faithful said, before I could flee.

Uh-oh. Here it comes.

"Have you accepted Jesus Christ as your personal savior?"

Damn. I knew it. Ugh. I *hate* that question. It always sounds as though Jesus Christ is moonlighting as a private accountant or my personal valet.

"Hmmm," I murmured. "Jesus and I are okay. We're on speaking terms."

"Stop by the church some time," he said. "For Thanksgiving dinner, perhaps, or to learn how Jesus can speak to you, instead of you just speaking to him."

"Okay. I'll do that."

Pastor Faithful opened the door and we stepped out. Next door the salt lady was inviting Stiletto inside her house. His magnetism was unbelievable. He could be covered with pig poop and wearing foil on his head and women would drag him to their boudoirs.

" 'Thou shalt not go up and down as a talebearer among thy people.' Leviticus 19:16," Pastor Faithful quoted. "Keep that in mind."

"By 'talebearer,' " I said, "I assume you mean 'reporter.' Not some fur trapper who goes around carrying tails."

This threw him for a loop. "A talebearer serves as the Devil's agent. You'd do well to aspire to another profession, Miss Yablonsky. Your soul depends on it."

And here I'd worked so hard to become a reporter only to learn that the fine print on my guild contract sent me to hell. First the lousy hours and the threat of jail and now eternal damnation.

I needed a raise.

"I suppose I could go back to being a beautician," I said. "Gossiping is optional when you're a beautician."

"A beautician?" Pastor Faithful didn't like that job, either. "Woe unto you. As Peter wrote in his first epistle, 'Let it not be that outward adorning of plaiting the hair, and of wearing of gold, or of putting on apparel; But let it be the hidden man of the heart, in that which is not corruptible. . . . For after this manner holy women are in subjection unto their own husbands.' "

"We didn't do much plaiting at the House of Beauty," I said, thinking back. "Mostly coloring and perms. A couple of bang trims."

To this Pastor Faithful was speechless. I guess the Bible didn't have a position on bang trims.

Stiletto met me on the sidewalk a few minutes later. He limped out of the salt lady's house, finishing a chocolate-chip cookie and acting pretty smug. "What was that all about?" he asked.

"Satan. Apparently I've been duped into doing his PR."

"You'd think with the boss being Satan the pay would be better."

"My sentiment exactly." I walked around to the driver's side of the Camaro. "Pastor Faithful had lots of quotes about how we're going to burn in hell."

Stiletto got in. "Not me. I'm an international reporter. 'As cold waters to a thirsty soul, so is good news from a far country.' Proverbs 25:25."

I stared at him in amazement. "Where'd you get that?"

"I used to date a nun."

"No." I leaned over and took a bite of chocolate chip. "The cookie."

Stiletto finished it off. "Mrs. Whatsherface. She lives next door. And she had some very interesting observations about your self-righteous minister's daughter."

"Did she now?" I pulled a U-ey and waved to Pastor Faithful.

"Turns out," Stiletto said, "that Ruth Faithful, who's usually in bed by nine, left her house around eleven and didn't get back until two this morning."

"Midnight mass?" I suggested.

"Only you pagan Catholics gather at midnight," Stiletto said. "My new best friend said the devout Miss Faithful returned with a woman. A woman with a suitcase. The neighbor saw her get out of the car."

Cerise May. Could it be?

"She's a real Mrs. Kravitz, this neighbor," I said. "Up at eleven and two, peeking through the window."

"She says she gets by on only three hours of sleep. As a fellow insomniac, I was invited to come over at any hour and keep her company."

"Watching TV?"

"In bed."

"Where else?"

Chapter Twelve

There was quite a shock waiting for us when we returned to the *News-Times* around two-thirty. Four white-and-black Lehigh Police cruisers were parked out front, and a crowd had gathered to discuss them.

"Shit," Stiletto said as I searched for a parking spot. "See what happens when you stay too long on your lunch break?"

I hesitated, unsure if Stiletto was telling the truth. This newspaper business was nasty, and I wouldn't put it past Notch to call the cops if I fudged my time sheet.

"Look." Stiletto pointed ahead. "Someone wrote 'gullible' on the parking spot."

After he defined 'gullible' for me, I got the joke.

But it wasn't any laughing matter when I killed the engine and Lorena flew out of a side door screaming for us to stay in the Camaro.

"You've got to get your ass out of here." She stuck her head in the window. "Burge and four cops are upstairs with an assistant DA looking for your notebook."

Even though this morning Burge had threatened to do a search, I never expected he'd actually go through with it. The idea of cops tossing around newspapers and opening my drawers was outrageous. I had important stuff in those drawers. At least three dollars in change, Tampax, and the other half of my Twix!

"Since when can the cops storm a newsroom?" I asked. "I thought we lived in a free country."

"That's Canada," Stiletto cracked.

"They got a search warrant and everything," Lorena said. "I offered to punch 'em out, but Notch wouldn't let me."

"Spoilsport," I said. "Who'd they get the search warrant from?"

"Judge Pincus Fortrand. Lawless said he's an ultraconservative wack job."

"Had no choice but to be an ultraconservative wack job with that name," Stiletto said. "Where are the lawyers?"

Lorena looked over her shoulder. "They're on their way. The cops just got here. You've got to split, Bubbles. Notch sent me out because he thinks they could haul you down to the station and detain you until you produce. By the way"—Lorena leaned in closer—"Lawless asked me to find out where your notebook is, in case . . . you know."

"You know what?"

Lorena ran her finger across her neck.

"That's not going to happen." Stiletto placed a comforting hand on my knee. "Don't scare Bubbles."

"I'm not scared." I was worried. Lawless may have been nicer to me lately and Notch may have instructed me to work with him, but I still didn't trust the fool. He was too chummy with the cops. All those beers with them at the Tally Ho and his fat-filled luncheons on the police department's tab.

"Tell Lawless my notebook's in a safe place. Not at the *News-Times*."

"Good enough for me." Lorena slapped the car. "Now giddyap."

"Wait. Before we go." I held up the orange envelope. "You didn't leave this in my car this morning, did you?"

"Never saw it before in my life," Lorena said. "What is it?"

"Photos. I'll show them to you later."

I had to because the front door to the *News-Times* opened and two cops exited, surveying the scene.

"I'll distract them," Lorena said, running off. "You just go."

"Cut across there," Stiletto said as I backed up the car. "Take the alley down to Second Street and follow Mechanic Street. You want me to drive?"

I laid a patch of rubber as I peeled across the lot and hopped over the curb. "Why? You nervous?"

"Hardly." Stiletto gripped the handle as I fishtailed down the alley. "What are you trying to do? Purposely draw the cops' attention? Take it easy."

"Liar. You *are* nervous."

"I've zigzagged through desert ambushes. I'm not nervous."

"Oh, sure. The desert ambushes line. That old fallback."

We swerved as I hooked a right into an alley behind the House of Beauty and parked in back of Uncle Manny's, the local bar that serves the men while the House of Beauty serves their wives.

"Last stop. You'll have to hoof it to your Jeep from here," I said.

"Probably be safer." We got out and Stiletto limped around to my side. "You have a plan."

"As always."

"Ditch the photos."

"One step ahead of you." I tapped his injured leg lightly. "Which, under the circumstances, isn't too hard."

"Hmmm." Stiletto's penetrating blue eyes betrayed naughty thoughts. I reached up and stroked his rough stubble, which managed to emphasize his deep-set crow's-feet. Even with his longish, unkempt hair and the vague, not entirely unappealing cologne of Shorty's dandelion moonshine, Stiletto was hard to resist.

He bent down and placed his lips softly on mine, wrapping me in a harder hug. For a fleeting instant, I wished for all the world that we really were engaged, that he had just pledged to spend his life with me—instead of six months until Jane graduated from high school.

"Remember," he said, breaking away, "you're the future Mrs. Stiletto. Let the whole world know."

"In case Chad Kent comes into town?"

"That guy would sell his mother to get that London assignment."

"I'd sell my mother to get ten percent off at Payless."

"And she'd probably be game if she could get a cut."

If it were buy one, get one free, sure.

He promised to call me later. I watched him fake a normal stroll toward the Polish section of town, my heart filled with hope and fear: hope that G had been able to tinker with Stiletto's car, and fear of what would happen to us if he hadn't.

Mrs. Pulieo was hunched in Sandy's chair, a pink plastic apron around her neck and perm rods in her hair, flipping through *People* magazine when I came in, Oscar nipping at my ankles. What had gotten into that yipping dog? It was like he suffered from doggie ADD. I'd worked there for more than a decade, but you would have thought I was the substitute mailman.

"Dan's been calling every half hour looking for you," said Sandy, who was at the front desk doing bills. *All My Children* was muted on the TV. "I told him you don't work here anymore, but it didn't sink in. Nothing sinks in with him."

"He wants me to do an investigation. Something's going on at his work and he won't tell me. It's really stupid." I tossed Sandy the orange envelope.

She stopped punching the calculator and regarded the envelope warily. "More lipstick samples?"

"Kind of. Why don't you check them out?"

Sandy unclasped the envelope and removed the photos. She flipped through them with the trademark calmness she displayed for frantic mothers of the bride and tempestuous teenagers in prom night fits.

"Interesting," she said, stopping at one photo. "Not an angle you see very often."

"Not in *Penthouse*, at any rate."

"Probably there is a porno magazine, though. *Foot Fetish Weekly*."

"With articles on 'How to Master the Toe Job.' "

(For that's what was going on in the photos. Toe sucking. Did your dirty mind suspect some other activity?)

"Well, it is going on in a podiatrist's office," I said. "Might be considered therapeutic. Maybe even insurance pays for it." I had a sudden, impressively insightful thought and filed it away. "See? That's the rug Doctor May has."

"Doctor May's where Principal Schmidt was murdered?"

"Doctor May who the police say now might be missing."

Sandy was hooked. "How did you get these?"

"Someone left them in my car this morning when I was covering a soap drawing of Madonna, before I was kidnapped by a couple of Polish mobsters."

She glanced up at me. "I might not offer the best benefits and you might have to work Saturdays, but, then again, you don't get hauled away by Polish mobsters as a staffer at the House of Beauty."

"I'm really committed to being a reporter. Thanks anyway. I might take up your offer if the devil schedules me for more overtime."

"Pardon?"

"Skip it. Do you have a magnifying glass?"

"Sure do." Sandy opened her top drawer and pulled out a large magnifying glass. She scanned the photo. "Fascinating."

I came around to her side of the desk. "You noticed that too, say?"

"Looks like that Raquel Welch wig. Breathless." Sandy put down the glass. "Why would she be wearing a wig?"

"I'm thinking so she can look like Doctor May. I saw a photo in Doctor May's office. She has the exact same haircut."

"So Doctor May wearing a wig would be pointless," Sandy said, thinking. "You should call around to salons and see if anyone's been buying the Breathless lately. That could be your woman."

"Not a bad idea. By the way, I have an update on Stiletto and me."

"He's already married?"

"No. He's marrying me."

Sandy's face brightened, but I snuffed that. "It's a fraud, so Stiletto can get a six-month extension on his London assignment. Something about AP policy allowing deferrals for weddings, babies, or deaths in the family. Stiletto's all upset because he has to lie and he's so truthful, but if we don't convince everyone we're legit, this AP weasel Chad Kent will run crying to his superiors and take Stiletto's plum assignment."

I could tell Sandy was trying to assemble an encouraging response. "Still, it's nice of him to make the effort, Bubbles."

"For six months, yes."

"It's something." She smiled weakly. "Besides. Stiletto might get to liking the idea. Maybe he'll marry you for real."

"Sandy." I lowered my voice so Mrs. Pulieo couldn't hear. "He used to date a nun!"

"Granted. But let me ask you, he didn't get engaged to her, did he?"

Sandy offered to cover the wig angle and insisted on contacting salons and wig shops in an effort to locate women who had ordered the Raquel Welch Breathless in recent weeks. I trusted Sandy to get the job done. Not only would she fulfill her duty quickly and thoroughly, but each woman would be identified by name, address, and age when she was finished.

Wait until I told Stiletto. Emphasis on the wait. Because as I rushed from the House of Beauty—where the photos were stashed under all the clean folded towels—to Stiletto's mansion in the posh Saucon Valley, I had one goal and one goal only: to search and destroy the answering machine tape on which I had pledged nights of slutty revenge.

This was no simple feat, as me and answering machines are like teenage boys and washing machines. Incommunicado. No speaky the language. *Que?*

I thought of dropping by Liberty and picking up Jane, she of the so-called technical generation. But Jane was sequestered in final preparations for Rudolph Schmidt's memorial halftime service on Friday. When I spoke to her on the phone from the House of Beauty, she sounded none too thrilled.

"This is a drag," were her exact words. "I've talked to a lot of people in putting together my eulogy and Schmidt wasn't such a nice guy. He was in that job so long he thought he was God. Used to make his staff get up at five and go jogging with him, even if it was winter."

This was the ultimate horror, as Jane despised jogging. And winter.

"One secretary quit after he made her stay until midnight typing and retyping a two-paragraph letter he was sending to his dentist complaining about a bill in which he claimed he was overcharged. I'm telling you, the guy was a jerk. He was mean to fat kids, poor kids, and especially Puerto Ricans."

"How about you?" I asked. "He thought highly of you if you were asked to deliver a eulogy."

"Not that highly. He didn't write me a recommendation for Princeton. He didn't write anyone a recommendation, except for a select few. As for me, he never approved of my nose rings or dog collar, even if I was at the top of the class. He was a real prig that way."

I found this galling, that Schmidt would have been so superficial, though I replied in the neutral way of a mother who is trying to raise her daughter to be fair and open-minded. "It is a eulogy, Jane. You're supposed to say only nice things about the dead."

"Supposed to is one thing," Jane retorted. "But talk to Consuela DeJesus, who runs the South Side Centro de Comunidad. She was asked to step off Friday's program because the memorial committee worried she'd slip in a negative comment. It's really fascist."

When I hung up, I called El Centro de Comunidad. Consuela DeJesus wouldn't be in until five-thirty. I made an appointment.

Then I questioned whether, in addition to fat kids, poor kids, and Puerto Ricans, mentally ill girls who dressed like Popeye the Sailor Man had been on Rudolph Schmidt's shit-list too.

Chapter Thirteen

Stiletto's answering machine blinked at me like a taunting playground bully. Damn this thing. All black plastic and digital. Digital! How stupid could I have been to have assumed there'd be a tape? Of course, no one had tape answering machines anymore. No one but me.

The mission seemed easy enough. Hit the play button to hear messages and then erase the one I wanted. Yet I was unsure. This was Stiletto's machine. What if I heard a scary message (i.e., one from another woman that hadn't been intended for my ears)? Then again, why were other women calling him? What happened to our so-called monogamous relationship? Heck. We were engaged now, and other women were still calling him?

What was up with that?

I put my hands on my hips, mad, and curled my lip at the machine. "Two-timing, low-down man," I heard myself say before shaking back to reality. Get a grip, Bubbles.

I glanced around to make sure no one was listening. Eloise, Stiletto's housekeeper, had answered the door when I arrived, let me in, and then scuttled away to do laundry. Her husband, Frank, was at the hardware store to buy pipe to fix a storm drain. The coast was clear.

It's not like Stiletto's AP salary could pay for Eloise and Frank or this historical stone mansion, by the way. Stiletto had inherited the estate from his very corrupt stepfather, Henry Metzger. A man who so loved me he tried to kill me—twice. Metzger was dead now, shot before my very eyes, though when I was here alone once, I saw his ghost. Watching me with derision as he had on Earth.

I shivered and pressed the play button. The first message started with an ear-piercing beep.

Twelve . . . new . . . messages, the machine announced. What a popular boy Stiletto was. *Playback . . . newest . . . message . . . first. . . .*

Message . . . number . . . one. . . . A fluttery voice came on. Just what I'd dreaded to hear. *Hi, Steve, this is Ebony.* Ebony? What was she, a runway model? *I just got off the runway in Paris* (Ohmigod. I was right!) *when I heard your big news. So sorry to hear. . . .*

I pressed skip and went to message number two. *Steve? Steve, are you there, you old dog?* This one was not so fluttery. This was a woman who packaged herself as the kicky fun type. The sort who slugs back shots and rides rodeos in hip-hugging jeans. *What's this about you getting hitched? I can't stand it, cowboy. One last night, that's all I ask. . . .*

Skip. *Message . . . number . . . three. Steve, hon-neee. Pick up so I can . . .*

Skip. *Message . . . number . . . four. Baby! Say it ain't so. . . .*

I sighed. Now I knew how salmon felt swimming upstream. Skip. *Message . . . number . . . five.*

Hey, Stiletto. You listen and listen good. I turned it up. It was the voice of Karol Smolak and he wasn't calling to congratulate. *Cute trick this morning. Biggie and Joe wanna thank you in person. Me too. Wanna meet the famous Steve Stiletto that put my brother in jail.*

I turned it up some more.

Instead of messing with my business, why don't you attend to your own? Ask your hot girlfriend why she sent that punk kid to mess with your Jeep.

He didn't know what he was doing so I took over for him. No problem. Not for me at least.

Click. End . . . of . . . message.

I pressed pause and froze.

Smolak had caught G tampering with Stiletto's Jeep and then "took over for him." What did that mean? Had he hurt G? Forget that. If there were four messages before his, did that mean all those women had called Stiletto in the past hour? Did I stand a chance?

It was difficult to decide which was more devastating. The former girlfriends after Stiletto . . . or G's condition at the hands of an irate Polish mobster.

My palms were sweating and my head spun dizzily. I felt like I was having a panic attack. Not the kind I usually get, when Mama shows up at seven A.M. on a Sunday when Jane is at her Dad's house and Stiletto and I are doing things banned by most religions in the Western World. The kind of panic attack that requires medication the soap operas advertise.

Smolak likely sabotaged Stiletto's Jeep as payback. Cut the brake lines or screwed with the steering, whatever it was Polish mafiosos did to Jeeps of photographers who put their brothers behind bars. Stiletto might be in a lot of trouble. I should call the police and ask Mickey Sinkler to make sure he was okay.

I picked up the phone and got as far as 9-1 when I was jolted by a shrill call.

"Who's down there?" A woman in a rose pantsuit appeared at the top of the stairs. "Make a wrong move and I'll blow your head off."

One of Stiletto's ex-girlfriends, I decided, sighing. Man, these women were peskier than the centipedes under my sink. Plus, unlike the centipedes, they packed heat.

I hung up the phone. "It's me, Bubbles. I'm a friend of Stiletto's."

"Of course you are." She slinked down the stairs. The first close-up look I got of her was her shoes. They were rose and white with a strap in the back. I'd seen knockoffs of them at Almart, so I knew they were expensive. "It's so wonderful to meet you. I'm Rosa, Stefano's cousin. From the old country."

"Sicily?"

"Actually, Bayonne."

I stood with my finger hovering over the answering machine's erase button. I didn't trust her. She was slim with thick brown hair and perfectly plucked brows, though she was well past thirty. Maybe pushing forty. There were so many silver bangles on her wrists that at first I thought she was handcuffed.

"Stefano and I haven't seen each other in years." She tucked her tiny pistol in her waistband. "I used to make passes at his stepfather, Henry. I can't resist a loaded . . . you know."

"Gun?"

"Man. Cute." She punched my shoulder slightly. "At first, I thought maybe I could get in on the action—snag me a financially secure sugar daddy—but the diamond leash around that old boy's neck was buckled and locked. His kitty-cat wife wasn't eager to share the wealth, either, and I couldn't blame her."

I didn't know what to say. I'd never met a gold digger before. Not one who spoke so much or so bluntly.

"Then again, with me being Stefano's cousin," she kicked off her shoes, "it would have been kind of incestuous, though we're not technically related. We're more like Dutch cousins. I'm the daughter of his late mother's best friend."

Here's trouble.

"Growing up, I used to dream of Stefano and me walking down the aisle, white dress, big Italian church wedding, caviar, champagne, and a nice, fat monthly allowance. *Ka-ching!*" She punched me again. "But you were quicker on the draw, sweetie. How is that dashing Stefano, anyway?"

"Fine." I rubbed my suddenly sore shoulder. "I have to . . ."

"Wanna drink?" She gestured toward the bar in the den. "It is the holiday season. Why don't we kick off Thanksgiving early?"

"You're staying for Thanksgiving?"

"Thank you. Finally someone was polite enough to ask." She sauntered off to the den and returned with a martini already made. "I mean, I've been hinting for days, ever since I heard about the engagement. But Stefano's so daft, like all men."

Somehow I had been tricked into inviting her and immediately I regretted it. I tried to picture Rosa mingling with Mama, Genevieve, G, and Jane. I tried to remember what bookies in the valley would take bets on the first musket shooting of Thanksgiving.

"How did you hear about the engagement . . . so fast?"

"Stefano's friend Chad called me."

Couldn't be. "Chad Kent? From the AP?"

"Yup. I met him last year in New York when I was visiting in the city. We had a one-night stand. At least I *think* we did. I woke up naked and Chad wasn't wearing underwear. Hard to remember after a few of these." She toasted with the martini. "He's coming too."

Wait until Stiletto heard this. "You invited him to Thanksgiving?"

"I hope that's okay. It is a holiday after all, and he was dropping lines like, 'How do you defrost a turkey roll?' and 'Maybe I'll just have a TV dinner.' "

Oh, he was good. He was very, very good. Stiletto was right. Chad Kent would sell his mother, and for less than a Payless discount.

"Though who knows if he'll actually show," Rosa continued. "AP photographers have a reputation for being chronically unreliable. I'm sure that's not news to you."

Thanksgiving was taking on new meaning, such as meaning I'd give anything to have it over with already.

She pointed to my hands. "No ring, I see. How come?"

I looked down at my fingers. "I don't know. You'll have to ask Steve."

"Absolutely. It'll be the first question. Right before how come he decided to get married so quick. You're not . . ."

"Pregnant?" I blushed. "No."

"That's a relief. Because Stefano's a Stiletto. In the field of women he grazes like a deer." She walked her plum nails across the table. "I wouldn't have kids for years, if I were you. Not until you're sure he won't be straying."

My neck felt hot. "Stiletto doesn't stray. He's extremely loyal. We have a very trusting relationship."

"Sounds like you're talking about a golden retriever instead of the scoundrel who used to play Doctor Goodlove to all the Saucon Valley girls in second grade. The touch of an ice-cold stethoscope still makes me hot."

"Excuse me?"

She downed the last of her martini. "Hey, don't let me stop what you were doing. You were picking up messages, right?"

"That's okay," I said, now stuck. "I can't work this machine anyway."

"Oh, it's easy. I have one like this at home." And before I could stop her, Rosa pressed the play button.

Hey, Stiletto, you lowlife. If you're there, pick up.

It was my voice, my insane message. "Let's press skip," I suggested. "It's not right to listen in . . ."

"Are you kidding?" She pushed my hand away. "Whoever this chick is, she's pissed. Nothing more entertaining than a bitch in heat."

I covered my eyes.

Of course you're not answering. Why should you when you're in the middle of a sex marathon? Oh, I know all about it. All about her. And let me tell you something, Stiletto, I'm glad you're getting married to someone else. Because frankly, I'm sick of you. I'm sick of your boring stories about your so-called international adventures and all the women you've slept with. . . .

Rosa looked at me, puzzled. And then her face dawned with enlightenment. She knew it was me. Bubbles. The bitch in heat.

I was tempted to throw up on her Jimmy Choos.

I'm sick of your short attention span. One minute here. One minute there. And me always wondering if you were with another woman. Hey. You know what? Despite your sophisticated worldly experience, you weren't even that great in bed. The RadioShack guy down on Stefko was better.

"Ouch," said Rosa. "That hurts."

Bigger, too. Much, much bigger.

"Is that true?" She opened her eyes wide. "I always imagined him having . . ."

I pressed the erase button. "Please. It was all a misunderstanding."

"If you say so." Rosa twirled her glass. "Now, how about that drink? You're behind one."

I was tempted to say yes when a car pulled up outside.

Rosa eyed me.

I eyed her back. "I'd appreciate it if you didn't . . ."

She put a finger to my lips. Her finger smelled like gin. "Your secret's safe with me . . . for now."

"Bubbles!" Stiletto crashed through the front door, tossing a duffle bag aside. "What are you doing here?"

Rosa spun around and opened her arms, all motherly warmth and affection. "Stefano. It's me, Cousin Rosa. Here for Thanksgiving."

Stiletto didn't have a chance to react before "cousin" Rosa had thrown her arms around him and planted a kiss smack on the lips.

I slipped over to the door and checked the driveway. The Jeep was there in one piece. Never looked better. I could have sworn it had even been waxed.

Well, I was jiggered. Maybe messing up meant something different in Polish.

"I see you met Bubbles?" Stiletto grasped my hand and pulled me to him, tight. "Isn't she wonderful?"

"Ach, such a love." Rosa pinched my cheek so hard it hurt. "But look. No ring?"

She held up my left hand.

"Hmmp," said Stiletto, scrounging for a reason. "I haven't had the . . ."

"You can't be very serious if you haven't given her a ring. A Stiletto man is never serious until he gives his betrothed a diamond. At least," she added, winking seductively, "that's what I'm banking on."

It was four-thirty when I returned to the South Side and I was pretty near exhausted. It had been a long day and I still had a township meeting to cover at seven-thirty, plus a story to file.

That was a party compared to hanging around with Rosa, whom I left languishing on Stiletto's couch, sucking down her second martini. Stiletto had fled to an AP assignment covering a candlelight vigil held by animal rights activists protesting doe season. I wasn't positive, but I think he volunteered to be with crooning vegetarians just to get away from Rosa.

I drove past Dr. May's office as I made my way to the *News-Times*. It was dark and shut down for the day. Ruth Faithful must have canceled her boss's patients, cleaned up the tossed files, and gone home.

The Lehigh PD, too, had crawled back to its cave. I parked the Camaro right out front and hustled up the stairs to the newsroom. No time to spare. I had one hour to write up the soaped Madonna scam and file background on the upcoming township meeting before my appointment with Consuela DeJesus, the snubbed Puerto Rican.

Notch and Mr. Salvo were in the afternoon edit meeting. Lawless had punched out early and had left a note on my keyboard saying that the final toxicology report on Popeye would be back earlier than expected. By ten A.M. tomorrow.

In a PS he added that he had set me up on a date with Detective McIntyre after my night meeting. Lawless was certain I would use my feminine wiles to elicit secret cop information he couldn't get through normal means.

JUST A BEER, his note concluded. WHAT THE FUCK?

Clever boy.

I crumpled the note and tossed it in the trash. As soon as I did, the phone rang. I answered it while booting up my computer.

Newsrooms were very unproductive places for those who didn't multitask.

"Where the hell have you been? You weren't in Highland Heights when I came to get my coat and you haven't returned any of my messages."

It was Dan.

"I have a job, remember?" I pulled out the Madonna notes. I could feel the other reporters looking at me, asking themselves if this was *the* notebook.

"The whole bar is talking about you, how you're skirting Fortrand's order. Are you crazy? Hand over the damn notes."

"What happened to me as the final protector of the First Amendment?"

"Let someone else finally protect it. You've got our daughter to think of. You don't want to raise our baby from jail."

I tried to draft a clever lead for the soap Madonna. "Jane would love it if I was sent to jail on a First Amendment issue. Heck, she'd join me."

"Sure, what does Jane care about jail? But you! Think of it. The noise. The drug-addicted cell mates. The thin mattresses and everyone sees you pee."

"I'd deal."

"No blow dryer."

Then again . . . "Why have you been bugging me all day?"

"Because I need to meet with you so we can discuss this dangerous case I'm working on," Dan said. "How about dinner?"

I started typing. "No good. I've got a five-thirty appointment and then I think I'll pick up Jane from school, stop off at home to get some clothes, and then drop her off at Mama's before my Mahoken Town Council meeting. I don't want her staying home alone. Not after that phone call last night."

"But there's been a new development in my . . . situation."

"Oh?" I wasn't really paying attention. I was wondering how

Lorena's photos of the Madonna had turned out. "You getting more death threats?"

"I haven't heard from my caller." Dan paused. "The caller came to me."

I stopped typing. I leaned into the cubicle so my colleagues couldn't hear. "What do you mean, he came to you?"

"When I opened my office this morning, I found a drawer open and a file missing. A very important file."

"Whose?"

"I can't tell you. Not over the phone. Let me just say it belongs to a client and it contained some very sensitive material."

"Dan, you've got to go to the police."

"I can't. Remember my self-compensation program?" His voice was strained, which was telling, since Dan was accustomed to putting on a show every day in the courtroom.

"I thought you promised to return the cash." I checked the wall clock. It was almost five. "I thought we'd agreed you'd pay it back in twenty-four hours. Didn't Wendy give you the money?"

Dan was silent.

Oh, no. "Don't tell me you haven't told her yet?"

"I haven't had time. And besides, you're missing the point, Bubbles. Someone's been threatening me and my family. Someone blew up my radiator. Now someone's broken into my office and stolen the most important file I possess right now."

"Possessed," I corrected.

"Either way I have more problems than alerting my wife to a potential financial mishap."

Financial mishap. Since when was $20,000 a minor checkbook oversight? "Why would they want that file anyway?"

"That's why we have to meet, so we can discuss it. I need you, Bubbles. You're the only person I trust right now." I heard him close the door to his office. "I have to confess, I've been blown away by what a good reporter you are, by how far you've come since I met you in Delta Upsilon. You're not the same shallow dimwit townie with the big hair and the big boobs. You've turned into a top-notch investigative reporter who writes hard-hitting, intelligent, and complicated stories."

"Like an exposé on Madonna in Ivory soap. I'm on deadline." I hung up, flattered and confused about what had gotten into Dan. And curious as to what was so wrong about being a townie with big hair and big boobs.

It didn't add up. Dan often made me use the back entrance when he had guests, and he didn't pay me alimony even though I'd put him through college and law school when we were first married and Jane was an infant.

He'd cheated on me with a makeup saleswoman on my very own living room couch while I was at work, and he'd changed his name so that his white-collar clients wouldn't suspect that in his prior life he'd been a flat-footed podunk who used to salivate over Tuna Helper.

Dan had spent a decade distancing himself from me, West Goepp Street, and all I represented. So how come he was being so nice?

Something smelled foul, and for once it wasn't sulfur spewing out of Lehigh Steel's smokestacks.

Chapter Fourteen

I was slightly late in getting to the South Side Centro de Comunidad because Mr. Salvo nabbed me as I was headed out the door.

"Nine a.m. tomorrow. Fortrand's chambers," Mr. Salvo said as we passed on the stairs. "Pack a toothbrush."

"What does that mean?" I rubbed my gums. Maybe I should buy that whitening gel I've seen on TV for those glow-in-the-dark teeth. "It's not my fault. It's coffee."

"Having a conversation with you I might as well be talking in Juju. Packing a toothbrush means Fortrand might jail you for contempt."

In which case I wouldn't have to worry about dingy dentures. "Really?"

"Don Markin's representing Garnet." That was the out-of-state corporation that owned the *News-Times*. "He's a top-notch attorney. Still, I'd be prepared."

"Bring a makeup mirror too?"

Mr. Salvo shook his head. "Forget it. Come as you are. Fortrand will get the picture."

El Centro de Comunidad was a colorful oasis of bright,

Caribbean-themed mosaics, lush plants, a couple of red parrots, and salsa music set in the gray sea that is the South Side in winter.

Puerto Ricans had flocked to the South Side, occupying the homes left by their predecessors, the Hungarians, Germans, Poles, and Lithuanians, two decades ago when Steel was still hiring and American success seemed easy pickings.

Lousy timing. The Puerto Ricans didn't inherit their predecessors' jobs, since they arrived right when Steel was closing down. The Lehigh plant had gone from 20,000 jobs in my youth to now only 1,600. And those 1,600 rattled with death. Steel was terminal and no one had a cure.

It was a disastrous formula for the South Side. There were too many young, energetic Puerto Rican men unemployed, and too many of the old holdovers unwilling to offer them what jobs were available. To the uptight babushkas who hadn't moved across town, the new Spanish-speaking neighbors with their growing families and backyard parties were nothing more than foreign intruders destined to dirty their scrubbed sidewalks.

The tensions were spelled out in the swirled graffiti along the walls of old garages and abandoned cars. The pink, blue, and orange scrawls glowed under the street lamps as I walked toward the community center. They urged revolution and love of all things hip-hop.

Consuela DeJesus had her work cut out for her.

I found her in the center's large industrial-strength kitchen, where I was nearly knocked unconscious by the aroma of fried garlic. She was standing at an eight-burner stove supervising two teenage girls in a giggle fit and trying not to laugh herself.

"What can you do?" Consuela threw up her hands. "They don't know the difference between a tablespoon and teaspoon. A very bad mistake when it comes to adobo."

"Keep you from getting fatter than you already are, old woman," shot back one of the girls.

Consuela pretended to look stern. An effort that was rewarded by a stuck-out tongue.

"Kids," she said. "Ungrateful nothings. Wait till I make them wash the floor."

After I introduced myself, she fired off rapid instructions in Spanish to which the girls nodded obediently. There was obvious love there. Impressive considering the age group she was dealing with.

"Getting ready for Thanksgiving?" I asked as we walked toward her office.

Consuela made a face. "You mean Anticolonialism Day? We don't celebrate Thanksgiving here. Thanksgiving is a lie."

"What do you mean, a lie?"

"Don't you know the true, nonwhite-male history?"

"I was taught in Lehigh public schools. All the history we got tended to be white and male."

"*Lo siento.*" Consuela took out a set of keys and stuck one into her door, raising questions about why it was locked. "It's not the people in the center I worry about," she said, reading my mind. "The front door is always open. Anyone can walk in. I have to be careful."

"Clearly." I sat in a wicker chair in front of her messy desk. The office was a monument to clutter. Papers were piled high and tamped down by oddly shaped paperweights haphazardly molded by children and glazed in pale green and pink. There were posters of Puerto Rico's sunny shores, and a straw piñata, and the walls were painted a deep orangish red.

"See, what most Americans don't know is that the first Thanksgiving was an accident." Consuela slipped off her shoes. "The colonialists invited one chief of the Wampanoags and ninety of his men showed up, uninvited. The colonialists didn't like that. Two years later, the colonialists invited more tribes and promptly poisoned two hundred Indians with Thanksgiving food and drink. Intentionally."

I thought of who would be at my dinner. Rosa. Mama. Genevieve. "We better stop," I said, "before I get ideas."

"I've got family too. I know what you mean. However, if you want to get away, you are invited to share in our anticolonial dinner. All turkey, stuffing, and nonnative food are banned."

It was an ideal alternative to the other Thanksgiving dinners Mr. Salvo would assign me to cover for a general feature. "Might just do that. I have to work that day anyway." I took out my notebook as someone knocked on the door.

Lorena walked in, not even waiting for an invitation. "You Consuela"—she stopped to read from a pink carbon photo slip—"Duh Jesus?"

Consuela looked at me questioningly.

"My editor's fault," I said. "I can't go anywhere without a photographer."

Lorena set down her bag with a loud clunk. "Don't mind me. Continue with what you were doing."

This was impossible as Lorena proceeded to do her job, to noisily open white umbrellas, activate test lights with blinding flashes, and swear repeatedly at both. Meanwhile I made my pitch. It was my understanding Consuela had been removed from the Friday halftime memorial service for Rudolph Schmidt. Why?

Consuela shrugged. "Ask the committee. They're the ones who made the decision."

So she *had* been kicked off. I wrote this down. "Sources"—read: Jane—"tell me that you were removed out of fear you might say something negative."

"Who, me?" Consuela thumbed her chest. FLASH. And then rubbed her eyes. "That was so bright. Did you have to do that right in my face?"

I gave Lorena a dirty look. She pretended not to notice.

"I'm inferring you and Mr. Schmidt butted heads occasionally," I said.

Consuela constructed a diplomatic response. "About five years ago when I first took over the center, I met with Doctor Schmidt."

"Doctor?" Lorena interrupted. "Since when was that coot a doctor?"

"I believe he has, excuse me, *had* a PhD," Consuela said.

Lorena snorted. "Might as well call *me* a doctor, then. I got a doctorate in that near-death-experiences course I took at Two Guys, say, Bubbles?"

Why couldn't Lorena vaporize like all the other bad witches?

"Anyway," Consuela continued, "I met with Doctor Schmidt to discuss some problems a few students and their parents were having with racism at the high school."

FLASH. "Aw, shit. My bulb broke." Lorena bent down and picked up the pieces. "You got a broom or anything?"

"In the kitchen," Consuela said, exasperated. "The girls will help you."

"What do you mean by racism?" I asked when Lorena had finally quit bothering us. "Was it racism from the students or him?"

"Him, though it was hard to pinpoint. For example, if I tell you one story, you could easily side with Doctor Schmidt instead of the students. It's that iffy."

"Try me."

"A typical situation would be a student on the edge, let's say a Puerto Rican male about fifteen, in and out of trouble with petty crimes but otherwise okay. He's in school. He makes a poor decision and goes down to Pine Street. Smokes a little dope."

I knew where this was going. "And he gets busted, but his white buddies don't."

"Exactly." Consuela sat back. "The difficulty is that it's so hard to file a complaint. Technically, as principal, Doctor Schmidt should alert the authorities whenever he finds a child using illegal substances. So what's the gripe?"

"The gripe in your mind is that Doctor Schmidt didn't have all the kids busted."

"Especially the kids who'd bought the drugs in the first place," she said. "The rich ones."

"Because they had money to buy the drugs."

"Which in Dr. Schmidt's view put them in a separate class. A white, Anglo, middle class."

I wrote what she said, hoping she wouldn't ask me to go off the record. Personally, I didn't like the term "Anglo." Then again, maybe that's what it was like to be called black or Spic or Polack.

"I read your story this morning about Doctor May," Consuela said. "I can't see how my infrequent disagreements with Doctor Schmidt could relate to his murder or to what I'm hearing is Cerise May's disappearance. Cerise is a good person. I have been praying that she is safe."

"How did you meet Doctor May?"

"I'm back!" Lorena threw open the door and immediately set to sweeping. "These light bulbs are a bitch to sweep up, and expensive, too. There's always a tiny piece you miss. Hey. You should put your shoes on there, Consuela."

The handle of Lorena's broom worked back and forth, bumping into the file cabinet and coming precariously close to the framed photos on the wall.

"Uh," Consuela said, rising slightly from her chair. "The photos—"

CRASH!

Consuela collapsed and covered her eyes.

"Oh, sorry. Shit." Lorena held up the picture. The glass was broken. "Hey. Look at it this way. At least I don't have to get a broom."

"It's our Año Viejo photo." Consuela touched the frame. "One of my favorites."

"The *News-Times* will pay for a new one. I'm so sorry." I was ready to murder Lorena. Consuela was on the verge of giving us the boot.

"You were saying about Doctor May?"

Consuela gingerly removed the photo. "I met her briefly. She came to one of our block parties last summer. She was with her boyfriend and didn't say anything. Sweet but very shy."

"Around Karol Smolak, who wouldn't be? Probably afraid he'd smack her in the kisser if she so much as opened her trap," offered Lorena, holding up a dustpan full of glass and dirt. "Where to?"

Consuela pointed to the wastepaper basket. "Who's Karol Smolak?"

"Cerise May's boyfriend," I said. "Her ex, though I think they were still going out last summer."

"They didn't break up until a few weeks ago," said Lorena.

"I don't know who Karol Smolak is," said Consuela, "but I know for sure he wasn't Cerise May's boyfriend last summer. I'm a good friend of her boyfriend. And a more thoughtful guy you'd never want to meet."

"That's not Karol," said Lorena. "He's got a temper on him like a bull with his nuts superglued."

Consuela blanched.

"Bob's been a saint to us here at the center. Toilet stopped up, he's on the spot. Gutters need cleaning out, he's there. He even drove Dora Colon to the hospital when she slipped in the kitchen and broke her ankle."

Lorena and I looked at each other. Whatever Karol Smolak was—Polish mafioso, flower fancier, low-down murderous thug—Good Samaritan he wasn't.

"Detective Bob McIntyre," Consuela said. "Maybe you know him? The other day, I heard he'd asked Cerise to marry him and that she said yes."

Chapter Fifteen

Would wonders never cease?

Detective McIntyre was Cerise May's boyfriend. How convenient, then, that he was also in charge of investigating Karol Smolak, his rival in love as well as war. That's a cop for you. Always got a game going on the side.

It was six-thirty when Jane and I arrived at my dark house. I flicked on all the lights, inspected every room including the basement, and concluded that, unlike Dan's office, the fort was secure.

Jane ran upstairs to get her clothes for the next day while I sorted the mail—electric bill, phone bill (second notice with the red stripe across the top), and an Avon catalogue. Yippee.

After I'd checked off two lipstick purchases (Matte Maraschino and Matte Heather) plus two matching Glimmersticks, I made myself a ham-and-Swiss-cheese sandwich with mayo and honey mustard on Wonder Bread. Cracked open a refreshingly cold Tab and dialed Mickey Sinkler, the one cop I could trust, at home.

Our relationship lately had been icier than my Tab, thanks to Mickey's discovery that Stiletto had managed to get under my pink satin Victoria Secret stretch mesh thongs. It had been a couple of weeks, though, and seeing as it was the Thanksgiving season and all, I had high hopes for a rapprochement (learned that word at Two Guys Community College: Overseas Relations isn't just Sex on a Cruise Ship).

I stood by the phone, eating and drinking while thinking about how my life had turned into one endless stream of multitasking now that I was a full reporter.

"What!" Mickey answered, a high-pitched kid's scream nearly splitting our phone line in two.

"I thought your kids were at your ex's." I pictured Mickey being attacked by his four juvenile delinquents, one of whom, at age five, was still in diapers.

"She went out to buy yams. Won't be back for another hour."

The last time Mickey's ex-wife bought vegetables, the grocery store turned out to be in Seattle and an hour turned into a year.

"What do you know about Detective McIntyre?" I bit into my sandwich and waited while Mickey ordered one of his brood to sit in the corner.

"Prick of the first order." I assumed he was referring to McIntyre and not the kid. "Super control freak. Wife left him two years ago because he used to insist that she have breakfast on the table and his uniform ironed before he got out of bed in the morning."

It's the little touches that make a marriage special. "You know if he got engaged recently?"

"I'd heard rumors to that effect." Mickey cursed under his breath about a flying PlayStation that had nearly hit the TV. "I keep my distance from McIntyre. Unless we're on a case together, we never communicate."

"You're some help."

"Why do you care, anyway? He one of the cops out to get your precious notes?"

I decided to ignore the veneer of sarcasm. "I have a date with him tonight."

"No way. What happened to Stiletto?"

"This is more like a business meeting slash date. Lawless set it up against my will."

"Hold on. I gotta kill this kid."

Jane came down the stairs and cringed at my Tab while Mickey engaged in what sounded much like a murder in the making.

"Death," she mouthed as she walked by, pointing at my soda.

I shrugged. Tab was a monkey on my back, I admit it. The way I looked at it, there were worse monkeys.

"Whatever you do, don't let McIntyre get you alone," Mickey said when he got back on. "We've had complaints from a number of women about his blow-pass offer in exchange for a dropped ticket."

"I assume you're not talking about blowing into a Breathalyzer."

"Indeed I am not."

I finished my sandwich. "One last thing, you catch the name of the woman he's engaged to?"

"I told you. I keep my distance. All I heard is she's some chick he met while investigating Karol Smolak. I assume she's an early riser."

As soon as Mickey hung up, I called McIntyre and left a message on his answering machine, feigning a sudden headache. It was unoriginal, but that's what I loved about the excuse.

Mama and Genevieve lived downtown in a new senior citizen high-rise made out of orange brick. It was close to the city center, bus stops, the library, the American Legion Hall, and the VFW, though most of its residents never made it farther than the wooden benches bolted to the sidewalk out front.

What the senior citizens high-rise did not permit was hookers and babies, the latter being too noisy and the former being considered counterproductive to the future financial prospects of widows like Mama and Genevieve.

The apartments inside had white walls and were crammed with overstuffed, faded furniture left over from previous lives in real homes. As a result each room looked like a storage locker. It was not the kind of place where the term "minimalist" held sway.

It was also not the kind of place where you expected to find Vo-Tech dropouts with bleached blond hair oozing nose rings and cigarette smoke and testing firearms, but there he was: G, my daughter's beloved, taking musket lessons in Genevieve's apartment.

"Yo, yo, Mrs. Y. Sorry I couldn't deliver on your old man's vehicle." G wrapped a wad of cotton around a metal rod and shoved it down the musket as Genevieve looked on approvingly. "Course you still owe me fifty since I nearly got my ass kicked by that Polish putz."

Jane dropped her school stuff on Mama's kitchen counter. "What did my mother make you do now?"

"Asked me to disable her old man's Jeep, that's what. Chuck the carburetor. Trim the brake lines. Mumble a little mumbo jumbo on the hot rod's gumbo."

"Tamp it down good. Don't take any shortcuts," Genevieve barked, barely able to contain her pride as G carefully loaded the musket.

"You asked G to sabotage Steve's Jeep?" Jane was irate. "Mom. That does not sound like you. Even if you were mad."

"Long story," I whispered to her. "It's not what it appears."

"Serves the Italian gigolo right, I say." Genevieve helped G place a pin. "What with him running off and getting engaged to some Twinkie. If I'd been Bubbles, I would have stuffed his tailpipe with fertilizer and lit a match."

That was not as shocking as it sounded. Genevieve regularly went around stuffing tailpipes. Usually with mashed potatoes, but occasionally fertilizer, depending on whether Agway was running a sale.

"All this violence, guns, and sabotage—I need to get out of here. I'm going upstairs to see Grandma." Jane left with a slam.

That was too bad because G and Genevieve were just getting to the good part: blasting out the reverse alarm of a garbage truck parked forty feet away.

"Why should I have to wake up every morning to that racket?" Genevieve guided G's arm as he leaned out of her fourth-story window and sited the musket. "Beep. Beep. Beep. At five a.m. I'm sick of it."

"Is this okay?" G aimed for the truck's cab, which, as Lady Luck would have it, was conveniently parked under a streetlight.

"Move it toward the tail there, Butch. That should stifle its tweeter."

I couldn't look. G fired a musket ball. It missed the garbage truck and flew over the wooded hillside behind the parking lot. I prayed there were no innocent groundhogs skipping hibernation.

"Aww, that's a shame. So close." Genevieve yanked the musket out of G's hand and began the gunpowder, ball, tamping process all over again. "Let's leave it to the pros."

Mama flew in, complaining of noise and what the super would say.

We ignored her. "You mind telling me, G, how you sabotaged Stiletto's Jeep so it was better than ever?" I asked.

"Sugar in the gas tank." G juggled a musket ball. "Really gums up an engine."

"That's a lie," Mama said. "Sugar doesn't dissolve in gasoline. It's one of those urban myths. I read about them in *Reader's Digest*."

"But . . . ," G said.

"Aw, sure it does. It flows to the filters, carmelizes, and cruds those up." Genevieve poured in enough gunpowder to blow up the Lehigh Valley Mall. "It's hell to clean. Expensive, too."

"But . . . ," G tried again.

"Not to mention illegal," Mama interrupted. "Irma Kline, she's a secretary in 5B, dumped five pounds of Domino in her boss's Monte Carlo when he sent her on a personal errand to have the oil changed. Her boss stalled on the Macungie Road, figured it out, fired her, and had her cited, too."

"But . . ." G waited for the interruption. When he saw we were listening politely, he said, "But I didn't dump in sugar. LuLu's right.

You can go to jail for that. All I did was make it *look* like I dumped in sugar.

That was G. Half-assed.

"I wet down the side of the car and threw on a boatload of sugar *around* the gas cap, figuring when Stiletto saw the white stuff, he'd know better than to drive the Jeep. He'd have it towed and cleaned out. Cost him no more than a hundred bucks, but it'd delay him for half a day."

I was surprised by G's brilliance, not to mention consideration. The savvy clientele at Hess's must be rubbing off.

"I was pretty much finished," G continued, "when this Smolak dude runs out of his flower shop and demands to know what's going on. Threatens to beat me up and all. I told him I was messing with Stiletto's Jeep and then he stops reaming me out and starts cursing Stiletto and saying he's been looking for a way to pay him back for what he did to his employee and his Ford. Only Smolak says I've gone about it all wrong."

"Uh-oh."

"Yeah. He says I've been sloppy, leaving sugar on the side of the car. Says Stiletto will see it and be onto me. Next thing I know, he's got a rag and water, wipes it all off. Finally he brings out the wax so there's not a trace."

I couldn't believe it.

"Stiletto comes by. Gets in his Jeep and drives off like nothing's happened." G shook his head. "I spend one hour losing time from work and Stiletto gets a free polish."

"That's what we call a Polish, not a polish, Butch." Genevieve sited the musket for another go. "And them Polacks wonder why the rest of us make fun."

Chapter Sixteen

The Mahoken Town Council meeting was its usually exciting event. Much of the evening was spent sitting on uncomfortable metal chairs in the Mahoken Town Hall, trying to stay awake while the council embroiled itself in hot discussion about the road-salt budget and whether or not a Quick Mart was absolutely necessary at the corner of Deiter and Doherty, since the sewer lines didn't go out that far.

I watched for fireworks between Councilman Arthur Youngman, a Republican Rotarian who sold cow feed, and Councilwoman Tracy Inuzzi, a housewife from Lower Mahoken. They'd been caught last year in embarrassing circumstances after the two continued an executive session on a king-sized spring coil at the Bide-A-Wee Motel.

Unfortunately, I spotted only a shared wink and that might have been a speck in Councilman Youngman's eye.

When I wasn't scoping for town council lust, I was learning way more about sewerage than a human being should need to know. Then I lost interest and ended up doodling an impressive rendering of the photos that had been left in my car earlier in the day. When I was finished I decided that something in the picture was definitely off.

But what?

The meeting ended early at nine-thirty (I assumed so Youngman and Inuzzi could suck face) and I found myself a half hour later back at the *News-Times* where the usual nightly chaos was under way. Reporters on deadlines, blaring police radios, and Mr. Salvo loosening his tie, sweat popping out on his forehead, looking like he was on the verge of a myocardial infarction.

I updated the Mahoken story I'd filed earlier and made a call to Al Girard, a "tech ed" teacher at Liberty who was serving as chair of the Rudolph Schmidt Halftime Memorial Committee. Girard was grumpy because I'd awakened him, and he was downright livid when he found out I'd awakened him to ask why he'd disinvited Consuela DeJesus.

I let him deny it with a fudge that was so thick they could sell it on the Jersey Shore Boardwalk. Something about Ms. DeJesus providing valuable input, but her schedule not permitting her to speak on Friday. He was stone silent when I said that was kind of odd because Ms. DeJesus herself had said she'd been excused out of fear she might mention Mr. Schmidt's clear ethnic preferences.

It was all dull "no comment" after that. I took down his non-denial denials and popped them in the story, which turned out to be a short-but-sweet eight inches. Mr. Salvo proclaimed it great page-one material, found a file photo of Ms. DeJesus and Schmidt hugging at "Community Day" last year, and moved my Mahoken Town Council piece to deep inside beyond sports. Shows what you get for attending night meetings.

"You got your fluff pieces lined up for Thursday?" Mr. Salvo asked. It was our nightly ritual, him making sure I was progressing on my assignments before he'd let me go. "You'll be the only one on staff, you know."

"I'm doing All God's Children's Church. Tom Faithful's holding a traditional Thanksgiving supper for the homeless." Two birds with one stone, there. "And El Centro De Communidad, their Anticolonial Day celebration."

Mr. Salvo chewed his gum. "Anticolonial Day celebration? I don't know. I hate politically correct."

"You hate politically correct like Consuela DeJesus hates Pilgrims. They slaughtered a bunch of Indians. Did you know that?"

"Liberal propaganda." Mr. Salvo handed Billin a corrected layout page. "What about your other feature?"

"The madness of getting your kid into an Ivy League college." I made the okay sign with my fingers. "One more interview and I'm done."

"I don't want this being a first-person narrative. No 'how hard it was to get *my* daughter into Princeton.' "

"No, boss."

"I want figures. Stats. Helpful hints. Talk to graphics for a chart."

This was an inside joke, since the *News-Times*, unlike every other news organization in the world, had no graphics except for a high school student named Jim Bob. Seeing Jim Bob was at his grandmother's for the holiday, though, we required other art besides a high schooler's rendition of ivy.

"I'll send Ludwig to do a head shot of your interview." Mr. Salvo snatched a photo slip. "Who is it?"

"Jonas Walker. Liberty High's top guidance counselor. And Mr. Salvo?"

"Yes?" He scribbled out the photo slip.

"The way Lorena interrupts during interviews, she's kind of"— what was the right word?—"distracting."

"I'll speak to her." He dropped the slip in the photo drawer. "She's been hard to contact lately. Supposedly she's gone undercover at the Polish-American Club. Some top-secret mission. You know what it is?"

Digging dirt on Karol Smolak, I thought, though I said, "Free Rolling Rock?"

"Either that or she has the hots for fat men in black pants and white shirts."

Could be that, too.

Around eleven I was set free. I took out my time sheet and filled in all the hours. Seven to eleven. Off until around 7 P.M., then on until 11. Out of the corner of my eye I could see Neal Everston ready to pounce.

Neal was the local rep for the reporter's union, quaintly referred to as the Guild. I couldn't be a member of the Guild because I was still on probation, but that didn't mean I could be spared Neal's nagging. He caught me at the door as I pulled on my fake rabbit fur coat.

"Split shift again?" Neal was gangly, with fuzzy gray hair and ripped jeans. He considered himself a hippie intellectual. The worst kind. "You're making us look bad."

"I'm not in the union yet." I had to make up my mind whether I ever would be. It was not a closed shop.

"Doesn't matter. I've got my eye on you. Split shifts. Overtime. Even if you're not in the Guild, you have to apply for overtime. A learning curve is not an excuse."

"Not to you, maybe, but to me it is."

"What I'm trying to tell you is to watch out." He pushed up his wire-frame glasses, the nerd equivalent of fingering the trigger on a gun. "Reporters who don't, uh, comply can run into difficulty. You're on our radar screen."

I brain waved him a big "whatever," unlatched the glass door, and left. All I wanted to do was go home, make sure Jane was safe, stir up a big glass of chocolate milk, and catch David Letterman.

But it was not to be. As soon as I turned the corner, I was in another man's arms.

And for once that was a good thing.

"Funny meeting you out here."

Stiletto looked down at me with his gorgeous eyes that sparked with mischief. He wrapped me in a hug and kissed me as I soaked up the heat of his body and the smell of leather from his bomber jacket.

The rock-hard thighs in his tight jeans pressed against mine in a most masculine way.

"My Jeep's waiting right here."

I felt a pang of guilt regarding G's pranks at Smolak's. Not too sharp a pang, though. Stiletto did get a free wax, after all.

"Let me take you home."

"But my Camaro," I said, foolishly not picking up on his hint. "I'll need it tomorrow. . . ."

"Then I'll drop you off in the morning."

I smiled and Stiletto grinned, and between the two of us there wasn't a morally proper thought in the house.

"Saves on gas," I said, "what with the oil shortage and all."

"Yes." He opened the passenger door to let me in. (Note, ladies, how far he had come from our first encounter.) "Very environmentally conscious of you."

"That's me." I got in and observed that Stiletto had been thoughtful enough to put up the top. This never happens. Stiletto is a true fresh air addict. It could be pouring and he would have to consider long and hard about the advantages of not getting wet.

"So to what do I owe the occasion?" I asked as Stiletto hooked left on Fourth and headed in the diametrically opposite direction from my house.

"Just wanted to be with you and seeing as Smolak had sent around his goons to chauffeur you around this morning, I didn't want you to get the impression I wasn't holding up my end."

"In other words, Cousin Rosa's driving you mad."

"Cousin Rosa's passed out. But not until she managed to flash her cleavage numerous times and make suggestive remarks about what tricks she picked up on a cruise around Thailand."

"Oh, brother." I leaned my arm against the door. I was up against a pro.

"Cousin Rosa's pathetic, Bubbles. You, on the other hand, are a sweetheart."

"And don't forget I'm your betrothed."

"Which is why I have to play your bodyguard. It's my husbandly duty."

Whenever Stiletto is worried about my safety, which has been more and more often lately, he starts popping up in places. Never announced, just there. It's kind of nice. Makes me feel as though I've got some support besides Wonderbra underwire.

"You realize," I said, "that you are going in the wrong direction."

"Maybe I'm taking you back to Saucon Valley, to my house."

"With Rosa there?"

"Then it's a surprise. A big surprise."

The big surprise turned out to be the dank underbelly of the Hill to Hill Bridge. Okay, the Hill to Hill Bridge is technically *our* spot, but twice in one day and the magic had worn off. Near midnight in November after a long day and a Mahoken Town Council meeting, and it smacked of torture.

"I thought this place was fitting." Stiletto leaned in the back and brought out a kerosene lamp. Lighting it, he put it on the dashboard and reached in the back again, this time producing a bottle of real champagne and two plastic cups.

"Had to hide this from Rosa," he said, unwrapping the lead top. He pointed the bottle toward the back and uncorked it with a loud pop. "Have you noticed that privacy for us is hard to come by? Jane's at your house. Rosa's at mine."

"Makes our get-togethers all that more meaningful."

"So for this occasion, I'd like it to be just the two of us."

He poured the champagne into the cups and handed me one. "A toast." He held it up. "To a whirlwind engagement."

"To a whirlwind engagement."

He sipped and I sipped and then I wondered what the hell he meant by that.

"You're a good sport, Bubbles, to put up with a bogus betrothal."

"Ditto. And thanks for sacrificing your no-lies rule so we could be together."

"It's not a sacrifice. I'm beginning to enjoy it, really." Stiletto reached into his pocket. "Which is why I decided you need this."

What he held out was a tiny black velvet box. Granted, I'd grown up in Lehigh, where high-end jewelers answered the phone, "Van Scoy Diamond Mine," but I could spot class.

"Stiletto," I gasped, "you don't have to . . ."

"I want you to know I bought it in New York way before Rosa started yapping about how you needed a ring. I'd be damned if I was going to give it to you like that, in front of Rosa, with her adding up its carat weight."

I kept staring at the closed box. "We're just faking it. You don't need to . . ."

"Please, Bubbles. That is . . . unless you don't want to."

Oh, I wanted to all right. I wanted to very much.

I'd always dreamed of someday wearing a genuine engagement ring. Dan had asked me to marry him while I was studying *So You're Having a Baby* pamphlets in the ob-gyn's office. We were at City Hall two days later, a slip of gold no wider than telephone wire on my finger, which turned green a week later.

I had to remind myself that the ring would be temporary. That this whole charade we were playing was merely Act II of *Scenes from an Engagement*, a one-woman play slated for a six-month run—Off-Off-Broadway—culminating in May when Jane graduated from high school and I had to decide whether I should stay or I should go.

"What are you waiting for?" Stiletto asked. "Is the ring too much?"

The stalling was over. With a deep breath and fortification from another sip (let's be honest, gulp) of champagne, I opened the box, half expecting a cigar band and a gag.

It wasn't no cigar band, as they'd say in Lehigh. What it was was the most dazzling ring I'd ever laid eyes on. Even in the flickering yellow light of the kerosene lamp it danced and sparkled. Two pear-shaped diamonds, perfectly cut, set off a sizeable, but not garish, round-cut diamond on a platinum band.

I was speechless.

"I thought it looked like you." Stiletto took it out of the box and slipped it on my finger. It fit like Cinderella's slipper and I scrunched up my face so I wouldn't cry and come off like a sappy fool who couldn't accept a bogus engagement ring with bored approval.

"It's gorgeous," I said. "It's . . . it's the most beautiful thing . . ." I almost said I'd ever owned, but that would be wrong, as surely I would have to give it back to him when the act was over.

"It's from Harry Winston."

So I was right. It was a loaner. "He let you borrow it?"

Stiletto took a second to absorb this and then laughed. "No, um, Harry Winston is a jeweler in New York."

"Oh." I splayed my fingers. The diamonds were brilliant. "He does good work. Almost as good as Van Scoy Diamond Mine."

"Yes," Stiletto agreed. "It looks beautiful on you, too. The diamonds on either side remind me of this lovely place right here." And he kissed the spot where my collarbone met my neck. "You're like a swan. Such perfect symmetry." There was a slight choke in Stiletto's voice. It caught me off guard.

I kissed him and he kissed me back with a power I hadn't felt before. If it wasn't a sense of love and commitment, then it came damn close.

"Anyway," he slugged back the rest of his champagne, "you more than deserve it after going through this ordeal."

"Thank you." I watched him closely. He was acting oddly, not his usual cocky self.

"De nada." Stiletto started up the Jeep and we were silent for awhile, me recovering from the excitement of having a genuine engagement ring, and Stiletto? Who knew? Maybe suffering from the lack of nookie.

"This is perfect." I fingered my ring. "When Chad Kent sees it, he'll be convinced we're really engaged."

"I hope Chad never sees it."

We were zipping down the Spur Route going around seventy-five (slow for Stiletto). I waited until we passed a truck and I made sure my safety belt was secure to say, "Yes, he will. Chad's coming to Thanksgiving dinner. At your house."

Stiletto wrenched the wheel into the right-hand lane, traversed another lane of traffic, and took the Union Street exit.

"What?" he exclaimed when we were safely off the highway. "You're kidding me."

"I am not. Rosa invited him. Apparently they're chummy from what might or might not have been a one-night stand. Too many martinis to remember."

"Rosa," Stiletto said.

We turned onto West Goepp and Stiletto killed the engine.

"She's against me." He rubbed his brow. "Rosa's always stirred up trouble. She's a catalyst for disaster. Even when we were kids she used to say or do something that would cause me to punch another boy for no reason."

Would have liked to have seen that. Just imagining Stiletto defending a woman's honor—even Rosa's, even years ago—was tantalizing. He was so . . . hot when he was fired up. Maybe it was the raging Italian within him or how he kept that raging passion controlled. I didn't care. I wanted him. I wanted him alone and preferably naked.

"Are you listening?" he asked.

"Un-huh," I lied. I hadn't realized he was speaking.

"I said it's like we're playing with fire."

I shrugged off my rabbit fur coat and then I reached over and unzipped his jacket.

"What are you doing?" He blinked as I pushed off his jacket and then slid my hands up the hard silkiness of his abs. Before he could say anything else, I crawled over the gear shift and onto his lap, my mouth firmly on his.

Stiletto tasted wonderful. He had the best lips. Whenever I kissed him my brain turned to Silly Putty. All I could think was, Oh, boy. I'm kissing Stiletto! Yahoo!

"Jesus, Bubbles. Is this what champagne does to you?" he said when he managed to catch a breath. His mistake, because I took his weakness for oxygen as a chance to pull his turtleneck off him and, as luck would have it, mine off me, too.

Stiletto grinned and finally stopped talking.

In the week that he'd been away I'd forgotten how broad those shoulders were. Muscular and smooth. Not a hair on them. Just defined tendons that continued up his strong neck.

Wouldn't you know it, next thing I knew the only thing covering my thighs were Stiletto's hands. Like in a bad movie, the windows were fogging up and we found ourselves in the back entwined between his ratty photo bag and half a month's worth of *New York Times* scattered over our naked bodies.

Part of my mind was conscious of not kicking over the kerosene lamp on the floor and the other part was wondering how Stiletto was able to thrill me in what had to be the least comfortable of circumstances, though I'd had plenty of encounters in the backseat of cars. (See RadioShack technician as impetus for chastity vow.) Let me say right now, the RadioShack guy did not have answers for my questions. Stiletto was born with the ultimate cheat sheet.

It wasn't just what Stiletto did or stroked or kissed. It was how he moved and what he whispered as we got closer and closer, unable to tear ourselves apart from each other. It sounds corny but the only word I can use to describe it is "electric." What we had was electric.

Charge! Stiletto slid into me and my mind went blank as my head hit the door handle, and I swear I heard a *rap, rap, rap*. Either I was suffering the effects of a minor head injury or gosh darnit if someone wasn't at the door.

Stiletto and I both froze.

"Shit," he said, echoing what I was thinking. "Who could that be?"

"Bubbles?"

My mother's high-pitched dog call pierced through the Jeep's cloth cover straight into our backseat of romance. The electricity fizzled and so did Stiletto. He handed me my turtleneck and bra and I fumbled as I tried to untangle the two.

A flashlight went on and my tiny mother was outlined against the steamed windows.

"Bubbles, are you in there?" The beam flicked across the interior. I felt like a prison escapee in the warden's searchlight.

"It's okay, LuLu," Stiletto called out, zipping up his jeans. "It's just us. Bubbles and me."

"I *know* that. What I want to know is what you two are doing in there."

"She knows that, too," I murmured as I wriggled into my tight leather pants. "It's okay, Mama. You can go inside."

"Not until you come out of there. What will Jane think?"

"If you'd stopped yelling at the top of your voice, she wouldn't even know." *Zip.* Stiletto and I exchanged one last look of longing just as the door flew open and Mama's flashlight nearly blinded me.

"I thought so." She directed the beam to my tousled hair and down to my bare feet. "Bubbles. How could you?"

Stiletto started laughing as I turned red. I couldn't see her, just the sheen of Crisco reflected on her face (see page 292). That was a good thing because I would have strangled her tiny body if I could have found the neck.

"And what's that on your finger?"

It took a nanosecond, but it was too late. Mama had seen.

"Oh!" she gasped. "Oh my! Is that what I think it is?"

Stiletto and I were silent, hoping that she'd be mistaken or confused. Both of which she is often.

We didn't stand a chance.

"Is that an *engagement* ring? I can't believe it. I wish Genny were here. I have to tell someone. Mrs. Hamel!" Mama stuck her fingers in her mouth and whistled. "Mrs. Hamel, get out here!"

The Hamels's front porch light flicked on and Mrs. Hamel ran out carrying her own flashlight. "LuLu, is that you? Everything okay?" Behind her Mr. Hamel stood in his boxer shorts and flabby belly, his hair sticking up like crabgrass.

Mama hopped up and down. "She's engaged. Come look. Bubbles has a ring."

Mrs. Hamel screamed and the DeNofrios's light went on, as did the Salabskys's.

Stiletto gripped my hand. "Be strong."

"It's Armageddon," I said. "It's the end of us."

"Never." He leaned over and kissed me, and when he was done, half of West Goepp was there to witness it.

There was no going back now.

Chapter Seventeen

Judge Pincus Fortrand's chambers in the Court of Common Pleas were paneled with dark wood, carpeted with a burgundy rug, and so dimly lit that candles would have caused snow blindness.

This was not an invigorating environment for a woman who was operating on five hours of restless sleep haunted by previews of LuLu Yablonsky's wedding plans. A boombas band, scrapple turnovers, and a dollar dance. What crime had I committed in a previous life to have deserved this?

I fingered Stiletto's ring, which dangled from a chain around my neck, while we waited for Fortrand to make his appearance. The *we* in this case was District Attorney Reggie Reinhold, Detective Burge, and Don Markin, the local lawyer acting on behalf of the Garnet News Agency, which owned the *News-Times*.

Markin had filed briefs with Fortrand yesterday, as had Reinhold. The argument Markin made was that Pennsylvania's "shield law" protected not just anonymous sources, but also a reporter's unpublished materials, such as notes and quotes that weren't used in a news story.

I knew what the DA's argument was: my notes were evidence in a murder investigation and withholding evidence was a crime.

Kuntz wasn't at the hearing. Markin told me that since Julia Simon was dead and she had possessed previously undisclosed assets, Kuntz, as a state-paid public defender, was no longer eligible to represent her.

One attorney down, I thought, regarding Reinhold. One to go.

"All rise!" the bailiff announced.

We jumped up as Fortrand entered, a packet of briefs under his arm. He was dressed for the judge part. Long black flowing robes and jowls. He sat in a high-backed leather swivel chair and motioned for us to sit too. We didn't have leather chairs; we had wooden ones.

Fortrand slipped on a pair of half glasses and opened the file, which set off a sudden nervous reaction. I wished I'd dressed differently, and I suspected Markin wished I had too. My leopard-print scoop-neck T didn't quite fit the mood. And the black miniskirt? Kind of a clash with the bust of Thomas Jefferson and the framed law school diploma from Penn over Fortrand's chair.

Peering over his half glasses, Fortrand told us that he had read the briefs and come to a decision. He offered us an opportunity to make any last-minute pleas.

Reinhold stood and reiterated the "gravity of the situation," noting that Rudolph Schmidt had been a pillar of Lehigh, and that his murder had "disrupted the fabric of safety that blankets the Lehigh Valley."

I didn't know what fabric he was talking about, unless it was Visqueen. Nearly every home in Lehigh has at least one window or car covered with plastic.

"That sense of safety cannot be restored until this case is solved and the murderer is brought to justice," the DA said. "By withholding her notes from the last interview with the key suspect, Miss Yablonsky illegally hides evidence and impedes that process."

Markin interjected. He was an imposing man, six feet or so with silver-gray hair that I knew from my professional experience had been chemically treated.

"I can't imagine how Miss Yablonsky's notes will affect the safety of the community, since the suspect in Mr. Schmidt's murder has not only been arrested, but also has committed suicide."

That's the kind of zinger you get for four hundred bucks an hour.

"New evidence, Your Honor," Reinhold said.

Markin looked at me questioningly.

"Final laboratory test results my office received last night from the state medical examiner conclude that Julia Simon suffered from a significant overdose of her antipsychotic medication. Much more than she'd been prescribed or had access to. This overdose induced neuroleptic malignant syndrome, severe dehydration, and sudden death. . . ."

"In short?" Fortrand said, impatiently.

"According to the medical examiner and the Lehigh Police Department, Ms. Simon was murdered."

It was a startling statement, the ramifications of which took a moment to sink in. Popeye had been murdered, and I had witnessed her murder. I had been there when she began to feel ill and confused. When she had suddenly stiffened and died. And I had done nothing.

I rubbed my shoulders and Markin, who apparently harbored a rare attorney gene for sympathy, patted my arm. I'd never witnessed a murder before and I was shaken. I was also alarmed.

Who killed her? And why?

Everyone was looking at me and I realized that was because Judge Fortrand had asked me a question.

"Miss Yablonsky, I'd like to hear from you."

Markin helped me stand. My legs shook slightly, and I had to steady myself by leaning against the chair.

"Was there any statement made to you by Miss Simon that has not been published, but that, in light of the district attorney's revelation today, you in your judgment might consider to be evidence?"

Hell with it. Popeye's dead, I thought. Take the damn notes. Read how Popeye had been locked in the bathroom, how she'd heard voices before someone—her murderer, perhaps?—unlocked the door. How she was convinced everyone was against her. I wanted to give up. I wanted to run away. I was feeling dizzy myself. Dizzy and sick.

"I'm sorry, Your Honor," I said, parroting what Markin had instructed me to say, "but under the protection of the First Amendment, I respectfully decline to answer that question."

"I see." Fortrand had expected that answer. "Then I am afraid—"

Suddenly the big mahogany door behind us burst open and one of the judge's law clerks entered, apologizing for the intrusion. He said an attorney representing Cerise May was insisting that he be allowed in the hearing.

We faced the door. Dr. May was still missing or on the lam. No one knew which, and the whole town was buzzing. If I'd known Dr. May had a lawyer, I would have called him myself.

"I'll allow it," Fortrand said, "though he should have filed an amicus brief."

The law clerk opened the door wider. I nearly fell over when Dan rushed in wearing a crisp gray suit, a glaring bright blue tie, and retouched hair. I could sense Burge trying to make eye contact with me, but I ignored him.

"Dan," I said under my breath to Markin. "He's my ex-husband."

"What's he doing here?" Markin said out of the corner of his mouth. "Representing May?"

"Not that I knew."

"Chip Ritter, from Ritter and Ryjeski," Dan said, handing out briefs to the judge, Reinhold, and Markin. He pretended not to know me. "I represent Doctor Cerise May, a potentially harmed party in this case."

I could tell Dan was nervous because he was playing with his cufflinks. Otherwise no sweat, thanks to a trick I'd taught him long ago (see Dan's No-Fail Antisweat Method for Men, page 292).

"Where is your client?" Fortrand asked bluntly.

"I have no idea, Your Honor." Dan straightened his tie and patted down his hair. "I haven't heard from Doctor May since Sunday night and I fear for her safety."

I noticed he didn't mention the break-in at his law firm. And for good reason, besides his skimming from the law firm till. Now that I knew Dr. May was his client, I had a clever hunch that the "most important file he possessed," which had been stolen, was probably hers. And it probably contained the photos that showed up in my Camaro in Highland Heights.

"Attorney Ritter, I have already—" Fortrand began.

"Please let me enter a brief statement," Dan interrupted, not waiting for Fortrand to respond. "In light of Doctor May's disappearance and the possibility that she has met with foul play, I strongly urge the court to consider that producing Miss Yablonsky's notes at this time would be. . . ?"

He sucked in a breath.

Prudent, I guessed, mentally concluding his sentence. *Imperative. The right thing to do.*

"Highly irresponsible."

I was hit by a wave of disbelief. Was Dan defending me?

"Given that those notes might put Doctor May in jeopardy," Dan continued, "I would ask the court to respect the Commonwealth's shield law and agree with Garnet in this matter."

"What kind of load of crap was that? That didn't make any sense," said Markin under his breath. Nevertheless, he made no move to object. Why should he? Dan was on our side, though I wasn't sure if in this situation that was a good thing.

"Your Honor . . . ," Reinhold started.

Fortrand cut him off. "Mr. Ritter, you may sit down. Miss Yablonsky, come forward."

I knew that was bad. Markin gave me a stiff upper lip as I confronted Judge Fortrand.

"In reviewing the material, I see no reason why you should not produce your notes to the prosecution and the police in this matter."

Sarah Strohmeyer

Lead fell to my stomach. In the back of my mind, I'd predicted this would be his ruling. Nevertheless, the words were hard to hear.

"Your interview with Miss Simon was on the record and, as such, does not fall under Pennsylvania's so-called shield law. I am asking you one last time, at the risk of being charged with contempt of court, will you produce these notes?"

I looked back at Markin, who shook his head subtly.

That was *not* the signal I'd hoped for. I really didn't want to go to jail. In jail they wore itchy orange prison jumpsuits, and orange definitely was not my color. It's hard to be brave when you're facing a stint as an orange person, scratching endlessly behind bars, no soap, no makeup, no Stiletto. And what would Jane do?

I checked Markin one more time, just in case he had changed his mind.

He gave me the thumbs-up.

"I'm sorry, Your Honor." I swallowed. "I can't."

"Aw, jeez," I heard Dan say. "Give it up, Bubbles."

"Then I find you in contempt of court." Fortrand clicked a pen. "Do you understand?"

"You're sending me to jail," I whined. "But it's almost Thanksgiving and . . ."

"No, Miss Yablonsky, I am not sending you to jail. I am, however, fining you one hundred dollars."

One hundred dollars. I was stunned. One hundred dollars wasn't so bad. It was more than I could spare, but one hundred dollars was definitely doable. A few weeks of moonlighting at the House of Beauty . . .

"A minute." Fortrand scrawled this on a piece of paper. "One hundred dollars a minute for every minute you don't produce the notes."

I was in shock. No, really. I think my heart stopped and crazy dots appeared in my eyes. One hundred dollars a minute! I'd never heard of such a thing. Didn't Fortrand know I could barely pay my five-dollar parking tickets?

"Excuse me, Your Honor." Markin approached the bench. "This is a fine to be paid by Garnet or. . . ?"

"By Miss Yablonsky herself." Fortrand regarded me squarely. He went in and out of my vision. "With a maximum set at fifty thousand dollars. Case closed." He pounded the gavel and swung back into his private office, his black robes flowing behind him.

Dan caught me as I swooned. "I did what I could," he said. "I tried my best. I've been trying to help you all along. Didn't you know? I left you those photos."

Suddenly it came together, the facts congealing like hair gel in ice water. Dan represented Dr. May. And the photos of Schmidt getting the toe job came from Dr. May's office. They were found in my Camaro when it was parked in Highland Heights. Dan had gone to Highland Heights that morning to retrieve his coat from the back of my car.

"You gave me the photos from Doctor May's office," I hissed, fighting to remain conscious. "You put them in my car when it was parked in front of the Taylors for the Madonna story."

"Yes." He sat me in a chair. Markin ran off to get a cup of water from the hall cooler as Reinhold and Burge passed, smug and victorious. "Cerise gave them to me and I gave them to you."

"Why?"

"Because, Bubbles." Dan grasped my hand and looked deeply into my eyes. "Because as insane as it sounds, I can't help myself. I want you to succeed, and I want to be with you when you succeed. I want us to be a success together."

"Huh?" Had Dan turned into a motivational speaker?

"Don't marry Steve Stiletto. Marry me, Bubbles. Marry me all over again and be my wife."

"Dan?" I thought I might be dying, that maybe Popeye's leftover medication had been slipped into my morning coffee and I was hallucinating. "Don't make fun of me. Not now."

"I've never been more serious. If you won't do it for us, do it for

Jane. Ivy League schools prefer kids from nuclear families. They get five points added to their application if both parents file jointly. It must be true. I read it in *Newsweek*."

Dan proposing? *Newsweek*? I wasn't being poisoned. I was being solicited.

Thankfully, it all turned black after that.

"He lost his mind." Sandy handed me a Diet Pepsi as I recovered on her couch.

"Do you mean Dan or Judge Fortrand?"

"Both."

"Judge Fortrand is a doofus," announced Mona Sprague, who came in every two weeks to retouch her acrylic nails. "He gave full custody of both my kids to my ex-husband even though I was bringing home the bacon."

Sandy and I were too polite to point out that as an exotic dancer who didn't get home until 4 A.M., maybe Mona didn't keep a June Cleaver schedule. Or perhaps Fortrand took issue with her string of boyfriends, who came with their own string of arrest records, and her numerous citations for loud parties that often ended in mid-street rumbles.

"Let's see those nails." Sandy bustled over to the table. "Hey, I think they're dry."

Mona blew on them. "No, they're not."

"A five-dollar discount says they are."

"Well, what do you know? Dry as my granny." Mona made her way to the cash register as Sandy rang up her bill.

I sipped the Pepsi and parted the blinds with two fingers. The day was gray and drizzling, classic Thanksgiving weather. All over Lehigh, families were reuniting. College kids were being met at bus stations. High school students would go home at noon and stay out late. There'd be cooking and football and, in my neighborhood, more Christmas decorations.

At my house, bread was being pulled for stuffing and pies were in the oven. Pumpkin, apple, and mincemeat. A twenty-pound turkey tomorrow. Mama's watermelon pickle, of course, carrots, celery sticks, and olives. Reconstituted dried corn (blech), a Pennsylvania Dutch dish that Mama claimed came straight from the Indians. Mashed potatoes. Green beans with that fried onion glop on top and cranberry sherbet.

It was the same dinner we always made, except I'd be working and my family would be at Stiletto's—with Cousin Rosa and Chad Kent. Aside from the house, Stiletto's contribution to the holiday had been several bottles of fine wine to celebrate or, as he put it, sedate.

"Finally!" Sandy shut and locked the door, then flipped the OPEN/CLOSED sign to CLOSED. "I couldn't wait to get her out of here. So what are you going to do about Dan?" She plunked herself in the flowered chair opposite me and opened her cigarette case.

How I would have loved to have had a cigarette. The smooth feel of it between my fingers, the anticipation of lighting it and then the deep, satisfying inhale. I breathed in deeply. If I hadn't promised Jane I wouldn't smoke, I would have sucked down one of those babies so fast my fingers would be on fire.

"I'm not going to do anything about Dan." I distracted myself with a coffee stirrer, flicking it around like a minibaton. It was a pathetic substitute. "Dan's going through a midlife crisis. That's all."

"I was thinking it was one of those grass-is-greener situations. Stiletto's proposal put you under contract and now Dan wants to make an eleventh-hour offer. This is why bulls have horns and not cows."

"Bulls don't have cows?"

"You know what I mean. How did he hear about the make-believe engagement anyway? Jane?"

"Mama. She caught Stiletto and me fooling around and saw my big engagement ring and called Dan right away to tell him. Woke him up, even."

"What ring? You didn't tell me about a big ring."

I pulled out the chain I'd hidden under the leopard-print top. The platinum and diamonds lit up the salon with dazzling color and shards of light.

"Yowzee!" Sandy leaned over and pinched it between her fingers. "That's gotta cost a mint."

"I didn't ask. It's made by some guy in New York. Harry Winston."

"He's not so shabby, this Winston." Sandy held the ring to the light. "He's just as good as Van Scoy."

"That's what I told Stiletto."

"Why aren't you wearing it?" Sandy slipped it on her finger so her nail stuck into my neck.

"I don't want to become attached. I'm going to have to give it back someday."

"To Harry?"

"Yeah, him. You're hurting me."

"Oh, sorry." She pulled off the ring with a look of regret.

"Knowing Stiletto, he'll give it to the homeless, the way he gave away almost all of Henry Metzger's money to charities and families of workers who'd been injured at Steel."

"Listen to you. Mother Theresa and her vow of poverty. Boo-hoo-hoo." Sandy took another drag of her cigarette. "You ever think that this scam might be Stiletto's only way of easing into a lifetime commitment?"

"No. A morphine drip would be Stiletto's only way of easing into a lifetime commitment. What time is it?"

Sandy checked the clock over the coat rack. "Eleven forty-five. Why?"

I did the math as best as I could. The judge's order went into effect at nine-thirty. It was now two hours and fifteen minutes later, which meant, "I owe $1,350."

"I thought it was a hundred dollars a minute."

"It is."

Sandy exhaled. "Then try $13,500."

Yipes. I clamped my head between my hands. That was more than last year's 1040EZ.

There was a knock at the door. Sandy jumped up. "Who do you think that is?"

"Probably a walk-in," I said. "Someone who wants to get their hair done for the holidays. I'll do her. Cheap. Six hundred dollars an hour."

"I'm not taking chances." Sandy closed the blinds on the alley windows and shut the office door.

"Nervous?"

"You have to admit it's somewhat disturbing." She adjusted the peach acrylic sweater around her shoulders. "Everyone's after your notes. The district attorney, the cops, and who knows who else. And where are they? Right here. In the House of Beauty." She glanced behind her as though the DA himself had entered the room.

I decided now was not the moment to reveal that Popeye had been murdered—*during* our interview.

"Don't think of them as notes," I said. "Think of them as lipstick samples."

"Right. That reminds me." She ground out her cigarette. From underneath the cash register she pulled out a notebook of her own. "I called all the salons around town that sell the Raquel Welch Breathless wig."

"Whoever bought it could have bought online," I suggested. "Or Allentown. Then we'd never be able to track it down."

"Have no fear." Sandy pointed to an entry in her orderly note-book. "Leila's Hair Heaven. Leila herself told me the wig was pur-chased over a month ago, by none other than a Mrs. Grace Schmidt."

"Rudy's wife?" I thought of Grace Schmidt. Petite, wrinkled, and constantly smiling. A full foot shorter than her husband, who she'd admired with worshipful doe-eyed gazes. "What did Mrs. Schmidt want it for?"

"Who knows? Who cares? Maybe Principal Schmidt made her buy it. Maybe he snitched it from her personal collection."

Which, if true, confirmed him as the photos' geezer. "I have to talk to her. Stiletto's right. I have to confront Mrs. Schmidt."

"Don't get Leila in trouble." Sandy closed the notebook. "Make up something, like you'd heard Mrs. Schmidt had bought the wig and you wanted to check it out. Nothing specific."

"Oh, yeah. That'll work." I rapped on a make-believe door. " 'Hi, Mrs. Schmidt. So sorry to hear of your husband's passing. Hey? What about this wig you bought a month ago?' Come on, Sandy."

"Won't know until you try."

I gathered my stuff, my faux rabbit fur coat and purse with its new notebook. That brought back familiar worries. "My lipstick samples. If someone's followed me looking for them . . ."

Sandy smiled wisely. "You can thank Martin. He had the idea to hide them in full view. He saw it on *Masterpiece Theatre*."

"How do you hide notes in full view?" The salon looked the same to me.

"Don't worry." Sandy hummed a delightful ditty. "It'll do."

Chapter Eighteen

My agenda for the day, besides racking up one-hundred-dollar-a-minute profits for the county court system, included finishing the background on my college admissions feature, since no one would be available to interview on Thanksgiving, when I would be writing it.

The last on my list to interview was Jonas Walker, Liberty High School's top guidance counselor. As I was not eager to repeat the Consuela DeJesus fiasco, I managed to schedule Lorena an hour before my interview. She was assigned to take a head shot of Walker, ideally advising an Ivy-bound student. Though with Liberty closing after lunch, Jane might be the only Ivy-bound student sticking around, waiting for a ride from me.

Back at the *News-Times* I had enough time to punch the clock, pick up my mail, sneer at the Guild ninnies, and check my schedule. I did all of those and more. Then I called Stu Kuntz.

Kuntz answered the phone directly. No secretary. "She's out to lunch," he said. "I eat at my desk."

Of course he did. "I wanted to convey my condolences," I said, feeling awkward. "I didn't know Popeye . . . I mean, Julia, very well. But she seemed okay. It's awful that she was murdered. I want to do a story."

"Hmph," Kuntz said. "The story is that if she'd been Martha Stewart she wouldn't have been left unprotected in the courthouse tank. But as a homeless woman Julia had no clout. Didn't matter that she was an obvious target, that there was palpable outrage in this town over Schmidt's murder. She was left defenseless."

I opened my notebook to a clean page and started writing.

"The sheriff's department has a lot of explaining to do. Lookit, they even let *you* in with her. And who knows who else?"

I tried not to be offended. You would have thought I was a leper pushing smack, the way these lawyers referred to me.

"The coroner's office released her remains into my custody today, even though I'm no longer her attorney. On Friday morning I'm going to scatter her ashes around the South Side. She loved that neighborhood."

That seemed a bit off. Couldn't Kuntz find a peaceful meadow? Why did he have to pick the gum-splattered sidewalks of the South Side? Now I'd have to be careful wherever I stepped. "She had no family?"

"None that I've been able to locate. Julia was a late-in-life baby for the Simons and they were overjoyed when she was born, she once told me, because they'd tried so hard to conceive. But she was uncontrollable as a child and they had her institutionalized. As a parent I can't imagine."

Nor could I.

"Took its toll. Mother and father became alcoholics." Kuntz sighed heavily. "Both died fairly young. In a car accident on Thanksgiving, ironically. Apparently Julia's father was drunk. Over on the Hilltop Road, behind the university."

The Hilltop Road was a winding, steep, and sinister road that had taken the lives of many intoxicated college students. I remained mum and let Kuntz dump what for lawyers passed as grief. I'd hold my questions about what would happen to Julia's trust fund for later.

"After I scatter her ashes, I'm going to the halftime memorial service at Liberty. My son's delivering a eulogy to Schmidt. How's that for irony?"

As I had never quite grasped the nuance of irony, I didn't know how to answer. "See you there," I said. "My daughter's speaking too."

"Kids are what it's all about. They're our future and our hope. They keep you going, say?"

"Yes," I said, thinking kids draw with crayon on your walls and keep you up nights worrying what party they had snuck off to. Kids put holes in your pockets so you never can figure out where the money went. "Children are a joy."

I thanked him for the interview and hung up. I typed up my notes and copied them for Lawless, adding a request that he check if any records had been filed in Probate Court regarding Julia Simon's trust fund and who got the money. I was delighted to give *him* something to do for a change.

It was another page-one story. The sad life of Julia Simon. Abandoned. Orphaned. Wrongfully accused of murder and then murdered herself.

Mr. Salvo was thrilled.

I stopped off at Henny Penny for a BLT and called Stiletto from the pay phone. No way I was calling him from the *News-Times*. That place trafficked in the currency of relationship gossip.

"I heard about Fortrand's ruling. It's bullshit," he said. "I'd hash it over with you, but I've got an assignment."

My gut clenched. As journalists we both had assignments, but Stiletto's were usually dangerous. Mine were narcoleptic. Stiletto shot hostage situations and hung out of helicopters. I detailed sewer ordinance amendments and risked butt sores.

"Nothing interesting," he said. "It's a feature for the AP." Which meant it was none of my business and that meant I was curious.

"What about Cousin Rosa?"

"She's planning an invasion. Your mother and Genevieve are here with her setting the table and reviewing the china like they're reviewing the troops. When I look at them I think of the Axis."

"The Axis?" Was that a heavy metal band I missed?

"Like World War Two Axis. Your mother's Hirohito. Rosa's Mussolini, and Genevieve . . ."

"Watch it, Stiletto."

"You have to admit," he said, "she does share his love of bunkers."

I had to admit, that she did.

It was still too early for my guidance counselor interview. I had just enough time to squeeze in a courtesy call to Grace Schmidt. This was not going to be fun.

Fun would be dropping by and surprising her with an oversized check from Publisher's Clearinghouse.

Fun is not asking an elderly woman why she bought a wig that her husband then put on a much younger woman with an abnormal interest in podiatric oral exams.

The Schmidts lived over by St. Anne's in a stunning colonial. It was shingled with mullioned windows, two screened porches, a swimming pool, and extensive plantings. It was a real house, the kind you see in movies and on TV commercials for lawn equipment.

I parked and counted the cars in the driveway to determine how many kids and grandkids might be comforting Mrs. Schmidt during her mourning.

There were four, not including the light blue Saturn sedan that had followed me all the way from the *News-Times*.

After two weeks on the job and several months freelancing, I'd become accustomed to folks following me when one of my stories got hot. Frankly, I'd be disappointed if they didn't.

There's just not that much to do in Lehigh. Entertainment opportunities are slim to none, and slim just left town. Bowling on Friday night, a movie on Saturday, Mass on Sunday. There's a tendency, then, to tag behind others who are engaged in more interesting activities. If I weren't so freaked, I'd be flattered.

I pretended to lock my car as I checked out the sedan behind me. A woman was behind the wheel, down low so I couldn't make out her face. Obviously she wasn't used to this stalking business. Most stalkers I've come across like to park across the street so they can check me out in the side mirror and I can't see them.

I walked up the walkway, the photos retrieved from Sandy's under my arm, and knocked on the door. A woman with a baby answered. She was an upper-crust type, straight thick golden hair, big diamond studs in her ears, and a matching pendant.

After introducing myself, the woman identified herself as Mr. Schmidt's daughter, Elaine, let me in, and called for her mother. The hallway was big with a white center staircase. I waited as other family members drifted in and out. Another sister, Claire, and her toddler, Brian. The place smelled of Thanksgiving, of sage and apple. The mood was merriment mixed with grief.

This was going to be tougher than I thought.

"We're going through with Thanksgiving because that's what Daddy would have wanted," another one of Rudy Schmidt's daughters, Arla, informed me. Arla was the biggest of the bunch, though she, too, had the thick golden hair. A genuine Brunhild. "I feel as though Daddy will be with us in spirit. Only he won't be cutting the turkey."

Yes, this was going to be a lot tougher.

When Grace the mother arrived I found myself surrounded by Arla, Elaine, Claire, and her toddler Brian, who was spinning himself on the floor out of excruciating boredom. He was the only one who wasn't curious to know what I wanted.

"May I speak with you alone?" I asked Grace.

Grace stuck out her chin. She was shorter than all her daughters, but it was evident she was the boss of the applesauce. "Whatever you want to say to me alone, you can say to my daughters. We're a family."

I looked out the window. The woman in the Saturn had pulled up closer to my Camaro. She was leaning toward us, trying to peer in.

"What I have in these photos," I said, "is not fit for your daughters to view."

Grace's hand flew to her turkey neck. She glanced at Arla, who nodded. "Arla will stay with me."

Elaine started to object until Claire nudged her, and Brian ran out of the room. When they were gone, I handed the envelope to Grace and clasped my hands. Grace slid out the photos and studied them intently, Arla looking over her shoulder.

Grace was a solid matriarch, I had to hand it to her. If she was shocked by seeing a nude man—possibly her husband—getting his toe sucked by a naked woman, she didn't let on.

"This is gross," Arla announced, incensed. "Why are you doing this to my mother? Mom, don't look at them anymore." She snatched the photos out of her mother's hand. "I want to talk to your superiors."

Grace regarded me coolly and said nothing. That's when I knew that Stiletto was right. Grace had to confirm that the geezer was Schmidt.

"Arla," she said, "could you get me a sherry? I need it."

"Absolutely," said Arla, shoving the photos into my hand and flashing me a dirty look. I predicted Arla couldn't wait to blab to her eavesdropping siblings. I gave myself five minutes, tops, before I got the heave-ho.

"What do you want me to say about those?" Grace asked.

"I was hoping you'd confirm that the man is your husband."

Grace felt behind her for the arm of a chair and sat down. "Where did you get these?"

"They were given to me anonymously."

Grace snorted in disgust.

"Though I concluded they came from the security tape off Cerise May's camera." That's all Dan had told me, that Cerise had sent them to his office asking him to handle the photos she'd downloaded off the camera. "I don't know when they were taken."

"I see." Grace tapped her fingers together. Her nails were bright red, and the silver charm bracelet on her wrist jingled. "But you're not going to publish them in the paper."

An exclamation of horror had burst from the kitchen. Arla must have dropped the bomb.

"It's a family newspaper," I said. "What I'm interested in is finding the woman in the photo. I believe she's wearing a wig you purchased from Leila's Hair Heaven two months ago. Whoever she is, she might have information about your husband's murder."

"You've been busy." Grace stared at me levelly. "And the police?"

"Don't know about the pictures. At least I haven't showed these to them. I was waiting to hear an explanation from you."

Grace said nothing, but bent her head and tapped her slippers on the foyer floor. Her slippers were black velvet and elaborately embroidered, and the floor was expensive green slate. The Schmidts lived high on the hog for a school principal, unless Grace had been a trust-fund baby, like Popeye.

"My husband," she began quietly, "resembled many men, in that he had needs that I, as his wife, could not fulfill. If you read between the lines, then you'll understand this is a personal matter and has nothing to do with my husband's murder."

I had no idea what she was talking about. What needs that a wife couldn't fulfill? Maybe she couldn't leg wrestle worth beans and she was a lightweight at holding beer. Not fun to shoot skeet with and had no interest in football.

"I don't mean to pry," I said, "but I'm not following."

"Think about it. You're a mature woman. If you analyze those photos you'll figure it out. And I would ask you to promise that you'll keep them out of the papers. My husband is dead, after all. There's no purpose in exposing these except to forever tarnish a good man's name and a beloved father's reputation."

"I'm a reporter. I can't promise to keep this out of the paper. That's my job. To get things *in* the paper," I said, resenting the cheap "beloved father" line.

"So much for being sensitive." Grace stood and called for Arla. She rushed in hurling darting looks.

"Call Frank Donches." Turning to me, Grace said, "Frank Donches is our lawyer. He'll put a stop to this."

My life, I decided, was single-handedly keeping the Lehigh Valley Bar Association in business.

Elaine and Claire followed, also excelling in the hot looks department.

"I better go," I said.

"Yes," said Grace, opening the front door. "Frank will be in contact. I'll have him call Dix Notch."

"Of course." Our extreme formality struck me as very odd. "And for what it's worth, Mrs. Schmidt, I'm sorry you had to see those."

Grace said nothing, but Elaine called out, "I just bet you are" before the door slammed, leaving me on the front walk feeling downright cruddy, Pastor Faithful's voice quoting Scripture in my mind.

"Thou shalt not go up and down as a talebearer among thy people." Leviticus 19:16.

I was doomed. Then again, I was also satisfied.

Rudolph Schmidt was the geezer.

The blue Saturn followed me to Liberty High School, occasionally so close I could make out some details of the driver. I lost her when I neared the school as it was letting out. Kids were jaywalking like they were rabidly confused dogs, blithely entering traffic and dodging cars. I decided I better pay attention so I wouldn't end up with a cheerleader as a hood ornament.

I parked one block down from Kosta's Drugstore, across the street from the high school, locked the photos in the car, and headed straight for the store's soda fountain. Kosta's made fantastic cherry Cokes, plenty of cherry, not too much Coke. I ordered two in paper cups with lids along with two straws. Paid for them, went outside, and knocked on the window of the blue Saturn parked in a driveway.

A familiar face peeked out and then she rolled down the window. I handed her the cherry Coke. "It's on me." I gave her a straw. "I figured you must be pretty thirsty sitting in the car all this time."

Ruth Faithful smirked, took the cherry Coke, and asked me to get in. She was fairly harmless as far as I could see. Thinner, too, than the photo on her desk. She was wearing a good cloth Republican tweed coat and black leather driving gloves.

I could take her.

"I've got ten minutes until I have to be at an interview." I slid into the passenger side. "So you better tell me fast why you've been following me."

"More like I should be asking you that question." Ruth pulled the paper off the straw. "My life has been in complete disarray since you showed up at our doorstep."

"Father displeased?"

She rolled her eyes. Ruth wore very little makeup. I bet that Reverend Faithful had total dominance over her life, such as it was. Clerking in a doctor's office. Home in her twin bed by nine every night. Church all day Sunday. Unmarried at thirty-two. She'd reverted to conservatism since her wild days at Liberty.

"Father's full of questions. He always thought I was the devil's offspring, and now he's sure of it."

"Join the club. I'm the devil's spin doctor."

A hint of a smile flickered before she got serious again. "I was going to ignore you and hope you'd go away, and then I read your story this morning about Consuela DeJesus."

"And you thought maybe I wasn't giving up so easy."

"I thought maybe Consuela DeJesus better watch out." Ruth put her cup on the dashboard and crossed her arms as if she were freezing. "Even with Mr. Schmidt dead, I'm not sure anyone in this town is safe to speak against him. You should tell her to leave Lehigh for a while."

"Oh, come on." I opened the lid and sucked out an ice cube. "Who's going to harm her?"

Ruth shrugged. "Look at Doctor May. Last Thursday night, the night Mr. Schmidt was murdered, she made an appointment to meet him in her office."

"Nothing unusual about that. She is a doctor."

"It wasn't a medical appointment. She wanted to confront him about"—she ran her leatherized hands along the steering wheel, searching for a neutral term—"stuff." "Stuff" was a great word. Both noun and verb signifying nothing.

"What kind of stuff?"

"I better not get into it. Anyway, she showed up fifteen minutes late and found Mr. Schmidt dead, Popeye leaning over him. Thing was, someone had already called the cops and they caught Popeye with her hands down his throat."

I took mental note of that.

"So Doctor May started thinking maybe she'd been set up. That if Popeye hadn't been there, she would have been busted. Especially since there are these dirty photos that would have looked bad." Ruth eyed me. Did I know?

"I know," I said. "I have copies. I brought them to your house yesterday for you to see. The woman looks like Doctor May, at least from behind. . . ."

Ruth nodded, as though my confirmation had answered a nagging question. "But it isn't Doctor May."

"I know that, too. Whoever she is, she's wearing a Raquel Welch wig. I used to be a hairdresser so I know these kinds of things."

Ruth sat back a bit. "How did you get the photos?"

"They were given to me anonymously." Before Ruth remembered I'd been married to Dan, her boss's lawyer, I quickly added, "When did Doctor May get them?"

"They popped up on the security tape four days before the murder. We never look through the tape unless there's a break-in, like there was two years ago when the office was robbed and Doctor May bought the camera. Anyway, I came into the office the Monday morning before the murder and it was clear someone had jimmied the lock. We ran the tape and that's what we saw."

"You didn't call the police?"

"Sure we called the police. Doctor May talked to Detective McIntyre."

Dr. May's fiancé.

"Detective McIntyre came over, took photos and stuff. He said he'd look into it, but he didn't think it was a big deal, you could tell. He kept saying that nothing was taken, and he had other cases that took precedent."

Like Karol Smolak, McIntyre's one obsession.

"You didn't show Detective McIntyre the tape, did you?"

"No," Ruth stirred her Coke. "We told him the machine was broken."

"Why?"

She hesitated. "Doctor May didn't want Detective McIntyre to get the wrong idea, that she was the woman on that tape." Ruth checked the rearview.

"Because Doctor May is engaged to McIntyre."

"How do you know all this?" Ruth acted surprised.

"Like they say in the movies, I have my sources. But"—I scratched my ear in an effort to appear stupid—"I'm confused. It seems Karol Smolak's still in love with Doctor May. Are they over or what?"

"I hope so," Ruth said firmly. "Smolak's the last man Doctor May needs in her life. He came in as a patient, and she just fell for him. She's a sucker for tall blond men with muscles. It wasn't until much later, when they got really involved, that she found out the truth."

"That he's got a bit of an anger management problem?"

"That he's what you might call an extortionist."

I could never remember if that was someone who shook down someone else for money or a circus act. I went with the former. "Who does he extort?" If that was the right way to put it.

"I don't know, exactly. I just overheard Doctor May last week talking on the phone to her lawyer. She was crying and really loud, kinda hysterically screaming into the phone. I heard her say it wouldn't surprise her if Karol tried to extort money from her. It's what he does to everyone else. He's a blackmailer, she said."

I thought of the incriminating photos and made a mental note to ask Dan if Cerise May had ever cried to him about Smolak trying to extort money from her. Then again, knowing Dan and his much-ballyhooed lawyer/client confidentiality, I wouldn't get so much as a speck of dirt from him.

"Why did she date the guy for so long, if he was an extortionist?" I asked

"Doctor May didn't have the courage to break up with Smolak until she started dating Detective McIntyre. He let her do it over the phone from his office at the Lehigh Police Department. Karol knew he was being recorded and that a cop was listening in, so he held back from throwing his usual tantrum."

That got me to thinking. "You suppose Doctor May is on the lam to get away from Smolak? Or do you think she's afraid of Schmidt's murderer?"

Ruth mulled over her answer. "I don't know who killed Principal Schmidt, but I know as sure as the Lord is my Savior that Karol Smolak is so filled with rage that he wouldn't think twice about snapping her neck. Doctor May told me she started sleeping with a knife under her pillow, she was so scared."

Karol Smolak was a real problem. And growing realer every minute.

"How'd you find out it was Principal Schmidt in the photos?" I asked, moving on.

"That was easy: bunions. Doctor May's been treating him for years. He's a real regular. We matched the photos from our files to the security tape and, sure enough, it was dead on. Though we have no idea who the woman is."

I checked my watch. I was now officially five minutes late for my interview. Oh, and I also owed a total of $34,500 to the county. "You have no idea?"

"No idea. That's what Doctor May was hoping to find out, since all those photos came from a ten-minute interval after midnight on the Saturday before the murder. But then . . ."

"But then Rudolph Schmidt turned up dead, so he wasn't giving out answers."

"Yup." Ruth slurped the last of her cherry Coke. "And our office was broken into again two nights ago. The police think whoever intruded was searching for something specific. Files were tossed all over the place."

I kept mum on that one. I saw no reason to tell Ruth Faithful that she could spare me a detailed description since I'd seen the trashed office firsthand.

"By then the security camera had been busted. For real," she said.

"It had?"

"Mr. Schmidt broke it on Thursday when he showed up for his appointment, before Popeye and Doctor May arrived. It's the last image the camera took. Him smashing the camera with his size twelve shoe. Makes me wonder if Mr. Schmidt was such a nice guy after all."

Chapter Nineteen

Why would Rudolph Schmidt have smashed Dr. May's security camera minutes before he was murdered? In an attempt to answer that question, I backtracked.

Schmidt chose Dr. May's office for his sexual dalliance because he knew no one would be in there around midnight the Saturday before he was murdered, which was when the security camera documented his escapades à la Monica Lewinsky meets Dr. Scholl.

The following Monday he received a call from Dr. May. Her office had been broken into over the weekend and the security camera—of which Schmidt must not have been aware—caught him on tape. She made an appointment to confront him on Thursday after hours. He arrived early. Perhaps the office was open, perhaps he broke in again (doubtful). He smashed the security camera and waited.

Only instead of Dr. May, Popeye arrived, looking to use the bathroom. Or maybe . . . maybe Popeye had a key.

In our interview Popeye mentioned that "Doctor May lets me use her bathroom whenever I want. Lets me sleep in her waiting room, even." To do that, Popeye must have had unlimited access.

In the meantime, a crucial question was left unanswered. Why did Schmidt break the camera? Had he been planning to do more than converse with Dr. May? Had he, as Ruth Faithful suspected, meant to harm her?

These were my thoughts as I hustled up the wide stone steps of Liberty High, that bastion of higher learning where the debating team consisted of four guys with brass knuckles, and advanced math class graphed the increasing prices for a nickel bag.

I yanked open the heavy doors to the school's marble entranceway and was stopped short. Liberty High had been transformed into a mausoleum. A Graceland, if you will. Only, instead of Elvis, it was Rudolph Schmidt.

Black-and-white photos blown up so large that I could make out the dots lined the hallways. There was a six-foot-high Rudolph Schmidt, his thin rectangular face in the trademark bowler and mackintosh raincoat, presiding over football games, handing out diplomas, meeting with members of the faculty, dipping into the icy Lehigh for his annual Polar Bear swim.

Banners in Liberty's navy and crimson crisscrossed the lobby quoting Schmidt's typical platitudes: TRUTH BEGINS WITH DISCI-PLINE. Or TO STRIVE, TO SUCCEED IS ALL. And his most famous (not to mention most obvious) THE ONLY WAY TO VICTORY IS BY CON-QUERING DEFEAT.

Or "the feet" I thought wryly, thinking of the May photos.

"Bizarre, isn't it?" asked Jane, who had been waiting for me by the guidance office under an EXCELLENCE IS THE REWARD OF LABOR banner. She was wearing a navy peacoat and ripped jeans. Her hair was spiked and her hands were hennaed. Cool, relaxed, pierced, she would never be pegged as an excellence laborer.

But this was untrue. Jane was poised to graduate at the top of her class because she was into learning. Always had been. A project she conducted on cells in seventh grade once led to a summer study on the effects of sodium imbalance in athletes. Five years later she was immersed in university-level studies of molecular physics. For Jane, each question inspired others, and there never was a final answer.

Still, despite her As and awards and the devotion of her teachers, she hadn't been one of Schmidt's pets, largely because she never bought into his motivational jargon. Schmidt despised her messy black clothes, her casual attitude, her pink hair, and her punky personality.

Schmidt liked straight arrows. He liked button-down shirts and plenty of "Yes, sirs." (Preferably those followed by salutes.) Schmidt, above all, had valued order. And order was not a word in Jane's vocabulary.

"I'm sick of it," she said, pointing to a photo of Schmidt saluting an ROTC recruiter. "Okay. So he was principal for thirty years. Does that mean we have to rip our shirts and beat our chests?"

Is that what kids were into these days? "No matter how you feel about him, Jane," I said maturely, "Principal Schmidt was a good man. A good man who was murdered."

"Yeah, well, maybe he had it coming."

"Jane!" How had I raised such a heartless child? "I'm amazed by you. . . ."

"Miss Yablonsky?" Jonas Walker opened the door to the guidance office. He raised an eyebrow at Jane, indicating that he'd heard more than just voices.

"I won't be long," I said to Jane as she returned to the book she was reading.

"Sorry about that." I trailed Walker to his office. "Also sorry I'm late. I ran into an unexpected interview."

"Been having lots of those, from what I've been reading." He closed the door.

Walker's office was lined with books about college entrance exams and how to choose careers. It was exactly like every guidance office I'd been in with the exception of my other alma mater, the defunct department store that had been transformed into Two Guys Community College. There the guidance office was in Sheet and Towels, and smelled vaguely of boiled hot dogs.

"Jane's openly proud of you," Walker said, sitting in a chair opposite mine, instead of at his desk. "That's a rarity among teenagers. Most teens admire some quality in their parents, but they can't bring themselves to admit it."

Walker was a light-skinned black man whose youthful appearance I decided was due to having more in common with kids than adults. He was wearing a Looney Tunes tie, and on his desk was a Homer Simpson electric pencil sharpener. I swear they didn't make adults like him when I was a kid.

After small talk we got down to business. The feature I was writing was on college admissions, why college was tougher to get into than ever before, and what parents were doing to make sure their kids were admitted to the Ivies.

"I could tell you stories," said Walker, getting up to look for a book on college stats. "Parents these days are desperate. They'll do anything to get their kids into a status college. Push them into endless extracurriculars, send them overseas and down to the soup kitchen. They give me nightmares."

He found the book he wanted and started turning the pages. I took notes.

"The problem is all in the numbers. This country had a record number of high school graduates seeking college admission last year thanks to the baby boom echo—the baby boomers having babies of their own. Here's Harvard's facts." He read from the book. "Last year nearly twenty-one thousand kids applied to Harvard. Of those about three thousand were class valedictorians."

I wrote this down. I thought of Jane. "How many slots did Harvard have?"

"A little over twenty-five hundred. That's a lot of rejection letters. Liberty sent one kid to Harvard that year. And there were seven hundred fifty students in that class. Of those, thirty had applied to Harvard."

I sucked in a breath. I had no idea. "So these annoying parents who successfully push their kids to get into Ivy League schools . . . what did they do right?"

"What didn't they do?" He shut the book. "The most savvy are prepping their kids as sophomores. I've had parents actually transfer their kids from private school to Liberty in tenth grade just so they'll improve in class standing."

Class standing. Jane's class standing was good. I felt better.

"Then there are the SATs. Harvard, Princeton, Stanford, and Yale turned away a large number of students with perfect SATs last year. I'm talking sixteen hundred here."

Hello. Jane had a 1,600 and I'd figured that made her a shoo-in.

"So you've got a kid with a high standing, perfect SATs, and still he has a better than average chance of getting turned down. How do you beat the odds?" He shoved the book into the shelf. "In order to be admitted into the top schools he has to be an outstanding talent. For example, it might behoove him to be a good musician and I don't mean playing clarinet for the Liberty Grenadiers. I mean semiprofessional."

I jotted down "semiprofessional." The only musical instrument Jane could play was her Walkman.

"When our prodigy isn't earning debating medals or receiving standing ovations in Carnegie Hall, he should be rushing passes on his way to a Heisman. Because athletics, dynamic athletics, is what the Ivies want."

Jane hated sports.

"Let's look at our candidate now. Top standing. Perfect SATs. Musical ability. Athletics. Mix in the three other must-haves: community service, international travel, and recommendations from school administration."

Jane's recommendations came from her favorite fifth-grade teacher. Her community service amounted to little more than handing out free ice cream. As for international travel, did a field trip to Delaware count?

"Think he's in?" Walker folded his arms. "Nope. Even if our over-achiever applies early decision, the traditional guarantee that's allowed plenty of ambitious kids Ivy admission, he's wait-listed. A mere thirty percent of students who apply for early decision get in, on the average."

I felt a trickle of sweat run down my spine. Jane had applied early admission and hadn't heard.

"Our overachiever needs to be a legacy," Walker said.

"A Subaru?"

"The offspring of alumni. Take Yale."

Locks, I thought.

"Yale's not satisfied with the son or daughter of one of its graduates. It wants four generations. That's great-grandparents. It also wants aunts. Uncles. Brothers. Sisters. That is a Yale legacy."

I tried to remember what the Two Guys legacy policy was. Difficult to be a legacy as the school had been around only since the department store went bankrupt in the late seventies. Then again, with the number of teenage mothers . . .

"In conclusion," said Walker, tapping Homer on the head, "the horizon is depressing. And we haven't even discussed financial aid or the cost of paying for a private college to the tune of one hundred and fifty grand."

I felt defeated. So defeated, Schmidt's idiotic line about the way to victory by overcoming defeat was making sense.

"Is something wrong?" Walker sat in his chair, his brows furrowed with guidance counselor sympathy.

"It's not exactly ethical for me to bring this up, but I can't help thinking of my daughter, Jane."

"Jane will be fine. She's a devoted student."

"Yes, but she doesn't have sports, music, international travel, community service, or stellar recommendations from the principal."

"Schmidt didn't give her one?"

"Not that I'm aware."

"That's because he made it a policy of not writing many." Walker fingered his tie. "I hope Jane hasn't put her eggs in one basket."

"Princeton," I said.

"That's a pretty lofty basket."

"Two Guys was just as good, I told her. Its Physics for Physicians' Assistants course is tough. I know because I took it. Twice."

Walker coughed. "There are plenty of excellent schools for physics besides Princeton and, um, Two Guys. What's important is that Jane find one that fits her interests and personality. She might be happier at Rutgers or Carleton College. Great physics programs at both. Bryn Mawr, even, right nearby."

I wrote this down. Walker was trying to tell me something, and I was afraid his news was not good.

"Jane didn't get into Princeton, did she?"

He returned to fingering his tie, and the soothing tones adopted by morticians. "I talked to the director of admissions this morning. They were leaning toward one student for early decision and I'm afraid Jane was not that student."

My pen froze over the tablet. "Could she still get in if she's wait-listed?"

"Unlikely. Wait-listing really is just a college's polite way of telling a candidate their application was great, but they didn't make the cut. Like a pillow to soften the blow."

"At Two Guys," I said, "no one is wait-listed. That's what makes it such a comfortable place to go to school. Also, if you need pillows, they're in the English department."

Walker stared at me. "How long did you go to Two Guys?"

"Eight years." I smiled. "It took me sort of long, since I failed every course except one, but it was worth it. I got this nifty reporting job."

"Walker," he said, bending over my notebook, "is spelled W-A-L-K-E-R."

"Thanks." I included the *L*.

"And Jane is your biological child?"

"She wasn't conceived in a petri dish, if that's what you mean. Otherwise, yeah. She's my kid. Though her father was a total jerk. The night he knocked me up he was wearing two beer cans strapped to either side of his head."

Walker leaned back and stroked his chin. "Interesting. For the first time in over twenty years of education, I finally have the answer to the age-old debate of nature versus nurture."

"Hmm." I thought about this. "Jane wasn't much for the woods. She spent a lot of her childhood reading. So I'd go with nurture instead of nature."

"Yes," said Walker. "Exactly."

"What did Walker say?" Jane asked eagerly as we crossed the street to my car. The rain had stopped, and it was beginning to snow. "Did he mention me?"

"It was a professional interview," I fibbed. "I wasn't supposed to bring up personal business. How about a cherry Coke at Kosta's? We can talk about Carleton College or maybe Bryn Mawr. It's not just for pearls and tea dances anymore."

Jane quit on the corner. Her complexion lightened from a healthy pink to a deadly gray. "Oh. God."

"Jane, please."

"Oh. God."

I reached to hug her and she fell into my arms. Her body shook with sobs. Sobs that no cherry Coke could allay.

"It's okay, Jane," I said, trying to mimic Walker's soothing. "Princeton isn't the only horse in town."

"But it's the best. I *love* that place. I love the trees and the courtyard. I love Nassau Street. I loved the professors I met and the students I saw. It was home to Albert Einstein!"

"There, there."

"If that stupid twit Brooke Shields got in, why couldn't I? Did Brooke Shields take college-level physics courses in eleventh grade? Did she win Math Challenge four years in a row?"

"That's not fair, Jane." I regarded her seriously. "Brooke Shields was an established actress. She had made sophisticated films like *The Blue Lagoon* and *Pretty Baby* before she got admitted to Princeton."

"Whaaaa!" Jane buried her face in my fake rabbit fur.

People passing by frowned at us, at me in my black miniskirt, and at my wailing daughter with pink spiked hair. I didn't care. I wanted to be a sponge and mop up Jane's pain.

"I did everything I could," she mumbled into my coat. "Why didn't I get in?"

"Because your mother went to Two Guys," I said, leading her slowly to my car. "And your father wasn't a legacy. I'm so sorry. It's not the end of the world. You have to believe me."

I opened her door. Jane didn't budge. "Who got the slot?"

"I don't know. Walker didn't tell me. It was one of those confidentiality issues."

I started up the car and we hooked a right onto Linden. Yes sirree. This was going to be one happy Thanksgiving. Rosa seducing Stiletto by the creamed corn. Jane bleary-eyed and depressed. Genevieve and G taking turns firing musket balls at the turkey carcass.

Jane was staring out the window at the bleak day.

"Why aren't you wearing the engagement ring?" Her face was still turned to the window.

"Because it's not a real engagement. You know that." Jane was the only person I'd confided in. She deserved the truth. "The fewer people who know, the less explaining I'll have to do when you graduate from school and Stiletto and I break it off."

She wiped a tear from her cheek with the back of her hand. "You don't have to continue with this farce. I'm not going back to school."

This pronouncement was so alarming I ran right through a red light, setting off a cacophony of angry horns in alarm.

"What do you mean by that?"

"I'm not going back to school." She sniffed. "After Thanksgiving vacation, I'm dropping out. I'm hitchhiking out west with G."

"Not to pick grapes." I thought we'd been through that.

"No. Now he wants to go to California and try to get a job as a stylist on a movie set. Until now I haven't . . ."

"Screw G and don't you dare drop out. I dropped out of school and it took me years to recover. Oh shit." In my rearview a set of flashing blues appeared. The red light. The goddamn red light. I'd run it and now I was busted.

"What's wrong?" asked Jane as I slowed and pulled to the side.

"Cops." I reached over and opened the glove compartment for my registration. How much more could I add to the local coffers? Wasn't one hundred dollars a minute enough?

The blue uniform appeared by my door. I rolled down the window and handed the officer my ID without being asked.

"Good afternoon." He took it. "You realize what you did back there?"

"What?" I said innocently.

"Ran a red light clocking thirty in a twenty-five-mile-an-hour zone." He started copying down the info.

"I had no idea."

Jane shook her head in disgust as I launched my no-woman-busted routine. "My husband's going to kill me," I began.

"Really?" He examined my license.

"Yes." I pinched my thighs and willed myself to cry. It's cheap and low-down, I know, but it works. It works almost every time. "We'll have a horrible fight over the insurance rates. And the day before Thanksgiving, too."

"Hmm, hmmm. And which husband would that be?" The cop bent down.

I stared into his mirrored glasses. "Pardon?"

"Last I checked, Miss Bubbles Yablonsky, you were unmarried."

He took off his shades and I found myself face to freckled face with Detective McIntyre. Cerise May's fiancé.

And, oddly enough, the man Lawless had set me up to have a date with just last night.

"Are you married? Or were you lying?" he asked. "Lying like you do about everything else. Including, where you were the night Doctor May's office was raided?"

"I wasn't lying," I lied.

"Don't even waste your breath, Yablonsky. Get in my office. Or else I'll take you to jail myself."

Chapter Twenty

Detective McIntyre's office was the front seat of his cruiser. The seats were a plush dark blue, not a crumb on them. A laptop computer hung from the dashboard along with a handheld radio and the gauge on his radar.

It was not the kind of atmosphere conducive to so-called cruising, in my opinion. There were no fuzzy dice from the mirror, no sheepskin on the seats. No Van Halen blaring from the speakers. Very subpar as far as cruising was concerned.

McIntyre got in. His shiny leather belt and boots crinkled as he settled into the seat. I wondered when we'd get to the part where he'd demand oral sex in exchange for pretending that red light was green. I wondered what he'd look like with a black eye on his Howdy Doody face.

"I didn't want to ask you this within earshot of your daughter," he said. "She might not understand."

Jane was waiting in the passenger seat in my Camaro. Every once in a while she shot us nervous glances. From what I knew about what high school kids did at parties, she'd understand all too well.

"Lookit, Detective," I said, "just give me the ticket. The way my bank account is draining today, the city's gonna have to wait in line for its cash anyway."

"What I'm offering is a favor."

"A favor? Is that what you call it?" I could feel my blood getting hot, along with my fists. "Since when is demanding a blow job a favor?"

McIntyre was speechless. His lower jaw dropped, and his face turned really bright red, like it often does in fair-skinned redheads. "A blow job? What makes you think I'm asking for a blow job?"

"Word on the street is that's your MO."

"That's a lie. That's a lie started by an old partner of mine who didn't get promoted when I did. I lost my wife because of crazy talk like that."

"I heard you lost your wife because you made her iron your shirts and cook you eggs before you got out of bed."

"Amy never woke up before eight!" He put up his hands. "Whoa. Did Lawless tell you this bunk?"

Lawless's reputation as a cop reporter, such as it was, could be in jeopardy if McIntyre got the misimpression he was spreading dirty rumors. "No," I said. "Lawless has nothing but praise for you. Says you're set to rise through the ranks."

This calmed him down. "That's more like it."

"So what's the favor, then?" I asked. "Unless your idea of a good deed is slapping a hardworking single mother with a hundred-dollar ticket."

McIntyre turned down his radio. "Word on the street is that Karol Smolak's put a hit out on you. I thought you should be forewarned."

I said nothing. What was there to say? No one had ever put a hit out on me before. It was frightening, like the time in Northeast Junior High when word got back to me that Teresa Colon with the big green plastic comb in her hair wanted to beat me up in the basement bathroom after I accidentally tripped her in the hall.

As far as I could remember, I had never tripped Karol Smolak. I hadn't even so much as extended my foot.

"Why?" I said. "What did I ever do to him?"

"Apparently something. You met with Smolak, right?"

"Right. One of his men picked me up Tuesday morning. Smolak had read my story about Cerise May and wanted to know where she was."

"What did you tell him?"

"I was honest. I told him I didn't know."

McIntyre ran his finger over his upper lip. "What I'm about to divulge to you goes no further than this cruiser, you understand?"

"I understand."

"Because if I see this in the paper, you're in deep shit."

"I hate deep shit. It's so . . . icky."

"And this is a matter of life and death."

"You're scaring me."

"I've been investigating Karol Smolak for some time. Smolak's nothing like his brother. He doesn't deal in drugs or prostitution. He doesn't run numbers or ship weapons."

I waited for the big "but" that hung in the air.

"He deals in information." McIntyre pursed and unpursed his lips. "He is a blackmailer. In fact, I came to investigate Smolak after receiving a case involving a prominent citizen who shall remain nameless, from whom Smolak was allegedly extorting money."

This jibed with what Ruth Faithful had said about Smolak being an extortionist, though in this case the prominent citizen sounded like someone besides Dr. May. I tried to think of other nameless prominent citizens who might fit the bill.

"Schmidt," I guessed. "Smolak had dirt on Schmidt."

McIntyre remained neutral. "No comment."

Definitely Schmidt.

"This prominent citizen was not the only one," McIntyre continued. "Another was a city councilman, a judge, and even"—he smiled—"a local lawyer."

"I don't get it," I said. "Smolak's a blackmailer. What does that have to do with his hit on me?"

"My same informants tell me Smolak's convinced you've put it all together. His back is up against a wall and he's not thinking straight. He's panicking. He's eliminating anyone who could send him down the river." McIntyre became intense. "First he took care of his old girlfriend, because she knew too much."

"Cerise May?"

"Cerise May." McIntyre nodded somberly. "In August, Doctor May discovered Smolak's illegal enterprise and, like a good citizen, reported it to the police. She took a risk coming to us, but we provided her with some protection."

Some protection, I thought. Lehigh's finest in action.

"Unfortunately, Smolak discovered her secret last week. Before Doctor May could contact us, we believe he had her kidnapped and killed. It's a black mark on our department and I'll be damned if he gets away with her murder. For me it's more than another case. It's a mission."

"Because you two are, um, together?"

McIntyre fiddled with the radio button. "It's personal. I'd rather not go into it. All I can say is that the day we find Cerise's body is the day Smolak wishes he'd never been hatched, the reptile."

I caught Jane out of the corner of my eye. She was tapping her watch, impatient to get going. I held up five fingers.

"Smolak or his men should be attempting to make contact with you in the next twenty-four hours." McIntyre reached in his pocket and pulled out a small black box. "This is a beeper. If you hear from him, page me immediately. Just press this button and then that button and I'll be there as fast as I can. It's easy."

He handed it to me and I stared at the black box dumbly. I didn't trust its buttons, and I definitely did not like the looks of the digital screen. This thing was worse than the answering machine. It was equally evil, but also smaller, like an elf on the take.

"I'd put a tail on you, but with municipal budget crunches we can't afford to lose an officer to a stakeout. The beeper's the best I can offer."

I felt unsure about this beeper, and not just because electronic gadgets scare me more than bill collectors issuing their third "friendly reminder." I felt unsure because I was a reporter now and notifying the cops as soon as I heard from Smolak smacked of being a snitch.

"I don't know," I said. "Being a reporter, I don't think I can do double-duty undercover."

"Cerise would be alive today if she'd gone undercover sooner. And Smolak would be in jail." McIntyre gestured toward Jane. "And it's not only you who's not safe, it's your family. All their lives are in danger too."

As if on cue, Jane beeped the horn.

"My daughter?" I was almost unable to comprehend that possibility.

"If I know Smolak," McIntyre said, "she's first on his list."

Our drive back to West Goepp was morosely quiet. Jane was beyond glum, her mood darkened by the realization that Princeton, the home to Albert Einstein and alma mater of Brooke Shields, was beyond her reach. No eating clubs. No quads of green. No free screenings of *The Blue Lagoon*.

My temptation was to lean over and say, "You think that's bad, let me tell you about Karol Smolak, the Polish florist/mafioso and what he'd like to do with your dog-collared neck." But I didn't because I'm a mother and like most mothers I try not to threaten my child with Polish florists/mafiosi. Well, not usually.

I fingered the beeper McIntyre had given me and plotted my course. I would have to be open with Jane and Mama. They were my family and they had a right to know, not to mention a vital need, that Karol Smolak might try to murder them. The more I thought about

McIntyre's conversation, the more I became convinced that Karol Smolak was a very dangerous man and that I needed to protect my family.

Karol Smolak, I had a hunch, was the guy sitting in the sedan on Monday night when I visited Dr. May's apartment. Even more frightening, Karol Smolak might have been with Dr. May when I called from the *News-Times* requesting an interview. Who knows? He could have had a gun to her head at that very moment.

I shivered. The image alone gave me the willies.

Yes, I would have to break the bad news to Mama and Jane. Thanksgiving preparations be damned.

Mama, Genevieve, and, lo and behold, Rosa were in my kitchen when Jane and I got home. They were arguing. Big time. Mama and Rosa were in a face-off, hands on hips, a Dutch oven worth of stuffing on the stove. Bread crumbs lay scattered on the floor, the counter, even on Mama's head. And if this wasn't bad enough, Genevieve loomed over both of them with a cast-iron skillet in her mitt.

"Genevieve, no!" cried Jane, dashing to the kitchen.

"Put down the pan," I ordered, tossing my keys on the counter. "Mama, make nice."

"I will not!" She stamped her tiny foot, and the fat along her middle rippled in repercussion.

"All this over stuffing?" Jane jumped and grabbed the pan. "You're being ridiculous."

"This has nothing to do with stuffing," Mama said. "This has everything to do with your wedding."

"*My* wedding," exclaimed Jane, forgetting. "I'm not getting married."

"No, but I am." I poked Jane in the ribs. Hard. "*Remember.*"

"I don't blame her for forgetting." Mama pointed to my hand. "Where's that gorgeous ring Steve gave you?"

"Oh, yeah." I unclasped the chain, slid off the ring, and slipped it on my finger. It sent rays of light across the kitchen, the diamond was so big.

Rosa's eyes bugged at the sight of it. "That's some rock. When did you get that?"

"When they were up to no good in the back of Steven's Jeep, that's when," Mama answered for me. "Now let's get back to this wedding."

Rosa, who was domineering in a dark purple suit etched in gold thread, waved her hand dramatically.

"All I'm saying is that Stefano must be married where his mother was baptized and where all Stiletto weddings have taken place: in Sardinia. The holy chapel of Madre de Dios in Porto Cervo, a thousand years old, built into the rock cliffs of Costa Smeralda." She kissed her fingertips.

"Sounds great," I said, getting excited even if I wasn't getting married. But what was the hook? I couldn't see how Rosa stood to make a buck at a thousand-year-old chapel.

"Followed by a sunset reception at the Hotel Cala di Volpe." Rosa sighed. "So romantic."

Jane helped herself to a handful of pecans. "Isn't Costa Smeralda supposed to be some jet-setting place crawling with slimy Eurotrash and slimier Eurotrash wannabees?"

Rosa smiled. "I can smell the Armani now."

Which answered how she stood to make a buck.

"What about St. Bart's on Haupt Street?" asked Mama, insulted. "They got a new organ and they don't care if Bubbles was divorced or nothing as long as she slips Father Mack an extra fifty. And how are we gonna get Kowalski's to cater in Sardinia? I bet they don't even know how to make scrapple."

"That's true," Rosa said.

"Not to mention getting the boombases on the plane," added Genevieve. "It ain't practical, not to say nothing about cheap."

"Kowalski's offers a twenty-buck-per-person buffet." Mama liked the financial angle and was running with it. "Roast chicken, ham, potato casserole, and rolls. All-you-can-eat, too."

Of course.

"Stefano can pay for everyone to fly to Sardinia!" Rosa offered.

Genevieve looked skeptical. "With boombases?

"With the boombases. He's loaded. Right, Bubbles?"

"Enough!" I pointed to the couch. "All of you. Sit. It's a matter of life and death."

Genevieve, Mama, Jane, and even Rosa shut their traps and did as they were told. I sat on the coffee table and gave them the skinny starting with how Karol Smolak had me kidnapped. I ended with Detective McIntyre's warning that Smolak wanted to bump me off and might even go for members of my family.

When I was done, everyone sat stone-faced. Cousin Rosa asked if there was any booze in the house besides Bartles & Jaymes strawberry spritzer. Genevieve eyed her musket in the corner. Mama patted Jane's ripped knee.

"So that's why you were so silent in the car," Jane said. She fingered a stud on her left ear, her usual worry signal. "I thought you were disappointed about Princeton."

"Are you talking about Cosmo Smolak's brother?" Mama asked. " 'Cause I can't believe that. Karol was always the wuss. If you ask me, I thought he was loose in the loafers."

"You mean light," Rosa corrected.

"No, I mean loose." Mama held up her hands. "Tiniest feet you ever saw."

"You know what that means," Rosa said, nudging Mama.

Mama nudged her back and the two started giggling until I whistled for them to shut up. Geesh. My life is threatened and they crack themselves up over sexual innuendo.

"You don't know the Karol Smolak I'm talking about," I said. "The Karol Smolak I'm talking about is a cold-blooded killer. You must be confused."

"Sure," Genevieve said. "Little Karol Smolak with the boogers."

I thought of how Karol towered over me, booger free. "I don't know how little he is. He's about six feet."

"Has to be Jeanette Smolak's kid." Mama turned to Genevieve. "Wasn't his brother named Cosmo?"

"You mean that snot-nosed bruiser with the potty mouth? More than once I wanted to spank his be-hind, that twerp. Spare the rod and spoil the brat, is what the problem was there."

"The problem there was that Jeanette's husband ran off with a rose supplier and she had those two boys to raise," Mama said. "You can't blame her for not spanking. She was overburdened."

"Overburdened my fanny. It was Doctor Spock." Genevieve huffed. "Those two hellions were jumping on couches until they were eight and all Jeanette would say was, 'Now, Karol and Cosmo. Mommy doesn't like it when you stand on other people's furniture.' Hmph."

It was hard to envision this freethinking Jeanette as the Russian stacking doll who'd snapped the whip at Karol to speed up with the holiday baskets.

"Worthless," agreed Mama. "That whole Spock generation was a waste, what with their arms-are-for-hugging-not-for-war. And we're the ones who've had to clean up their messes."

"Ain't that the truth," agreed Genevieve. "Should've been weaned earlier. That would have showed them who's boss."

The two old biddies folded their arms and clucked in disgust. The fact that my life—and possibly theirs—was precariously close to being blown apart by a .357 Magnum was peanuts compared to Dr. Spock's appalling theory that breast is best.

"What Spock are they talking about?" Jane asked. "*Star Trek?*"

"Not that Spock, another," I said. "And apparently your grandmother and Genevieve knew Smolak when he was a boy."

"In diapers," said Mama. "Used to be in the Saint Anne's nursery school. Don't you remember, Bubbles? He ate paste."

"Paste?"

"A bucket of it. Had to go to Saint Luke's and have his stomach pumped."

I would have remembered a budding Polish mafioso florist who ate a bucket of paste and had to have his stomach pumped.

Genevieve was still fixated on Spock. "Because of Spock and his no-spanking, no-bottle crackpot ideas, one of Jeanette's boys is in jail and the other's threatening our Bubbles."

"Not for long." Mama stood and untied her apron strings. "Come on, Genny. Let's straighten this out once and for all. If we hurry, we can get back in time to soak that bird in salt brine before supper."

"Hold on." I put myself in front of them. "What do you think you're doing? Karol Smolak's a killer. A serial killer."

"Oh, don't be so dramatic, Bubbles," Mama said. "You said the same thing in second grade when you tripped Michael Smith with that bebop thingy on the playground and you wouldn't go to school because you were afraid he'd beat you up. You called him a monster and he was just a squirt. Three feet tall."

In all fairness, Michael Smith was a monster. At least to me.

"And then I spoke to his mother and got it ironed out in a jiffy." Mama pushed me aside. "Sometimes when kids don't get along, you need a couple of adults to step in and make everyone play fair."

"Cover the stuffing," Genevieve said as she and Mama waddled out the door and piled into Genevieve's Rambler, leaving me and Jane dumbfounded in the living room and Rosa in the kitchen, resigning herself to the Bartles & Jaymes.

I stared at the stove clock. It was 2:44. In one minute I would owe the county $31,500.

Karol Smolak, shoot me now.

Chapter Twenty-one

Of course I didn't let them drive over to Smolak's Flowers alone. I covered the stuffing, dropped Jane off at her friend Gracie's, and hightailed it as fast as I could to Little Warsaw. Despite my errands, I was still able to beat Genevieve, who's been known to cause accidents on Route 22 by driving thirty-five in the left-hand lane.

Sitting in my Camaro parked across the street from Smolak's, I kept an ear cocked for gunfire or feathers flying as I monitored the crusty broads. Mama and Genevieve filed into, then out of, the flower shop and knocked at a house next door to Kaminski's. Mother Smolak answered, smiled broadly, and let them in like they were there for a weekly bridge party.

I got out. Mother Smolak lived in a red brick row home much like my own, except I had some vinyl on mine and Mother Smolak's porch had been weather-coated a durable high-gloss gray. Okay, so I was jealous.

I knocked on the door and Mother Smolak answered, smiling not so much. Her ankles were more swollen than the day before, and she smelled vaguely of mildew.

"So you're LuLu Yablonsky's daughter. I didn't know you were *that* Bubbles Yablonsky," she said, letting me in.

I swear. In the thirty-something years I've been alive, I've never heard that line before.

"Your mother's in the kitchen." Mother Smolak pointed to the rubber mat. "Don't make no mess. Wipe your feet." She squinted at my head. "Where'd you get your color done?"

I scraped my feet. "House of Beauty."

"Ain't you fancy, then. I use Clairol. That's 'cause I was born in the Depression."

Always with the Depression.

Mother Smolak directed me to the kitchen, where Mama and Genevieve stood stiffly, not so cocky now that they were on another dog's turf.

"Okay," Mother Smolak said, returning to a pile of onions on the cutting board. "I got lots of chopping so make it quick." She stuck a slice of Wonder Bread between her teeth as a barrier to the fumes.

From upstairs wafted the unmistakable musical intro for *General Hospital* and my heart yearned. It would be the usual boring Thanksgiving episode, I consoled myself. A saccharine, meaningless dinner of minor characters who'd been on the phaseout. Felicia and Bobbi. The hospital president and the Quartermaines bickering.

Still . . .

"What we come here to tell you," Mama began, smoothing down her skirt, "is that we want your boy to leave my girl alone."

Mother Smolak pulled out the bread. "Karol? What's he done now?"

"He's trying to kill her is what." Mama gestured to me like I should say something. "Tell her, Bubbles."

Mother Smolak turned to me with a sour mug that gave new meaning to the concept of "protective mother." The message that I better not say anything about her precious baby was written into the pouches under her eyes and the frown under her nose.

"It's nothing, really, Mrs. Smolak," I said, now thoroughly embarrassed. "Let's go, Mama."

"Oh, ho, ho," countered Genevieve. "I beg to differ. I don't think putting a contract out is what you'd call nothing."

"He did that?" asked Mother Smolak. "My Karol put a contract out on you? I told him not to do contracts no more. . . . Wait till I get hold of him. Karrrrooolllll!"

Mama gave me the thumbs-up. Genevieve winked. And I decided to flee fast, only because the laws of physics did not permit me to melt into the floorboards.

"I'll go get him," I lied.

It was too late. Karol Smolak with his muddy green apron and massive brown hands that could strangle oxen was stomping up the front stoop. He looked angry to be called out of work and I didn't blame him.

I swung around the banister and scrambled up the green carpeted stairs to the second floor where in a very feminine bedroom I found a woman reposing, her feet propped up on a chenille-covered bed, munching popcorn and watching *GH*.

"Who are you?" she asked, punching the mute button. "You with that crazy group downstairs?"

Her hair was black and cut short. She was dressed like Jane, though she was my age. The silver rings on her fingers were too numerous to count.

"I'm sorry to bust in here," I apologized. "I had to get away."

"Don't blame you. Mama wanted me to come down, but I told her nothing makes me miss my soaps. I can't live without *General Hospital*."

Amen to that, sister.

"I'm Donna. Donna Smolak," she said.

"Karol's sister?" I thought of Mrs. Taylor, aka Karol's sister Sophie. She didn't look anything like this woman. "You must be Sophie's sister, too."

"Younger," she insisted. "Sophie's much, much older."

"You mind if I . . . ?"

"Sure. Why not?" She unmuted it. "It's a real snoozer so far."

Donna didn't offer me any popcorn, but kept the bowl in her lap. For a late-in-life punker, she had oddly normal nails. Short, neatly manicured, and pink.

I kept one ear tuned to what was happening downstairs and one ear tuned to *GH*. As I expected, it wasn't such a hot episode. It was damn dull, in fact. Downstairs Mama was yelling and Karol was grumbling.

"Is Thanksgiving dinner at Felicia's this year or the Spencers?" I asked.

"Mmmm," she muttered vaguely. "Not sure."

"Probably Laura's throwing it this year," I said. "It's Laura's turn to throw Thanksgiving."

"That's right." She popped a kernel in her mouth. "Laura . . . I think."

Laura hadn't been on *GH* for three years, and now I was intrigued. Whoever this Donna Smolak was, she didn't know bupkes about Port Charles, and that didn't sit right with me.

"That's a great cut," I said, testing the waters. "Where'd you get it done?"

"Hess's." She inched over a bit.

"You always been a natural brunette? Or is that color?"

"Natural." Her gaze was fixed to the TV as she speeded up the popcorn inhaling. "I'm kind of the black sheep of the family."

Bull. If that wasn't a Tess by Noriko wig in Espresso, then my bustline was silicone-enhanced. What we had here was not Karol's long-lost sister Donna. What we had here was the woman in the Schmidt photos. The Monica Lewinsky of the Lehigh foot fetish community. The wig wonder woman of wayward pedantries.

"You're not a natural brunette," I accused before leaning over and giving her bob a nice neat tug. It didn't budge. Boy, that was some tight-fitting wig. Noriko really knew their stuff.

"Oww!" She sat up and grabbed the back of her hair. "What are you doing?"

"What am I doing?" I refused to let go. "I'm getting to the truth is what I'm doing. There's only one other woman your size who wears wigs and she was captured on tape performing certain acts on certain toes in the office of one Doctor Cerise May. Acts that I don't think her mother would be too pleased to see."

"Get real." She clicked *GH* back to mute. "*I'm* Cerise May. Let go of my hair."

What? I let go and tried to comprehend this. Cerise May had a shag and wore fancy suits. This chick was a punker with studs on her pants where buttons should be. She wore a chain belt.

Besides . . . Cerise May was dead!

"You can't be Doctor May," I said, fumbling for the words. "Doctor May is dead. Detective McIntyre told me so."

"Detective McIntyre is a bozo." She stood and opened a bureau drawer, pulling out a wallet. She retrieved a driver's license and held it to her face. "See?"

The woman in the photo had blue eyes. This woman had purple. "No," I said, "I don't see."

She pinched her hair. "This is a dye job. The eyes, contacts. And my clothing? It's a disguise, duh."

"Oh." I didn't know what to say. I'd never met a living dead person before.

"I'm Doctor Cerise Marie May. I'm thirty-eight years old. I graduated from Temple University and the Merrick School of Podiatry. And I am very much alive."

All of a sudden it hit me. Dr. May was alive! We had to beep Detective McIntyre and tell him. He'd be thrilled. I pulled out the beeper from my purse.

"Hold on there, kiddo," Dr. May said. "What do you think you're doing?"

"I'm going to beep Detective McIntyre. Or you can, if you want.

He'll be so happy. He'll come right over and save you from Karol. . . ."

She snatched the beeper right out of my hand. "Nothing doing. What do you take me for? A chump?"

"I thought he was your boyfriend."

Dr. May's shoulders began to heave as she suppressed a laugh. "A boyfriend, sure. And monkeys secretly rule the world."

They did? Who knew?

"The reason why Karol hasn't been hauled down to headquarters is because of my so-called boyfriend, my future life partner, my one and only Bob 'Bozo' McIntyre. My very convenient fiancé."

I tried to wade through the saturation of sarcasm. "You mean, you and Karol are still together?" My mind was swimming, along with my stomach. I was both hungry and confused. Also, still a bit hopped-up on cherry Coke from Kosta's.

"I haven't done anything wrong." She sighed as though she was too bored to recite an explanation. "Karol and I had been dating for two years when McIntyre started investigating him. The way the police pea brain works is if your brother's a criminal, then you must be too."

She tossed the wallet back in the drawer and slammed it. "McIntyre started dropping by my office asking all sorts of nosy questions. What did Karol and I do with our spare time? What was in his basement? Whom did he associate with?"

Dr. May said "whom." That's what you get with a Temple University education.

"Finally, Karol and I decided to stage a breakup. I made out like Karol was a violent-tempered Polack so I could run to McIntyre's protective arms. McIntyre, the macho protective cop, as predicted, ate it up. For a while, I got great information, and Karol stayed clear of trouble. Problem was, McIntyre turned out to be the violent-tempered one."

Dr. May was now pacing the room. She was in bare feet, and her toenails were painted dark red. I admired the choice in color and its chip-resistant qualities. I also kept quiet while she continued.

"After the Schmidt murder and the break-in and that disgusting tape, I was ready to throw in the towel as far as podiatry and under-cover police work were concerned. It was too much stress." She peeked through the sheer curtains at the window. "All I wanted was to marry Karol and be a housewife anyway. Is that so wrong?"

"A housewife?" I said, unable to hide my amazement. "I haven't heard a woman say that since I was in grade school."

"It's true. What can I say?" She shrugged. "The only reason I be-came a podiatrist was because my mother thought I could meet rich, eligible executives with tired feet. Turns out I should have been a proctologist, since rich, eligible executives never stand. They sit all day."

"You went to podiatry school to meet men?"

"It's a jungle. A girl's gotta use her resources."

"Guess so." I made a mental note. Matchmaking through Podia-try. Two Guys might want to add that to its curriculum.

"I had kind of a nervous breakdown when you called my office Monday night. A newspaper interview was like the last straw, and I couldn't stop crying after you called. Karol was there and took me to my apartment. He said I needed to get away, but I didn't think so.

"Then the cops left a message on my home answering machine saying that my office had been broken into. That files were scattered everywhere, probably people looking for something. I don't know what."

I knew what and Cerise knew what. But each of us was pretend-ing we didn't know what was what. I didn't want to mention the pho-tos because that could give away Dan, who had violated the sacred rule of lawyer/client confidentiality by leaking them to me. That didn't mean I wasn't dying to ask her all about them, though.

"That Monday-night break-in convinced me Karol was right. I needed to drop out for a while. He hid me here. When we read the next morning that you'd been in the office the night before, he had you brought over to pick your brain."

"I hope not literally."

"Karol might break a few skulls. He's not inclined to pick brains. He has other people do that for him."

"I'm so relieved."

She threw herself onto the bed. "Karol's still not happy about what your boyfriend did to Zbigniew and his Ford, by the way. He's writing up a bill for damages."

"Stiletto will get right on that." I pushed aside a strand of hair and Dr. May zeroed in on my ring.

"Oh my God. What a rock."

"Rocks," I clarified cattily.

"Service Merchandise?"

"No. A guy in New York. Harry something. He loaned it to Stiletto."

"Oh." She frowned in disappointment. "Still, it's pretty."

"Thanks."

She leaned over my hand for a better look. "Engagement?"

"You could call it that." I splayed my fingers while Dr. May gawked.

"That's it," she said, sitting back. "That's exactly the kind of ring I want Karol to get me. I've been trying to describe it, but the jewelers around here are such hicks, all they can imagine is boring solitaires. Karrollll! Come here quick!"

She was a young Mother Smolak in the making.

Returning to her breathless voice, Dr. May said, "Karol and I are going to get married as soon as Mother Smolak gives us her blessing. I think she's warming up to me, even if I am part Albanian."

A cacophony of footsteps drummed up the carpeted stairs. Karol burst into the room followed by Mother Smolak, Mama, and Genevieve. They seemed to be aghast to find us there, with Dr. May clutching my hand.

Seeing Karol in the flesh was more disturbing than I had antici-
pated. He was so big, and the way he scowled at me gave me goose
bumps. I remained outwordly unflustered, but I was a mass of jelly
inside. The only comfort I took was in knowing Jane was safe at
home.

"Look, Karol," Dr. May exclaimed. "This is the exact ring I was talking about. Two pear-shaped diamonds on either side of a round cut."

"It's beautiful," said Mother Smolak. "But so expensive."

"Are you insane?" asked Karol, his ire momentarily turning from
me to Cerise May.

Dr. May pouted. "You saying I'm not worth it?"

"No!" said Karol.

"Ohhh!" She dropped my hand and rushed to the window, biting
her finger and willing herself to sob dramatically. Like I didn't know
that routine.

Karol shook his head, flustered. "I don't mean no about the ring.
Well, I do. Kind of. I mean . . . do you know who this is?"

He grabbed me by the shoulder.

Mama stepped forward from the back of the pack. "Hey, hey, hey,
big boy. Keep your hand off my Bubbles."

"I know who she is. I'm not dumb," said Dr. May. "I told her
everything."

"Everything?" Karol dug his thumb into my shoulder. "Now what
am I going to do? She's a goddamn reporter. You know how that
McIntyre is out to frame me. He'll use Yablonsky as a witness to say
I kidnapped you. He'll lock me away for years so he can get you for
himself. It'll be the end of us."

Cerise whipped her head around, giving Karol a long, love-struck
look.

"You could whack her," Mother Smolak suggested. "That'd put an
end to it."

I gave her a dirty look. "What about telling him not to put out
more contracts?"

"Contracts is messy. Too many people involved." Mother Smolak stuck her chin out. "If you're gonna whack somebody, whack 'em fast and at home around family."

"No one's whacking nobody," Mama said.

"I bet he don't even got a gun," Genevieve taunted

"Sure I do." Smolak pulled out a small pistol from his pants pocket and waved it in the air.

Thank you very much, Genevieve.

"That puny thing?" Genevieve scoffed. "Wait till you see what I got. And it's oiled, too." She turned and galumphed down the stairs to get her musket.

"Ahh, you're too much of a weenie to shoot her," Mother Smolak said. "Now your brother Cosmo, he would've pulled the trigger already. Cosmo's a real man."

"You saying Cosmo's better than me?" Karol sounded hurt.

"It's okay, babycakes," Cerise soothed, gently stroking his arm.

Karol shook her off and the next I knew the barrel of the gun was pressing into the temple of my forehead. Polish mafia sibling rivalry and I got to be caught in the middle. Why couldn't the brothers have fought over bunk beds?

"Not so fast," Mama said, reaching up to practically garrote me with some sort of chain. My Lord, she's going to do me in first.

"What are you doing?" I screamed. "Help! My mother's strangling me!"

"Knock it off, Bubbles. I'm saving you. See?"

I looked down. From the slim chain, a tiny golden figure bobbed. Mother Smolak gasped. "Saint Dorothy!"

"Patron saint of brides and florists," Mama announced. "It would be a sin for you especially, Karol Smolak, Polish florist/mafioso, to shoot a bride-to-be who has the protection of a Saint Dorothy around her neck. All your flowers would wilt for an eternity."

"Damn." Smolak lowered the gun. "Now we're gonna have to go on the lam."

"Why, babe?" Cerise asked, not so smart.

"Because he held a gun to a reporter's head and then was too chicken to finish the job, that's why." Mother Smolak slapped him upside the head. "You ain't got no sense of media relations, do you?"

"Hey, I want one of those," said Dr. May. "I want a patron saint of brides. I *need* it."

"What are you standing around for, toots?" Mama whispered to me. "Skedaddle."

Before anyone could sing "Bring Out the Barrel," I slipped past Karol and down the stairs, clutching my Saint Dorothy all the way, vowing never again to tease Mama about her idol worship.

I was now a firm believer.

Chapter Twenty-two

Detective McIntyre was on the case within the hour, to no avail. Smolak had fled, as promised, along with Dr. May.

Mother Smolak pretended she didn't know what the detective was talking about. She claimed "no one pointed no guns at nobody's head" and that Mama, Genevieve, and I stopped off for a holiday "social call." As for Karol, he had gone to his hunting camp in the Poconos to catch the last weekend of whitetail season. She didn't know "nothing about no Doctor May."

Detective McIntyre related all this to me in the empty lobby of the *News-Times*, where I had returned to file my story about seeing Dr. May and to prepare for my Mahoken Board of Adjustment hearing on a five-unit PUD proposed for the Smalley Farm. I felt faint from the prospect of so much excitement.

McIntyre was looking mighty depressed. There was a spot of coffee on his uniform, and his eyes were red from crying.

"Tell me again," he said, his expression listless. "Tell me what she said."

I finished my bag of popcorn (from the vending machine, cooked in the paste-up room microwave), crumpled it, and tossed it in the trash can. "She said she used you so she could get information to Karol about your investigation. She wants to marry Smolak. She wants to be a housewife."

McIntyre winced. The freckles on his nose popped up. "I could have made her a housewife. That's all I've ever wanted too. To be a cop and have a family in the burbs."

All cops say that. I got up and brushed the white popcorn detritus off my skirt. "I've got to go back to work. I got a board of adjustment meeting to cover."

"Tonight? It's Thanksgiving Eve. I thought maybe I could take you out for a drink or a sandwich, maybe."

"Sorry." I held up my left hand. This ring was coming more and more in handy. "I'm spoken for."

McIntyre regarded the ring vacantly. "You're engaged?"

I nodded. It was the closest I could come to a lie under the circumstances.

"Lawless said you were single."

"Lawless doesn't know bupkes about my private life."

McIntyre looked even more dejected. "I'll have a patrolman assigned to tag you tonight. If you have another emergency, don't forget to use the pager," he said finally. "I'm gonna go home and zap Lean Cuisine."

It was one of those awkward Christian moments. Awkward because I sensed he had one horrible holiday awaiting him. Christian because if I were a decent one, I'd ask him to join us.

"Detective," I called as he creaked toward the door, "you doing anything for Thanksgiving?"

The question took a moment to register. When it sank in that I was being nice to him out of pity, McIntyre hitched up his pants. "Working. We, uh, bachelors do a trade-off with the family men."

"That's considerate of you."

"Yeah." And he left.

Mr. Salvo came down the stairs. Although it was only six, he had his overcoat on and the day's paper under his arm.

"You're leaving?" I'd never seen Mr. Salvo leave before midnight. "I worked the day shift. Billin's doing the desk tonight." He plunked a tweed cap onto his bald head. "I'm driving to my cousin's in Massachusetts for the turkey. Very Arlo Guthrie."

"Who's he?"

"Jon Bon Jovi's illegitimate stepfather. By the way, Ludwig got some nice shots of Walker advising a student. She might be okay as a photographer. You set with the college-admissions story?"

"Uh-huh. But I have to tell you something. . . ."

Mr. Salvo stopped at the door. "Notch read over your May piece. We're running it page one left. Billin's got a couple of questions, so check with him before you go to your meeting. McIntyre any help?"

"No."

"Figures." He tapped his cap. "Happy Thanksgiving, Yablonsky."

"But, Mr. Salvo!" I ran to the door. "Karol Smolak's still at large. The police haven't a clue where he is, and I'm worried he's going to kill me. Worse, I'm going to be the only one in the newsroom to-morrow."

"If you think that's gonna get me to change the schedule, forget it. I've heard all the Thanksgiving, Christmas, weekend excuses, and then some. Steve Stiletto could be in the hospital suffering from mul-tiple stab wounds and I'd still want you to make cop calls. Now good-night."

As I had expected, the Mahoken Board of Adjustment was a rip-per. The PUD vote was tabled, partly because one board member was picking up her kin at the airport and because another member was in deep depression over the loser boyfriend her daughter had just brought home for Thanksgiving. It lasted all of fifteen minutes, yet had managed to kill my evening.

From the Mahoken Town Hall pay phone I called the office and spoke to Billin, who took my one-sentence lead and pasted it on top of the story I'd written earlier.

"No need to come back to the newsroom tonight," he said, kindly. "Go home and enjoy what you can of the holiday. I'll leave a beeper here for you."

I reached for the beeper in my purse. "Another beeper?" This was like putting a pair of nuclear reactors in the hands of Baby Leroy. I couldn't handle one, let alone two.

"Notch will be on call tomorrow, so beep him if there's an emergency," he said. "But only in an emergency. Don't beep him if the Pepsi machine runs out of Diet Pepsi or if there's a paper jam in the copier."

Glad he told me that, because in my world those *were* emergencies.

"Beep him if that Smolak guy shows up. We can't change your schedule, but we don't want you dead, either."

"Kind of you."

"Don't thank me. It's newspaper policy."

I was the last one out of the Mahoken Town Hall, except for a janitor who couldn't wait for me to exit. When I left, he slammed the door, locked it, and zoomed away in his pickup truck, leaving me to fumble for my keys in the dark.

I started the car and turned on my headlights, as did someone else behind me.

Perfect.

Where had that car come from? Either the chairman of the Mahoken Board of Adjustment was itching to play deep throat about the groundhog problem under town hall, or Karol Smolak was on my ass.

I guessed the latter.

Lucky for me Mahoken was a community of three hundred people, fifty miles west of Nowhere. And if you had told me that my Saturday nights spent drag racing when I was sixteen would someday amount to a skill, I would have laughed.

Until now.

Simply put, I floored it. My wheels spun crazily as I hauled ass across the gravel lot and out onto the dirt road. I actually wished a state cop was hiding in the bushes waiting to nab me for speeding.

Karol was no slouch, either. As I tried to remember which turns to take, zipping left and then right, running one blinking red light and bouncing over a set of dangerous potholes, he stayed on my tail, bouncing with me.

I had no idea what I was doing. I was too panicked. I felt like a rabbit in a night field, zigging and zagging crazily as a faster-than-I-was fox pursued its evening meal.

Karol's lights filled my rearview, blinding me and illuminating my face, which was sweating despite the thirty-degree temperatures of the November night.

I came to a T and hooked left, then hooked right into what I thought was a road, but turned out to be a driveway. Leaning on my horn in desperation for aid, I decided not to risk stopping. Instead I careened over those poor people's lawn and headed back to the road.

Karol did the same.

My speedometer read eighty-five and, worse, my tank read almost empty. Being a Lehigh Valley girl, the lyrics to the 1977 Jackson Browne song "Running on Empty" automatically sprang to mind, which was okay. As long as I was trying to remember them, I wasn't hyperventilating at the increasing probability that Karol Smolak was going to run me off the road into a ditch, where my body and incinerated car would not be discovered for two weeks.

An abrupt impact caused my body to hit the steering wheel and the Camaro to swerve. Karol Smolak had tapped my bumper. A warning. The chase was almost through.

Not quite. Ahead of me I saw flashing red lights and heard the *ding-ding-ding* of a train crossing. White gates with reflective red stripes lowered slowly. The nightly Norfolk Southern on its Allentown to Easton route coming through.

God bless it.

The train was a quarter mile down the track. Actually, I didn't know if it was a quarter mile *exactly*, since I'm really bad with measurement, but I gunned it on the off chance that in the land of trains, a quarter mile meant I could cross.

I was wrong.

In a blur of lights and a deafening locomotive engine, I circumvented the gate and hopped the tracks. I do not. Repeat. *I DO NOT* Recommend doing this at home. I only recommend it if you are in Mahoken and if Karol Smolak is fulfilling an earlier dare to blow your brains to bits.

I managed to cross the tracks and reach the other side safely. Behind me all I saw was darkness. All I felt was the terrific rumbling of the Norfolk Southern barreling up the tracks. All I knew was that Smolak was dust.

I turned left on a road with cheerful signs to Route 22. In less than two minutes I was on the highway weaving in and out of traffic on my way home.

In an hour I was back at West Goepp, the doors bolted, Jane safe in bed with her windows locked, and an oh-so-kindly Lehigh patrolman snoozing in his cruiser outside my front door.

Bliss.

Chapter Twenty-three

Thanksgiving Day dawned gray and cloudy, as a Thanksgiving Day should. I awoke to the aroma of roasting turkey and burnt butter wafting from Mrs. Hamel's kitchen next door and realized I'd met the county's goal of $50,000. I should put one of those United Way thermometers on my front lawn.

I had to be in the newsroom by nine. A squishy nine, in my view. This was a tree-in-the-forest approach to employment. If a reporter fails to show up to an empty newsroom, does anybody notice?

The patrolman, figuring Karol Smolak wouldn't attempt to kill me in the light of day, had left. This was good, because otherwise Mrs. Hamel and the entire neighborhood would have been on his case about noise problems with the extended and growing Violetti family, whose unmuffled cars and nightly fights had put everyone on edge.

After fixing myself a cup of coffee, a semistale glazed doughnut, and a bowl of Special K (weight control), I showered, blow-dried my hair, and picked out a festive harvest outfit of a brown leatherette skirt, an orange V-necked T with leopard-print cuffs, and a fake amber necklace.

My lips were Autumn Dawn matte. My lids were chestnut with matching liner and sable mascara. On my cheeks I dabbed a subdued rose with a touch of gold glitter, because I have very little patience with subdued. No Puritan I.

Then I woke Jane, who managed to basically stay asleep all the way from West Goepp to the senior high-rise, despite her own shower and cup of coffee. When I dropped her off, she asked, "Where am I?"

"See you at Stiletto's around three," I said, pushing her out to the sidewalk. "Don't let Mama bring that cooked corn crap."

"It's the only stuff G and I can eat, besides mashed potatoes."

Vegetarians. More out of place at Thanksgiving than Easter bunnies at Christmas.

I headed down Main Street toward the Hill to Hill and decided Lehigh was dead to the world. Almost no one was on the street. The Wednesday before Thanksgiving was historically a party night in this town, as was the Friday after, which was an even bigger party night. It started with the Liberty/Freedom football game and continued well into the wee hours of Saturday morning with lubricated Liberty alumni either toasting their victory over Freedom or drowning their sorrows over their loss.

I wondered if this year would be more low-key, what with the halftime ceremony dedicated to Mr. Schmidt's memorial. If there'd be an aura of respect and grief. If there'd be beer. If there was beer, the aura of respect and grief might take the form of a few overturned cars.

My shiny brand-new key allowed me to open the back door of the *News-Times*. The cramped, tiled staircase echoed as I climbed to the second-floor newsroom. The inky odor of newsprint was stronger than I'd ever smelled it, possibly because there was no other aroma like coffee or cologne to compete. Or possibly because I was keenly aware how much responsibility weighed on my shoulders.

I was slightly frightened and awed by the duty of being the only reporter in charge of gathering the day's news. May all the criminals be good today. May they stay in their houses and eat turkey and not bother anyone until we were back to full staff.

The empty newsroom was cluttered and dirtier, too. I ratcheted up the volume of the scanner so I could hear reports of any fires or homicides and went to Billin's desk to read the headlines from the competition. The only story on the Rudy Schmidt murder in the *Morning Call* was one highlighting tomorrow's memorial service. A sidebar mentioned the *News-Times* contempt case and noted that I had passed the milestone of $50,000 without turning over my notes.

Lawless had written a similar sidebar to my story about the resurrection of Cerise May. Karol Smolak must have read it. None too pleased, I supposed, by the part about him pointing a gun to my head. I pictured him in his undershirt, sitting in a cheap motel room, tossing the paper onto the floor and swearing to Cerise how he'd get me if it was the last thing he'd do.

Lawless had also left me a note on my computer. According to Probate Court, there'd been no action on the Julia "Popeye" Simon case aside from a fairly routine notice that Stu Kuntz, her defense lawyer, had been appointed the estate's executor. The will had not even been filed, so there was no way to glean how much she had been worth.

Damn.

Bang! A gunshot went off in the darkroom and I nearly collapsed from fright. When my mind cleared, I decided it was nothing more than the darkroom's shut-off timer and that hardly sounded like a gun. Academic theory confirmed: I was going nuts.

I made cop calls, typed up the college-admission story, sent it to Mr. Salvo's cue, and printed out a copy for Mr. Notch. (Notch insisted on reading all my stories before they went in the paper, for some odd reason.)

Cautiously I opened the door to Notch's office. The heavy green drapes were drawn shut, and the room smelled of his Cuban cigars and spicy aftershave. I flicked on the light and dropped the printout on his desk, right by the fishbowl of fireballs.

His dark red leather high-backed chair beckoned. With a quick glance to the door, I went around to the other side of Notch's desk and plunked myself down. I was rewarded with a satisfying hiss of escaping air as the seat molded itself perfectly to my rump. I sat back and surveyed Notch's office. The massive bookshelf and brass award plaques, the oil painting of some dead British prime minister.

So, this was what it was like to have a view from the top.

I reached into the fishbowl and pulled out a fireball, Mr. Notch's "macho candy." Tough on the teeth, tough on the tongue. A jawbreaker for men who break jaws. I rolled it around in my mouth and winced as the overpowering cinnamon stung straight up through to my nostrils.

A few minutes later the cinnamon had mellowed, and I had my feet up on his desk, firing underlings left and right. "Lawless, you're canned. Outta here." I reached into Notch's top drawer and pulled out a cigar, imagining Lawless slinking to the door. I could get used to this bigwig status. Yessirreee.

"Yablonsky," I proclaimed, "you're doing a hell of a job. How's fifty grand sound? Not to cover the fine, dear girl. Garnet will pick up that tab. I'm talking salary. Yes. Why not? You deserve it. Sky's the limit."

I called Sandy at home. "Guess where I am?"

"Las Vegas," she said. "Married by Elvis."

"I'm sitting in Mr. Notch's chair and he doesn't know."

"Naughty girl. I'm jealous." She lowered her voice. "Think of me. We're about to leave for Grandmother Moron's."

"Yipes!" Grandmother Moron was Martin's grandmother. Grandmother Moron rocked in her rocking chair and complained constantly about the government while producing enough gas to power Pennsylvania Power & Gas. She forbade televisions, phones, microwaves, and all things technological, believing that her life expectancy would be cut short should she come in their contact. She was pushing eighty-five, so maybe she had a point.

"Sorry."

"I made Martin promise he'd take me on a cruise next Thanksgiving. You get great rates this time of year. Watch a football game for me." And she hung up.

Wheee! I twirled in the chair until I accidentally swallowed the fireball whole and started coughing, spraying bits of red sticky fireball juice all over Mr. Notch's neat green blotter.

"Bubbles. Are you okay?"

I looked up, red faced and oxygen deprived, to find Stiletto standing over me, holding a pair of tongs that grasped a set of wet photographs. He was in his usual tight jeans and a plaid flannel shirt over a black T-shirt. The combination sounds like it was straight from a Sears advertising insert, but it was so sexy I temporarily forgot that I was choking.

"Stiletto," I sputtered, feeling like a fool. "When did you get back?"

"Last night. I left three messages on your machine."

"Little good that'll do you. You know how I am with machines."

He smirked. "Having fun playing king shit?"

I slid out of the chair, clutching my throat. "Had to drop off a printout."

"Yes." He eyed the cigar. "I see that."

"Oh, buzz off. What are you doing here?" I stood and dropped the cigar in the drawer.

"I was in the darkroom blowing up the Schmidt photos." He took me in from head to toe. Apparently my outfit met with his approval, because he got the evil grin that meant he wasn't thinking about baseball scores or how the Dow had done today.

"Did you say the Schmidt photos? You mean the one from May's security camera?"

He pulled them out of the tongs. "I figured Dan, being a lawyer, had made copies of the photos Cerise May gave him, and I was right.

He gave me a set this morning and I blew them up. Where's the ring I gave you?"

I showed him the chain around my neck.

"Why don't you wear it? It looks beautiful on you."

I explained my rationalization about having to inform as few people as possible when it would be revealed that he really didn't want to marry me after all. The way I said it sounded kind of pathetic, like I was auditioning for prima wallflower, and it made Stiletto frown.

"Come here." He opened his arms and kissed me in his usual gentle, sensual way. "You know I love you."

"Uh-huh." I pointed to the photos. "Can I look at those?"

"Absolutely."

We spread them out on the leather couch. There were ten altogether, magnifications of various body parts. Some body parts were more tolerable than others, and I wasn't talking about legs and feet.

Unable to bring myself to examine my former high school principal naked, I shoved those photos over to Stiletto and concentrated on the woman.

I was right about the hair. It was definitely a wig. Her body was trim, but also muscular. Whoever she was, she worked out. And her hips were narrow. I couldn't imagine that she'd ever had kids.

Ruth Faithful, I thought, until I traced my finger over her buttocks and down her thighs, over the calves, and reached the feet. That's when I came to a new conclusion.

"I've come to a new conclusion," I said,

Stiletto looked over my shoulder, ostensibly to see what I saw, but really to caress my bare neck with his lips. I shivered. He put his strong hands around my waist and pressed into me. I tried to keep my mind focused.

"What's your conclusion?" he asked out of sportsmanship.

"It's that . . ." Stiletto found the sweet spot under my ear. His breath was warm and inviting. I felt dizzy and tingly, especially when his hands explored under my top.

"Did you ever make love on your parents' bed?" he asked.

"If I had," I said, "I wouldn't be here to tell the tale."

His hands roamed farther. "It's the same thing, making love in your editor's office."

"Stiletto!" I found the concept both appalling and thrilling. "In a newsroom? It's the least romantic place I can think of."

"Really? Have you ever seen my masthead?"

"Your mind really is in the gutter."

I spun around and kissed him back, and before we knew it, the photos were off the couch and we were on it. He was right. There was something thrilling and very naughty about having sex where the editors argued every night about story placement and cropping photos and who should order in Chinese.

Vaguely I worried that Mr. Notch might make a surprise appearance, or that one of the editors might walk in to check the morning's wires. But I was beyond caring, because Stiletto's chest was hard and bronzed and looming over me and the rest of him I could not be responsible for.

As for me . . . I was stripped across page one.

When our rush of passion had peaked and subsided, Stiletto and I lingered lazily on the couch. I rested my head on his bare chest, and he fingered the ring around my neck. After a few thoughtful minutes, he unclasped the chain, slid off the brilliant ring, and slipped it on the third finger of my left hand. He held up my hand and smiled as the diamonds caught the light.

I said nothing. But I dreamed.

"Okay," he said finally. "What's this new conclusion of yours?"

It took me a few seconds to remember what he was talking about.

"Oh, yeah." I leaned over and retrieved the photo that highlighted the calves of the kneeling woman. "Look." I pointed to the dark black hair that covered the back of her legs.

"Yup."

"What do you think?" I asked.

"I think maybe she's a free spirit who sees no reason to shake hands with a razor."

"Oh, she shakes hands with a razor. Only on her face, not her legs."

Stiletto sat up. "Come on."

"No, really. I think our hostess is a man."

Stiletto took the photo out of my hand and gave it a good hard look. "So Rudy Schmidt was into guys sucking his toes."

"Guess that's what Grace Schmidt meant when she said her husband had needs she as his wife couldn't fulfill."

"Poor Grace."

"Yes, poor Grace," I agreed, recalling her tight-knit family and gracious home. "I'm sure she had no idea that when she bought the wig, her husband would be using it for this perversion."

"Do you mean toe sucking or the humiliation of another man?"

"Both," I said, "and maybe more."

Chapter Twenty-four

The new question now was, who was the guy giving the toe job? It was imperative to find out, fast, because he might also be Rudy Schmidt's murderer. If Dan would let me release the photos to the cops, I could turn them over to Detective McIntyre. The hour had arrived for me to leave this matter to the professionals.

After Stiletto left, I called Dan at home and found Wendy filled with a rare abundance of holiday cheer.

"Bubbles! I was going to call you."

She was? The last time Wendy called was to complain that G had infested her den with fleas.

"Yes. Congratulations about your engagement to Steve Stiletto. What a catch."

I groaned. Dan had blabbed to Wendy, the last person I wanted to know. I could picture her face this summer when I'd have to tell her the engagement was off, while she wore the smug smirk of "I knew a guy that wealthy and handsome and charming wouldn't settle for you."

"Thanks," I said. "Is, um, Dan there?"

"Hold on. You're not getting off that easy." She giggled. "I mean, okay, I'll admit it, even I find Steve handsome. But forget about that. Good-looking guys are a dime a dozen. Call me a gold digger, but what I want to know is how much is that guy worth?"

"Gold digger," I said.

She laughed.

I didn't.

"Now that you two are making it official, I can unload a terrible secret," she said. "Girl to girl."

"No, Wendy, really . . ."

"Dan is *sooooo* relieved that you're marrying Steve."

"Because now he won't be tempted by me?"

She giggled again, a bit too loudly.

"No. Because, well, he had one hundred thousand dollars or so set aside for Jane's education . . ."

My fingers twisted around the cord. I did not like where this was going.

". . . which we could really, really use, you know?"

"Williams-Sonoma's Christmas sale?" The sarcastic question felt bitter on my lips. As an heiress to a cheeseball empire, Wendy wanted for nothing. Her cashmere bedroom slippers were bought in Philly and cost more than my monthly food budget. Everything she owned was fancy, right down to the lotion-soaked toilet paper and hard English soap in her bathroom.

"Second home, actually," she said. "In Avalon two blocks from the beach. Costs a fortune and we're going to need a jumbo mortgage, but as Daddy said, it's not like they're making more beachfront property. Now Dan can put the cash toward it. Every bit helps."

"How much?" Dan had a lot of nerve buying swanky beachfront property when he was pilfering in the five figures from his firm.

"The asking is $1.5 million. Sleeps nine. Three decks and an outdoor shower. Dan needs it to entertain clients, Bubbles. It's an absolute must. So you can see how positively over the moon we are that he doesn't have to pick up the tab for Jane's education."

"But . . ." I was so livid, my vision started to blur. "But, Wendy, this isn't a real engagement. And even if it were, it wouldn't be Stiletto's responsibility to pay for Jane's tuition any more than it would be yours. Dan's her father."

Wendy said, "Huh?"

"We're not getting married." How much more blunt could I be? "It's all a fraud. For Stiletto's career."

"Oh." She cleared her throat. "Oh. Well, that *is* disappointing. I so had my heart set on the house in Avalon. I already contracted a decorator."

"Is Dan there?"

"No." Her voice was dreamy. "He's grouse hunting with Sherman." Sherman was Dan's best friend. "Though in all likelihood they're parked in Sherm's Hummer passing the flask. You think Stiletto would be willing to pitch in for the tuition even if you two aren't getting married?"

"No, Wendy. And when Dan comes in, please have him call me."

"No point. He's not coming home before Thanksgiving dinner. You can bug him then."

"I'll be at Stiletto's."

"I know," she replied, "so will we. Stiletto's Cousin Rosa called yesterday and invited us. I said yes but, of course, that was before I knew this engagement was phony. If I'd known it was a sham, we would have gone to the Lehigh Inn."

I closed my eyes and rubbed my forehead. Dan and Wendy were coming to Thanksgiving. Could the holiday get any worse?

"Listen, Wendy, I know this sounds weird, but if you could do me a favor, please don't say anything at Thanksgiving about this being a fake engagement. Mama and Genevieve and Rosa don't know. Okay?"

"Sure," said Wendy. "What do I care?"

I stepped on the gas and hightailed it to All God's Children Church, the Reverend Tom Faithful presiding, for my fluff piece on what

Lehigh soup kitchens were up to over Thanksgiving. Pastor Faithful was reading from the Good Book as church members set long tables covered with white paper and tilted, haphazard cardboard turkeys.

It was the usual Thanksgiving fare served from steaming chafing dishes onto paper plates. A few select members of Lehigh's homeless sat side by side with All God's Children's flock, making small talk as they picked through dry turkey, tepid mashed potatoes, and overly sweet pumpkin pie. Still, I was envious. The gathering was so merry, so without homicidal and/or gun-toting family members, that I found myself with a lump in my throat.

"Stay," urged Pastor Faithful, "and praise the bounty." He swept his arms wide. "We are all one family in God."

I certainly hoped so, because my family was turning out to be a bit of a no go.

"Where's Ruth?" I asked, speaking of family.

Pastor Faithful answered me with a granite stare. "Ruth has gone her own way."

I looked left and right. "Which way is that?"

"Not the way of the Lord, I'm afraid." He pasted on a bright smile as a nodding and bowing worshipper passed with two plates of pecan pie. "Save some for me, Joy!" This was punctuated by a chuckle.

"Do you mean Ruth has left home?" That kind of worried me, what with Karol Smolak and Ruth's boss on the rampage.

"I can't quite say. We had a tough discussion and I guess she didn't appreciate my blunt advice. She left yesterday."

Would have been interesting to know how to translate a "tough discussion" and "blunt advice."

"Aren't you worried about her?"

"Ruth is over thirty. She is a grown woman. I have raised her to be a God-fearing child, a humble and sober adult. What she does now is out of my hands." And he excused himself to get another slice of pie.

Ruth might very well be in God's hands, I thought as I got back into the Camaro and headed to the other side of town. And that would be comforting, as long as I could be assured that God's hands were wringing Karol Smolak's neck.

El Centro de Communidad was a very different scene from All God's Children. Who knew that *arroz con pollo*, red beans and rice, and fried plantains were official Anticolonialism Day fare?

And whereas All God's Children had hummed to the melodic murmur of polite conversations and Faithful's sonorous recitation of the Bible, El Centro de Communidad was bouncing off the map with a salsa band. I could hear it two blocks away.

"Feliz liberdad!" shouted Consuela DeJesus as we weaved in and out of the red-, green-, blue-, and yellow-covered tables. "Why don't you grab a plate? There's plenty."

"Thanks but no," I shouted back. "I've got dinner in an hour."

"Bueno!"

That was easy for her to say.

Consuela danced with a toddler who was swaying to the music. "Detective McIntyre called me yesterday to ask me my impression of you," she said. "I told him you were very nice. Trustworthy. I told him your photographer was another story."

Yeah. Another story straight out of Stephen King.

Consuela danced away and I interviewed three families, two of whom were not Puerto Rican, about why they came to the center. I talked to a lonely old man and a widow and then I went back to Consuela DeJesus.

"Why would Detective McIntyre ask about me?"

She stuck out her lower lip. "I don't know. You could ask him yourself. He was supposed to stop by already, but . . ." She scanned the crowded hall. "I haven't seen him. I worry. It's not good for a man like Detective McIntyre to be alone on a family holiday. He told me what happened with Cerise."

"Oh?"

"Yes. Some women can't help but fall for the wrong men, is what

I said to him. They think bad men are more interesting, although bad men only end up as trouble. It makes me sad for Detective McIntyre. A good man is hard to find."

Though my mother swore it was the other way around.

On the way to Stiletto's I spawned a brainstorm. I should get Ruth Faithful and Detective McIntyre together. They were an ideal match. Ruth was modest and chaste. McIntyre yearned for a devoted mother to raise his children, to settle in the suburbs and grow kids who wore starched shirts and said, "Yes, sir" and played on Little League teams.

It was a delightful vision. A safe world where children were protected and loved and where a woman driving alone down a deserted country road on Thanksgiving night wasn't being tailed by a maniac in a black BMW.

As I was now.

In addition to feeling that old rush of adrenaline and fear, I was also annoyed. I mean, it was Thanksgiving, for heaven's sake. Over the river and through the woods to Stiletto's house we go. But not at one hundred miles per hour!

Couldn't Smolak give it a rest for a day? Didn't he have respect for family?

I checked out the BMW in my rearview. It was the kind of car that was so obnoxious you wanted to punch its lights out. Low slung, shiny black. Faster than a car needed to be.

It bore down so hard that the Camaro's speedometer, still not recovered from the previous night's workout, hit close to sixty, which was twice the speed limit on the winding Saucon Valley Road. Plus the other car had those irritating headlights, the ones that are purple and blinding.

I released the accelerator and yawed to the right, to give him a chance to pass. Still he sat on my tail. I gunned it to sixty-five and there he was.

Beep. Beep. The BMW issued a nasal, European command. His right blinker was on, indicating, I hazarded a guess, that he wanted me to pull over. Forget it. I wouldn't stop this car if Mel Gibson was behind me with an order from God himself.

I was still a good five miles from Stiletto's. I needed McIntyre. Reaching into my purse, I depressed the beeper. It flickered red, then green, but I couldn't take my eyes off the road long enough to pay attention to its signals. I was too focused on gripping the steering wheel and did the best I could, swerving left, then right, trying to remember how the road banked.

Beep. Beep. Beep.

My muscles felt taut and my vision sharp. It seemed as though I could see better, hear better. I listened for gunshots. I hugged the curves. *Just get to Stiletto's. He won't dare follow you to Stiletto's.*

Before I knew it, we were there. The stone gate appeared in my headlights on the right. I turned into the driveway so fast my brakes squealed and the Camaro went up on two wheels. Surely Smolak would speed off.

He didn't. He was right behind me.

I downshifted into first. The BMW pulled in front of me and parked. I turned off my lights. He turned off his. I waited.

He got out and slammed his door. I heard the crunch of gravel and a tall figure coming toward me. I slouched behind the wheel and planned my next move. It was a move I'd seen in a *Magnum, P.I.* episode, and if it worked for Tom Selleck, it would work for me.

"Hey!" he said, approaching my door.

It was now or never. *Bam!* I swung open the door and hit him right in the face.

"Ugh!" He doubled over, holding his nose.

Leaping out, I grabbed him by the shoulders and kneed him in the crotch as hard as I could. He fell to the ground, writhing on his stomach and screaming, "Oh God. Oh . . . my . . . God."

Stiletto's front door opened, sending out a golden stream of light. Rosa ran down the steps, shielding her eyes.

"What's going on?" she cried.

"Get back in the house, Rosa. Call the cops."

"Stefano's already on the phone."

"Why?" my stalker shouted, but I stamped my booted foot on his back.

"Shut up. Shut up, scum."

I heard a click. Genevieve was by my side, her musket aimed squarely at his spine. "Make another move and you'll be joining the cranberry sauce in the compost heap tonight."

Shoot. Cranberry sauce. I'd forgotten to bring it.

"Cool," said G, smoking a cigarette. "Can I hold the gun?"

"Leave it to the professionals, Butch."

Rosa put her hands over her ears. "Stop! Stop! This is a horrible mistake. I know that car."

"Puhleeeze, Rosa," I said as politely as possible. "This doesn't concern you."

"Rosa?" the scum squeaked. "What have I done?"

"Nothing, darling." She knelt and cupped his face.

Needless to say, it wasn't Karol Smolak. It was a pretty boy prepper with blond hair and a $4,000 black leather jacket to match his $40,000 Beemer.

I was shocked and I was mad at the same time. Who was this jerk?

"Hi, Chad." Stiletto put his arm across my back and kissed me on the cheek. "I see you met my fiancée, Bubbles."

"Ugh." Chad slowly rose, clutching his gut. "Yeah."

"Chad works with me at the AP," Stiletto said dryly, as though I'd never heard of him before. "I'm so glad Rosa invited him for Thanksgiving. Aren't you?"

"Absolutely," I gushed. "Thrilled."

Chad Kent wanted the London assignment and suspected that Stiletto was faking our engagement. One wrong move on our part and he'd be blabbing to the AP higher-ups. Stiletto would be out of the London assignment and out of a job. He might even be blacklisted from the industry altogether for lying.

"I promise I won't beat on your friends when we're married, dear," I said, pursing my lips for a domesticated kiss.

"I understand, honey bunch." He chastely kissed me back.

"Thing is, he was on my tail so hard, I thought he was Karol Smolak."

"So did Dix Notch." Stiletto handed me the portable. "And if you don't talk to him soon, he's gonna call out the cavalry."

Chapter Twenty-five

$\mathbf{D}$ix Notch had been immersed in football on his wide-screen TV, sated with turkey and what he described as an "absolutely breathtaking sauvignon," when his beeper beeped, causing him to spill his pecan pie and miss the Dallas Cowboys' touchdown that won the game.

I tried to explain over the phone about how the beeping had been a mistake, though it was hard to concentrate on Notch since I was in Stiletto's foyer. Every few minutes a member of my family bustled by, showing how hard they were working to get Thanksgiving dinner on the table, while all I could do was gab on the line.

"I got confused," I said as Mama ran past, muttering under her breath about how she could "use a set of manicured hands around here, thank you very much."

"I thought I was beeping McIntyre because there was this insanely fast driver tagging me," I told Notch. "I assumed it was Smolak, but it turned out to be an AP friend of Stiletto's."

Dix Notch didn't care. All he knew was that there was no Karol Smolak, only a buddy of Stiletto's with a lead foot. And that he had to explain the entire mess to the Lehigh PD, which he'd put on hold, waiting for an update.

"You've made a fool out of me. Out of the paper!" Notch bellowed, adding that he wanted to see me in his office bright and early Friday morning. "On my couch!"

I winced. Not *that* couch.

I got off the phone and Stiletto handed me a Rolling Rock. "Here, you deserve it."

"I can't. I'm on duty."

"Dan and Wendy just pulled up and they're sitting in the car ripping each other's heads off. Dan's three sheets to the wind and Wendy's pissed and I just caught Chad in my office ostensibly looking for a bathroom, but actually checking out my date book to see if we really are getting married."

I took a swig.

Jane turned the corner, her eyes red rimmed. "I don't want to eat dinner," she sniffed. "I just want to go home."

"You and me both, kiddo." I punched her lightly on the shoulder. "What's wrong?"

She folded her arms and shook her head. "I don't want to talk about it."

"The hell with you," said G, stomping past her and heading out the door.

"Ohhh!" Tears welled in her eyes.

"There's a library on the second floor," said Stiletto with sensitivity. "You should check it out. No one will bother you there."

"Thanks." She managed a half smile and headed up the stairs.

I felt a pointed tapping on my shoulder. I turned around and looked down. Mama had outdone herself. She was wearing a tight-fitting tan top that plunged too low and a flowered apron that was already stained with gravy.

The thick liner around her eyes extended to the corner of her brows. Her eyelashes were false. Her lips were thick, almost puffy, and painted a reddish brown. It looked like she'd been aiming for a bad Sophia Loren impression and ended up with a cat on steroids.

"Where's the cranberry sauce?" she said.

"I completely forgot. Sorry."

"That was your assignment. To bring cranberry sauce. You go to the store, buy a couple of cans, and dump them on the plate." She frowned. "Genevieve, Rosa, and I have done everything. Everything. Turkey. Stuffing. Beans. Watermelon pickle. All the polishing. Even ice water. And you can't find ten minutes to stop off at ShopRite and get cranberry sauce?"

"No cranberry sauce?" hollered Genevieve.

"I'll get cranberry sauce," said Stiletto, putting down his beer. "What's open?"

"Nothing!" my mother and Genevieve screamed in unison.

"Don't you touch me!" Wendy yelled as she and Dan shook off their coats. "I don't want you to ever touch me again."

"Oh. Like that's a threat. I *wish* I never had to touch you again." Dan tossed his coat onto the rack and missed. He was holding an extremely large bottle of champagne. I think it's what they call a magnum. "Happy Thanksgiving, everybody. Let's drink up."

Stiletto rushed to the rescue. "Tell you what, Dan." He slapped him on the back. "This fire's getting pretty low. How about we go out to the shed for more wood."

"You can't!" screamed Mama. "Dinner's almost on the table."

Yippee. This was fun.

"Yeah. To the woodshed. That'll fix him," snapped Wendy. "Better yet, why don't you sleep out there, Dan. For the rest of your life."

"Witch!" hissed Dan.

"Dinner's ready!" screamed Rosa.

Stiletto gave me a conspiratorial wink and led Dan out the door. I steered Wendy to the dining room. In twenty steps I got an earful about how Dan was a self-centered pig, a low-down insensitive creep who always put his needs first and her needs last.

Like this was news to me.

"And to think we could have eaten at the Lehigh Inn if it hadn't been for this so-called engagement," Wendy said, completely forgetting her prior agreement not to mention that our upcoming wedding was a fraud.

"Who goes out to eat on Thanksgiving?" asked Mama, leading the way with a bowl of carrots cooked in honey.

"People who haven't been snookered by their husband's ex-wives into—" Wendy entered the dining room and froze in awe.

Chad Kent, all cleaned up except for a couple of scrapes on his cheek, stood behind one of Stiletto's gorgeous high-backed dining room chairs. He wore a yellow Ralph Lauren Polo shirt and gray wool slacks. His jawbone was so angular it could cut butter.

"And who do we have here?" asked Chad, flashing a very J. Crew grin.

"Ah," said Wendy with approval.

They were like the last two members of a nearly extinct species that had been devastated by a sudden ice age. Words were unnecessary. Their highbrow genes allowed them to communicate telepathically.

"Wendy, this is Chad Kent. He works with Stiletto at the AP. Chad, this is Wendy." I had to think quickly of a subject to get Wendy off my fake engagement. "Wendy is a retired tennis pro."

"Oh, really?" Chad stepped closer.

I couldn't look. It was so much WASP concentrated in one small space, I felt my skin shrink with Protestant dehydration.

"Nice, say?" Mama waved to the table. "Course, it would have been more colorful with cranberry sauce."

The white room was set with the most exquisite plates etched in blue and gold. Stiletto's mother's pattern, I assumed. The silver wasn't silver, but gold. The napkins were white linen, and instead of my mother's usual crappy centerpieces of boy and girl Pilgrim candles and a Hallmark tissue-paper turkey, there were vases of gold and purple mums.

"Wow!" I said. "This must be Rosa's doing."

Mama stood on her tiptoes and whispered in my ear, "I found my paper turkey in the trash. Can you believe it?"

Genevieve brought out the last of the dishes, the dreaded baked dried corn. Stiletto returned with Dan, who seemed no more sober, and we were ready.

Mama was at the head of the table. Rosa was at the foot. The rest of us sat in a boy/girl arrangement, me between Stiletto and Chad, Wendy between Dan and Genevieve. Yes, I know Genevieve is a girl. But, honestly, does anyone else?

"Where are Jane and G?" Mama asked.

"Engaged in a teen melodrama." I shook out my napkin and felt Stiletto's hand caress my left knee.

Then I felt Chad's on my right. I gave it a tiny pinch.

"How about a prayer?" said Mama, holding out her hands.

"Sure." Chad took mine in his. Wendy didn't bow her head. To do so would require taking her eyes off Chad. Her eyes started to tear, either because her marriage had hit the rocks, or because Genevieve was bone crushing her knuckles.

"Dear Lord," Mama began. "Thank you for the food we are about to receive. And forgive us for not having cranberry sauce. Amen."

We let go hands. "I don't think it's a sin not to have cranberry sauce," I said as everyone passed around plates of sliced turkey.

"Yes, it is," said Genevieve with authority. "It's like the wine in communion."

"What?" Where was my rational Jane when I needed her?

"Speaking of wine." Stiletto offered to pour some for Mama.

Mama used her hand to cover the glass. "Oh, perhaps a smidge. I'm not much of a drinker."

"I am," said Dan, holding out his glass. "Fill 'er up."

Wendy cleared her throat, so Stiletto took care of her first, conveniently bypassing Dan for Genevieve.

"Cabernet Sauvignon," Genevieve said. "Hmph. Where's that dandelion I brought?"

"Probably in the trash with my paper turkey," Mama muttered.

"You'll like this, I promise." Stiletto moved on to Rosa.

Dan passed a dish of green beans with onions across the table. His mouth moved silently in exaggeration and it took me a moment to realize he was pantomiming words to me.

"What?" I pantomimed back.

"Bubbles . . . I . . . love . . . you!"

Oh, brother. I took the dish and mouthed, "Cool . . . it."

Chad caught us. "Interesting," he said under his breath.

"Not really." I scooped out the green beans. "Dan's just affectionate."

Wendy, ears attuned like a bat's, picked up on this. "Dan affectionate with you? You should hear what he says when you're not around."

"Really?" said Chad. "Do tell."

Stiletto and I looked at each other. Stiletto said, "Did anyone see the fox this evening? Ran right through the backyard."

Dan's fork dropped on the beautiful china with a clang. "For your information, Witch Wendy, Bubbles was a better wife than you ever were. Better in the sack, too."

"That's my girl," Stiletto murmured.

"I bet," Chad echoed.

My stomach clenched. Genevieve coughed. I was glad Jane wasn't present to hear this.

"Bubbles never came home with six-thousand-dollar Visa bills, either. She never threw a hissy fit over not having the biggest, bestest, newest sixty-thousand-dollar Volvo. She never withheld sex because I wouldn't buy her a diamond tennis bracelet."

"I think I did see that fox," Mama said. "Red, wasn't it?"

"In fact"—Dan pushed back his chair—"Bubbles put me through law school. She worked two jobs and then suffered eight years at Two Guys while raising our daughter and now she's a goddamn investigative reporter on a goddamn newspaper and no daddy got her that job."

I covered my eyes and wished that transmogrification had been invented. Next to me, I could sense that Chad was keen for the next blow.

"Well, if you love her so much"—Wendy tossed down her napkin. Her nose was red and her eyes teary—"why don't you marry her all over again?"

"I would. In a heartbeat. If she wasn't already getting married."

Stiletto gripped my shoulder. Wendy zoomed in on me. Then on Dan. Then on Chad. Then on Dan again. She waited. We waited. For one brief instant I thought maybe Wendy might do the right thing.

And then she opened her mouth. "Actually, Dan . . ."

I couldn't take it. Pushing back my chair, I slid past Stiletto and ran out of the room, bounding up the stairs to look for Jane. As I turned the corner, I heard Wendy drop the bomb: "They're not really engaged at all. It's just a fraud so Steve can buy some time before going to England. Bubbles told me so herself."

"I thought as much!" Chad exclaimed.

We were ruined.

I wanted to get as far away from this place as fast as possible. This fake engagement hadn't been my idea. Stiletto had hated lying and now he was going to pay the huge price for his deceit. It was a stupid, stupid risk for us to have taken.

"Jane!" I called, rushing down the carpeted hallway to Stiletto's study. "Come on, Jane."

I opened the door. The room was dark. She must be sleeping. I flicked on the light, but the couch was bare. Not a book was disturbed.

I headed down the stairs and across the slate foyer to the front door. G was outside finishing a cigarette, looking cold. I had a very sickening feeling.

"Where's Jane?"

"Dunno." He pointed with his cigarette. "She just drove off with some guy."

My heart quit beating. "What guy?"

"Dunno. We were hashing it out and she stormed off and then this car pulled in the driveway. I figured it was someone she knew or he was asking for directions. She stuck her head in the window and then got in."

Who could it have been? A friend from Liberty, I thought optimistically.

"I'm splitting," said G, getting into his beat-up pickup truck. "This Thanksgiving bites." He started up the truck. "If you see Jane, tell her I'm sorry."

The phone rang.

"Phone's ringing," G said helpfully, shifting the pickup into reverse.

I heard Stiletto say, "Hello." And then, "Okay. She's around here somewhere. Hold on."

I ran inside. "It's Jane, isn't it?"

Stiletto handed me the phone. He looked serious and I knew it was bad. I grabbed it, my hands sweating already.

"Jane?"

"Mom." It was her little-girl voice. A voice I hadn't heard since she was six and got lost in the women's department of Almart. "Mom, I'm on a cell phone. I'm okay. I'm really, really sorry about being such a snot about Thanksgiving."

"Where are you?"

Jane didn't answer and then there was a rustling as the phone was taken away from her. A man got on and immediately I recognized his voice, though I couldn't place it. All I knew was that he was *not* the voice who had called me the night Lorena and I had been to Cerise May's office.

"I'm going to say this once, so listen good."

I closed my eyes and teetered. Stiletto held me and bent his ear to the phone. "Get your notes from the Julia Simon interview and deposit them in the waste receptacle in the far stall of the girls' bathroom in the basement of Liberty High before midnight tonight."

"But it's not—" *Open* I wanted to say, but he interrupted.

"Do not call the police. I have a police scanner in my possession and I receive every call, including the nonpublic frequencies. If I so much as hear that you've made a donation to the Policemen's Benevolent, Jane will end up just like Julia and Rudy Schmidt. Dead. And no suspects."

He hung up.

I dropped the phone so it clattered onto the slate floor and buried my face in Stiletto's chest.

"No!" I found myself shaking. "No. Stiletto. They have my baby!"

Chapter Twenty-six

Dan was useless. We found him with his head in his turkey and mashed potatoes, passed out, drunk. Personally, I was relieved. Dan would have overreacted and called in the posse. He would have blown everything.

I was both dazed and energized. I would have hopped in my car and searched all Lehigh for Jane, except my feet wouldn't move.

Stiletto sat me in a chair, got me a glass of water, and promised it would be all right. We would handle it together as soon as he shooed everyone away.

"I'm afraid Thanksgiving's over," Stiletto declared, somehow managing to be charming while giving my family the boot. "We have an emergency and Bubbles and I need to attend to it immediately."

"Thanksgiving's not the only thing that's over," Wendy said, marching to the coat closet. "Dan's all yours, Bubbles. You two deserve each other."

"I'll drive you home," offered Chad, getting his own coat. "I have a BMW."

"I should hope so," Wendy said, sliding a finger under his chin.

"See you back at the office," Chad said to Stiletto. "Though I might be in England when you get back."

Stiletto would have knocked his lights out if the situation were different. Chad knew that too.

They left and we were faced with Mama and Genevieve, who started to clear the table. Nuclear bombs could have been falling from the sky, fire could be raging across the countryside, and still Mama and Genevieve would insist on clearing the table.

"That's okay," Stiletto said, taking a plate from Genevieve's hands. "I'll take care of it."

"You can't just leave all this food here out in the open," protested Mama. "Besides, it'll only take a few minutes. I'll clear and Genny will scrape. We can't let that turkey go to waste."

"Don't worry about it," Stiletto said.

"Botulism!" Mama suddenly remembered. "If you leave it at room temperature with the stuffing . . ."

Stiletto steered them to the door and got their coats. "LuLu, if you could be so kind as to invite Rosa to your house for dessert, I'd appreciate it."

"That's okay." Rosa was helping Dan stand. "I'll take him up to bed and let you two talk. You have a lot to discuss, I know."

"What with the engagement being called off and all, say?" Mama kissed me on the cheek. "You didn't have to fake it for me, Bubbles. I don't care if you get married or not."

"They think the emergency is the big news that our engagement was a fraud," I said when they left. "If they had any idea of the truth, they'd be hysterical."

Stiletto sat next to me and took my hand, giving it a reassuring squeeze. "I guess it would have been an emergency too, if Jane hadn't been kidnapped. Funny how that bogus engagement pales in comparison now."

"What are we going to do?"

"We're going to find those notes and then we're going to do as he said. After that we're going to hunt him down and beat the crap out of him. If we can find him."

"If we can find the *notes*," I said. "Because right now I have no idea where they are.

Stiletto and I used the back door to the House of Beauty and turned on the light in Sandy's perpetually neat office. Oscar was in the kennel, his empty bed and chew toy by Sandy's desk. We combed through the stacks of towels, bottles of shampoos and conditioner, the various tints and dyes, and, of course, cartons of Clorox. Boxes of foil, clips, bobby pins, and razor blades

I looked in the washer and dryer, the paper towels, and collection of plastic aprons. I even did a cursory examination of the contents of Sandy's desk, but found only Post-its, paper clips, paper, pens, a couple of accounting books, a check register ($8,568.63 in the House of Beauty checking account), and insurance forms. Finally I looked under Oscar's sheepskin bed. Nada.

Stiletto, meanwhile, attacked the salon, starting with the drawer where I had originally tossed the notes and ending with the cash register. Together we checked the cushions of the couch and the *TV Guide* by the TV, and we flipped through all the magazines. We worked silently, tension building every minute as my fears increased. What if Sandy had taken the notes home?

Worse, what if by accident she had thrown them out?

"Explain to me again why you can't call her?" Stiletto said.

"Because she's visiting Martin's grandmother, who lives without a phone in some hellhole in central PA."

"What's the name of this hellhole?"

"East Bumfuck, Sandy calls it."

"There is no East Bumfuck."

I opened a drawer in the coffee table. "Are you sure?"

"Almost positive."

It was now past nine and I felt as though I could climb out of my skin. I'd left countless messages on Sandy's home machine on the off chance she might check her messages on Thanksgiving.

I was trying to be strong for Jane. I wanted to be clearheaded and focused. But suddenly my whole body went weak and I started shaking. Stiletto brushed back my hair and held me. It made me feel better for half a minute. Then I had to move. I could not stand still.

"Why don't you call Sinkler at home?" Stiletto asked. "If the caller is Karol Smolak, then maybe the cops already know where he is. A call to Sinkler's house won't be picked up on the guy's scanner."

I bit my red acrylic nail so hard it cracked. "I'll call Mickey after I get the notes and drop them off. After that, I'll think about it."

"Think. That's what you need to do, Bubbles. Think." Stiletto grabbed me by the shoulders and searched my puffy eyes, which were desperately in need of treatment (see Bubbles's Under-Eye Cream, page 293). "What did Sandy say—exactly—about where she hid the notes?"

"I told you. She hummed this tune." I hummed it, but it made no difference to Stiletto. It was foreign to him. "And then she said Martin came up with the idea to hide it in full view."

"Where were you when she said this?"

I pointed to the couch. "There."

"Okay. Do what you were doing on the couch."

I lay down. "Also, I had a Diet Pepsi."

Stiletto opened the minifridge by Sandy's counter and got me a Diet Pepsi, popped it open, and handed it to me. "And where was she standing?"

"Right where you were." I tried to remember. "I think she was smoking."

"Forget that. That's not going to happen." Stiletto positioned himself where Sandy had been and tried to look . . . effeminate. Hands on hips à la Sandy. Fluffing up his hair.

"Sandy doesn't do that."

"Humor me." Stiletto cleared his throat and parroted what Sandy had said, only in a girlish high-pitched voice. "Martin had the idea to hide it in full view."

"He saw it on *Masterpiece Theatre!*" I shouted, sitting up. "Does that help?"

Stiletto closed his eyes. "*Masterpiece Theatre.* Full view. It's got to be a literary reference, seeing that it's *Masterpiece Theatre.*"

"Poetry?" I suggested.

"Not poetry." Stiletto smiled. "Poe. Edgar Allan Poe. 'The Purloined Letter.' "

"The Pearl-Loined letter? Sounds obscene."

"Your loins are pearly, Bubbles. But 'purloined' means 'stolen.' And in 'The Purloined Letter,' a letter in question was framed in full view, and none of the investigators could find it because it was so obvious."

We scanned the walls and hit upon Sandy's framed beauty license, Board of Health Certificate, and first dollar bill. We explored the backs of every family photo in the joint and came up with nothing.

Humming Sandy's tune, I suddenly saw with new eyes the House of Beauty's most famous decorations. The Dippity Do! posters. They'd hung in the salon for so long the colors had faded, pink to cream, black to brown.

I yanked the posters off the wall and ripped off the backing. It was easily removed because Sandy had just done the same, securing each note page with a single dab of mucilage and lining them up in perfect order.

"That's half the battle right there," Stiletto said. "All we need to do now is get them to the school and then get Jane."

I stared at the crumpled pages in my hand, the scrawls of ink on white, lined paper, barely coherent, almost impossible to decipher. It was incomprehensible to me that notes held such power, that prosecutors, a cop, a defense lawyer, and finally a judge would be so desperate to possess them that they'd search my office and fine me $50,000.

That an unknown man would steal my daughter to get them first.

"What are you thinking?" Stiletto asked.

"How no one told me when I was growing up that of all the powers in the world, few were more threatening than the written word."

"What power did you think was the most threatening?"

"Money," I said.

"Chump change," said Stiletto, "compared to the truth."

Chapter Twenty-seven

The massive fortress that was Liberty High School stood white and dark in the cold November night. Street lamps and security lights illuminated the doors, one of which, I hoped, would be open so we could drop off the notes.

A giant stage had been built out of plywood on Liberty's side at the fifty-yard line in preparation for the next day's halftime memorial celebration to honor Rudy Schmidt.

"Jane was supposed to be the first student speaker," I told Stiletto as we walked along the racetrack that surrounded the field.

"Not *was*," Stiletto said. "Will be. She'll be there, Bubbles. Never you fear." He gripped my hand firmly. I gripped back.

Stiletto had let go of my hand only to shift gears in his Jeep. He hadn't said many comforting words except for the occasional, "It will be okay. We'll get her home. We'll get through this."

We did not discuss who the caller might be or how Jane's kidnapping could have been prevented. We did not lay blame. Stiletto had not gotten angry. He did not demand answers.

He had been solid, determined, and silent. And in his silence I found more strength than in his words.

At some point we would have to tell Dan. I didn't know when that point would be. Tuesday, I was thinking. Tuesday would be a good point.

A cold wind whipped down the field and hit our faces as we crossed the end zone. We were heading for the boys' locker room entrance, the most likely spot, since it was largely hidden by the bleachers and led to the basement.

The cement hallway to the locker room was pitch black and damp. Stiletto turned on his flashlight and led the way to the double doors. Which were chain locked.

"Damn," I said.

"Lots more doors to try," said Stiletto.

We ended up trying them all. My watch read 11:25 and my anxiety was in the red zone.

"It'll be the last door," said Stiletto. "Murphy's Law." And he was right. The band entrance, on the other side of the stadium, had been left slightly ajar. Intentionally. A thin strip of metal had been placed between the lock and the frame.

"He's been here," Stiletto said. "He's probably watching us."

I was glad I hadn't called Mickey.

Now self-conscious, we headed down the green tiled hallway. Stiletto turned off his flashlight so that the only illumination came from the red exit lights over the doors and fire alarms. Neighbors around here were known for keeping guard over the school and would readily report any signs of vandalism. We'd have to do this in the dark.

The girls' bathroom was on the right side of the band room. I pushed open the dark green door. Stiletto handed me the flashlight.

"Want me to go with you?"

"It's the ladies'," I said. "No men allowed."

Stiletto laughed. "Good to see you've kept your sense of humor."

Actually, I was serious. It *was* the ladies'.

"Jane?" I called, entering the bathroom. "Are you here, Jane?"

The basement girls' bathroom hadn't been upgraded since I'd been at Liberty. The same old pink tiled walls and cruddy white sinks with soap dispensers that were never full, along with those brown paper towels that the shop class depended on when they ran out of sandpaper.

The far stall was nearest to a small window set up high and facing the courtyard. It was open, providing a space large enough for an agile man—or woman—to climb through, yet was hidden from the view of neighbors. So that was how he did it.

I entered the stall and opened the metal waste receptacle on the side. It had been cleaned and lined with a fresh brown bag that held a white envelope. I deposited the notes and ripped open the envelope, sitting on the john to read its contents. The note was written in Times New Roman font, clearly from a computer.

DO NOT CALL THE POLICE. JANE REMAINS ALIVE PRO-
VIDED NOTES ARE SUFFICIENT AND POLICE ARE NOT IN-
VOLVED. RETURN IMMEDIATELY TO PHONE WHERE I
REACHED YOU TONIGHT. STAY TUNED.

My hands shook as I read it over and over. I was both furious and disappointed. Part of me had banked that Jane would be waiting, although I knew intellectually that would have been a foolish move on the kidnapper's part. Even so, why hadn't he said where I could get her? Where was she?

Plus something was off.

Stiletto cracked open the door. "Everything okay?"

I stepped out of the stall and showed him the letter. Stiletto read it and said, "Fine. If that's the game the SOB wants to play, we'll do what he says. We'll go back to my house and wait by the phone."

"Read it again," I said.

Stiletto read it. "So? There's not much there."

"The photos. Why didn't he ask for the photos?"

Stiletto thought about this. "Because," he said, "he doesn't know they exist."

"Or," I added, "he doesn't know we have them."

Next to Jane's incredibly difficult and long birth, it was the most agonizing seven hours I'd ever spent. Stiletto and I sat on the couch, staring at the fire, all the phones in the house turned to full volume, waiting.

Stiletto napped briefly, his chin nodding into his chest, while I counted the second hand as it inched across my watch face. There were so many impulses I fought, aside from calling Mickey and Dan. I wanted to call McIntyre. I didn't because McIntyre was so hot for Smolak's ass, there was no telling how he might respond.

I wanted to call Mrs. Smolak and appeal to her, mother to mother, to find her son and intervene. Stiletto talked me out of that.

"Don't rock the boat," he said, waking from one of his catnaps "Let it be. Besides, what makes you think the caller is Karol Smolak?"

"Because Karol Smolak vowed to kill me, and McIntyre said he'd go after my daughter first. McIntyre said Smolak's back was up against the wall, and he was afraid this might be the final blow to bring him down."

"McIntyre's obsessed with Smolak," Stiletto said. "He's unreliable."

I sat back and thought about this. It was now five-thirty. Dark. It's always darkest before the dawn. "Who else could it be besides Smolak?"

"My guess is, judging from what the caller said, he's the guy who killed Rudy Schmidt and then Popeye."

"That was Smolak," I said.

Stiletto turned to me. "Are you sure? What evidence do you have? And why would Smolak care about your notes? He knows where Cerise May is. They're together."

I could feel myself becoming ill-tempered and beyond exhausted. I did not need to be cross-examined by Stiletto, not now, while my daughter was missing and every last nerve in my body was frayed like a split end.

Karol Smolak was a known entity. A neatly packaged murder suspect. Karol Smolak was my man. I was jiggy with that.

As Cerise May's boyfriend, Smolak had access to her office. Cerise would have tipped him off that Schmidt was waiting and possibly she set up the meeting. Smolak had been using the photos to blackmail Schmidt, was my wild theory, but Schmidt wouldn't back down. So Smolak had him murdered. Wasn't that the way blackmailers worked?

In truth, I didn't know how blackmailers worked. The only person I'd ever met who'd been blackmailed was . . . Dan!

Holy mackerel. There might be a connection.

I left Stiletto on the couch and ran up the stairs to one of the guest bedrooms, where Rosa had put Dan to bed. He was in his dress shirt and boxers, face flat on the pillows, oblivious to the torture his daughter was enduring.

"Wake up!" I shook his beefy shoulders. "Wake up, you fool."

Dan cocked open one eye. "Wha . . . ?"

I had to cover my nose to keep from being overwhelmed by his stale whiskey breath. "Tell me about the blackmail. It's important."

"Wha' blackmail?"

"You know. The blackmail and the death threats. You couldn't talk about it then, but I know now the caller wanted you to hand over Doctor May's photos." I poked his ribs to rouse him more.

He flinched. "No blackmail. Let me sleep."

"Remember, you idiot?" I turned on the light and Dan cringed. "First you got those death threats. Then they blew up your radiator. After that they broke into your office, but by then you'd given me the photos so they couldn't find them."

"Hmm?" He started to snore softly.

"Dan! This is a matter of life and death." I so wanted to say Jane's life and death, but the last thing I needed was Dan in this condition asking questions and butting in. "Tell me now. Who do you think the blackmailer was?"

"No blackmailer."

Oh, he was so literal, a typical lawyer. "Then who called in the death threats?"

"Me." He yawned. "Just me."

I stared at his lump of a body. His legs were pale against his black socks, and where the pants rubbed against his calves, hairless. His ass had gotten big and round, middle-aged looking. I couldn't believe I'd once been married to him.

"What do you mean '*just me*'?"

"Because I luff you." He raised an arm, his lids still shut. "Come here and give us a kiss."

I pushed his arm away. "I will not. Are you saying to me, Dan Ritter, that you lied to me about those death threats?"

His arm fell back on the bed. "Yesh."

"And about the break-in?"

"Mm-hm."

"Why?"

"Because I wanted me to be more exciting so you'd luff me. I'm a man of danger, don't forget." He raised his head, his two red bleary eyes focusing poorly on my face. "And by the way, it's Chip."

With a thump, his head fell back onto the bed.

He'd lied, that moron. He'd lied about his life being in danger so I'd pay attention to him. Apparently me having my own busy career and a worldly boyfriend had been too much for the dope. Dan felt left out and so he created a bogeyman. Then he leaked me the photos as though he was being noble, all in the effort to become included in my go-go world.

At that moment I knew the truth. Dan, aka "Chip Ritter," was the most self-centered man on God's green earth. Wendy had him pegged.

A splintering ring shattered the silence. Dan sat up and instinctively reached for the phone, but I got it first. From downstairs I could hear Stiletto taking the steps two at a time. I quickly prayed for strength, guidance, and Jane's safety, and then spoke into the portable.

"Hello?" The alarm clock by the bed read six o'clock. On the dot.

It was the now-familiar voice. "Have you called the police?"

"No."

"Who iss it?" lisped Dan.

I put my finger to my lips.

"Who's that?" the caller asked nervously.

"Her father," I said. "He doesn't know."

"Good." The voice paused. "Jane will be at the Liberty halftime ceremony by noon."

"Where?" I asked, panicked. "There'll be so many people. Hundreds. Let me speak to her. Put her on the phone."

There was silence, and then he said, "I see one cop . . ."

That was followed by a disconnect and, at the sound of it, part of me died.

"It's okay." Stiletto gently took the phone from my hand and sat me on the bed. He brushed back my hair. "It's okay, Bubbles. It's almost over."

Dan stared at us, mouth agape. "Who was that?"

"The blackmailer," I said bitterly.

"What blackmailer?" he asked. "There is no blackmailer."

"Yes, there is. And he's taken our daughter."

Chapter Twenty-eight

Since dawn, Stiletto and I had been sitting in his Jeep, parked inconspicuously behind a barrier on Pine Street. The morning was brisk and cold, the gray sky giving way to blue. Pine Street residents dragged garbage cans full of turkey carcasses, bottles, and cracker boxes to the curb, oblivious to the horror that somewhere near them a kidnapped teenage girl's life hung by a thread.

I hoped that G, who I had called on a last-minute whim, had followed my instructions and would be waiting by Kosta's, where he had a good view of the front door, in case Jane should be dropped off there. He was overcome with feelings of guilt for not having stopped Jane from getting in the car. I assured him that he couldn't have known, but he was a mess. Nothing gets to me more than a crying teenage boy.

Dan, showered, shaved, and caffeinated, was by the band entrance. He had complained repeatedly about my not calling in law enforcement until I had agreed to compromise and notify Mickey Sinkler.

Mickey, and Mickey alone, was staked out on the other side, by the tennis courts. Mickey had offered to put ten patrolmen undercover, but I put my foot down. He wasn't to tell a soul. Not his kids. Not his supervisor. Not his ditzy ex-wife. I just wanted him.

"It would be perfectly understandable for you to be at the halftime ceremony," I told him, using Stiletto's cell phone while we drove, so that our signal couldn't be picked up. "You've got kids in high school."

"No, I don't. My high schooler is at juvy hall."

"Maybe he's aspiring. The point is that this guy might know the cops. If he sees a few of them, he'll panic."

"What guy are you thinking of, exactly?"

"I'm exactly thinking of Karol Smolak."

"Then we need to call McIntyre," Mickey said. "McIntyre will be pissed as hell if we finally apprehend Smolak in a major felony and he doesn't make the nab."

"Then McIntyre will be pissed as hell, because I won't risk him flying off the handle at Smolak so Jane ends up dead."

"Suit yourself," Mickey said. "You're the mother."

"Yes, I am."

Now we were left with the awful task of waiting. First the neighborhood was empty. Then the rival band and football team from Freedom arrived on buses to begin practicing. That was followed by the peddlers. Hot dogs. Cotton candy. Hot chocolate.

A crew tested the stage microphone and draped the stage with the American flag and Liberty's logo. The Liberty Grenadiers started up, the thump of the bass drum echoing my own heart as "Rule Britannia" filled the stadium. I burst into another round of tears as the lonely wail of the bagpipes finished "Waltzing Matilda" and segued into "Amazing Grace," in honor of Schmidt.

There were so many ways in which I'd been responsible for Jane's kidnapping. The first and most obvious was that if I had remained a hairdresser at the House of Beauty, Jane would be safe at home. Karol Smolak or whoever the kidnapper was wouldn't have known my name, much less attacked my daughter. Right now we'd be sitting in the stands, waiting for Jane to deliver her eulogy. I'd have the day off!

And it wasn't like I hadn't been forewarned. Sandy repeatedly told me this job was dangerous and I disregarded her, all because of my brewing ambition. There was no escaping the truth. I'd been selfish. I should have put Jane first. Dan was right.

Dan. Okay, so he was a louse. He left me for another woman when he was making good as a lawyer. And as a lawyer he was the scum of the scum. A slip-and-fall attorney. Ambulance chaser. WASP wannabe.

Then again, Dan had always been a devoted father. He did put Jane first, unlike me. He never gave me grief when Jane had to stay at his house because it was unsafe for her to stay at mine. He would drop any case, any client at a moment's notice to rush to her aid. He brushed aside Wendy's protests and pulled every string he could to get Jane into Princeton.

Yet the biggest sacrifice Dan was willing to make was to remarry me for the sake of our daughter. Jane deserved a home with two parents, he claimed. She deserved to feel secure and loved.

I hated to give Dan credit for anything, but on this issue he had a valid argument, especially in light of the crisis we were going through now. I couldn't predict what shape Jane would be in should she survive this kidnapping. I expected she'd be rocky and scared, unsure and depressed for months to come. It would be hard going.

Would a stable home with two parents help?

I studied Stiletto, who was deep in thought, surveying the crowd as it flowed past our Jeep. Though he, like I, had not showered or changed clothes since the day before, he seemed more put together. The collar of his bomber jacket was up to keep out the cold, and the day's growth of beard made him rustic and masculine.

I was so in love with him.

"What happens after this is all over?" I asked, pouring from our thermos of coffee. The cup in my hand shook and I gripped my wrist to steady it. That's when it suddenly hit me how frightened I was. How frightened of the future.

"Jane and you go home. The kidnapper is caught and prosecuted and we all live happily ever after." Stiletto winked encouragingly.

"Do *we* live happily ever after together?" I had to know. At least one dreadful unknown in my future had to be answered. "Or apart?"

Stiletto put his coffee cup on the dashboard. "Let's not talk about this now, Bubbles. Now is not the time."

"Listen, Stiletto. I am experiencing the worst moment of my life and I need to get a few things straight before I make a big decision."

He folded his arms and bowed his head. "I've got an obligation to go back to New York as soon as possible and explain what happened. Kent may have beaten me to the punch. There's nothing I can do about that now."

In other words, my keeping him here as support might have cost him his job. I sipped my coffee. "You can go now. As you keep telling me, it's almost over. And Dan and G and Mickey are here."

"I want to see the mother and daughter reunion." Stiletto focused ahead at nothing in particular. "Besides, even if I explain my lie, I may not get the London assignment. I may not have a job."

The London assignment was the plushest honor an AP photographer could receive. Doubly so because he'd be heading up the bureau.

"If you still have the assignment, I want you to go to London."

Stiletto turned to me. "What's this? Are you trying to get rid of me?"

"I want you to go, Stiletto. I mean it. I'm not being girly or coy. I know what it's like to have ambition, to want a career and fight for it. If you don't go to England, you will resent me forever and I won't stand for that."

"But—"

I held up my hand. "Resentment kills a relationship. Ask me. I know. I resented Dan. I resented waiting tables and washing hair while he studied and got a degree. Two degrees. In a way I resent him still."

Stiletto and I were silent. More people filed into the stadium. They were carrying picnic baskets and blankets, seat cushions and big foam fingers. A few stared at us, wondering why we were sitting stupidly in the Jeep. I scrutinized each for a familiar face that might have crossed my path in the past week.

I searched for Jane.

"I'll stay until you find her, Bubbles." Stiletto dropped his voice. "After that I'll take your suggestion. I'll go."

For a while we were silent. Then I said, "We all make sacrifices for what we love," before I slipped the gorgeous engagement ring off my finger, put it on the dashboard, and slid out of the Jeep to look for the most important person in my life.

My daughter.

At noon there was still no sign of Jane. Stiletto and I had split up, him taking the Freedom side and me surveying the Liberty end. I walked back and forth examining each row, fan by fan. There were so many faces. Fat, thin, jowled, and old, young, and fresh. Women, grandmothers, men, boys. It blurred into an absurd human jigsaw puzzle.

I decided I knew no one until I saw Stu Kuntz in a button-down wool coat, standing proudly with his wife, Rita, in the far right bleachers, two benches from the field. They were beaming at their son, Jason, sitting on stage where Jane should have been. I felt pangs of jealousy and sadness, seeing the empty chair next to him. Jane's chair.

"Stu!" I called out, running up to him. "Stu! Have you seen Jane?"

They didn't hear me, though Estelle Cameron had. Estelle Cameron taught drama at Liberty and was somehow involved in putting together the halftime memorial service. Out of the corner of my eye I saw her flying toward me in a panic, her black tunic flowing in the breeze, her many beaded necklaces dangling around her neck.

"Wait, wait, Bubbles," Estelle trilled. "You're just the person I'm looking for."

Maybe she had news. "Have you seen Jane?" I shouted.

Estelle put her hand to her chest. "I was just about to ask you. Where is she? She's the next speaker. This is highly irresponsible and not like her."

I was so frayed and brittle, I could have slapped the drama queen on the spot. "There's been an emergency, Estelle. Jane's not . . . available," I heard myself say calmly.

"For heaven's sake." Estelle pushed back her graying hair. "Well, then the Kuntz boy will have to go on."

Without pausing to ask what kind of emergency could have caused a responsible girl like my daughter to miss a big event like this, Estelle ran back to the dais, waving her hand and gesturing for Jason Kuntz to step up to the podium.

I headed toward the bleachers, taking the stairs two at a time until I was on the same level as Kuntz.

"I'm sorry to bother you, Stu," I hollered, cupping my mouth, "but I'm looking for Jane. It's important."

"Jason's just about to speak," said Stu, turning on his Canon video camera.

I inched down the row, much to the irritation of several spectators. Rita, who would have had a flawless view of her son had I not been in her way, scrunched down, annoyed.

"Jane's in trouble," I said, "and I need to find her. It involves Karol Smolak."

For all his concern back in Notch's office about bringing Smolak to justice, Kuntz now couldn't have cared less. "No, I haven't seen Jane." He put his eye to the viewfinder.

Rita clapped hysterically as Jason, carrying two papers, walked to the podium and nervously adjusted the microphone. He was being introduced by Estelle, the intercom echoing badly, drowning out my screams of, "PLEASE! YOU HAVE TO HELP!"

Stu and Rita remained deaf to all but their son's sappy speech.

It was like a bad episode from the *Twilight Zone*, until I saw the tinge of raspberry in a throng of teenagers promenading by. My maternal vision tunneled and I pushed Rita Kuntz over as I leaped the bench in front of her and landed in the crowd below.

"Jane!" I cried, shoving aside astonished students. "Jane!"

The raspberry head turned and at once I knew the nightmare was over.

"Mom!" Her face was pale and her black mascara streaked. "Mom!"

With arms outstretched I caught her and held her tightly. Jane was sobbing into my neck. I patted her head. My heart swelled with gratitude and overpowering love. "It's all over, baby. It's all over. Are you . . . okay?"

She lifted her tearstained face. "I'm not raped or anything, if that's what you mean."

That's what I meant, all right. A small crowd had gathered around us. Shielding her with my body, I rushed her behind the bleachers. Dan and G could wait. I needed answers, fast.

"Did he hurt you?"

Jane's eyes fluttered. They looked strange. "He drugged me. I don't know with what. I slept most of the time. I woke up in this cart behind the bleachers. I was so confused."

"What cart?"

"I think it was a hot dog cart. It smelled like hot dogs."

"Show me."

Jane took me by the hand and led me to the back by the fence that lined Pine Street. "It's gone," she said, confused. "It was right there. I woke up and the door of the cart was open. I got out and I couldn't believe I was here at school. I should have called you or something." She rubbed her head. "I was so dazed. I just started wandering."

To think that Stiletto and I had been but a few feet from her the entire morning.

"I'm so sleepy," she said, her eyelids fluttering again. "I don't feel right."

She needs to go to the hospital, I thought. I led her back to the stage, the agreed-upon meeting point for Stiletto, me, Dan, and G.

"Who was it?" I said. "Come on, Jane. Try to think."

"I can't think." She massaged her temple. "I never saw him. He was wearing a beard and glasses last night. He took me to a room. One of those rentable storage spaces, I think it was. That's where we called you. Then he gave me a drink. I went to sleep and woke up here."

Oh! This was so frustrating. I couldn't believe this murderer was going to get away with kidnapping my daughter.

Stiletto sprinted toward us, calling Mickey on his cell. G was already by the stage, looking dumbly up at Jason Kuntz.

"G," said Jane, swaying. "You came."

"Oh, man." He grinned. "I am so fucking glad to see you. I thought you were a goner."

"Yeah, me too." Jane managed a smile. I was glad G was there, even if he was leaning down to kiss her.

"Don't kiss me," she said, covering her mouth. "I haven't brushed my teeth."

He planted an awkward kiss on her cheek. "Are you okay?"

"I'm okay. Not raped or anything."

"That's good." G nodded. "Who took you?"

Jane shrugged. "I don't know."

"I should have done something," G said. "Last night."

"Yeah," Jane said bluntly. "You should have."

Stiletto, seeing us, slowed to a trot. He flashed me a thumbs-up and I flashed him one back. Our eyes met and my heart clutched. The moment had come. Stiletto, not wanting to make a scene in the midst of Jane's remarkable reemergence, slipped off diplomatically.

I watched him go, sifting among the crowds. My eyes began to burn. Not now. Pull yourself together for Jane.

I turned away and saw Dan hustling toward us, his belly jiggling. Mickey, I noticed, was keeping his distance, hidden behind the stage. His steely-eyed gaze met mine. He had us covered.

I was okay. Mickey. Dan. Sandy. G. Genevieve. Mama and Jane. They were my extended family and I was thankful for them. An odd extended family, sure, but a family nonetheless. They would have to do.

"Dumb ass up there is the one who took your Princeton spot," G said, thumbing to Jason Kuntz. "I could climb up and punch his face in. That might make up for letting you get kidnapped."

Jane squinted at Jason. "Jason Kuntz? He's a total dud. Good boards and grades, but none of the outstanding extracurriculars Princeton wants. I'd liked to know who he blew to get that." Embarrassed, Jane turned to me. "Sorry, Mom."

"It's okay." Everything was okay.

"I don't know whose dick he sucked," said G, "but he just thanked Schmidt for writing him a recommendation that got him in."

G's words hit me like a blast of Arctic air as the truth became crystal clear. Not whose dick.

Whose toes.

G accompanied Jane to the hospital, where she would be examined and interviewed by female police officers. Dan and I would join her later. As soon as Stu Kuntz was arrested.

"You positive it's Kuntz?" Mickey asked as we watched three plainclothes detectives position themselves near Kuntz and his wife.

"I'm not positive, but I know a surefire way to verify."

A dozen police officers, half undercover, had infiltrated the stadium. The ones in uniform were scattered about, chatting with spectators. To the unaware, they served no more important role than crowd control.

If Kuntz was concerned, he didn't let on. He and Rita cheered Liberty. They were so enthusiastic and so charged that I was riddled with doubt. What if I was wrong?

Then I remembered what Dan always said. A quality courtroom lawyer is a performer. Putting on a trial requires smoke and mirrors to bewitch a jury, as well as facts.

"You reach McIntyre?" I asked.

"He's on a call in Plainfield. I think he's got a lead on Smolak," Mickey said, adding, "What I don't get is why Stu Kuntz resorted to kidnapping in order to get your notes. What's the big deal?"

"Because my notes were the only proof that Popeye suspected him. Her last words to me were that everyone was against her, especially her own lawyer. And with Kuntz on the short list for state defender general, he had a lot at stake. He couldn't risk her blowing his cover."

Mickey brought up a pair of binoculars. "Yeah, but Popeye was insane. She was a paranoid schizophrenic."

"And no one knew that better than Kuntz. He represented her when she was charged with killing the garbageman. He got her committed to an insane asylum instead of jail."

"Uh-huh."

Kuntz looked directly at us and we backed into the shadows.

"Popeye told me that she'd been locked in Cerise May's bathroom during Schmidt's murder. And then she was let out. While in there she heard voices. Lots of voices."

"Again," Mickey said, "paranoid schizophrenic."

"Not in this case," I said. "Police scanner. Kuntz's police scanner. When Popeye collapsed in the courthouse holding tank, Kuntz rushed in. He had a portable scanner and was on it fast as lightning to call for backup. It was the same scanner he used to listen to the cops when Jane was kidnapped. And he was the only one with access to Popeye's meds."

"If Kuntz overdosed Popeye on her medicine, why would he try to save her?"

"He was sure he couldn't. What Popeye didn't know was that Kuntz had given her enough antipsychotics at the appropriate time so she'd collapse during her arraignment, in front of the press."

Mickey nodded. "The prosecution doesn't need motive, but it'd be nice."

This was the bombshell. I took a deep breath. "Cerise May gave Dan photos to hold that showed what appeared to be a naked woman in a wig sucking the toes of Rudy Schmidt in her office."

Mickey started to laugh and then caught himself as I continued.

"The woman in the photos is no woman, Mickey. It's Kuntz. And for whatever reason, he was sucking Schmidt's toes. For Schmidt it was a game, I'm guessing. Kuntz would humiliate himself and in return Schmidt would use his influence to get Kuntz's kid into Princeton. I don't know." I shrugged. "Maybe Schmidt was into humiliation. For some people that's better than sex."

"In my case," Mickey said, "sex *is* humiliation. The two are synonymous."

I let that one go. "When Cerise saw the photos on the security tape, she told her boyfriend Karol Smolak, who was heavy into blackmail."

"That's McIntyre's theory, at least."

"And if McIntyre's right, then my guess is Smolak contacted Schmidt and suggested a sum to keep the photos quiet. Cerise, meanwhile, trotted them over to her lawyer, none other than Dan, for safekeeping, which is how I got them."

"Jeez," said Mickey. "Talk about walking into the fire, say?"

"Say. But no one was thinking murder until Schmidt told Kuntz. Maybe he even asked him to make a contribution to the blackmail payoff. Kuntz couldn't risk that. He was up for state defender general. His appointment was assured by the Court of Appeals Third District."

"Not if he's sucking the toes of naked principals," Mickey observed.

"Nor if he's succumbing to a mobster's blackmail. Worse yet," I went on, "when Kuntz found out Schmidt would be in Cerise's office to discuss the terms with Smolak, he got there first and killed him. Lucky for Kuntz, Schmidt had smashed the security camera."

"So why didn't Kuntz hold Jane until he got the security tape stills as well as the notes?"

That was a good question. "I can only assume that he either didn't know I had the photos, since I never told him, or that those weren't important as long as there was no one to identify him. And there was only one other person who could do that: Schmidt."

"What about Popeye? How did she get messed up in this?"

I hadn't figured that out, exactly. "Knowing Kuntz, my assumption is that he was so familiar with his own long-standing client that he was able to arrange for her to be in Doctor May's bathroom. Popeye was a very convenient scapegoat."

Mickey nodded. "Kuntz looks like he's making ready to split."

Indeed, Stu and Rita were hurriedly gathering their belongings. It was the last bit of confirmation I needed.

"Go time," Mickey said into his walkie-talkie.

In a flash, Stu and Rita Kuntz were surrounded. People had stopped cheering for Liberty and were pointing to the couple as officers detained Kuntz at the gate.

"I know my rights!" Kuntz yelled. "I'm a goddamn defense lawyer and this is an outrage! This is unlawful arrest!"

Mickey and I approached him. Kuntz glared at me. I glared back. Rita said something stupid, but I ignored her.

"Sorry to do this, Stu," Mickey said, "but could you please lift up the left leg of your pants?"

"No. I'm not doing anything until I get a lawyer. What am I being charged with?" His beady eyes twitched above his scratchy mustache.

"You are under arrest for the murder of Julia Simon, the kidnapping of Jane Ritter, and"—Mickey raised his voice—"the murder of Rudolph Schmidt." The people near us gasped. Only the football team seemed not to know that all hell was breaking loose in the stands.

"Show me your leg right now and we can make this all go away."

"Show him, Stu," Rita pleaded. "For whatever ridiculous reason, show him."

Kuntz stood motionless. "I have the right to remain silent. I have the right to an attorney."

"I see," said Mickey. He nodded to a plainclothes, who slapped a cuff on Stu's wrist. "Then by the power of the Commonwealth of Pennsylvania . . ."

"I don't get it," Rita screamed again. "What's with the leg?'

"Shhh, Rita," Stu said.

I turned to her. "Does your husband have a six-inch scar between his knee and his ankle?"

Rita blanched. She covered her mouth and stared at her husband. "What have you done?"

I backed off and walked away. If I had stayed a moment longer, I would have strangled both of them.

Dan, too livid to face Kuntz, was waiting by Gate E.

"It's over," I said. "Stu Kuntz definitely took her. The police arrested him."

"I know." Dan was pale and drawn, not his usual polished self. "I just talked to Burge. Mrs. Cressman across the street noticed a car coming and going out of the band parking lot last night. She took down the plate. It matches Kuntz's."

I appreciated the confirmation. "I'm surprised he was so sloppy."

"Screwed up. Guy's fucking screwed up." Dan looked off. His eyes were red rimmed. "I'm going to kill the bastard someday."

"Enough violence." I reached out and took his hand. Unlike Stiletto's, whose hands were sinewy and almost artistic, Dan's were white and puffy from years spent behind a corporate desk.

"About your offer, you know . . ." I had no idea how to put this. "The *Newsweek* article and all."

Dan brightened. "Yes?"

"That was decent of you to think of Jane. You've come a long way, what with the family stuff and all." I wasn't feeling exactly eloquent. What I was feeling was waterlogged with stress.

"So . . . your answer?"

"I have to think about it." I could barely believe those words had come out of my mouth. After all those years of loathing Dan and his money-grubbing, class-climbing ways, of enduring his insults and callous treatment, here I was actually saying I would consider marrying him. "But I can't marry you just to get Jane into college."

"It's more than that." He cleared his throat and tried to look earnest.

I kept in mind his courtroom training in drama.

"It's . . . it's the right thing to do," he said. "Jane needs our love and support, considering the trauma she's endured today. She needs us to be there for her." And then, squeezing my hand, he added, "Maybe it was too much for us in the beginning. The work. The bills. The baby. Us not really knowing each other that well. We had a lousy start."

I said nothing. The beginning of our marriage had been a blur. In a snap, I'd had to quit being a high school girl obsessed with Aerosmith so I could become a mother saddled with car payments and diaper changes. It was as though I had been the butt of a cruel joke.

"What does Stiletto have to say about this?" Dan asked, probably thinking Stiletto was the only barrier preventing me from whooping a joyful "Yes!" to his proposal.

"He's gone."

"I see." Dan swallowed a triumphal grin. "We'll take it slow. We'll start over, Bubbles. It'll be tough, but it'll be worth it."

"I'll think about it," I said again.

Dan continued as if my hesitation was inconsequential. "And this time around I'm getting you a real engagement ring and a big wedding. It's what you deserve."

I shoved my hands in my pockets, suddenly cold and sad.

I knew all too well what I really deserved. But what I deserved had left me for London and was never coming back.

Chapter Twenty-nine

The walk home was what the doctor ordered. The wintry air cleared my brain, so starved for healthy oxygen and a regular schedule. My whole body ached, and I longed for a hot shower with lots of soap, a tall, cool glass of water, and a warm, comfortable bed. I could sleep for years.

Sleep heals, Mama always said. My memories of Stiletto, the pain in my heart for him, would not disappear with a nap or even months of dreamless nights. But time, life, work, and family would go far in healing this deep, deep wound. At least that's what I was counting on.

I turned down West Goepp and walked past the blinking Santas, twirling elves, the porches with their multicolored icicle lights, the fake snow sprayed on the windows, and the plastic wreaths on the doors. Now that Thanksgiving was over, my neighbors were coming out of the closet, overjoyed at being finally free to show their true colors, which, in this season, were red, white, green, and sometimes blue.

I was too blue to get in the spirit, really. I shuffled through the leaves to my front porch and emptied the mail from the mailbox— bills and five catalogs. My house seemed particularly small. There was a disturbing odor coming from the kitchen that I decided was a stopped-up disposal.

Tossing my fake rabbit fur coat to the couch, I planned my evening. I'd take a shower, get dressed, and pick up a pizza at Angelino's for Jane. Then I'd visit her at the hospital, where Dan and I had arranged to meet. Then I'd go to the paper, write my story, and come home.

After that, and only after that, could I lie on my bed and have a good cry.

The answering machine blinked, but I ignored it. I called the *News-Times* and got Mr. Salvo, back from his Massachusetts Thanksgiving. In a first, he gushed sympathy about Jane and how he'd wished he'd known so he could have helped.

He said Notch wanted me to know I could have the weekend off. (Say it ain't so!) He also said Notch received approval from Garnet. It would pay the $50,000 fine, though the company was still going to appeal Fortrand's order.

"Probably won't win," said Mr. Salvo. "There was no reason why the cops couldn't see those notes, is what they're going to argue. We'll see."

I yawned. "At least it's over. Schmidt's real murderer has been caught. Kuntz is in jail, and Jane's safe. I have no idea where the notes are."

"What about Smolak? He held a gun to your head just yesterday, don't forget. You shouldn't be home alone without a patrolman standing guard."

"The cops don't know where I am."

"I'll call them and get someone over right away. In the meantime, Yablonsky"—Mr. Salvo cleared his throat—"I got the scoop from Steve. If it'll make it any easier for you, I'll break it to the staff that you two are over so they won't bug you when you come in to write the Kuntz piece."

"Okay." I yawned again, so tired I could barely stand. "Thanks."

"And for Christ's sake, get some shut-eye."

We hung up and I rummaged around the refrigerator for leftovers. Nothing looked or smelled edible, so I resorted to a peanut butter and jelly sandwich, passing on the pickles. Made myself a glass of chocolate milk and flicked on the TV.

There was a half hour to go on *GH*. Carly and Sonny were at it again. Luke was still searching for Laura and, per usual, the Quartermaines had recently discovered a buried fortune underneath a boathouse. I sighed, glad to be back with old friends. When the show was over, I looked out the window, saw a cruiser parked by my curb, and felt slightly better.

To be safe, though, I left McIntyre's beeper by the sink before I stripped and took a shower. I ran the water as hot as it could get, filling the room with steam and turning my flesh red. I was lathering up when I remembered that my car was still parked at Stiletto's house, the last place I wanted to return to. I was debating whether to call Mama and ask her for a ride when I heard McIntyre's beeper fall off the sink and clank to the floor.

I remained stock-still, letting the shower drench me. Slowly I put down the soap, rinsed off, and pulled aside the curtain.

A woman stood shrouded in steam and in her hand was a large butcher knife. My knife, from the kitchen.

My chest tightened and I started to let out a scream until Ruth Faithful clapped her hand over my mouth and held the knifepoint to my throat.

"Shut up or I'll slit your neck right here," she said in a calm voice. "This is what you're going to do. You're going to get out of the shower and walk to your bedroom. You're going to wear the clothes on the bed and then you're going to go with me. If you so much as peep, I will kill you. Make no doubt."

I made no doubt. I felt woozy and disconnected. This was a dream, wasn't it? But then the tip of Ruth's knife grazed my carotid artery and I did as I was told. I slowly picked up a towel I'd dropped on the floor, managing to secure Detective McIntyre's beeper as I did so.

Ruth and I did a slow march to my bedroom. I debated whether I could take her until I saw the clothes she'd picked out and decided I'd have to.

"I can't wear those," I said, pinching a pair of faded blue jeans and a bulky gray sweatshirt that had once been Dan's and was stained with paint, what Jane whimsically termed my "pretty" clothes. "They'll put twenty pounds on me."

Ruth pressed the knife to my spine. "No one's going to see you . . . alive. I wouldn't sweat it."

"That's more of a reason." I got into a pair of underwear and a bra. "I don't want the last sight of me to be my"—I swallowed—"corpse in this." I slid into the jeans anyway. So much heavy cotton and big seams. What kind of woman wore this stuff?

I balked at the sweatshirt. "How about a V-necked T? I have one in the right-hand drawer."

"You probably have a *gun* there too." She sneered. I couldn't wait to find out what her story was, but I held off from asking.

"How about makeup?" I asked. "I can't go outside without makeup. I have a reputation."

"No makeup." Ruth checked her watch. "We're late already. Move it."

I shrugged on the sweatshirt. "You're not going to go very far with a cruiser parked outside. He probably didn't recognize you as the enemy because you're Ruth Faithful. But when you come out of the house holding a knife to my throat and me looking like a slob, then he'll know something's up. I never look like a slob."

Neither did Ruth, who was dressed in a blue wool crewneck over a pink oxford cloth shirt and khaki pants. The knife was the only sinister touch. Needless to say, it didn't go with the outfit.

"I'm not worried about the cop," she said. "Just brush your hair and we can go."

Like a snail on dope, I reached slowly for the brush and combed a strand of hair with painstaking care. "How'd you get mixed up with Karol Smolak, Ruth?"

She smiled, revealing a set of pearly white teeth. "Karol Smolak is no one, Bubbles. He's a decoy. Always has been. A big Polish stuffed deer at the shooting range."

Her words didn't make sense. "What do you mean, Smolak's a decoy? He put a gun to my head. He's a blackmailer. Detective McIntyre said so."

"McIntyre." Ruth's shoulders started heaving. I supposed she was laughing, but it was hard to tell. Her body was simply convulsing. "Who do you think fed McIntyre that line of bull about Smolak? I told him what he wanted to hear, and he ate it up. He desperately wished the rival for his affection to be a thug, a criminal not worthy of his precious Cerise, and I gave him that. It was a lie, of course, but people—even cops— will believe anything they want to hear when their heart's involved."

I stopped brushing. "McIntyre said he had sources."

"Me!" Ruth raised the knife like a spear. "One source. Good, sweet Ruth Faithful. Pastor's daughter. Never said a lie for fear of burning in eternal hell. How could he resist?"

Which is why in Journalism 101, Mr. Salvo taught us that reporters need three sources. Not one. You can't go on one even if it's a pastor's daughter.

"I'd have let you live, except I decided that sooner or later you'd figure out my role," Ruth said, now back to pointing the knife menacingly. "You're not so dumb, even if you are blond."

"I'm dumb, all right," I said defensively. "You ever look at my checkbook? It never balances. Ask my old boss, Sandy. I'm a ditz of the first order. I always forgot to bring my own shampoo to work."

"Right." She waved the knife. "You done yet?"

"Almost." I studied a split end. "So *you* were the blackmailer?"

"I set up the security camera. I arranged for Rudy Schmidt and

Kuntz to meet in our office Saturday night. Kuntz would have done anything—anything—to get his kid into Princeton, and I wouldn't be here now if Kuntz had just accepted our offer."

"What offer?"

"Our discount. A hundred grand for the security-tape photos. Cheap. Kuntz should have paid. If he had, his kid would be in the Ivy League, and he wouldn't be facing murder charges."

The brush drooped in my hands as I played over Ruth's words in my mind. *Our* offer, she kept saying. But if Smolak wasn't involved and Cerise May had been surprised to see the tape, then that left only one other person who could have been in on Ruth's blackmailing scheme.

"You mean you and Rudy Schmidt were working together?"

"Hey, don't sound so surprised. Rudy was a pro. He was at it long before I ever got on board."

I thought back to Principal Schmidt's ramrod posture and constant calisthenics. Of Liberty's corridors draped with banners echoing his motivational platitudes, one of which should have been YOUR LUNCH MONEY IS MINE, PUNK.

"I can't believe that my high school principal would be involved in such scummy work."

"Scummy work!" Ruth was back to waving the knife. "I'll have you know it takes a lot of research. As principal, Rudy had access to everyone's vitals. Social Security number, birth date, mother's maiden name. All you need to get unlimited info on a person. But it was me who taught him how to set up the compromising scenes, who made the tapes."

"How long had you two been in cahoots?"

"Ever since I worked in the county clerk's office. He kept coming in to look up records, and I figured it out. We worked out a deal. There are a lot of secrets in this town involving very high-profile people, who have been squashed, thanks to me. . . ."

"And Rudolph Schmidt."

"He was beginning to get in the way." Ruth smiled. "Just as well that he's out of the picture now."

"Your doing?"

"No. That was an accident. We never counted on Stu Kuntz murdering Schmidt. We thought it'd be the other way around."

Which was why Schmidt broke the security camera.

A door slammed next door in Mrs. Hamel's house. Ruth looked over her shoulder, giving me the perfect opportunity to crack the hairbrush onto her skull. She teetered and I grabbed the knife, tossing it in the hall. Ruth lunged for it, but I tripped her and pinned her to the ground. Then I activated my beeper. A minute later, I heard a beep in response.

It was the best sound I ever heard. McIntyre was out of the cruiser and on his way.

"You're cooked now," I said, sitting up. "That's McIntyre's beeper. I just paged him and he's coming to help me."

Before I could utter Hulk Hogan, Ruth kicked me off and spun me around, twisting my arms behind me in a WWE special. That's when I noticed that the beeping was coming not from McIntyre, who hadn't appeared, but from Ruth's pocket.

"Huh?" I said as Ruth removed the beeper and clicked it off before dashing it against the hall wall. "What are you doing with that? That's McIntyre's."

"Not anymore." With my hands still bound, she grabbed the knife and pointed its tip into the base of my skull. "McIntyre's still in the car. Dead."

Ruth and I did not talk on the way to the Bide-A-Wee Motel in what Sandy would have called East Bumfuck but what other people called my very own beat, Mahonek. Ruth spent the drive thinking about how to spend her blackmail profits while I pondered life after death.

We were headed for a rendezvous with Karol Smolak and Cerise May, two innocent parties after all, who were holed up in the Bide-

A-Wee in fear of imminent arrest on bogus murder and kidnapping charges by McIntyre, the duped—now deceased—cop.

Ruth in her khakis and Sears sweater and I, dressed like I was cleaning out the basement, made it from my front door to her car without so much as a glance from the neighbors. Along the way I caught sight of McIntyre's cruiser and his body, head slumped forward as if he were filling out paperwork or taking a nap on another boring stakeout.

It was a disconcerting image to witness right before Ruth pushed me into her sedan and flashed her silencer-equipped gun as a warning. Popeye may have accidentally killed a garbageman once in a fit of delusions, but Ruth was much worse. She was a calculating murderer simmering with rage.

The plan, as outlined by Ruth, was to have her take me to Karol Smolak's room at the Bide-A-Wee Motel. Pushing me inside, she'd lock the door, sever the telephone lines and hold Karol, Cerise, and me at gunpoint while she called the police on her cell phone, claiming that Smolak had just murdered McIntyre outside my house on West Goepp and was now holed up at the Bide-A-Wee with her boss, Dr. May, and me, his latest hostage.

As McIntyre's favored tipster, Ruth's word was gold, she asserted confidently. The cops wouldn't stop to question. They'd race to her rescue.

When the cops arrived, Ruth planned to hide in the locked bathroom so Karol, Cerise, and I could conveniently die in a shootout. When the smoke had blown over, they'd find Ruth cowering like a hostage, Cerise May's gun at her feet—the same gun that had been used to kill McIntyre.

Ruth told me she'd stolen it Monday evening from her boss's office, which she had trashed to make it look like a break-in. She would have done more damage except that Lorena and I had shown up, thereby giving her an opportunity to hear our conversation from her hiding place.

"So you were the one who called me when I got home," I said.

Ruth didn't answer. She kept driving. Hands on the wheel. Eyes on the road. Brain on the fritz.

It was dark when we arrived at the Bide-A-Wee. Ruth zipped around to the back and parked her car, the blue Saturn. We got out and Ruth put Dr. May's gun to my back as she led me around to the motel room where Karol and Cerise were staying.

The Bide-A-Wee Motel screamed, Hold Your Next Shoot-Out Here! It was the kind of establishment where recently furloughed prisoners watched cable TV until they decided which gas station to rob and which jail they'd be in next.

There were three cars in the lot. One was a nondescript Caprice. One was a fancy Acura that I judged was Cerise's rental. And the other had a raised rear end and a license plate that said 8ME. It was parked in front of room 6.

Holy Batman.

"Come on." Ruth pushed me. "What's wrong?"

"Stomach cramp," I said. "I get that when people put guns to my back."

"Don't breathe so much air."

We had arrived at room 7. The thick vinyl curtains were drawn shut and a TV blared inside.

Ruth knocked efficiently. "Open up, Doctor May. It's Ruth. I have, um"—she smiled at me—"someone to see you."

The TV turned off and Cerise opened the door on a chain. I tried to send her eye signals: Don't open the door—gun in my back. Though I think I ended up looking like a nearsighted woman with sand in her contacts.

"What's she doing here?" Cerise asked.

"Bubbles needs to talk to Karol. She has new information that can clear his name. She knows who killed Schmidt. Don't you, Bubbles?" Ruth pressed the gun into my spine.

"Oh, sure," I said.

Cerise mumbled something to Smolak and then let the chain go. Big mistake, I thought as Ruth forced me in.

Karol Smolak was in a neat black shirt and jeans, sitting on the bed, his hands on his thighs. He looked nervous and I felt bad that I'd thought so meanly of him. I remembered him loving his cactus. Any man who loves a wilting cactus has to have a heart, right?

"What's this about clearing my name?" he said.

"Ruth's got a gun," I said. "She's setting us up to die. She already shot McIntyre dead."

Karol jumped up, but Ruth held out the gun. "Whoa there, hotshot." He turned to Cerise. "I told you she was in on it."

"No," said Cerise. "Ruth's too nice."

"You don't know anything about me," Ruth said. "I worked with you for only two months. That was long enough."

"Why?" asked Cerise. "What's going on?"

Ruth didn't answer. She was too busy calling in a tip to the cops from her cell phone.

"I know. I know." I waved my hand excitedly. "Ruth worked with you just long enough to set up a blackmailing arrangement with Schmidt. They set up Stu Kuntz with a wig to make him look like Doctor May, and then they tried to extort him for one hundred grand, unless he wanted his identity revealed.

"Stu didn't like that, so he strangled Schmidt and had Popeye take the fall. The cops might have investigated that angle, except our buddy Ruth here snitched to McIntyre that Karol was to blame. She had McIntyre convinced that Karol was the blackmailer and Schmidt's murderer."

"Shit!" Karol swung his fist and punched a hole in the dresser, causing Ruth to nearly fire off a round.

"We just got off the phone with Doreen," Cerise cooed. "Remember your new calming words."

"Screw calming words," I said. "Next time hit Ruth, not the furniture. What did the furniture ever do to you?"

Karol rubbed his fist. "McIntyre's ruined my life."

"No," I corrected. "Ruth Faithful ruined your life. McIntyre was just a lackey. It's not good to speak ill of the dead."

"I'll keep that in mind at your funerals." Ruth closed her cell phone and raised the gun. Sirens filled the parking lot, along with the squeal of brakes. I heard the door at number 6 open and close.

Lorena Ludwig had emerged to check out the action. And who said there wasn't dish to dig at the Polish-American Club? Here the newsroom had been buzzing that Lorena was a sucker for fat men in EZ-Waist pants when all along she'd been at the Polish-American Club with her ear to the bar, learning Karol Smolak's hiding place.

I needed to get to Lorena, but how? Ruth kept the gun pointed squarely at us as she backed toward the phone. Taking a pair of scissors out of her pocket, she cut the line. Then she backed toward the bathroom.

"So long," she said. "See you in hell." And she slammed the door.

Karol and Cerise looked at each other. Stupefied. "That's it?" asked Karol. "We're free?"

"No," I said. "You're dead. Step out that door and the cops will gun you down. You may not know this, but you're armed and dangerous."

"Am not," he said.

Unlike double chins and anger problems, genes for intelligence did not run rampant in the Smolak family.

"What she means," Cerise explained, "is that Ruth's set us up to die in a shoot-out."

"What she just told the Lehigh PD is that you're a cop killer," I added. "You killed McIntyre with Cerise's gun."

Cerise covered her mouth in horror. "It was *Ruth* who stole my gun?"

"She's dead," Karol declared, clenching and unclenching his fists. "You're dead, do you hear me Ruth?!" He banged on the bathroom door and kicked it in with his foot.

Sarah Strohmeyer

"Go fuck yourself, Smolak," Ruth shouted back.

Such language from a pastor's daughter.

"Forget her, Karol. We have to think." Cerise tapped her temple as though it might loosen a bright idea.

"There's only one way to tip off the cops to hold their fire," I said. "A *News-Times* photographer is in the next room—Lorena Ludwig. . . ."

"I know Lorena," Karol said. "She's in my anger management group. What's she doing here?"

I peeked out the window. The parking lot was a mass of red and blue flashing lights. "Maybe the Bide-A-Wee's such a happening place. Might be the luxurious decor."

"Doreen," said Cerise, flinching as another siren swung into the lot. "That's Karol's anger management counselor. She probably told Lorena where we were."

"If I can get Lorena's attention, we'll be safe." I patted my clothes. "I don't even look like myself, though. She won't recognize me."

There was a knock on the door. Cerise scrambled to chain it. "Who is it?" she singsonged.

"Open up. It's the police," a strong, masculine voice demanded.

"We didn't do anything wrong! Karol didn't kill McIntyre!" Cerise shouted.

I winced. In the minds of the police, there'd be no way Cerise would have known about McIntyre unless her boyfriend had shot him.

"Stand away from the door," the cop said.

There was a second set of footsteps. We weren't alone.

"We want to speak to the photographer," Karol yelled. "From the *News-Times*."

Cerise and I gave Karol the thumbs-up while the cops discussed this. A different cop said, "What photographer?"

"Goddamn it," came Lorena's voice. "You think I'm just wearing this camera for decoration? Let me talk to them."

"Get behind the police line," the police on the other side of the door ordered. "This is a volatile situation. We have reason to believe Karol Smolak is armed and dangerous. . . ."

"Bullshit." Lorena was right outside the door. "Karol's not dangerous. He's just pissed. Karol, is that you? Talk to me, baby."

"Lorena!" I shouted. "It's me, Bubbles!"

"Bubbles!" Lorena paused. "Oh God. This is too cool. We're gonna . . ."

From the bathroom Ruth Faithful primed the fire by letting off a startling shot. Then another, right through the bathroom door.

"Karol!" Cerise screamed stupidly as Karol Smolak rushed to shield her body.

I clamped my hands over my ears and hurled myself over the double bed. With a deafening crunch of splintered wood, the cops kicked open the door and the bright light of gunfire echoed through the room.

Cerise screamed again and so did Lorena. I tried to roll under the bed, but couldn't, because it was one of those hotel beds with the frame down to the floor.

"Hold your fire!" someone yelled, though no one seemed to be paying attention because the bullets kept coming.

I was trapped between the two double beds, blinded by a snowstorm of shot-up mattress and tossed covers. Cerise went down, and I saw Smolak fall against the television, sending it to the floor with a resounding crash. A lamp fell, and someone kicked over a chair. A bullet shattered a mirror. Another ricocheted off the wall.

They were going to get me.

"NO!" I cried. "Please!"

Then something big and hard hit me with a bone-breaking *thump*, and it was over.

Chapter Thirty

I slipped in and out of consciousness and finally woke with a splitting headache to find that I was in a speeding ambulance headed for St. Luke's Hospital. I also discovered I was slightly delusional, as, in addition to a young and pretty paramedic, none other than Steve Stiletto was by my side, clutching my hand and looking beyond concerned.

"Ugh," I said, wincing from the sudden stab of pain in my head. "Not in these clothes. And no makeup."

Stiletto came in blurry, but his voice was clogged with emotion. "You're alive. Thank God."

"I wish I were dead. Am I still . . ." My fingers touched the cruddy sweatshirt. "Oh yeah, I'm still in it. Tell me something. Be honest."

"It's okay, Bubbles. You're going to live. You were hit with a table lamp and you should be okay."

"No." I pinched the sweatshirt. "Does this make me look fat?"

He grinned. A bit clearer now.

"Smolak?" I asked. "Is he . . ."

"Don't know. He's in the other ambulance," Stiletto said. "He's shot but not bad. Cerise is okay. Shoulder wound. Told the cops everything. They caught Ruth Faithful in the bathroom."

Good, I thought, feeling instant relief—from worry if not pain. "Lorena's acting like she hit Powerball."

"She did." I smiled to think of how great our scoop was. The *Morning Call* was going to be livid. "Goddamn, did we ever."

"Keep her quiet," the paramedic said in an almost childlike voice. What was my life doing in the hands of someone so young?

"Good work, today," Stiletto whispered, kissing my forehead. "Nailed Kuntz and survived this. You're some woman."

I watched as the black blood pressure balloon automatically inflated. If I was some woman, if I was such hot stuff, then how come Stiletto could drop me like a bag of garbage for a job overseas? How come he could "pretend" to be engaged to me, but not for real?

Boy, was I pissed. It took seeing him again to realize that. Lorena had taught me a valuable lesson. When anger bubbles up, don't tamp it down. Acknowledge it. Deal with it. Let it out.

"I bet they don't have great women like me in England, say?" I said bitterly.

Stiletto caught the whiff of resentment. "I suppose I deserve that."

"Yup."

I tried to look away but the paramedic cupped my chin and shined a bright light into my eyes. "I need to ask you a few questions." That girly voice again. "What's your name?"

"Bubbles Yablonsky."

She checked this with Stiletto. "For real?"

Stiletto nodded. "For real."

"Who's the president of the United States?"

"I dread to think." I closed my eyes. Spots danced.

"What year is it?"

"I forget."

The paramedic cleared her throat. Apparently I wasn't acing her test. What she didn't know is I never knew what year it was.

"How many fingers am I holding up?"

I opened my eyes. "Five."

"Who gave you that ring? It's gorgeous."

I raised my head slightly and looked at my hand. The glistening diamond was back on. "I don't know."

"*I* put it there," Stiletto said. "I thought you should keep it."

"What for? Old times? To remember what a great guy you were before you jetted off to London and other women?"

"Ouch," said the paramedic.

"Does she have a head injury?" Stiletto asked. "Sometimes it's hard to tell."

"That's not a head injury," she said, wise beyond her few years. "That's a heart injury."

Truer words were never spoken.

"I'm sorry, Bubbles." He took my hand. "What I did . . ."

"Save the speech." I sighed. My chest ached. "Why did you come back, Stiletto?"

Startled by my uncharacteristic brusqueness, he got straight to the point. "I drove halfway to New York and thought, What the hell are you doing, Steve? She's the best thing that ever happened to you. I tried to picture living in England without you and I couldn't. It just wasn't conceivable. So I turned around and pushed that Jeep to the limit. But when I got back, I found you'd gone and gotten yourself in a shoot-out."

"Never a dull moment," I said.

"Never a dull moment. That's why I want us to be together. Forever."

I fingered the stiff white sheet and let that word sink in. "Forever?"

"Forever. Bubbles." He swallowed hard. His dark blue eyes were piercing as he looked into mine. "I'm a little nervous so please hear me out."

He brought my hand to his lips. "I have completely fallen in love with you. Madly. Deeply. Wildly. I need you and I'll take care of you. I'll do everything in my power to give you the happiness you deserve.

And you deserve it all. Joy, love, security, and great sex. I'm going to make sure you have that and more every day for the rest of your life. I guess what I'm asking is . . . will you marry me?"

The paramedic gasped. "Ohmigod. That was the most touching proposal I've ever heard and we hear a lot of them in this ambulance." She dabbed her eyes. "He's gorgeous. Say yes! Heck. If you don't, I will."

You know, this is what happens to women my age. We go through a desert of men. In my case, for a decade. No guy worth spending five minutes with trips into my life. And then, bam, two marriage proposals in one day.

I was not twenty, like the paramedic, gaga over sparkling diamonds and a dashing man. I was a woman in her mid-thirties coming into her own. A bit delayed, perhaps, but arriving nonetheless, baggage in tow.

I finally had a career that was stimulating and challenging. I had my house, as lousy and small as it was. Jane and I had managed to survive smaller traumas and we would handle this huge one.

So why should I screw it up by getting married again?

I loved Stiletto. He was the best. But did I have to wash his socks? Could I see us sitting at the kitchen table to pay the bills or us grocery shopping for a week's worth of food? I had witnessed him take out a man who tried to kill me, but I never saw him take out the garbage.

These things were important.

"Thanks," I said, slipping the ring off my finger and handing it to him. "I'll think about it."

Stiletto stared at the ring, stunned. "I thought . . ."

"I know what you thought." I closed my eyes and smiled, at peace and happy. "But you'll just have to wait for my answer and you will," I cocked open one eye, "if you really are Steve Stiletto like the knife . . . and not the heel."

Recipes for Beauty Products Mentioned in *Bubbles Betrothed*

Jane's Homemade Pimple Remedies

What's a teenage crisis without a zit? Whether it's the evening of the prom or your college interview, if the event's important and there will be strangers staring at your face, then you can count on a spot appearing inconspicuously—like on the tip of your nose.

There are lots of really effective acne creams on the market. There's even cover-up made with that all-important salicylic acid, a very effective zit zapper. For those moments when salicylic acid's not at hand, however, consider these easy-to-make remedies that adults—not just teenagers—have used for decades.

Honey

Apply a dab of honey, preferably warmed, to a pimple before going to bed. Place a Band-Aid over it. The theory is that the honey kills the bacteria in the pimple and the Band-Aid keeps the honey in place.

Vitamin E

Pierce a vitamin E capsule and apply it to an emerging pimple before going to bed. Not only does vitamin E ward off the pimple, but it also helps reduce scarring from recent pimples when applied regularly.

Tea Tree Oil

Tea tree oil, found in the health-food section of grocery stores, keeps pimples from becoming inflamed. Make sure to *dilute* the oil first by wetting either a cotton ball or Q-tip and then dipping it into the tea tree oil. Keep a saturated cotton ball handy and dab on several times a day. (Note: Shampoo made with tea tree oil is also a common lice preventative, though what that has to do with pimples is anyone's guess.)

Desitin

It's far-fetched, but Desitin, the widely used ointment for diaper rash, can be applied to pimples before going to bed. Who knows why it works? Perhaps it's the cream's zinc oxide. One word of warning: Desitin is made to have staying power on baby bottoms. Don't put on too much cream to begin with and have a good cleanser ready the next morning.

Mother Smolak's Strawberry Rub

While Mother Smolak insists that her son cultivate fresh strawberries, the rest of us can happily purchase them at the grocery store, thanks to Florida's nearly year-round strawberry production.

In this simple scrub, sea salt and strawberries—which have more vitamin C than citrus fruit—are combined and applied to dry spots, such as on the elbows and heels, for smooth skin. Try adding a few drops of aloe gel to soften particularly dry skin.

Mix:

1 cup fine sea salt
3 ripe strawberries, mashed
1 tablespoon canola oil

Rub into dry areas before showering. Store one week in a closed, refrigerated container.

Mama's Crisco Face Mask

Crisco All-Vegetable Shortening is one of the most inexpensive and effective moisturizers on the market. It is preservative- and perfume-free, and each tablespoon contains 15 percent vitamin E. To use it as a moisturizer on the face, hands, or dry spots, massage in a thin layer.

To make an excellent exfoliant, mix a quarter cup of Crisco with three tablespoons of sugar. Massage into skin and rinse off. The sugar removes dead skin cells without irritating the skin, while the Crisco acts as a moisturizer.

Dan's No-Fail Antisweat Method for Men (Especially Bald Men)

Makeup artists for television news programs often have to ensure that middle-aged men under the hot lights of a TV studio don't sweat, even though the questioning might be tough. One trick is to apply a thin layer of gentle, unscented clear antiperspirant to their faces before applying foundation. Almay is a favorite. This stops sweat from rising to the surface of the skin, just like it does on underarms.

For bald men, a common treatment is to use spray antiperspirant on the dome. Just make sure the spray does not leave a white residue. Wipe off any excess.

Bubbles's Under-Eye Cream

There are plenty of home remedies to remove under-eye bags. The old fa-vorites work, such as ice cubes, chilled slices of cucumbers, and wet tea bags placed on each eye for ten minutes. But did you know that many actors pre-fer sardines? Each evening, place one canned sardine under each eye and relax for a half hour. Make it a routine and you'll see those bags disappear in days.

But what if it's an emergency and you don't have time to lie around with dead fish on your cheeks? Preparation H, which contains shark liver oil and is famous for shrinking delicate tissue, provides a quick lift fast.

AUTHOR'S NOTE

In 2000, Pennsylvania Common Pleas Judge Jane Cutler Greenspan fined former *Philadelphia Inquirer* reporter Mark Bowden and former *Philadelphia Tribune* reporter Linn Washington $100 per minute each for every minute they did not turn over their notes from an interview with accused murderer Brian Tyson. Tyson was on trial at the time for a 1997 fatal shooting in North Philadelphia.

Prosecutors in Tyson's criminal trial had subpoenaed the notes. Bowden and Washington, who had interviewed Tyson during the trial, fought the subpoenas. At the trial's end each reporter had racked up fines totaling $40,000 apiece and were cited for contempt by Greenspan.

Lawyers for the newspapers and the reporters sought to overturn the fines and Greenspan's contempt ruling, arguing that Pennsylvania's shield laws and the First Amendment protected reporters from having to turn over notes from interviews with confidential sources.

However, in a 5–2 decision issued on December 19, 2003, the Pennsylvania Supreme Court ruled that the shield law does not protect reporters from having to disclose the content of unpublished notes as long as the source's identity has already been made public.

The appeals court said the sanctions were justified but sent the case back to the trial judge to reconsider the fines.

ABOUT THE AUTHOR

Sarah Strohmeyer is the bestselling author of the Agatha Award–winning mystery series that includes *Bubbles Unbound, Bubbles in Trouble, Bubbles Ablaze,* and *Bubbles A Broad.* A former journalist whose work has appeared in the *Boston Globe,* the *Cleveland Plain Dealer,* and on Salon.com, she lives with her family outside Montpelier, Vermont. She can be contacted through *www.SarahStrohmeyer.com.*